DEAD SPACE™

MARTYR

DEAD SPACE™

MARTYR

B. K. EVENSON

TITAN BOOKS

Dead Space™: Martyr
Print Edition ISBN: 9781835414347
E-book Edition ISBN: 9781835414354

Published by Titan Books
A division of Titan Publishing Group
144 Southwark Street
London
SE1 0UP

First Edition April 2025

10 9 8 7 6 5 4 3 2 1

www.deadspacegame.com

Design by Greg Collins.

A CIP catalogue record for this title is available from the British Library.

EU RP
eucomply OÜ Pärnu mnt 139b-14 11317
Tallinn, Estonia
hello@eucompliancepartner.com
+3375690241

Typeset in Adobe Caslon 11.3/15.7pt.

Printed and bound by CPI Group (UK) Ltd, Croydon CR0 4YY.

The creature charged and he dived out of the way. It slammed into the side of the circular chamber with a loud crunch, the wall panel buckling. He pulled himself up, aching all over, and limped to the other side of the chamber.

It was twice the size of a man. It moved forward by swinging from its spiky, chitinous arms to its feet and back again, with incredible speed.

He watched as it turned around, oriented itself, and then charged again, the floor shaking.

He waited until the last possible second and then leapt again, his arm torn open this time by one of its spikes. The creature bellowed in rage or frustration, turning all about, trying to locate him. By the time it finally did, he was on the opposite side of the chamber, as far away from it as he could get.

Okay, he thought, gripping his injured arm, now it's my turn.

It charged him again. This time, instead of throwing himself sideways, he dived between its arms, sliding under it and up against its soft abdomen. He pulled his knife out and slit across its dead flesh, tearing it open as much as he could, then scrambled quickly up and away, stumbling across the room.

∎

Before he got far, it caught him by the foot and swung him like a doll and let go. He smashed into the wall, hard. He tried to get up, but he couldn't move. He had felt the air rush out of him when he hit the wall, but it was more than that. Perhaps his back was broken.

He expected the creature to charge again, but it didn't. Instead, it approached him leisurely, almost curiously. He watched it approach, and his fear began to build.

The grotesque creature loomed over him. It struck him once, brutally, knocking him back against the wall. For a moment he thought he might pass out, but suddenly the room took on an intensity and crispness that it hadn't had before.

The creature lifted him up in the air, gave again its bellowing call. It shook him violently before bringing his head into its maw.

A moment later it tore his body in half. A moment after that he was dead.

PART ONE

PUERTO CHICXULUB

1

Chava woke up earlier than usual that day, just before the sun rose. His mother and sister were still asleep. His father was gone, traveling again. When the boy asked him where he went, he was always evasive, and Chava had learned not to ask further. He took a ladleful of water from the bucket and drank it, careful not to wake his sister. He poured another into the basin and washed his face and hands and arms before quietly slopping the rest onto the dirt floor.

He was still sleepy. He watched his sister move restlessly, giving a little moan. Why had he woken up early? He had been in the middle of a frightening dream. There was something chasing him. A strange, stumbling creature, something that moved in lurches and starts, something that seemed at once alive and dead. He shook his head, wondering how something could be both alive and dead.

He slipped into his clothes and left the shack, careful to stop the piece of aluminum that served as a makeshift door from clacking behind him. Outside, he could smell the salt in the air, could see, a few hundred meters away, the slate gray waves.

The tide was out, the waves gentle now, hard to hear from this distance.

Something lingered in his head, a noise, a strange sound: a whispering. It was saying words but in a language he couldn't understand, so softly that he couldn't even tell where one word stopped and another started. He tried to force the sound out, but though it receded, it didn't go away. It just hid itself somewhere deep in the back of his skull, nagging at him.

His dream rushed forward to fill the space. The creature had been large, just a little bigger than a man. He was watching it from behind. In the dream, at first he had thought it was a man, but when it turned, he saw that it was missing part of its face, the jaw. There was something wrong with its arms as well, but the dream was blurry and he couldn't make out what it was exactly. It watched him with eyes as blank and inhuman as the eyes of a fish. And then, in a single bound, hissing, it had been on him, its slavering half jaw trying to sink broken teeth into his throat.

He was wandering, not really aware of where he was going, trying to fight off the bits of dream playing out in his semiconscious mind. He was surprised to find himself down at the shoreline. To the left, the coast was empty. Down the coast to his right, far in the distance, were two or three fishermen, standing in the surf, trying to pull something in. Whatever it was, the boy knew, would almost certainly be deformed and taste of oil. It would be a challenge to choke down. It was no longer safe to fish. The sea here was polluted and starting to die, and similar problems were working their way inland as well.

He'd heard his father talking angrily about it. Crops that even a few years back had been healthy and strong now came up stunted if they came up at all. The only supposedly safe food was the patented foods grown in controlled environments by mega-corporations, food that few could afford. So the choice, his father said, was either to eat food that slowly killed you or go broke on food you couldn't afford, while everyone went on destroying the world.

He started walking toward the fishermen, but something hindered his steps, slowly turning him. He began moving down the beach in the other direction, where it was deserted.

Or almost deserted; there was something there, something rolling in the surf.

A fish maybe, he thought at first, but as he walked forward, it seemed too large to be a fish. And the shape was wrong. A corpse maybe, a drowned man? But when it flopped back and forth in the tide, he knew he was wrong. That *it* was wrong.

The hair started to stand on the back of Chava's neck. He walked toward the thing, trying not to listen to the rising cacophony of whispers taking over his head.

2

Michael Altman rubbed his eyes and looked away from his holoscreen. He was a tall man in his early forties, with dark hair going just a little gray at the temples and lively blue green eyes. Normally, he had a keenly intelligent gaze, but today his face was a little drawn, a little weary. He hadn't slept well the night before. He'd had bad dreams, visceral stuff—all death, blood, and gore. Nothing he wanted to remember.

"That's odd," said James Field, the geophysicist whose lab he shared. Field ran stubby fingers through his thinning white hair and leaned back, his chair creaking beneath him, as he stared across the room at Altman. "Altman, did you get these same readings?"

"What readings?" Altman asked.

Field spun a copy of his holoscreen Altman's way. It showed a Bouguer/Salvo gravity map of the 110-mile diameter of Chicxulub crater. The crater had been left when a ten-kilometer bolide had struck the earth 65 million years ago.

James Field, now in his late fifties, had spent most of his career micromapping the crater for the state-owned Central American Sector Resource Corporation (CASRC). He focused mainly inland along the perimeter of the trough, where small concentrations of key minerals might be found and quickly extracted. Since people had already been doing the same for hundreds of years, this mainly meant going back for quantities small enough that earlier teams, before the resource crisis, had deemed them unworthy of retrieval. It was slow, tedious work, as close to being an accountant as you could get and still be a geophysicist. That Field actually seemed to *enjoy* this job told Altman more than he wanted to know about him.

Altman, on the other hand, had been in Chicxulub only a year. His girlfriend, Ada Chavez, an anthropologist, had gotten funding to study the contemporary role of Yucatec Mayan folktales and myths. He'd managed to pull just enough strings and call in enough favors to get a small grant so he could follow her to Mexico. He was supposed to be profiling the underwater portion of the crater, providing a map of likely geological structures beneath the half mile or so of sea muck by gathering data from both satellite imaging and underwater probes. It was, in theory, a strictly scientific project, but he knew that whatever information he gathered the university would sell to an extraction company. He tried not to think about that. The work was slow and not very rewarding, but he tried to tell himself it wasn't quite as pointless as what Field was doing.

He looked at Field's holoscreen carefully. It looked normal to him, the gravity readings typical.

"What am I looking for?" asked Altman.

Field furrowed his brow. "I forget you're new," he said. "I'll zoom in on the center."

The center of the crater was in deep water, about a half

dozen miles from their laboratory. Altman leaned toward the monitor, squinted. A darkness at the heart of the crater revealed a gravitational anomaly.

"Here's what it looked like a month ago," said Field. "See?"

He flashed up another profile. In this one, the darkness in the center wasn't there, Altman saw. He checked the first profile. The readings everywhere but the center were the same.

"How's that possible?" he asked.

"It doesn't make sense, does it?" said Field. "It wouldn't just change like that."

"Probably just an equipment malfunction," said Altman.

"I've been working here a long time," said Field. "I know an equipment failure when I see one. This isn't one. The anomaly appears both on the satellite images and the underwater scans, so it can't be."

"But how could it change?" asked Altman. "Maybe a volcanic eruption?"

Field shook his head. "That wouldn't give this sort of anomaly. Plus, the other instruments would have sensed it. I can't explain it. There's something wrong," he said, already reaching for his phone.

3

As he got closer, Chava became more and more nervous. It wasn't a fish or anything like it. It wasn't a sea turtle or a dog or a jaguar. He thought maybe it was a monkey, but it was too big to be a monkey. He crossed himself and then crossed two fingers for protection, but kept moving forward.

Even before he could see it clearly, he could hear it breathing. It was making a strange huffing noise, like someone trying to retch up something he was choking on. A wave pounded in and for a moment the huffing stopped, the creature swallowed up by the water and foam. Then the water ebbed and left it panting on the damp sand. It flopped over and swiveled something like a head in his direction.

It was like the creature in his dream, but much worse. It was not human, but seemed as though it once had been human. Its neck looked like it had been flayed free of skin, the reddish pith underneath flecked with white splotches, oozing slowly. What looked to be eyes were only empty sockets covered with veined, opaque membranes. The jawbone seemed to have vanished entirely, leaving only a flap of loose skin and a hole where the mouth should have been. The huffing noise came from that opening, along with a bitter, acrid smell that made Chava cough.

The creature was hunched over, its fingers webbed, a thin leathery membrane running between its elbow and hip like a bat's wing. It tried to stand, then fell back again into the damp sand. There were two large red lumps bigger than his fists on its back. They were growing.

Mother of God, thought Chava.

The creature gave a sound like a groan, the lumps on its back pulsing. The bones in its arms cracked, the arms themselves twisting, becoming less human. It coughed up a milky liquid that hung in strands from the hole in its face. The back split open with a loud cracking sound, spraying blood, and exposing spongy gray sacs that filled and deflated; filled and deflated.

Chava was unable to move. The creature suddenly swiveled its head, staring at him with its eyeless face. Its muscles tightened and the gaping hole pulled back into a poor imitation of a smile.

Chava turned on his heel and began to run.

4

A few minutes later, Field had spoken to Ramirez and Showalter, two other geophysical scientists working in the area. They had confirmed it: they were getting the same readings as Field. It wasn't an equipment problem: something had changed at the heart of the crater itself.

"But why?" asked Altman.

Field shook his head. "Who knows?" he said. "Showalter thought it might have to do with seismic activity focused directly at one of the sensors, but even as he suggested this was already talking himself out of it. Ramirez is as confused as we are. He's talked to a few others, none of whom seem to know what's going on. Something's shifted, something's different, but nobody knows why it's changed or even what it could be. Nobody has ever seen anything quite like it."

"What should we do?" asked Altman.

Field shrugged, thought for a moment. "I don't know," he said slowly. He sat running his fingers through his thinning hair, staring at nothing. "Nothing much we can do on our own," he finally said. "I'll file a report with CASRC and see what they advise. Until I hear back, I suppose I'll just keep on with the readings."

With a sigh, Field turned back to his screen. Altman just stared at him, disgusted.

"What's wrong with you?" he asked. "Are you even curious?"

"What?" said Field, turning back. "Of course I am, but I don't know what to do about it. We tried to figure it out, and everybody else is just as confused as we are."

"And that's it? You're just going to give up."

"Not at all," said Field, his voice rising. "I told you: I'm filing a report with CASRC. They'll be sure to have some ideas. That seems the best way to handle it."

"And then what, you wait a few weeks for someone to read the report and then a few more weeks for a response? What goes on in the meantime? You just keep taking readings? What are you, a company man?"

Field's face flushed dark. "There's nothing wrong with following protocol," he said. "I'm just doing my job."

"This could be huge," said Altman. "You said yourself it's not like anything you've seen before. We've got to try to figure it out!"

Field pointed one shaky finger at him. "You do what you want," he said in a low, quavering voice. "Go ahead and be a maverick and see where it gets you. This is a big deal, and it needs to be handled properly. I'll do my job the way that I know it should be done."

Altman turned away, his lips a tight line. *I'm going to find out what's going on,* he vowed, *even if it kills me.*

. . .

Hours later, Altman still hadn't gotten any further than Field. He called every scientist he knew in or around Chicxulub, anybody at all with an interest in the crater. Each time he hit a wall, he'd ask the person on the other end who else they thought he should call and then called them.

By a quarter to five, he still hadn't gotten anywhere and had run out of names. He ran back over the data and correlated it with what he could get his colleagues to send him. Yes, there definitely was a gravitational anomaly. Something had shifted with the electromagnetic field as well, but that was all he knew.

Field, who like any good bureaucrat quit promptly at five every day, had begun to transmit his data and to pack up.

"You're leaving?" asked Altman.

Field smiled and heaved his pear-shaped bulk out of the chair. "Nothing left to do here today," he said. "I'm not paid overtime," he explained, and then walked out the door.

Altman stayed on another few hours, going over the data and maps again, searching for precedents for shifts like this in records about the crater itself or about similar sites, records that stretched all the way back to the twentieth century. Nothing.

He was just on the way out the door himself when his phone sounded.

"Dr. Altman, please?" said a voice. It was barely louder than a whisper.

"This is Altman," he said.

"Word has it you've been asking around about the crater," said the voice.

"That's correct," he said, "there's this odd anomal—"

"Not over the phone," the voice whispered. "You've already said too much as it is. Eight o'clock, the bar near the quay. You know where that is?"

"Of course I know," said Altman. "Who is this?"

But the caller had already hung up.

5

By the time Chava came back, dragging along his mother and a few of the other people from the nearby shantytown, the creature had changed again. The wet gray sacs on its back were larger now, each almost the size of a man when fully inflated. Its arms and legs had somehow joined, melding into one another. The flayed quality of the neck had changed, the flesh now looking as if it were swarming with ants.

The air around it had taken on an acrid yellow sheen. It hung in a heavy cloud, and when they got too close, they found it difficult to breathe. One man, a small but dignified-looking old drunk, wandered into the cloud and, after staggering about coughing, collapsed. Two other villagers dragged him out by the feet and then began to slap him.

Chava watched until the drunk was conscious again and groping for his bottle, then turned back to stare at the creature. "What is it?" Chava asked his mother.

His mother consulted in whispers with her neighbors, watching the thing. It was hard for Chava to hear everything they were saying, but he heard one word over and over again:

Ixtab. Ixtab. Finally his mother turned to him. "Who is Ixtab?" Chava asked nervously.

"Go fetch the old *bruja*," she told him. "She'll know what to do."

The *bruja* was already heading toward the beach when he came across her. She was moving slowly, leaning on a staff. She was old and frail, most of her hair gone and her face a mass of wrinkles. His mother claimed that she had been alive when the Spaniards killed the Mayans, a thousand years before. "She is like a lost book," his mother had said another time. "She knows everything that everyone else has forgotten."

She carried a pouch slung over one shoulder. He started to explain about the creature, but she silenced him with a gesture. "I already know," she said. "I expected you sooner."

He took her arm and helped her along. Others from the shantytown were coming down the beach as well, some walking as if hypnotized. Some wept; some ran.

There was no reason to go, Altman thought. It was silly, probably someone's idea of a joke. You ask enough questions, and it was inevitable that someone would screw with you. The last thing he needed was to start thinking espionage and conspiracy. He needed to figure this out rationally and scientifically. So instead of going to the bar, he just went home.

When he arrived, Ada was already there. She was sitting at the table, leaning back in the chair, asleep, her long dark hair tucked behind her ears and cascading over her shoulders. Altman kissed her neck and woke her up.

She smiled and her dark eyes flashed. "You're later than normal, Michael," she said. "You haven't been cheating on me, have you?" she teased.

"Hey, I'm not the one who's exhausted," he said.

"I didn't sleep well last night," she said. "Had the worst dreams."

"Me, too," he said. He sat down and took a deep breath. "Something weird is going on," he said. He told her about what he and Field had discovered, the calls he had made, the general sense that he felt, and that others seemed to share, that something was *off*.

"That's funny," said Ada. "And not in a good way. It was the same with me today."

"You discovered a gravitational anomaly, did you?"

"Kind of," she said. "Or at least the anthropological equivalent. The stories are changing."

"What stories?"

"The folktales, they're starting to change, and quickly, too. That doesn't happen, Michael. It never happens."

Altman was suddenly serious. "Never?"

"Never."

"Shit."

"They keep speaking of the devil's tail," she said, "a kind of twisted pronged thing. When they mention it, they cross their fingers, like this." She raised her middle and index fingers, crossed them. "But when I try to get them to talk about it, they fall silent. They've never been like that with me before. It's like they don't trust me anymore." She brushed the top of the table with her hand. "You want to know what's strangest of all?"

"What?"

"Do you know how they say 'tail of the devil' in Yucatec Maya? Same name as the crater: Chicxulub."

Altman felt his throat go dry. He looked at the clock. A quarter to eight. Still time to make it to the bar after all.

7

For a while, nobody spoke. They just stood there, watching the *bruja,* who, in her turn, steadying herself on Chava's shoulder, just watched the creature.

"You see," she said in a whisper that was nearly drowned out by the creature's wheezing. "It is growing bigger."

She reached deep into her pouch and pulled out a handful of something. She began to dance, tracing a slow circle around the creature, just at the edge of the cloud the creature was creating for itself. She dragged Chava along with her, sprinkling something in the sand before her. It was a wandering dance, off-kilter, almost drunken. At first the others just watched; then slowly one or two began to follow, then a few more. Some shook their heads, as if breaking out of a trance.

When she stood directly across from the creature's head, she stopped and began turning in place. Soon everyone was doing this, watching the *bruja,* falling into place, slowly forming a complete circle. They turned around the creature, some of them standing knee deep in the surf.

She swung her staff before her, stepped back, and stepped forward again. The others followed. Chava stepped too far and found himself coughing, having breathed some of the gas the creature was emitting. His eyes stung; his throat itched.

The *bruja* lifted her hands, her index and middle fingers crossed. *Chicxulub,* she murmured, and turned again. The word went up mangled from the mouths of the others, like a groan.

The *bruja* slowly turned and walked away, her back straighter and her stride firmer than on the walk over. She walked a few yards back from the circle and dug into the sand until she unearthed a piece of driftwood, then turned and rejoined the circle again. She nodded and gestured at Chava until he, too, left the circle and came back with driftwood. One by one the others followed, wandering out of the circle and coming slowly back.

The skin that formed the gray sacs on the creature's back had thinned and thinned as the sacs grew. Now it was almost transparent. The sacs slowly billowed up until they were taut and then deflated, going about halfway slack before swelling again. It was a terrible thing to watch. Chava kept expecting them to burst.

The *bruja* was dancing again. She lifted her chunk of driftwood high, gave a toothless smile, and threw it at the creature.

It struck the creature softly in the face and fell to the sand just below it. The creature didn't react at all.

"Now you," said the *bruja* to Chava. "Higher. And harder."

He threw his piece of wood high and hard, at the leftmost sac. It struck the sac near the bottom and tore it just slightly. Air began to hiss out. The *bruja* raised her hands and brought them down and the others threw their pieces of wood as well.

One or two missed, one or two bounced off, but more than a few tore the sacs, some quite deeply. Air rushed out of them; the acrid cloud slowly began to disperse.

"Now, go," the *bruja* said to Chava, her voice hoarse. "You see the nameless man there, stumbling drunk as usual. Run to him and take his bottle and bring it back to me."

He ran quickly around the circle and to the small but dignified dark-haired drunk who had gotten too close to the cloud earlier and almost died. The man turned and smiled at him. Before he could react, Chava grabbed the bottle he'd posted between his feet and fled back to the *bruja*.

She took it from him and uncorked it. Behind them the drunk was protesting, some of the others holding him back. "Hold your breath," she said to Chava as she gave him the bottle. "You must pour this on the wood and on the creature itself."

His heart pounding, Chava took a deep breath and rushed forward. The torn skin of the sacs had already begun to knit itself back together. The bags were still mostly deflated but were beginning to rise. He upended the bottle, splashing the creature and the wood around it, and then rushed back to the bruja, his eyes swollen and stinging.

The *bruja* lit the top of her staff on fire and carefully moved forward, touching it to the creature's head.

Both the creature and the driftwood caught fire immediately. She dropped her staff, letting it burn, too. The creature hissed and thrashed, but never tried to escape from the flames. The gray sacs on its back turned to ash and blew away. Eventually it stopped moving altogether.

The *bruja*, swaying, led them once again in a slow, stuttering dance. Chava found his feet naturally following it, adapting to it, almost as if someone else were moving his legs. He wondered how many of his fellow villagers felt the same way. The village drunk, he saw, wasn't part of the circle; he stayed at a little distance, swaying slightly, staring at the fire, his brow furrowed. They kept on, tracing slow curving motions in the air, until all that was left of the creature was a charred, smoldering skeleton. Stripped of its flesh and burnt to a crisp, it looked almost human.

He ordered a bottled beer and made sure it came with the cap still sealed. As he waited on his change, he scanned the bar, trying to determine who might have telephoned him. The small bar's only inhabitants were half a dozen scientists from the North American sector—it could have been any one of them.

He sat down at a table. He'd just opened the beer and taken a sip when a man approached him. The man was pale skinned and thin, wearing a jumpsuit, his hair cropped short. Altman guessed he must be a technician of some sort.

"You're Altman," the man said. It wasn't a question.

"That's right," said Altman. "And you are. . ."

"I only give my name out to friends," he said. "Are you a friend?"

Altman stared at him.

"All right," said the man. "Maybe you don't make friends right off the bat. Okay, whatever you think of what I tell you, if anybody asks, you didn't hear it from me."

Altman hesitated only a moment. "All right," he said.

"Shake on it?" the man suggested.

The man extended a hand. Altman took it, shook. "Hammond," the man said, "Charles Hammond." He pulled out the table's other chair and sat down.

"Nice to meet you," said Altman. "Now suppose you tell me what's going on."

Hammond leaned in closer. "You've been noticing things," he said. "You're not the only one."

"No?" said Altman coolly.

"I'm in communications. Freelance, mostly industrial installations." He reached out and poked Altman's chest lightly with a finger. "I've been noticing things, too."

"Okay . . ."

"There's a pulse," Hammond said. "Slow and irregular, and very weak, but strong enough to fuzz up other signals just a little. I'm a perfectionist. When I set something up, I like it to be crystal clear. Things that don't bother other people bother me. That's why I noticed it."

He stopped. Altman waited for him to go on. When he didn't, Altman took a sip of his beer and asked. "Noticed what?"

Hammond nodded. "Exactly," he said. "At first I thought it was a problem with the communications terminal I was installing for DredgerCorp."

"I didn't know DredgerCorp had a place here," interrupted Altman. That, as much as anything, was an indication to him that something odd was going on. DredgerCorp was one of the shadiest of the resource retrieval corporations, the sort of company willing to swoop quickly into an area under the radar of the local government, strip-mine or bore and take as much as they could before it was noticed, and then swoop quickly away again.

"Officially they don't. Just got here. Very hush-hush," said Hammond. "I'm not supposed to know who they are. Anyway, at first I thought it was a loose connection, something off just enough to give a minor electrical discharge that gave the line an occasional slight hiss every so often. So I took the thing apart.

Nothing wrong with it. So, I put the thing back together. The hiss still came. Sometimes once or twice a minute, lasting a few seconds, sometimes not even that. *Maybe you missed something,* I told myself. I was just about to take the fucker apart again when I thought maybe I better check another terminal in the same system. Same problem. I was just about to tear DredgerCorp's whole system apart when something dawned on me: maybe it wasn't just in this system but in other places as well."

"And?"

Hammond nodded. "Everybody's picking it up, but nobody's noticing. It's not a problem with one system. It's an electromagnetic pulse, weak and irregular, broadcasting from somewhere."

"So what is it?"

"I did some investigating," said Hammond, ignoring Altman's question. "I set up a few receivers, triangulated the pulse. It's irregular enough that it took me a little while to figure out where it's coming from. And when I did, I decided it couldn't be right. So I moved the receivers, triangulated again, and this time I was sure of where it was coming from."

"Where?"

Hammond leaned even farther in, putting his arm around Altman's shoulders and bringing his lips close to Altman's ear. "Remember," he whispered. "You didn't hear this from me."

Altman nodded.

"From the crater," whispered Hammond. "From the exact center of Chicxulub crater, under a kilometer or two of muck and rock. Right where you found your anomaly."

"Oh my God," said Altman. He explained to Hammond what Ada had been hearing. "Three different things," he said. "All of them leading back to Chicxulub crater."

Hammond leaned back, nodding his head. "My thoughts exactly," he said. "Maybe the pulse has been there all the time and nobody noticed it until now. Maybe we're only hearing it now because our equipment is more sensitive. But I think I would have noticed it before now. That's not the kind of thing I miss. But here's my question to you: Is it a pulse or is it a signal?"

"A signal?"

"It's a little irregular, but it still has a pattern to it. I can't swear to it, but I think it's something that's being deliberately made. Down there, under millions of tons of water and rock."

"That doesn't make any sense," said Altman.

"No," agreed Hammond. "And it gets stranger." He came in close again, and this time Altman saw something in his eyes, a haunted look. "I told DredgerCorp about the pulse, figure it's my job to do so. I don't want them blaming me for it, want to make it clear that it's something that everybody is experiencing, even if no one's noticing it. And what do you think they say?"

"What?"

" 'Have you told anybody else?' That's an exact quote. Before I know it, they've got me signing a gag order. In exchange for certain monetary considerations, I can't talk about the pulse, not to anybody. I haven't, until now, with you."

"What do you think it means?" asked Altman.

"What do *you* think it means? Let me ask you something. Who is the only person that a secure communications system isn't secure from?"

"Who?"

"The guy who installs it. From me. If you're putting a system in, you can loop yourself into it in a dozen different ways without anybody being the wiser. I do that from time to time as a matter of course, just to keep my wrist limber. A hobby, really." His voice grew almost inaudible. "I did it with DredgerCorp."

"And?"

"It didn't last long," he said. "Ten days after I put the system in, they tore it out. Flew someone in from the North American sector to do it, someone in-house this time."

"They must have known the system wasn't secure."

"No way for them to tell," said Hammond. "They couldn't have known for sure. They're on to something. There's something at the bottom of the crater, something valuable, maybe even something unique. Lots of speculation about it from the communications I was able to intercept. But after about three days, things went cryptic; they started coding everything." He reached into his pocket, took out his holopod. "Take a look at this," he said. "Up close. Don't let anyone else see."

"What is it?" asked Altman.

"You tell me."

Altman shielded the holopod in his hands, watched the image that appeared, rotating slowly between his palms. It was just a digitally imaged representation. It was impossible to know what it was made of or what it looked like exactly, but he could get at least some idea. A shimmering three-dimensional shape, in two parts, thick at the base and coming to two points near the top. It was clearly something manmade rather than a natural formation, no doubt about that. Or was that just the digital model making him think that? It reminded him of something. It looked like two separate strands, joined at the bottom, but twisted around each other, though it might have been a single tapering structure with a perforated center.

He stared at it a long time, watching it slowly turn. And then he remembered. It was the shape Ada had made with her fingers, crossing them over each other, the sign she'd said many of the villagers were now making.

"Tail of the devil," he whispered, not realizing he'd said anything aloud until he saw Hammond's startled expression.

He clicked the holopod off, handed it back to Hammond.

"I got that off the com system before they tore it out," Hammond said. "According to the message appended to it, they cross-indexed all the information they had—worked with the pulse and the anomaly and probably some other things that neither you nor I are aware of yet. And this is what they came up with. This is what's at the heart of the crater."

They sat in silence awhile, staring at their glasses. "So, a pulse starts up," said Altman finally. "Maybe a signal of some sort. Something at the center of the crater, something that appears to be not a natural geological formation but a man-made one."

"Constructed, yes," said Hammond, "but who's to say manmade?"

"If not man-made, then . . ." said Altman. And then

suddenly he got it. "Shit," he said, "you think it's something inhuman, something alien?"

"I don't know what I think," said Hammond. "But yes, that's what some of the folks at DredgerCorp thought."

Altman shook his head. "I don't know," he said. He looked nervously around the bar. "Why are you telling me this?" he asked. "Why me?"

Hammond jabbed his chest again with his finger. "Because you were asking. This stuff has been going on for a while," he said. "Others must have noticed it. But you're the only one who contacted everyone you thought might have the answer. You know what that tells me? That you don't work for anyone. That you want to know for yourself."

"Surely other people are thinking about it, too."

"Let me put it this way," said Hammond. "Someone is trying to suppress this. Maybe DredgerCorp, maybe someone bigger than that. A lot of people know what's happening, but nobody's talking about it. Why? Because they've been bought. Why did I talk to you? Because I don't think you've been bought." He drained his bottle dry, then gave Altman a steady stare. "At least not yet," he said.

It was only once he was walking the *bruja* back to her shanty that things really stopped making sense. One moment she was there, walking beside him, talking softly to him, and then the next she was gone. Not only was she gone, but as he looked back, the only tracks in the sand were his own.

He went on, ahead to her shanty. Perhaps she had left him and gone there. Perhaps he had simply not been paying attention.

When he arrived, he rapped lightly on the crumpled sheet of tin that served in lieu of a door. Nobody answered. He knocked again, harder this time. Still no answer.

He knocked again. And again. Still no answer.

In the end, curiosity won out over fear. He took a deep breath and carefully pulled the sheet of tin aside far enough for him to duck inside.

It was dark. It took a moment for his eyes to adjust.

At first, he couldn't see anything except the shaft of light entering through the crack of the door. But he smelled something, a rich and pungent smell, almost metallic—he couldn't quite place it. Then slowly he began to make out dim shapes. A table, scattered with indistinct objects. A basin, turned over on the packed earth floor. There, at the far end of the room, he saw a straw-and-grass pallet, and on it, under a tattered blanket, the shape of a body.

He called out to her. *"Bruja!"* The form in the bed didn't move.

He moved slowly across the room until he stood just over the bed. Cautiously he reached out and touched the form through the blanket, shook it slightly.

"It's me," he said. "Chava."

She was on her side. He tugged her over, flipped her onto her back, and the blanket slipped down to reveal the *bruja*'s wide staring eyes and her slit throat.

He found a box of matches and with shaking fingers lit the lamp on the floor beside the bed. He pulled the blanket off, saw the knife she held in her death-clenched fist. The blade was brown with her blood. He carefully tugged the knife free and laid it flat on the bed beside her. Her other hand, he saw, was badly cut, long gashes on each of the fingers.

Ixtab, he thought.

He picked up the lamp and held it close to her face. The cut was jagged and incomplete, the bluish white of her trachea jutting out. She had been dead for some time, hours at least, maybe days. The smell in the room, he realized, was the smell of her blood. How was this possible? He'd just been with her. Or thought he had.

Shaking his head, he turned and made for the door, then suddenly stopped. In the lamplight, he saw something else. The walls were covered with crude symbols, like nothing he'd ever seen, odd twisting shapes, inscribed in blood.

Shocked, he stared at them. Slowly voices crept into his head, the *bruja*'s among them. He turned and fled.

After Altman had left, Hammond stayed on drinking. His head ached. Had it been wise to tell Altman? Had he been right about him? Maybe he was a free agent, but then again, if he were someone fishing for information, wouldn't that be exactly what they'd want him to think, that he was talking to someone who was safe? But you couldn't be sure that anybody was safe. You couldn't be sure that someone wasn't watching you right at that moment. They were always watching, always looking, and the moment you felt safest was probably the moment when they were watching you most closely, most sneakily, the moment when they'd figured out how to worm into your skull. That's what they must have done—they must have implanted a recorder in his skull. His head hurt, had been hurting for several days now. Why hadn't he seen it before? They were recording his brain waves; then they transmitted them to some super-secret high-tech neurolab somewhere and plugged them into someone else's head and then knew everything he was thinking. The only thing to do was not think. If he stopped thinking, maybe he could keep one step ahead of them.

Someone was coming across the room toward him. A large

man with a bushy mustache and a wrinkled, liver-spotted face.

It must be one of them. He tensed his body but remained motionless. Was there time to get to the knife in his pocket and flick it open and stab the guy? No, probably not. But he had the beer bottle in his hand. Maybe he could throw it at the man's head. If he threw it hard enough and just right, it might knock him out. Or no, wait, he could grab the bottle by the neck and break it off. Then he'd have a real weapon. They'd never take him alive.

"Señor?" the man said, a concerned look on his face. "Is anything the matter?"

What was that voice? It was familiar: the owner of the bar. What was his name? Mendez or something. He relaxed. What was wrong with him? It was just the bartender. He shook his head. Why was he so paranoid? He didn't usually get like that, did he?

"I'm all right," he said. "I'd like another beer."

"I'm sorry," said the owner. "We are closing."

And indeed, when he looked around he saw that he was almost the last one in the bar. Everyone was gone except for one villager, the nameless town drunk who was sunk in the corner of the room, wrapped in a dark shawl, watching him.

Hammond nodded. He stood and made for the door. The drunk followed him with his eyes. *Don't pay any attention to him*, Hammond thought. *He's not one of them, he's just a drunk. They haven't gotten to him yet. Probably. Take a deep breath. You're going to be okay.*

He made it out into the dusty street okay. He could hear the surf against the shore, could smell the salt as well. *What now?* he wondered. *What else?* And then he thought: *Home.*

. . .

He was about halfway back to the complex he lived in, walking down a deserted street, when he heard something. At first, he wasn't sure he'd heard anything meaningful at all. It was just a clattering sound and might have been caused by an animal. When he stopped, he didn't hear it. But when he started up again, there it was, little traces of it, like a voice he couldn't quite hear in his head. After half a block more he was sure: someone was dogging his footsteps.

He turned around but didn't see anyone. He quickened his step a little. There seemed to be whispers coming from the shadows in front of him, but as he approached them they faded, continuing on farther along the road. He shook his head. *That's crazy,* he thought. *I'm going crazy.* He heard again a noise behind him and wheeled around again, this time seeing someone, a dark form, a little distance away.

He stopped, stared at it. It had stopped moving, and then as suddenly as it had appeared, it stepped back into the shadows and was gone.

"Hello?" he couldn't stop himself from saying. "Is anyone there?"

His heart had begun to thud in his throat. He reached into his pocket and pulled out his knife, opened the blade. It looked absurdly small, almost useless, in his hand. He started back toward the shadows where the figure had disappeared, then realized that that was probably exactly what they wanted him to do. He turned quickly around to continue the way he had been going.

Except when he turned around, he found the street in front

of him wasn't empty anymore. There were three men, two of them quite large, all faces he recognized from the DredgerCorp facility.

"Hammond?" said the smallest one, the only one of them wearing glasses. "Charles Hammond?"

"Who wants to know?" asked Hammond.

"Someone would like to have a word with you," he said. "Come with us."

"Who?"

"I'm not at liberty to say," the man said.

"I'm not on the clock," Hammond claimed. "Business hours are long over."

"You're on the clock for this," said another of the men.

He nodded. He pretended to relax, beginning to move toward them, then suddenly spun on a heel and ran as quickly as he could in the other direction.

Shouts rang out behind him. He ducked into an alley and ran down it, a ragged dog barking at his heels for half the length of it. He leapt over a makeshift fence and crashed through a pile of trash. Up and running again, he left the streets of the town proper and entered the shantytown.

His head was throbbing. He looked back—they were still behind him, gaining. He kept running, a stitch starting up in his side. Slower now, but still running.

By the time he reached the edge of the shantytown, they were close enough that he could hear the sound of their labored breathing. *They're going to catch me,* he realized, *there's nothing I can do.* He stopped suddenly, whirled around, holding the small knife in front of him.

The three men quickly fanned out, forming a triangle

around him. Hammond, panting, kept moving the knife back and forth from one hand to the other. The others kept their distance, their hands up.

"There's no need for that," said the man with the glasses. "They just want to talk to you."

"Who's they?" asked Hammond.

"Come on," said the man with the glasses. "Be a good boy and put down the knife."

"What's wrong with him, Tom?" asked the first of the other two.

"He's scared, Tim," said the second, said Tom.

"I'd be scared if I was him, too," said Tim. "Nobody likes a thief."

"Thief? Can you really steal secrets?" said Tom.

"Now, boys," said the man with the glasses. "You're not helping the situation."

There they were again, the voices in his head. But why did they need to send voices into his head if they were there in front of him? And then a terrible thought occurred to Hammond: What if there were two groups out to get him? DredgerCorp and another one as well? Or maybe even three. Or four. What did they want with him? Would they beat him? Would they kill him? Would it be even worse than that?

"Now just calm down," said the man with the glasses, looking a little nervous now.

Someone, Hammond realized, was making a noise, a high-pitched squealing. It was a terrible thing to hear. It took him a long moment to realize that that someone was himself.

"I told you something was wrong with him," he heard Tim say behind him.

"You're right about that, Tim," said Tom.

They were still there, the three of them, standing in a way that made it impossible for him to see all of them at once. He could turn and turn, but he couldn't see them all at the same time no matter what he did. And then there were the ones in his head, too, slowly extracting things from it. God, his head hurt. He had to stop them, had to get them out of his head.

"Put the knife down, friend," said the man with the glasses.

But that was the last thing Hammond was going to do. Instead he lunged forward and flashed his knife at the man with glasses. The man jumped nimbly back, but not nimbly enough; the knife opened a gash just below his wrist. He stood holding it, blood dripping through his fingers, his face suddenly pale in the dim light.

But Hammond had forgotten about the others. He turned and there they were, still a little way away, but moving closer. They stepped quickly back when they realized they'd been noticed.

He was still surrounded, both inside his head and outside it. There was no getting out of it. He would never get away.

And so, realizing this, heart thudding in his mouth, he did the only thing he could think to do.

"I didn't expect that, Tim," said Tom.

"I didn't either," said Tim. "This one was full of surprises. What'd they want him for, anyway?" he asked the man with the glasses.

"A few questions," said the man with the glasses. "Nothing serious. Just a few questions." He had wrapped his wrist in one of his shirttails. It was slowly soaking through with blood.

"Never seen anything quite like that," said Tom. "And I hope I never do again."

"Same here," said Tim, shaking his head.

He took a step back to avoid the puddle of blood that was spreading from Hammond's slit neck. He'd never seen anyone cut themselves quite so deep and so quickly. There was a lot of blood and it was still coming. He had to step back again.

How could anyone do that to himself? Tim wondered. He must have been very frightened. Or simply crazy. Or both. He squinted, massaged his temple.

"All right, Tim?" asked Tom.

"Better than him, anyway," said Tim. "Just a little headache."

"Me, too," said Tom. "Terry?"

"I've got a headache, too," said the man with the glasses. "Been one of those nights. Step lively, lads. Let's get out of here before the law arrives."

PART TWO

CONFINED SPACES

11

"He killed himself, just like that," the man on the vidscreen said. It was less a question than a statement. He had a square-cut jaw and white hair that was swept back and plastered down. Even on the small vidscreen, he was an imposing man. He was wearing a uniform, but his screen had been set to dither out his insignia, to make it impossible to say just what branch of the service he was part of.

"That's what they tell me, sir," said Tanner.

William Tanner was head of the newly established DredgerCorp Chicxulub, the semisecret branch of the organization that had been set up hurriedly as soon as they'd had some indication that something was going on in the center of the crater.

Tanner had a military background and specialized in running black ops through dummy corporations. He was running this one under the name Ecodyne. Enter the right command into the system at the right moment, and any sign of a connection to DredgerCorp would instantly vanish from the company files. Then Tanner would vanish and reappear under another name. So far, his operations had gone well, partly because of good luck, partly because he was very good at what he did, which was why he'd been with DredgerCorp for ten years.

He didn't know the name of the man on the screen. All he knew was that, three days before, he'd had a vid conference with Lenny Small, the president of DredgerCorp, who'd explained that they were bringing someone in from the outside. When Tanner asked who it was, Small had just smiled.

"No need for names, Tanner," he said. He flashed a vid still of the man onto Tanner's screen. "Here's your man," he said. "You tell him anything he wants to know. And you do anything he says."

Once Small disconnected, Tanner had shaken his head. Why bring someone in from the outside? Just one more possible way for something to go wrong. Just one more hole he'd have to plug after the operation was over. Small was getting soft in his old age, drinking too much maybe, getting sloppy. Which put everyone at risk. Which put *him* at risk. Tanner didn't like that.

But when he saw the guy on the screen, first heard him talk, first heard the coldness of his voice, he realized that he'd misjudged his boss. This wasn't just anyone. This was military, someone who'd clearly seen a lot and knew better than any of them what was going on. Privately, Tanner started thinking of him as the Colonel, though he had no idea what the man's actual rank was, or if he even had the right branch of the service. It wasn't even possible to guess at where he might be—the background had been deliberately pixilated out, which lent an odd shimmer to the edges of the Colonel's body. It was the Colonel who had taken the data they'd intercepted from various scientists' reports and generated a model that gave them an idea of what might be waiting for them at the heart of the crater. It was the Colonel who immediately had the security system replaced, who had seen the potential for the technician who had installed the first system to leave a back door for himself. And when that young geophysicist named Altman started asking around about anomalies in the crater, the Colonel immediately had his phone tapped.

A few minutes later, the Colonel was back on the vidscreen, telling Tanner that Altman had already had a call from the technician—Bacon was his name. Or no, not quite that, another kind of meat: Ham. Hammond.

"Too late to trace it," the Colonel said, "but let's bring this Hammond in and have a chat."

Which brought Tanner back to where he was now, impressed by how impassive and stern the Colonel's face remained as Tanner told him that Hammond was dead.

"Any chance they're lying to you?" asked the Colonel.

"I've seen the body myself," said Tanner. "He's dead, all right. They were just trying to bring him in, just talking to him, and he flipped and slit his own throat."

"He what?"

"Slit his own throat. Almost sawed his head off."

"Just talking to him, you say," said the Colonel. "What's that supposed to mean? People don't slit their throats when you're just talking to them."

Tanner swallowed. Talking to the Colonel made him nervous.

"Any chance they nudged him along a little too hard?" the Colonel asked.

Tanner shook his head. "I've worked with these men before," he said. "They're completely reliable. They had their orders straight. Trust me, they were as surprised as you and I."

The Colonel gave a curt nod. "You think this Altman's a threat?"

Tanner shrugged. "I was hoping to find that out from Hammond."

"Best guess," said the Colonel. "Threat or not?"

Tanner glanced down at the holofiles he'd spread before him, spun them through the holoscreen. Copies of them, he knew, were appearing on the other side of the link, where the Colonel could see them. "I don't think there's much to worry about with Altman," he said. "There's nothing special about him. Your run-of-the-mill scientist. No Einstein, not really the sort that stands out from the pack."

"In my experience," said the Colonel, "nobody stands out from the pack until they're given a reason to. It's not until then that you know whether they'll bend or break."

"I suppose so," said Tanner. "In my experience, very few people ever get that far."

The Colonel nodded, lips tight. "But if Altman does . . .?"

Tanner thought about it. "I don't know," he said. "He doesn't seem to be the hero type. He's not likely to be an industrial spy for another corp, I don't think, and not likely to opt to become one. He seems to have taken his current job exclusively so as to follow his girlfriend down to Chicxulub."

"Could be a good cover," said the Colonel.

"Could be," said Tanner. "But you'd probably know better

than me if it was, and, if so, for what. I don't think it's a cover."

The Colonel scanned quickly through the files. "No," he said, once he'd finished. "I don't think so either." He stayed for a moment, staring straight into the screen. To Tanner it felt like the Colonel was staring through him, not even seeing him.

Finally the Colonel said, "Let's move things forward quickly."

He turned to his own holobank, sent a rendering through his vidscreen to Tanner. A three-dimensional image. Some kind of vessel. At first Tanner thought it was a spacepod and experienced a brief wave of fear: he had been part of the shock troops for the moon skirmishes, part of the deadly fight over which nation had the right to the resources of the moon. He had spent harrowing hours with his oxygen running out, siphoning from the tanks of the dead and dying around him. Last thing he wanted was to be in space again. But then he noticed the screw engines and realized it wasn't a spacecraft at all: it was some sort of submarine. Deepwater, from the looks of it.

"What is it, sir?" he asked.

"The F/7," the Colonel said. "Prototype submersible, not released yet, even among our people. I'm sending it to you. Find two men to man it, people you can trust. And quickly. We need to get there first."

12

He chose Dantec, an ex-military man from his own outfit he'd brought with him ten years back when he'd first signed on, someone whom he trusted implicitly and who, in addition, knew how to pilot just about anything. Dantec was good at thinking on his feet, very quick. He also had no compunctions about doing something questionable as long as Tanner was the one asking. But he'd also been known to be a little too quick to resort to violence if something went wrong. Something had happened to Dantec during the moon skirmishes, something that had left his eyes steady but flat, as if nobody was home inside. Tanner wasn't sure what it was.

He's not a bad guy, Tanner told himself the few times Dantec had done something that he found hard to accept, even with his own fairly lax morals. *He just doesn't see things the way I do.* And then, as an afterthought, he would often find himself thinking, *I'm not a bad guy either.*

Tanner sighed. Bad guys or not, both he and Dantec would do what they felt, in their own way, they had to do.

He had to search a little for the other man, pulling him out of DredgerCorp's North American headquarters. His name was Hennessy and he was a marine geologist, also with quite a bit of submarine experience. He was bald although still fairly young, mid-thirties. He was also well respected, and if he was already with DredgerCorp, that probably meant he wouldn't object too strongly to something a hair outside the law. But the Colonel's question about Altman was still nagging at him: If push came to shove and Hennessy realized the full extent of what they were doing, would he bend or break? *No way to tell*, Tanner thought, but thought he was more likely to go with the flow than to protest or try to stop them.

Tanner made arrangements through President Small, got Hennessy on the next flight south. By the time the man had reached Puerto Chicxulub, the F/7 had arrived, was waiting for them under a tarp on the deck of an unmarked freighter about fifteen miles away from the center of the crater. Though a rusty hulk on the outside, the freighter was retrofitted with state-of-the-art equipment inside. It was crewed by either military or ex-military—they didn't wear regulation uniforms, but their training was clear from the tight economy of their movements, their meticulous haircuts, and the way they snapped to obey an order.

"Should we be careful what we say around the crew?" Tanner asked the Colonel over the vid linkup.

"You should be careful what you say around anybody," said the Colonel, and then showed his teeth in a way that Tanner guessed might be a smile. *Definitely a carnivore*, Tanner thought. Then the Colonel's lips slid over his teeth again and he said, "Don't say more than you have to."

The F/7 was a bathyscaphe. A prototype drilling model, something made to descend to great depths and then bore quickly down through solid rock. Hennessy responded to it like a kid waking up on Christmas morning to find a pony waiting downstairs.

He went around the craft with Tanner and Dantec in tow, babbling about the combination of the titanium alloy drill and the molecular pulverizers meant to keep the path clear. Tanner and Dantec just pretended to humor him.

"Don't tell me we're going down into Chicxulub," said Hennessy, excited. "I've always wanted to go there. What are we looking for?"

You'll know soon enough, thought Tanner grimly. "Just a few dives," he said as casually as possible. "Just something to run the F/7 through its paces. Routine."

Over the next few days, Tanner had them do just that. They put the F/7 through its paces, first seeing how maneuverable it was gliding along the surface, then testing it in deeper waters. and then finally testing the drill and the pulverizers. It wasn't the most maneuverable craft Hennessy had ever seen, but that wasn't the point of a bathyscaphe: it had to be solid and able to withstand tremendous pressure when it dived deep. On the surface it bobbed drunkenly along, slowly tacking in the direction it wanted to go. Underwater it was better, more responsive. And it was best of all once they had it boring through mud and into rock. Even when the drill was on full and biting into hard rock, the craft was stable, hardly shaking at all. Rear thrusters kept it up against the rock, and the drill itself pulled them forward if the threading had anything to grab. Meanwhile the pulverizers turned the remaining rock into a fine gravel and forced it back to where it caught in the thrusters and kicked away or dissolved entirely. Hennessy claimed he'd never seen anything like it.

They took the F/7 down seven or eight times, test runs. At first, Dantec just watched what Hennessy did, listened to him talk, observed him. And then one day, suddenly, Dantec informed Hennessy that it was his turn.

"But this is a delicate piece of equipment," cautioned Hennessy. "You need to have months and months of training before—"

"You're making my headache worse. Move," said Dantec. And Hennessy, turning away from the instrument panel and taking stock of his partner for perhaps the first time, seeing his dead expression and his steady eyes, did.

That night, just as he had sat down on the bed and begun to take his shoes off, Tanner heard a knock at the door.

"Come in," he said, continuing to work on his laces until he saw a familiar pair of boots appear. He looked up. *Why is it,* he wondered, *that Dantec always looks so predatory?*

"It's you," he said to Dantec. "Everything coming along nicely?"

Dantec nodded. "I've figured it all out," he said.

"You can pilot the thing if you need to?"

"After a moon lander, it's a piece of cake," said Dantec. "I won't have any problems."

"What about using the drill?"

Dantec shrugged. "Nothing too complicated to it," he said. "I know how to drill a bore tunnel and can probably figure out how to make it do anything else we need. Hennessy is no longer essential. If he gets cold feet or something goes wrong, I can take over."

"What do you mean if something goes wrong?" asked Tanner.

Dantec shrugged. "Just being prepared," he said.

"If something does go wrong," said Tanner slowly. "I prefer you don't kill him."

Dantec hesitated, then nodded. "Your preference is duly noted," he said.

The next morning found Tanner speaking to an image of the Colonel on the vidscreen. "We're ready," he said. "Anytime you want we can move the ship over the center of the crater and drop the F/7. Both pilots are trained and comfortable with the vessel. Both are eager to leave."

"Very good," said the Colonel. He seemed again to be looking through Tanner, as if Tanner weren't there. "Move the freighter into position tonight," he said.

"Tonight?"

"Weigh anchor just before dusk. I want you in position by 2100 hours and ready to go by 2200. No need to tell your two pilots anything or do anything to make them suspect or get word back to someone if you're wrong and they're spies. Just wake them up and get them on board in time to drop the F/7 well before midnight."

"Yes, sir," said Tanner.

The Colonel reached out to disconnect the link, then stopped. "You look tired, Tanner," he said. "Everything all right?"

"I'm fine, sir," said Tanner. "Just a little headache. I've been having trouble sleeping. But nothing to worry about."

"Tomorrow may be a historic moment," the Colonel speculated.

"Yes," said Tanner.

"What do you think is down there?"

Tanner had been wondering the same thing for days now. How could something seemingly man-made end up at the bottom of the crater, buried under miles of rock?

"I don't know," he said. "Maybe it's just a natural formation that somehow doesn't seem natural. Or maybe it's something man-made that's been placed there God only knows how. Or maybe . . .," he said, but couldn't bring himself to finish the sentence. It was too big to get his mind around.

"Maybe what?" asked the Colonel.

Tanner shook his head to clear it, which just made the headache throb more. "I really don't know, sir," he said.

"I'll tell you what you're thinking since you're not man enough to say it yourself," said the Colonel. "You're thinking, 'Sure, it may be constructed, but not by us, not by humans.'"

Tanner didn't say anything.

"Believe it or not, Tanner, it's a genuine possibility. That's what we're hoping for. The first contact with intelligent life other than our own."

It made Tanner dizzy to think about it, even scared him a little. If that was what it was, if that's what happened, it could change everything. "With a little luck, we'll know soon enough," he said in as steady a voice as he could muster. "I'll keep my fingers crossed, sir," he added, and then cut the link.

13

He was trying to run, but wasn't getting anywhere. His arms and legs were flailing in the air, but nothing was happening. He couldn't even feel the ground beneath his feet. And there was something wrong with the air. Every time he tried to breathe it, he ended up coughing, choking. He was slowly suffocating. He looked frantically around him, but on every side it was the same—an endless gray expanse, nothing solid, nothing definite, just he himself, alone, floating in a void, dying.

He knew he was dead, but he still, somehow, *was*. He was floating, his eyes open but seeing nothing, his body turning slowly around and around. There was nothing there but him, but he wasn't exactly *there*. He heard something. Quiet, like the sound of an insect scuttling over paper. It slowly got louder. It blossomed into a loud whisper. A human voice, speaking to him.

Hennessy, it said. It was a familiar voice. He wished it would speak louder than a whisper so he could be sure about who it was.

Hennessy, it said again. He heard it close to his other ear, and then in two slightly different whispers at once. It wasn't just one voice, he suddenly realized, but legion, all of them whispering, all of them saying his name. *Hennessy, Hennessy, Hennessy.*

And then, spinning around, the gray space around him suddenly didn't look so gray anymore. It was changing. Transforming. Becoming something else.

He knew he was dead, and he couldn't move. All he could do was stay there, floating, body spinning slowly about, listening to the voices, as the blank gray void that had been there all around him quickly became more and more textured. For a moment it was striated, run through with creases and lines, and then those shifted and crumpled in a way that reminded him of a human brain. And then these, too, tightened and shifted, beginning to take on vague features. It was not a void, he realized, but a tightly packed mass of bodies, stuck to one another, fading into one another, all of them dead.

He wanted to close his eyes but couldn't. There were thousands of them, maybe more, and as the faces became more and more differentiated, he began to realize that they were people he knew, all of them dead. There was his wife there, her neck broken from the accident, his mother and father, both withered and decrepit just as they had been after the cancer took them, and others, many others, whom he hadn't forgotten but who, upon noticing them, he knew were all dead.

Hennessy. The word came from one of those open and unmoving maws, like an echo from deep within a cave. But which? *Hennessy,* said another. And soon, they were all saying it, pressing closer and closer to him, and there was nothing that he could do to stop them. And then their fingers were sliding under his skin, threading through his bones, insinuating their way into him.

"Hennessy!" someone was yelling. "Hennessy!"

Something was grabbing him, shaking him. Hands. Someone was screaming, Hennessy realized, and then he realized that that somebody was him.

He lashed out and scrambled backward, out of the grip of whatever it was, until he struck a wall. It was only then that he was able to stop screaming and consider where he was. A normal room, in the DredgerCorp complex, in Chicxulub. There was his bed. It was his room. It was okay. He was back in the real world.

There was a man bent over near the bed. An ordinary-looking man wearing glasses.

"Jesus," said the man. He was covering his nose. Blood was dripping through his fingers and onto the floor. "What did you do that for?"

Behind him, Hennessy saw, were two larger men. They looked like they might be brothers, or even twins. He'd seen all three lurking around at various times within the complex, but never was quite sure what they did.

"You want us to rough him up a bit?" said one of the larger men.

"Soften him up a little?" said the other, and smacked his fist into his palm.

"You know we can't do that," said the man with the glasses. "We're just supposed to fetch him."

"I'm sorry," said Hennessy to the man with the glasses,

confused by what they were saying. "I was having a bad dream."

"Bad dreams seem to be going around lately. It must have been one hell of a bad one," said the man with the glasses. He tilted his head back and moved his hand away. The bleeding seemed to have mostly stopped. He gave an experimental sniff.

"What are you doing here?" Hennessy asked.

"We were sent to get you," said the man with the glasses. "Get dressed."

Maybe I'm still dreaming, thought Hennessy. "Get me? For what?" he asked.

"You're needed elsewhere. Just get dressed and come on. Or do you want me to let Tim and Tom work out some of their nervous energy on you?"

They took him down to the dock, Tim and Tom to either side of him, the man with the glasses leading the way. There was a large speedboat there, Dantec already inside it, seemingly at ease, sitting straight-backed, his arms crossed. Unlike him, Dantec didn't have an escort. One of the vaguely military men from the freighter was standing with one foot on the dock, the other on the deck, ready to cast off.

"Where are you taking us?" Hennessy asked the man with the glasses.

He was still rubbing the bridge of his nose. "We were told to bring you to the boat. That's all I know."

"Get on," said Tim, behind him.

"Or do you want us to put you on?" asked Tom.

Hennessy scrambled aboard, sat down next to Dantec. The soldier cast off, pushed away from the dock, and scrambled into the pilot's seat. A moment later the engine was screaming and they were tearing across the dark water.

"Do you know what's going on?" Hennessy asked Dantec over the roar.

Dantec gave him a hard, dead look. "We've been activated," he said.

Activated? wondered Hennessy. *What does that mean?*

With the wind and the spray of the water, Hennessy was soon freezing. His teeth were chattering by the time they arrived at the freighter. They climbed out and up the ladder to find Tanner waiting for them on deck.

"You made good time," said Tanner to the motorboat pilot. "Well done, son."

"Thank you, sir," the man said.

Tanner turned to Hennessy and Dantec. "Well," he said, "I bet you two are wondering what the hell is going on. Come onto the bridge and we'll talk."

After Tanner had finished explaining, Hennessy felt there was something wrong. Sure, he was excited to go down to the center of the crater, excited to find out what was there and see where it was from. It could, as Tanner said, be amazing, maybe even the first signs of intelligent extraterrestrial life. But maybe it was nothing, just an anomaly. He had to try not to get too excited.

Plus, something just didn't add up. Certainly DredgerCorp wasn't the only one to have detected the object. And even if they were, didn't they have an obligation to report it? Didn't they have to go through proper channels, consult with the Mexican government? Shouldn't it be a joint project, something that DredgerCorp was in on but which the government controlled, instead of a hurried and sudden operation in the dead of night?

No, they were definitely up to no good, and in a way that might have serious consequences. Maybe he was a little naïve, maybe in the past he'd sometimes looked the other way when things were questionable, but he wasn't *that* naïve. He knew that if anything went wrong, it wouldn't be either Tanner or DredgerCorp that got stuck with the blame, but he and Dantec. DredgerCorp would cut them loose without a second thought.

He looked over to Dantec, who turned and met his gaze. He seemed as cool as ever, his gaze dead, his eyes predatory. *He doesn't care,* Hennessy realized. *He'll do whatever he's asked.* So Hennessy took a deep breath and turned to Tanner.

"Why at night?" he asked.

"Why not?" said Tanner. "The F/Seven has lights. You'd have to use them anyway once you got far enough down, and would definitely have to use them once you started digging."

"I don't think that's what he's asking," said Dantec coolly.

"No?" said Tanner. "What's he asking, then?"

"If it's legal."

"Is that right?" said Tanner, turning to Hennessy. "Is that what you're asking?"

Hennessy hesitated a moment, then nodded. "It just seems a little odd to me," he said. "Isn't all this, this whole crater, owned by Mexico? Wouldn't it have been leased by a local retrieval organization? And what's going on with the crew of this freighter? Are they military or not? If they are, why aren't they wearing uniforms? Whose side are they on? If they're not, then what the hell is going on?"

"You don't need to think about that," said Tanner. "I'm handling all the details. There's no reason for you to worry."

"But we're the ones who will bear the brunt of it if things go wrong," said Hennessy.

Tanner didn't say anything.

"Aren't I right?" asked Hennessy, appealing to Dantec. "Shouldn't we be worried? Don't you have a problem with this?"

Dantec said nothing.

Hennessy turned back to Tanner. "Shouldn't I be worried?" he asked.

Tanner said, "I've already given you an answer."

Hennessy sighed.

"Look," said Tanner. "Don't you want to be in on this? It could be extremely important, but that's not to say there aren't some risks. You have to decide for yourself, Hennessy. If you don't want to go, you don't have to go, but you have to decide right now."

Hennessy hesitated a long time. Whatever this was, legal or not, it was big, important. He couldn't trust Tanner, but then again, he couldn't really trust anybody at DredgerCorp. He'd known that when he signed on. But he'd always managed to avoid getting into scrapes before. Whether what they were doing was legal or not, he told himself, he could make sure that his part in it was legal. Besides, if things got too bad, he could walk later. He'd go along with them, but he wouldn't trust Tanner as far as he could throw him.

He finally nodded.

"Good," said Tanner. "Off you go, then, the both of you."

14

He'd never been inside the bathyscaphe at night before. The fluorescent lighting, with darkness all around, struck him at once as harsh and dirty, like the office of a deranged dentist. It cast both his face and Dantec's in stark relief.

They strapped into their seats, Hennessy at the controls and in front, Dantec just behind and to his right, beside the ballast release. The hoist lifted them up and over the water. They hung there swaying for a moment and then, suddenly, were released.

They crashed into the water, and the darkness became even more total. Dantec flicked on the exterior lights, which dimmed the lights inside. Hennessy checked the controls. He put in his earpiece and adjusted the microphone so it wasn't scraping against the side of his cheek. He ran the F/7 briefly forward and backward, turned on the drill, and watched it swirl. He checked the sonar signal. He checked the fathometer and had Dantec verify the porthole seals. Everything seemed to be in order.

"This is Plotkin," Hennessy said, speaking his code name into the mic. "Are you there, dropship? Are you reading me?"

Tanner's voice crackled to life in his ears. The man was there on the holoscreen as well, his image crisp, well defined. "Hearing and seeing you loud and clear," Tanner said. "Everything a go?"

"Roger," said Hennessy. Dantec confirmed.

"Proceed when ready, Plotkin," said Tanner.

Hennessy stayed for a moment with his hands on the controls, then cut the vid link and dived.

Now it is just a matter of time, thought Hennessy, *four or five hours.* He leaned back and stretched. At first they went down slowly, then a little faster. He was careful to adjust. The air in the F/7 had grown thick and noticeably warmer. He had Dantec check the oxygen recirculator even though he knew it was just the climate system kicking in, that it was deathly cold outside.

There was, from time to time, the flash of a fish through their running lights, though as they descended farther and farther, this became more and more rare. Mostly it was just the two of them in the cramped vessel, breathing each other's air, waiting, just waiting.

His head hurt. It seemed like it was always hurting these days. He turned slightly in his seat and cast a brief glance at Dantec, who was staring at him, with steady eyes.

"What is it?" asked Hennessy.

"What's what?" asked Dantec.

Hennessy turned back. *That guy's enough to freak anyone out,* he thought. It seemed to get even hotter. The air became even more oppressive and difficult to breathe.

66

Another hundred meters. He'd never considered how small it was inside the F/Seven. But now that they were descending and the instruments didn't need much attention, that was all he could think about. He was sweating. It was really pouring off him, buckets of it. He felt as if he could drown in his own sweat.

He laughed.

"What?" asked Dantec.

He laughed again. He couldn't help it; he knew it was absurd to think of drowning in your own sweat, but what if it happened? It was absurd, but all of this was absurd.

"Take a deep breath and get a hold of yourself," said Dantec.

He knew Dantec was right. The last thing he wanted was to dissolve into hysteria here, in a craft hardly bigger than a winter coat, miles from help. No, he couldn't do that, no. But then, there it came, another chuckle.

He heard Dantec's seat belt click off and then suddenly the man was there beside him, leaning on the instrument panel, the bathyscaphe listing slightly for just a moment before correcting itself.

He chuckled again and Dantec reached out and clamped his hand around his throat. Suddenly he couldn't breathe.

"Listen," said Dantec. "We can do this two ways. We can do it with you alive or we can do it with you dead. It doesn't matter to me which way we do it."

He struggled, but Dantec was too strong. He had never felt anything like it, had never been so afraid. He was beginning to black out, red spots blotting out his vision. He kept gulping for air, but getting nothing.

Finally, when he was just on the verge of passing out, Dantec let go, gave him a long hard stare, and slowly returned to his seat as if nothing had happened. Hennessy sucked in air, panting, massaging his throat.

"All right now," asked Dantec, his tone flat. Less a question than a command.

"Yes," Hennessy said, and was surprised to find he did feel a little better, a little more in control of himself. Though his head now throbbed even worse than before.

Hennessy checked the controls. They were still on course. Had Dantec's actions really been necessary? It was just a little giggle after all, nothing to get upset about. But Dantec had overreacted, had made a big thing of it. Someone could have gotten hurt. What had Tanner been thinking, confining Hennessy to this sinking coffin with a madman? Maybe Dantec was stronger, maybe Hennessy couldn't do anything now, but let him get back on land and he'd know what to do. He'd file a formal complaint. He'd go to Tanner and tell him about Dantec's behavior and demand the fellow's dismissal. And if Tanner wasn't willing to do anything, he'd go over his head. He'd keep filing complaints until he'd gone to the very top, to Lenny Small himself. Surely President Small was a reasonable man. And if even Mr. Small wouldn't listen, then he'd show them all. He'd take a gun and he'd—

"A thousand meters," said Dantec.

Hennessy started guiltily, the thoughts dissolving. "A thousand meters," he repeated. He noticed a tremor in his own voice, but not too bad. Maybe Tanner wouldn't notice. He put the vidlink through.

"Mothership," he said. "Come in, mother."

Tanner's voice crackled in, weaker now. His image was present but less clear, eaten away at the edges.

"Here, F/Seven," said Tanner. "Still reading you."

"One thousand meters," he said. "Seals good, instruments good, no problems to report."

"Very good," said Tanner. "Proceed."

They kept descending. It seemed even slower than before. "Everything okay at your end?" Hennessy asked Dantec.

"Fine," said Dantec. "And for you?"

Hennessy nodded. When he did, it felt like his brain was rubbing up against the walls of his skull, getting slightly bruised.

"Is the oxygen okay?" he asked.

"You just asked if everything was okay and I already told you it was," said Dantec. "*Everything* included the oxygen."

"Oh," said Hennessy. "Right."

He was silent for a while, watching the water illuminated by their running lights. Nothing alive anymore, or if there was, he wasn't seeing it. Floating through a dark, undifferentiated world. It was like his dream, he suddenly realized, which struck him as a very bad thing.

"I have a headache," he said, as much to hear the sound of a voice as anything else.

Dantec said nothing.

"Do you have a headache, too?" asked Hennessy.

"As a matter of fact, I do," Dantec said, turning to him. "I've had a headache for days now."

"So have I," said Hennessy.

Dantec just nodded. "Stop talking," he said.

Hennessy nodded back. He sat there, staring out at the

blank expanse surrounding them and their craft, listening to the creaking of the hull as the pressure increased. There was something else, some other sound he was hearing. What was it? Almost nothing at all, but it was there still, wasn't it? Just loud enough to hear but not loud enough to interpret. What could it be?

"Do you hear something?" he asked Dantec.

"I told you to stop talking," the other said.

Did that mean he heard it or not? Why couldn't he just answer the goddamned question? He'd put it civilly enough, hadn't he?

"Please," said Hennessy, "I just need to know if you hear—"

Dantec reached out and cuffed him on the side of the head.

He doesn't hear it, a part of Hennessy's mind told him. *If he heard it, he'd be wondering about it, too. Which means that either it's something close to me, near the instrument panel or—*

But the *or*, when he identified it, was too terrible to contemplate. So he bent forward, tilting his right ear toward the panel, bringing it close to each instrument, listening. He kept expecting Dantec to ask him what he was doing, but the man didn't say anything. Maybe he wasn't looking at him or maybe he just didn't care. But, in any case, there was nothing. The noise was still there, but it didn't grow any louder.

Which meant, he realized, that the sound was in his head.

As soon as he thought this, the noise became many noises, and these quickly became whispering voices. What were they saying? He was afraid he knew. He tried not to pay any attention, tried not to listen and—

"Two thousand meters," said Dantec.

Yes, thought Hennessy, *pay attention to that, to your job.*

Don't think about the voices in your head, do your job. Pull yourself together, man, last thing you need is—

"Did you hear me, Hennessy?" Dantec asked.

"I heard you," said Hennessy, shaking his head. "Two thousand meters. I'll contact Tanner."

He called up the link. There was Tanner, very pixilated now. "Two thousand meters," said Hennessy.

There was a wait of about three seconds before Tanner replied. "Repeat that," said Tanner, only it came out as a burst of static and then "—peat that."

"Two thousand meters," said Hennessy again, slower this time.

"Roger," said Tanner, after the delay. "Proceed."

Another thousand meters, thought Hennessy. Maybe even a little less. They were more than halfway there. Once they were all the way down, he could occupy himself with running the drill. He'd have something to focus on. Everything would be okay. All he had to do was make it that much farther. Then they could bore down straight to the object as quickly as possible. They'd do as Tanner had asked and take a small sample of it and get back up to the surface immediately. And then—if whatever it was was worth taking—it would be out of his hands. He'd fly back to the North American sector, go back to his life, putting all this out of his mind. If Tanner and DredgerCorp wanted to put together a full crew and excavate the object completely before other organizations got wind of it, that was their business: he'd be long out of it, long gone. If he thought about it that way, things weren't so bad.

Maybe if he took short breaths, it would be better. Then he wouldn't use up the oxygen so quickly. He was still sweating, the sweat was still pouring off him, but he wasn't giggling about it now: he was afraid. He was afraid of what was happening and afraid of Dantec.

Hennessy, get a grip on yourself, he thought. Or, rather, a *part* of him thought. Another part was screaming in his head, over and over. Another part of him was trying to force that part down belowdecks and then batten the hatch down. But then there were also the parts that were speaking, or rather whispering, all the whispering going on within his head that he didn't even know for sure was him at all. *Hennessy,* the voices were whispering, *Hennessy.* As if trying to get his attention. They were both a part of him and not a part of him.

A wave of pain flashed through his head. He grunted and pushed his thumbs hard into his temples, and then looked back at Dantec to see if he'd noticed. Dantec, he saw, was clutching his head as well, his face pale and pearled with sweat. He was grimacing. After a moment his face slipped back into expressionlessness and he straightened, met Hennessy's gaze.

"What are you looking at?" he growled.

Without a word, Hennessy turned back to his control panel, hoping it had been longer, but not sure if any time at all had gone by. Maybe they still had nine hundred meters to go.

"How many meters?" he asked in as flat and noncommittal a voice as possible.

He watched the distorted, ghostly reflection of Dantec's face in the observation porthole. The man looked deranged.

"I'll tell you when it's time," Dantec said. There was a slight tremor to his voice now, unless Hennessy was imagining it. *Maybe,* thought Hennessy, *it's as bad for him as it is for me.*

On one level, the thought was comforting. On another, it made him realize that things might be much worse than he'd thought.

He kept looking out the observation porthole, sometimes watching the murky water, sometimes watching Dantec's phantom reflection. *How much longer,* he thought, *how much longer?* He shook his head. *Hennessy,* the voices said, *Hennessy.* They were voices he recognized but he wasn't sure from where, and then he realized they were the voices he'd heard in his dream. But one in particular was even more familiar. He knew who it was, he was certain, but couldn't picture a face to go along with the voice. How could you hear a voice and know it was familiar and still not know who it was? *They've gotten into my head,* he thought. *I must have done something to let them into my head. Something is wrong with me.*

Oh, God—oh, God, he thought. *Please help me.*

If he started screaming again, Dantec would kill him. He'd said as much.

There was a flash of something outside the bathyscaphe, down below them.

No, wait, he thought, *it's just Dantec's reflection. It's nothing.* But there it was again, coming out of the gray, something lighter, slightly textured. The ocean floor.

He slowed the bathyscaphe until it was moving at a snail's pace.

"Three thousand meters," said Dantec.

"We're almost there," he told Dantec, his voice suddenly confident again. "We're almost at the bottom."

He watched it approach. It was as barren as the moon, a thick layer of muck extending in all directions. They settled down very softly, raising almost no sediment. A flatfish that had been lying in the dust flicked its body and glided away, slowly settling again just outside the lights. In practice runs, there had been a fear that the craft would roll in landing and they'd have to struggle to right her, but she came down smooth and even.

"We've made it," he said to Dantec. "Should be easy from here on out."

Dantec just stared.

Hennessy contacted Tanner. Strangely enough, the signal here was better than it had been a thousand meters higher up, perhaps because of the new angle of the craft, though there were momentary pulses of energy that fuzzed everything out.

"We made it," he said once Tanner was on.

"What's it look like?" Tanner asked.

"Smooth, flat," he said. "First layer anyway shouldn't be too difficult to dig through."

"It looks like the end of the world," muttered Dantec from behind him.

Tanner nodded. "—say?" he asked.

"I'm sorry, sir, I missed that first part," said Hennessy.

"It doesn't matter," said Tanner. "Proceed when ready. And good luck."

Hennessy put out the struts for stability and to elevate the back half of the craft. The drill angled down until it was touching the ocean floor. He readied the controls.

15

He felt a hand on his shoulder, turned to see Dantec there, out of his seat and swaying, his eyes glazed over.

"I'll run the drill," he said.

"But I'm the one—"

Dantec squeezed and a sharp pain shot to his shoulder and neck; one of his arms went suddenly numb.

"I'll run the drill," said Dantec again, voice like flint. "Move."

It was a struggle to get the seat belt unbuckled with Dantec squeezing his shoulder, but in the end he managed. He stood up. Dantec was still holding on to him, but he made his way to the other seat. Only once he was sitting and buckled in did Dantec let go.

Hennessy breathed a sigh of relief and began massaging his shoulder with his fingers. Slowly feeling began to come back into his arm. He stared resentfully at Dantec.

"You hardly know what you're doing," he said. "You're going to get us both killed."

"Shut up," said Dantec, not even bothering to turn around to look at him. He powered up the drill and started it going.

The whole craft shook. With a jerk, they slowly began to burrow into the muck.

The F/7 performed better than expected, digging slowly but inexorably downward, the drill gouging a path forward and the pulverizers decreasing the debris. At first it was mainly mud and silt, particulate matter that had filtered downward over the years. It was easy to dig through, but also there was very little for the drill to grab, so the going was slow.

The real question, thought Hennessy, looking out the back through the navigation porthole at the way the tunnel was already filling up, was how easy it would be to get out again. The pulverizers were definitely getting rid of some of the debris, but not all of it, and they could very well get stuck if they just tried to reverse out the way they'd gone in. They'd have to dig a circle and try to rejoin the tunnel. Either that or just dig a second tunnel going up. As long as Dantec was careful, it'd be okay.

"Dropship, can you read me?" he heard Dantec say. "Dropship?"

All Hennessy heard on his own earpiece was static. He assumed from the fact that Dantec didn't continue speaking that he was hearing the same. Just the two of them, then, at least for the moment.

And me, said a voice within his head before scuttling away.

He groaned.

The F/7 lurched a bit. The sound the drill was making changed. They hit something harder—marl, he guessed, from what he'd seen of the geological maps. Calcium carbonate and mudstone. He'd be able to check the readings and the exact composition if he were in the chair he was supposed to be in.

He checked the readouts, looking over Dantec's shoulder. They seemed to be on track. So far, nothing to worry about.

You'll listen to me, said the voice in his head. *Before you're done, you'll listen to me.*

"I'm busy," he said aloud. He shook his head. He bit the insides of his mouth until he tasted blood, hoping that would distract him from the voice he was hearing. For a moment, it did.

"What?" said Dantec.

"Pardon?"

"What did you say?"

"Oh, that," Hennessy said. "Sorry. I wasn't talking to you."

He held still, phasing out a little bit, listening to the hum of the drill, feeling the bathyscaphe shiver around him. *I'm not here,* he started telling himself at one point. *This is all a dream. Nothing but a dream.*

He leapt into awareness again as the craft jerked and the sound of the drill changed again. The F/7 slowed considerably. He turned and plastered his face to the rear navigation porthole, trying to see the side of the tunnel. Darker rock now, a breccia amalgam and andesite glass. Here and there traces of shocked quartz, due to an impact.

"We must be getting close," he said to Dantec.

Dantec grunted. "Fifty or so meters to the tip of the target," he said. "It'll take some time still. You'll have to be patient."

Be patient, he thought. He couldn't promise anything, but he would try. All they could ask of him was that he try.

Then suddenly the drill stopped and the oxygen recirculator

died. The lights flickered out and the readouts on the control panels were reduced to lines of static. Not even the emergency lights were working. He heard in his ears, for just an instant, Tanner's voice, his tone terse: "—do you read, co—" and then nothing but dead air.

In the silence he listened to the sound of Dantec pressing buttons, trying to work the controls. Nothing. His hands, he suddenly realized, were doing the same.

"What's happened?" he asked, almost screaming it.

"I don't know," said Dantec. "It's not working!"

Hennessy felt the porthole and started pounding on it.

"Stop it," said Dantec. "Whatever you're doing, stop it!"

The darkness was thick all around him, too thick. He could feel it tightening its fingers around his throat, the air already growing warm and then hot. It was more than he could stand.

And then suddenly it got worse. There, briefly illuminated, on the other side of the porthole, was a face. At first he thought it was his own face, but it was pitch dark. How could it be his own face? Or maybe a deepwater fish, something with its own luminescence. But no, it was a human face, not a fish, and he was sure it was not his own face. It was there, just on the other side of the glass, pressed between the glass and the wall of the tunnel they had just dug, glowing softly. And it was a face he knew—a puffy and slightly pudgy face, curly hair that floated in the water, a somewhat slack mouth, crooked teeth. He and the face shared the same eyes—their father's eyes. It was his half brother, Shane.

Shane had been dead for years. He had died in college, a freak accident when he'd been driving down the highway and a restraint broke on an automobile transport vehicle in front of him, sending a car crashing off its top level to crush him. Hennessy was sure he was dead. He'd seen the body. Even seen, when the undertaker was looking the other way, how if you grabbed Shane's hair and tilted the head, a huge bloodless gash opened up just under the collar. No, it was impossible.

And yet, here he was.

Hello, Jim, Shane mouthed. Hennessy heard the words sound aloud within his head.

"Hello, Shane," he said. "What are you doing out there?"

"Shut up!" said Dantec. "What's wrong with you? Shut up!"

It's good to see you, Jim, said Shane.

Hennessy put his face very close to the glass. "I have to be quiet," he whispered. "If I don't, Dantec's going to throw a conniption."

Shane nodded and smiled, then pretended, as they had done when they were kids, to be zipping his mouth shut.

"I have to be honest, Shane," Hennessy whispered. He couldn't see his own face in the darkness, but he imagined his forehead to be wrinkled with worry. Hopefully Shane could see that and would take the question in the spirit it was intended. "I thought you were dead."

Of course you did, Jim, said Shane. *That's what they wanted you to think.*

Hennessy nodded. "Those bastards," he whispered.

Shane nodded. *They're not that bad,* he said. *They just don't know any better. But you know better, don't you, Jim?*

"I do now," whispered Hennessy. "God, Shane, it's really great to see you. But I have to ask you another question."

Go ahead, said Shane. *You can ask me anything.*

"What are you doing out there?"

Well, said Shane, looking down shyly, *to be frank, Jim, I was hoping you'd invite me in.*

Hennessy looked around at the darkness, trying to picture in his mind what the cabin looked like. "Shane, it's already pretty cramped in here. I don't know if there's room."

Trust me, there's more room than you think, said Shane. *Invite me in and you'll see.*

"But what will Dantec think?" he asked.

"Stop whispering!" shouted Dantec. "Stop it now!"

Shane gave him a sleepy grin. *He's not the boss here, Jim. I know how things really are. You're the boss. Dantec, he's just a big bully. He needs someone to put him in his place. I'll be quiet. I bet he won't even notice me.*

"You're right, Shane," whispered Hennessy. "He's nothing more than a big bully." He waited, pressing his face against the thick glass of the porthole. "Why not, then? Come on in, Shane. Come on in."

With that, suddenly the lights flickered and went out again, then came on in full force. The readouts went live again. Hennessy heard crackling in his ear, saw Tanner's ghost on his holoscreen before it was rubbed out by static.

The oxygen recirculators started up and the drill began to hum. Dantec gave a whoop. "We're okay," he said, casting a quick glance over his shoulder. His face, Hennessy saw, was slick with sweat. "We're going to be okay."

But Hennessy already knew it would be okay. His brother, good old Shane, was here now, sitting right beside him on a chair he hadn't remembered being there before. Shane must have brought it with him. He was smiling, holding Hennessy's hand in his own. Now that Shane was there, everything would work out.

16

He gently disengaged his hand from his brother's and looked at his chronometer. Six thirty-eight, it read, but he could tell by the way the numbers flashed and then slowly faded that it had stopped. Why wasn't it working? He showed it to Shane, who just nodded.

Nothing to worry about, brother, Shane said. *It doesn't really matter.*

Shane was right, of course, it didn't really matter, but he still wanted to know what time it was.

"What time is it?" he asked Dantec.

"Leave me alone," said Dantec. "We're getting close. I have to watch this."

Hennessy waited a moment and then asked again.

Distractedly, Dantec looked at his wrist, then held his chronometer to his ear. "It's stopped," he said.

"Mine, too," said Hennessy.

Dantec turned and looked at him. He didn't seem to notice Shane, even though he was right there, right next to Hennessy. *People see what they want to see,* thought Hennessy.

"Doesn't that seem weird to you?" Dantec asked.

Hennessy shrugged. "Nothing to worry about," he said. "It doesn't really matter."

Dantec narrowed his eyes. "And another thing," he said. "Why are you so fucking serene all of a sudden?"

Hennessy cast his eyes toward Shane, then realized what he'd done and flicked them back quickly to look at Dantec. Dantec's eyes moved to the side, stared through Shane, then moved back.

"It's just like that," said Hennessy. "I just feel better. I don't know why."

Rolling his eyes, Dantec turned away.

Just between you and me, Jim, should he really be doing this? asked Shane.

"I don't know," said Hennessy, "should he?"

Some things it's better not to mess with.

Hennessy nodded. Shane was probably right, but if he told Dantec that, he wouldn't listen. What could he do about it? Maybe it was a bad idea, but even if it was, he didn't know how he could get Dantec to stop.

After a few more minutes—or maybe it was longer, impossible to say—Dantec slowed the drill. He drilled forward slowly until they struck something and the drill made a whining sound. He reversed it, backed up a little, and then approached at a slightly different angle, shearing away the side of the tunnel wall. Hennessy just stayed smiling, glancing occasionally over at his brother, waiting.

Are you sure it's a good idea? asked Shane again. Hennessy shrugged.

Dantec backed up again, came in once more, then a fourth time.

I think it's a mistake, Shane said.

There was, Hennessy could see, a strange shape, still half enclosed in rock on one side. It was hard to see past the particles of rock and silt swirling through the water. Dantec pulled back a little, then turned off the drill.

"What's out there?" asked Hennessy.

"How the hell should I know?" said Dantec. "I've never seen anything like it before."

It's the Black Marker, said Shane.

The Black Marker, Hennessy thought. As the water settled, he began to see it more clearly. It looked like a monolith made of some sort of obsidian. It narrowed to a point at the top, the whole of it twisting slightly as it rose. It was horizontally striated and covered with thousands of symbols, symbols unlike anything he had seen before. Were they glowing, or did it only look like they were because of the way the light was catching them? He couldn't tell for sure. What he could see of it, of the part that was uncovered now, was probably three meters tall.

"Oh my God," said Dantec, his voice filled with an uncustomary awe. "Who put this here? Or what?"

That's the last question you want to ask, said Shane to Hennessy. *Better not to know.*

He remembered suddenly the schematic that Tanner had shown them of the Marker. He pulled it up on his holoscreen. There were two horns at the top, pointing out in either direction, and he could see the Marker went on much deeper below them, probably another twenty meters or more. "How big is it?" Hennessy asked.

Dantec, confused, said something, but Hennessy wasn't asking him.

Big, said Shane. He moved Hennessy's hand to the porthole, pressed it against the glass. Together they stared out. *You don't want to mess with this,* Shane said. *You're in danger.*

"I'm going to move us closer," said Dantec.

"Are you sure?" asked Hennessy, still staring out. "Maybe we shouldn't mess with it." Beside him, just at the edge of his peripheral vision, Shane nodded.

"Try calling Tanner," said Dantec. "See what he wants to do."

Hennessy tried, got only bursts of static, little bits of Tanner's voice spliced into it like it had been torn apart.

"I don't know," said Hennessy. "There's something seriously wrong here. Let's leave it alone."

"We came all this way," said Dantec. "We've been in this coffin for hours. Now that we're here, we have to get a better look."

Hennessy remained for a moment, staring at it, and finally nodded. "It wouldn't hurt to get closer, I guess," he said. "As long as we're careful."

He looked over at his brother, who was shaking his head. *It just might,* he said.

Dantec eased the ship forward, then cut the engines, let them drift. There they were, right up against it. The F/7 bumping softly against the Marker's side.

"It's marvelous," Dantec whispered.

It's not marvelous, said Shane, his face stretched into a strange rictus. *It's horrible. Dantec is becoming one of them, brother. I'm afraid we're going to have to get rid of him.*

17

So far, so good, thought Dantec, *or good enough anyway.* He'd probably make it through. His head had been aching ever since he got into the goddamn sub. Or, if he was to be honest with himself, for weeks now. Pills didn't seem to help. Whatever he did, it was still there, not unbearable, just always throbbing quietly, keeping him from sleeping, destroying his concentration. He hadn't felt so strung out since the moon skirmishes. For that matter, he hadn't felt this confined—this trapped—since then. He hadn't realized how much being in a sub underwater was going to feel like being in a jettison pod in space. It brought all sorts of things flashing back at him from the moon skirmishes, that weird war that wasn't officially a war, where all it took was one little tear in the fabric of your suit for you to die and where, by the end, if you wanted to survive, you had to stab a knife in a buddy's back just so you could steal what was left of his oxygen. How many men had he had to kill to stay alive? All that had changed him, hardened him. He thought at first that it had lifted him above things, had made it so he wouldn't feel fear, wouldn't be subject to the same emotional weaknesses as others. But he was beginning to realize that that wasn't quite right. True, he'd managed to avoid those parts of himself for a long time, but they were still there. And now that they were forcing their way up to the surface, they were raw and red, more sensitive than an exposed nerve.

And that bastard Hennessy. It didn't help being stuck with him. He was a real, genuine fucking chucklehead, that was for sure. First he had been like a kid in a toy shop, unable to contain his delight at the F/7, at his new toy. Then put him in the thing and he does a Jekyll/Hyde, becomes nothing but panic and nerves and slow collapse into madness. That was the last thing you wanted in a confined space like this. In the moon skirmishes, he'd killed men for less.

Not like the thought didn't cross his mind. But Tanner didn't want him to do it. Tanner had been good to him over the years. Though if Tanner had understood what had really happened during the moon skirmishes, Dantec knew, he might treat him a lot differently.

During the skirmishes, Tanner never realized that Dantec was not interested in saving him so much as stealing his air supply. Dantec had planned to kill him and take his oxygen tank, and he would have done it, too, except that, while looking for a safe place to kill Tanner, he'd stumbled onto a working transmitter, a technician's severed and frozen arm still stuck to it. So, instead of killing Tanner, he called the dropship to pick them up. Tanner never understood that the reason he blacked out and almost died before the ship arrived was because Dantec had turned the airflow on his tank down. Just in case the ship didn't come fast enough and he needed Tanner's air after all.

But loyalty and guilt toward Tanner weren't the only reasons that Dantec hadn't killed Hennessy. He didn't like the idea of killing someone in such a confined space, where he couldn't dispose of the body. He just couldn't imagine sitting there, knowing the body was behind him, feeling its dead eyes on his back. Add to that the fact that over the last six or so hours, he'd actually become a little afraid of Hennessy. Panicking, then whispering to himself, speaking to the bulkhead to his left as if there was actually someone sitting beside him. The man was out of his mind, and Dantec didn't want to do anything to provoke him. He knew, from personal experience, that when people went out of their minds, they became unpredictable. They could do things you'd never expect and they'd do them with a strength you'd never expect them to have.

He just wanted to come through this alive. They'd made it halfway. They were here now, right beside the monolith, which, he had to admit, also scared the shit out of him. But it filled him with awe as well. It had been there more than fifty million years if the geological data was to be believed. Which meant it predated humankind. But it was clearly man-made—or made by some intelligent life. It was mind-boggling.

Hennessy was staring out the porthole at it, lost in contemplation of the thing, looking like his brain had been switched off.

Dantec had the core sampler primed. It was readied and partly extended. He'd tested the molecular cutters that would slice into the stone. Carefully he extended the arm until it was touching the monolith itself, and then he thrust it forward and started to cut.

Almost immediately his head was filled with a piercing pain, so intense that he felt he was going to pass out. His vision first seemed as though it had been coated in blood and then it vanished entirely, being replaced by an empty white expanse. He gripped the control panel, struggling to breathe. Hennessy was screaming behind him.

Very slowly, the pain began to ebb away. His vision crept back. Hennessy was moaning, all but passed out behind him. The core sampler had kept cutting—very slowly, but it was still cutting. All they needed was a little bit, just a little bit, and then he could turn the F/7 around and get the hell out of there.

18

One minute, Hennessy was sitting there, looking at his brother, everything fine, and the next there was a piercing noise and his head felt like it was going to burst. His brother began to shake all over. His head tilted to one side, his neck tearing open just where it did when Shane had been killed. He shook more and in a burst his body exploded, spattering everything with blood. Hennessy began to scream, and suddenly couldn't breathe. A moment later the ship around him was spinning, and then darkness.

When he came to, Shane was back, looking just as he had before he'd dissolved into a burst of blood, the same strange fixed expression on his face. He'd moved, though, and was now sitting next to Dantec, facing the other way, looking back at Hennessy. Or not next to Dantec exactly: he seemed to be sitting, so it seemed, partly *on* Dantec. But as Hennessy pulled himself up, he saw. Shane was partly *in* Dantec, their hips fused together, his legs somehow jutting through the back of the command chair.

"You're all right?" asked Hennessy.

"Yes," said Dantec. "Except for my head. And you?"

He shouldn't be doing this, said Shane, his mouth moving soundlessly in the air, like a fish out of water. *It's dangerous. Looking's bad enough, but touching is too much. Neither of you should be doing this. Jim, I thought you were better than that.*

"Doing what?" asked Hennessy.

"I'm taking a core sample, of course," said Dantec. "What did you expect me to be doing?"

This is not something to be examined, said Shane. *This is not something to be understood. It needs to be left alone and untouched, where it's been lying undisturbed for millions of years. Do you think they would have buried it this deep if it was meant to be found?*

"What does it do?" Hennessy asked.

Dantec still wasn't looking at him. "It's a molecular cutter with a titanium cylinder behind it," he said. "The circular cutter makes a round hole and pushes slowly in. Once the cylinder is far enough in, the cutters rotate to shear off the end of the sample. I thought you knew all that. Don't worry, not much longer, we're almost done."

You don't want to know what it does, said Shane. *You shouldn't try to destroy it. You shouldn't listen to it. You should just leave it alone. You must resist Convergence, Jim.*

"Convergence?"

"What?" said Dantec, half turning around. "I guess that yes, the molecular beams converge, in a manner of speaking. But why are you so interested?"

Not to mention the Convergence, said Shane. *The last thing you want to do is get that started.* He stretched uncomfortably in his chair.

"Be careful how you move," said Hennessy to Dantec. "You don't want to tear Shane apart."

19

Oh, shit, thought Dantec. He turned fully around to face Hennessy, who immediately started screaming.

"Shane!" Hennessy screamed, *"Shane!* The blood! The blood! He's all over everything! He's all over you!" Making gagging sounds, he started rubbing his hands up and down Dantec's chest, a terrible expression on his face. "We have to get him off!" he said, and cast Dantec a desperate look. "Can't you see it?" he asked. "Can't you see the blood?"

Dantec slapped him hard enough to knock him down. "Just calm down," said Dantec. He was shaking. "Just relax."

"Easy for you to say," Hennessy was muttering. "It isn't your brother who just burst."

"Hennessy," said Dantec, "it wasn't your brother either. It's just you and me here."

But Hennessy was shaking his head. "I saw him," he was saying, "I saw him." His voice was more and more hysterical. "He was here, I swear, right here, right there, where you're sitting, there."

"But that's me," said Dantec, starting to get really frightened. "How could he be sitting here if I was here the whole time?"

"He was," said Hennessy. "He was halfway inside you. You tore him, and then he burst."

Oh, shit, thought Dantec again. "Try to get a hold of yourself, Hennessy," he said, keeping his voice level. "You're imagining things."

"We have to stop," said Hennessy. "Shane told me—we have to leave it alone. We have to bury it and get the hell out of here. Stop the core sampler!" He was screaming now. "Put it back!"

"It's okay," said Dantec, "I'll stop it," he said. "I'm stopping it now," he claimed. He reached out for the controls and then hesitated. It was nearly through, the sample nearly extracted. Just a few seconds more and they'd have it, and then they could get the hell out of there.

"Stop it!" raved Hennessy. "Stop it!"

"I'm stopping it," lied Dantec. "Don't shout, you're confusing me. It's almost done, I swear."

And it was done, for at that moment the molecular cutters finished and the core sampler began to withdraw with its sample in the extraction cylinder.

"There, you see?" said Dantec. "Everything's okay." He turned around, smiling, just in time to have his jaw broken by a metal bar. He raised his arm, felt the pain as the bar struck him there as well. He half slid, half fell out of the command chair. He saw the bar hit and crumple the armrest just above his head. It was a strut from the oxygen recirculator—he wondered how Hennessy had disassembled it so quickly. He kicked out, watched Hennessy lurch to one side and stumble against the bulkhead. Dantec started to scramble up, but his arm wouldn't support him. Blood was pouring out of his mouth and down his chest. He managed to heave himself to his feet, but Hennessy had already recovered and was coming at him, bringing the bar down. He raised the broken arm and Hennessy struck it again, the pain this time so intense that his vision faded to a dark blur. He slipped in his own blood and was down again. And then Hennessy struck him in the head.

As he lay there, the life leaking out of him, he began to feel people crowding around him. It was impossible. Even though he was dying, he knew it wasn't possible, it was only he and Hennessy there, and even if it were possible, there were too many people to fit. But even though he was sure it couldn't be happening, it was unbearable that it was. Particularly when he recognized the faces. They were all men he had been with in the moon skirmishes, men who not only had died, but died by his hand, so that he could take their oxygen and survive. One by one, they came forward while Hennessy continued to batter him with the iron bar, kneeling beside him and then leaning over him to suck the breath out of his mouth. When the last one finally came, he died.

20

He dropped the iron bar, exhausted, and limped back to his chair. He wiped the blood off his face with his sleeve and closed his eyes.

It was only after sitting there like that for a few moments, his breath gradually slowing, that he started to realize what he'd just done.

He opened his eyes and saw the mess on the floor and retched. It was barely recognizable as a human form anymore, the limbs twisted and turned in the wrong directions, the head flattened out and split open on the top. It was much worse than when his brother had exploded. He looked away. Had he done that? How? Dantec was a skilled and seasoned fighter, much stronger than he was—when Dantec had grabbed his shoulder, he'd been paralyzed with pain. No, he couldn't have done this, he couldn't have gotten away with it.

But if not him, then who?

And where was his brother? Was this really happening or was it just what *they* wanted him to believe?

"Shane?" he said.

His comlink suddenly crackled. Tanner's voice, unless it was someone pretending to be Tanner. "—eed me. Plea—spond. Hennes—"

He went to the screen, which was now spattered with blood.

"Tanner?" he said. "I've lost Shane."

"—aa—" said Tanner. Hennessy saw his face for just a minute on the scanner, looking grim; then a startled expression crossed Tanner's face and he was drowned out in static.

Hennessy turned away from the control panel to see, just behind him, his brother.

"Shane," he said, and smiled. "You're all right after all."

Of course I am, Jim, he said. *You don't think a little thing like that could hurt me, do you?*

It must have been a trick, Hennessy told himself.

His brother leaned against the control panel and stared down at him. *I need to speak seriously with you, Jim,* he said.

"What is it, Shane?" asked Hennessy. "You know you can talk to me about anything."

His dead brother looked straight at him, his face thoughtful, just as it had often been before, when they were younger.

You did good, brother, you stopped him, said Shane. *But this is a very dangerous time, you are too close. Too close to be able to hear clearly. The whispers, they may take you. You mustn't listen to them, Jim. Get free, stay clear, keep your mind to yourself. Or you may be no more. Tell all the others the same.*

"But . . . I don't . . ." Hennessey stuttered, groping for words. "I have to be honest, Shane. I'm not sure I understand exactly what you're talking about."

Let them know, said Shane. *The Marker is the past, and the past must remain undisturbed if we are to continue as we are. You have already awakened it. It calls out for you even now. But you must not obey. You must not listen. Tell them that.*

"Who am I supposed to tell?" asked Hennessy.

Everybody, said Shane. *Tell everybody.*

"But why don't you tell them, Shane?" he asked. "You know so much more about it than I do!"

But Shane just shook his head. *It's already begun,* he said. He reached out and touched his thumb to Hennessy's forehead. His touch burned like ice. And then, as Hennessy watched, his brother slowly faded and was gone.

21

He felt bereft, and very lonely. He went to the observation porthole, slipping on the carcass on the floor on the way. *Somebody should move that,* he thought. The whole cabin reeked of blood. *Maybe Shane's out there,* he thought, *like he was before,* but all he could see was the murky water, cut through by the light, and the edge of the Marker. Yes, it was definitely glowing now, its light pulsing slightly.

He stared at it. It was trying to tell him something. What had Shane said? That it had to be left alone, that they didn't need to understand it. But why, then, did he feel like he wanted to understand it, like he wanted to learn from it? Maybe Shane had been wrong.

He stared and stared. For a moment, he felt he could hear a voice again, maybe Shane's voice, but then it grew softer and softer and was gone. And then suddenly the glow grew brighter and it was as if his head had been cracked open and filled with light. He whirled around, his eyes darting back and forth. He needed to get it all down. He needed to record everything it was telling him. He could type it all into the computer, but that wasn't enough, there could be a power failure and then everything would be lost. No, he needed to write it, but he didn't have a pen, a pencil, paper. He hadn't used actual paper since he was a child. The computer would have to do.

On his way back to it, he slipped again, went partly down, soaking his knee and his hand in gore. He looked at his hand, dripping with blood, its bloody double inscribed right on the flesh of his thigh, and then he knew what to do.

He dipped his fingers in Dantec's blood and approached the walls, waiting for his mind to crack open again. When it did, it flared with symbols. He could see them perfectly in his head, shimmering there. Frantically, he began to jot them on the walls, writing as quickly as he could, stopping only to dip his fingers in blood again. At first there was something like an *N*, but only backward, with a bead on the bottom of its leg. Then an *L,* but upside down, with its horizontal bar crimped. Then something that looked like the prow of a ship, moving left to right, a porthole just visible, and a circle within a circle. After that he was writing so furiously, trying to keep up with the figures streaming through his head, that he couldn't keep track, could only let his fingers trace out the patterns and move on.

When he hit the porthole, he didn't stop, just wrote right over it. Anything that got in the way he wrote on. After a while, he was running out of space and started writing smaller so that there'd be enough room. When he ran out of room on the walls, he wrote on and under the instrument panels. When he ran low on blood, he stomped on what was left of Dantec's chest, trying to force more out. But only a little came out. So he stomped on a limb hard and blood began to leach out.

Before too long, Dantec's body had been torn to pieces, looking even less human than when he'd started.

The com unit crackled, sending out an angry hiss of static. "—in, co—F/Seven—othersh—" it said.

"Not now, Tanner," he said back.

"—ome in, come—o you read?" it said.

"Not now!" he shouted. The ceiling was already covered, the walls were already covered; all that was left was the floor. He piled the pieces of Dantec's body in the command chair. He tried to strap them in, but quickly realized it was useless. That was all right, he told himself. The vessel wasn't moving. They weren't going anywhere.

There was hardly any blood left, and what was left on the floor was beginning to clot. He dipped his fingers in it, kept writing in light, wispy strokes, conserving the blood. But very quickly, he ran out of floor.

He wished Shane were there to tell him what to do next. Had he done the right thing? Had he betrayed his brother? He stayed there on his knees, staring.

It was hot, almost too hot to bear. How could it be so hot? He stood up and took off his shirt, threw it on the other chair. It helped a little, but not enough. He was still hot. He took off his shoes, piled them on top of the shirt, then took off his pants, his underwear. Naked, he stared down at his body. *Pale,* he thought. *White as a sheet. No, not a sheet,* he corrected. *White as paper.* And then he knew where he would write next.

Only there wasn't any more blood. He'd used all of Dantec up; he hadn't saved enough to write the ending.

He looked around. Surely there was more blood here somewhere. Didn't they travel with bags of blood? What if they needed to do an onboard transfusion? How could they go anywhere without blood?

His eyes were scanning over the room, searching, when they passed over his arm, saw the pulse of a vein. "Ah," he said, breaking into a smile, "that's where you're hiding. There you are."

It wasn't easy to get the blood to come out, but in the end he managed, tearing the arm open with the sharp corner of the same strut he had used to discipline Dantec. At first, the blood came readily and he could simply rub the finger against his arm and then inscribe a symbol on his body. But quickly the wound slowed and began to clot. He had to tear it open again, and then a third time.

By the time he was done, it was as if he himself had become a representation of the Marker. He was beautiful, covered with a swarm of symbols, all the knowledge of the universe expressed on the surface of his skin. He stood straight, arms to his sides, and held still. He was the Marker. He could feel its power flowing through him.

How long he was like that, he couldn't say. He was snapped out of it by a sharp noise and an intense pain in his head. He swayed and fell down, clutching his temples. When the noise finally stopped, he stood and stumbled up. He had more to do, he remembered, confusedly. He had to tell them; he had to warn them.

He turned on the vidscreen and stood in front of it, set it to simultaneously record and to broadcast on all frequencies. The message was for *everyone*—Shane had been clear about that.

He needed to tell everyone, if the message could get through the rock and muck at all.

"Hello," he said to the vidscreen. "Officer James Hennessy here, acting commander of the SS *Marker*. I've been informed by my brother, Shane, that there's something we all need to know."

There was a stabbing pain in his head, as if someone were prodding his optic nerve with the tip of a dull knife. He clutched his head and leaned on the counter. After the pain had passed, he stood there for a moment, unsure of where he was. He opened his eyes and looked around him, unable to take it all in. And then suddenly he remembered: He was on TV!

He gave the camera his most winning smile. What was he doing again? Oh, yes, that's right: He was saving humanity.

"We've heard the wrong whispers," he started. "There's little time, and we're listening to what they say, but Shane says we should not obey. We are not following the right answers. We have to resist the past before it is too late. Too late for Convergence."

He gave his winning smile again, looking straight and intensely into the camera. Anyone watching would realize he was talking directly to them. They had to understand how important this was.

"I've drawn a map," he said, gesturing to his body. "I don't know if that's what Shane wants, but I looked at the Marker and looked at it and then I had to draw. We need to change our ways and learn to understand it," he said. He shook his head, confused. Had he gotten off track somewhere? "Or else not understand it," he said. It was like there were two forces inside him, fighting to claim him, and he was no longer sure which was which, and which he should listen to.

The Marker caught his eye through the porthole. He watched it pulse a long moment. He looked at his left hand, then looked at his right hand and slowly brought them together, in front of him. "Convergence," he said. He gestured at the Marker through the porthole, then gestured at the symbols on his own body. "We need to understand it," he said, even though a part of him was screaming at him to stop. "That's the only thing that's important right now, to learn from it. It is the way. We need to understand it, not destroy it."

He backed away and turned the vid off. He was so tired now. His head hurt. He needed to rest. He would rest for just a minute and then head for home.

He lay down on the floor. He felt both hot and cold. His bare body felt unnatural against the smooth floor. Slowly he folded in on himself, until he was curled into a ball, and started to shiver.

At the end he had a brief moment of lucidity, when he realized that he was tired because the oxygen was running out, when he realized that something else had controlled everything he had done, everything he had said. But by the time he realized this, it was far too late to do anything about it. *I'll get up in a moment*, he thought. *I'll get up and drill my way back up to the surface. And then I'll sort this mess out.*

A moment later he lapsed into unconsciousness.

Not long after, he was dead.

PART THREE

THE NOOSE TIGHTENS

22

"How long has it been?" asked the Colonel.

"Too long," said Tanner, his face drawn, his voice hoarse. "Nearly forty-eight hours now." He'd been awake almost two and a half full days. Most of that time he'd spent trying to get in touch with the F/7. There'd been a few scattered bits, moments when somehow everything aligned to let the signal through, and so he assumed there had been moments they'd seen him as well. But it never lasted long enough for them to communicate. And then, just when he was ready to give up hope, there had come a signal, broadcasting on all bands. They had gotten only bits of that, too, but others had picked up other bits of it on other channels. Tanner's team had gathered as much as they could and were working to sequence it all together to form something. He'd thought they'd have something by now, which was why he'd contacted the Colonel, but they were still working.

"Could they still be alive?" the Colonel asked.

"We already know one of them is dead."

"Hennessy?"

"No, Dantec," said Tanner. He rubbed his eyes. He'd had a headache for days now, maybe even weeks. He was starting to feel like he couldn't remember when he hadn't had one.

"That's a surprise," said the Colonel.

Tanner nodded. "We still don't know what happened, but we know he's dead." He spun the holofile through the screen, watched the Colonel take it up on his end. Tanner knew what it was: a grisly image capture showing a disjointed torso propped in the command chair, its limbs piled neatly on the chair just in front of it. The head was broken and distorted and hardly human. "It's a piece of one transmission that we were able to salvage. The last image we have, really."

"How do you know this is Dantec?" asked the Colonel. The Colonel was a hard man, Tanner thought: his voice was just as even as it had been before, like he was looking at somebody's wedding picture.

Tanner circled portions of the image on his monitor. "You can see here and there bits of hair. It's caked in blood, but we're reasonably certain it's hair."

"Ah, yes," said the Colonel, "now I see."

"Hennessy was bald," Tanner said simply.

The Colonel leaned back in his chair, thoughtful. "What happened?" he asked.

Tanner shrugged. "Something went wrong," he said. "Beyond that I can't say."

"If you had to guess, what would you guess?"

Tanner sighed. "Hennessy must have gone crazy and caught Dantec unawares. Maybe something wrong with the oxygen supply that had some effect on his brain, maybe the pressure of being confined in such a small space for too long. Or maybe he was already insane and we didn't know."

"Doesn't it strike you as strange?" asked the Colonel.

"Of course it strikes me as strange," said Tanner. "It's not normal behavior."

"No," said the Colonel. "Yes, of course, all that is strange, but it's even stranger that it happens now, just now, when they're on their way toward an impossible object found in an impossible location."

"Sabotage, you think?"

"I can't rule it out," said the Colonel. "But that's the least strange of the possibilities, Tanner. Show a little more imagination." He leaned forward again. "Contact me immediately once you've got some footage to show me," he said, and reached out to cut the link.

23

The power of the signal, Altman realized, had increased sometime during the night. The indicator he'd installed was reading higher than he'd ever seen it. The pulse ended and it fell back, still higher than it had been in its previous resting state.

He glanced over at Field, who seemed immersed in his own calculations. Just to be safe, he angled his holoscreen so that there'd be no chance of Field seeing what was on it. He scrolled back through the data log until he found the shift. There, sometime around six or seven in the morning, though he'd have to do a full correlation to make sure. The signal's increase wasn't gradual but immediate, as if something had suddenly and deliberately amplified it.

He hadn't heard from Hammond since the night in the bar, which concerned him a little but not too much. The security technician was probably lying low, being careful. When he wanted to get in touch, he would. In the meantime, it was up to Altman to find out what was going on.

He logged his results into the encrypted database and then looked to see if they correlated with work done by the others—

the others in this case being the three other scientists who had, like Altman, been intrigued by the gravity anomaly and the pulse and wanted to pursue it: Showalter, Ramirez, and Skud.

Showalter, who had more powerful equipment than Altman's simple sensor, had gotten the same readings. At 6:38 A.M., there had been an extraordinarily strong pulse, followed by a shift in the signal patterning. The signal was now perpetually amplified. There were still high and low points, but the basic profile of the signal was stronger, and had remained so ever since.

Ramirez had noted something else, something that he had picked up off the satellite images while trying to get a sense of whether there had been a change in the condition of the crater itself. A freighter, anchored about fifteen miles southeast of the crater's center.

"At first I didn't pay much attention to it," said Ramirez in the vidfile he'd attached. "But then, I go back a day and it's still there. I go forward a day and it's there, too. If it's really a freighter, what would it be doing sitting in the same place?

"So, yesterday morning, I hired a local man who called himself Captain Jesús to use his old motorboat to run me out for a closer look. I took a fishing pole with me. Once we were about two hundred meters from the freighter, I had Captain Jesús stop and cast my line into the water.

"The captain told me I wasn't going to catch anything. When I asked why not, he gave me a long hard look and pointed out to me that I hadn't bothered to put any bait on the end of my line.

"I didn't know what to say to that, so I didn't say anything. Captain Jesús made a point of looking at the freighter and then looking back at me, then told me that it didn't seem like it was fish I wanted to catch and that the kind of fishing I wanted would cost me extra.

"In the end, I had to promise to pay the good captain double his normal rate to stay there so that we could get a good look at the freighter. It didn't have any markings. Other than that, it seemed an ordinary enough freighter, except for the fact that it had a brand-new heavy-duty submarine lift attached to its deck.

"That was all I had time to ascertain," Ramirez said. "We'd been there all of five minutes, two of which I spent bartering with Captain Jesús, when a launch appeared from the other side of the ship and pulled up alongside us, manned by four muscle-bound boys with military haircuts, but without the requisite military garb.

" 'Move along,' one of them said.

" 'I'm fishing,' I claimed.

" 'Fish somewhere else,' he said. I was going to argue, but Captain Jesús threw the boat in gear and took us out. When I asked him why, later, all he would say was 'These are not good men.'

"Which left me with three questions," said Ramirez, concluding his vid-log. "First, what use would a freighter, if it really is a freighter, have for a submarine? Second, what makes them want to keep other boats at a distance? Third, what the hell is really going on?"

What indeed? wondered Altman.

The last report, from Skud, a laconic Swede, didn't arrive for another hour. It was a document instead of a vid-log.

So sorry, his report read. *Had to double check.* What followed was a series of charts with captions in Swedish, none of which

Altman knew how to read. After them, Skud had written: *Insufficient data for certainty.*

For certainty of what? wondered Altman. He tried to scroll down, but the report ended there.

He checked the network and found that Skud was still logged in to the system. *Skud,* he typed, *please clarify the conclusion of your report.*

By insufficient data I mean there is not enough data, he wrote. *Without enough data, we cannot be certain.*

Altman sighed. Skud was a good scientist, but a little lacking in communication skills.

What is your data concerning? he asked.

Seismographic data, wrote Skud.

And what were you trying to prove? Altman wrote.

That the seismic disturbance was something generated by a machine rather by ordinary seismological activity.

What kind of machine?

As I said in my note, wrote Skud, and then there was a long moment where the screen remained blank. *Very sorry,* he finally wrote, *I see now I left it off my note. A drill. I do not have enough data to prove it, and maybe it is only ordinary seismic activity. But I think maybe somebody has been drilling, and maybe in the center of the crater.*

Altman immediately disconnected from the system and went outside to call Skud. The man seemed startled, a little confused, but after a while, he started to fill in the details in a way that Altman understood. Skud was drawing his readings from multiple seismographs, some on land, some underwater, several very close to the center of the crater itself. Only those near the center had noticed anything. The reading, Skud said, was something that would normally be dismissed as insignificant, very minor seismic activity. But it was also possible, he claimed, that it could be from a heavy, industrial-scale drill. It was very regular, he said, which would not be typical of a seismic event.

"But you're not sure if it's in the center of the crater."

"No," said Skud. "Exactly, that is the problem."

"Where else would it be if not the center?"

"It might be as far as fifty meters from the center," said Skud. "I have done calculations but I am afraid they are inconclusive."

"But that might as well be the center!" said Altman, frustrated.

"No, you see," said Skud patiently. "As I said, it might be as far as fifty meters from the center. That is not the center."

Altman started to argue, then stopped, thanked him, and disconnected. He stayed there, looking out at the ocean awhile and then glanced inside to the window. Field was still keeping to his side of the room, talking on the telephone now, seeming no more and no less animated than earlier. Altman turned back to the ocean again.

Slowly things were beginning to take shape in his mind. He wished that Hammond would get back in touch, since he'd been aware of it before anyone else. He might have a perspective that Altman and the others didn't have yet. In the meantime, it was up to them.

There was nothing to say for certain that the pulse, the freighter, and the seismic readings were all connected. But then again, there was nothing to suggest that they weren't. And all three had something in common: the center of the crater. Something was going on down there. Maybe something had been discovered, maybe it was some sort of weapons test, maybe it was some incredibly uncommon but natural phenomenon. But something was happening, something weird, something that someone didn't want the public to know about.

He swore he would find out what it was. Even if it killed him.

24

"I've got it now," said Tanner, his eyes red-rimmed, his face noticeably pale. He'd reached the limits of the anti-sleep medication. He had only an hour at most before either he collapsed or it started doing serious internal damage.

"Let's see it," said the Colonel.

"I should warn you—" Tanner began.

"—I don't need any warnings," the Colonel interrupted. "Just play it."

Tanner sent the file through the screen and opened it. It started to play.

Tanner closed his eyes, but once the sound started, the dim hiss of static, the images flooded into his mind anyway, made worse by his imagination and his lack of sleep. He opened his eyes and looked.

There wasn't much. The image had been broadcast through layers of rock and it was, in a sense, surprising that anything had gotten through at all. Tanner wished that it hadn't.

At first there was only the sound of static, the image itself nothing but snow. Then, little bits and pieces started to emerge. In terms of the images, it was as if the snow was taking on texture, a vaguely human face forming and then dissolving again, what looked like a hand, what could have been a fist around a pipe or then again been nothing at all. The sound went from a staticky hiss to a whisper to something that sounded like a man was speaking through a mouthful of bees. Something that sounded like a scream, bloodcurdling. A dull rhythm that might have been someone talking. Someone singing, a wandering, meandering nursery rhyme.

And then, suddenly, a brief moment of clarity, a man's face, weirdly backlit and terrified, his skin covered with something, quickly bursting into fuzz again.

"Freeze that," said the Colonel.

Tanner stopped the vid and spun it backward. The man's eyes had an emptiness to them. His features were strangely distorted, as if he were screaming. His face was covered with strange markings, symbols of some kind, which extended down his neck and chest and arms.

"Hennessy? What's he done to himself?" asked the Colonel. "What did he use to write?"

"Blood, we think," said Tanner. "You can see it dripping off his hand to the left there, and there seems to be a cut on his arm. Maybe it's his own blood, maybe Dantec's. If you look behind him, you'll see traces of the symbols on the walls as well, which, we assume, is also blood."

The Colonel furrowed his brow. "What do the symbols mean?"

"We don't know," said Tanner. "Nobody has ever seen anything quite like them." When the Colonel didn't say anything, Tanner asked, "Shall we go on?"

The Colonel waved his hand. "All right," he said, "go on."

More hissing, more static, more vague and distorted images. At one point, a brief glimpse of an arm that had been torn free of its socket, its lifeless hand curled up like a dead spider. A bit of the command chair, spattered with blood. And then Hennessy was back, humming to himself, swaying slightly, covered with bloody symbols.

"Hello," he said, then dissolved again. He flickered in and out of existence, along with bits of words, nothing that could be sorted out, and then, something that sounded like *shame* or maybe was part of another word. And then "—something—eed to know."

Onscreen, Hennessy clutched his head and then was replaced by static, in color this time. When he reappeared, he was giving the camera a strangely ecstatic smile.

"—track," he said.

There was a long silence.

"—simply not en—" he said. Then, a little later, "—not care—will have le—usk."

Hard to make much sense of it, thought Tanner. *But whatever it was, it wasn't good.*

Then Hennessy was back again, with that same intense smile. He had moved closer to the camera, almost filling up the screen.

"—virgins," he said, and gestured offscreen. Then he was still there, still talking, but little more than a ghost in the static, the sound completely lost until, near the end he came back, the image almost clear now. "—understand the—" he said, then a microburst of static. Then "—destroy it."

Hennessy moved out of the way, revealing, in the command chair behind him, the bits and pieces of Dantec's body. And then the vid ended.

. . .

"How many people have seen this?" asked the Colonel.

"This particular version? Three or four technicians. But it was generally broadcast, so a lot of people may have seen different bits of it. No way to say who has seen what."

"So, no point killing the technicians, then?" asked the Colonel.

"Excuse me?" said Tanner.

"This is big, Tanner," said the Colonel. "Much bigger than you can even imagine. It's much more important than a life or two. There are billions of people on the earth. People are expendable. But this thing, whatever it is, this is the only one we've ever seen."

"Are you saying I'm expendable?" said Tanner slowly.

The Colonel gave him a shrewd look. "Don't take this the wrong way," he said. "At this point, you're less expendable than nearly anyone else. But yes, if the circumstances develop in the wrong way, you're expendable. Does that bother you?"

"Yes," said Tanner.

"Then don't let the circumstances develop in the wrong way," the Colonel said. He looked at his chronometer. "I'll give you until morning. Find out how widely the vid is spreading and how much of it people have seen. Get some people on the ground who can ask the right questions without raising suspicions. Once we know where we stand, we'll figure out what to do."

25

The call came around 1 A.M. Altman lay in bed, watching his phone buzz on the table beside the bed, like a trapped insect. It buzzed and buzzed and then stopped. He checked it—no number listed and the hologram image was blocked. Almost immediately it started buzzing again.

It could be Hammond, he thought, *I should answer it. Or Showalter, Ramirez, or Skud.* But he just watched it buzz until it stopped.

The third time, it woke up Ada. She yawned and stretched, her body arching. "What time is it?" she asked drowsily, and then she sat up in bed, tucking her hair behind her ear. "Michael, aren't you going to answer that?"

He watched his hand reach out and flip his phone open, bringing it up to his ear.

"Hello," he said. Even to him his voice sounded dry and crackly, as if he hadn't spoken for years.

"Is this," said the voice, and then paused. "Michael Altman?"

"Who is this?" asked Altman.

The man on the other end of the line ignored the question. "I have a simple question I need you to answer," he said.

"I'm curious if you've managed to pick up anything unusual lately. Intercepted something."

"Like what?" he asked.

"I can see that you haven't," said the voice quickly. "I'm sorry to have wasted your time."

"Do you mean a signal of some sort?" he asked, thinking of the pulse.

There was a silence on the other end of the line.

"Some sort of transmission?" said Altman.

"Maybe," said the voice slowly. "Do you have something in mind?"

"Who is this?" said Altman again.

"That doesn't matter," said the voice.

"What kind of transmission are you talking about?" he asked. "A pulse of some kind?"

The voice suddenly turned nasty. "You'll have to do better than that, Mr. Altman," it said, a harsh note to it.

"Wait," said Altman. "Let's make a deal. If you tell me what you're looking for, I'll tell you if I come across it."

The line went dead.

"What the hell was that about?" asked Ada.

"I don't know," said Altman. "I wish I did. Someone trying to pry something out of me."

"Like what?"

"I don't know," he admitted.

He got out of bed. He went into the bathroom and washed his face, stared at the man looking back at him from the mirror. There were dark circles under his eyes, his eyelids puffy and swollen. He barely recognized himself. He hadn't been sleeping well. Bad dreams and, on top of that, all the excitement and fear associated with whatever was going on in the crater. Plus a headache that seemed to go on and on.

What if something had happened to Hammond? he wondered. What if they had killed him? What if they were coming after him now?

No, that was crazy. There was no point being paranoid. It was just a phone call.

He went into the other room, switched on the computer, connected to the secure server. Nothing new from the others since he'd last checked.

"What are you doing?" Ada asked him. She was sitting up in bed again, hair falling partly over her face.

"I have to check on something," he said. "It won't take long."

"Michael," she said, her voice stern now, "I want to know exactly what's going on. You shouldn't keep secrets from me. You're not in trouble, are you?" she asked.

"I don't think so," he said.

"If you were in trouble, you'd tell me, right?" she said.

"I'd like to think I would," he said.

"What do you mean you'd like to think you would? What kind of answer is that?"

"I mean yes, of course I would."

"There," she said. "That's better."

She ran her fingers through her hair and twisted it so it fell behind her shoulders, then got up and went into the bathroom. He turned to the screen and quickly typed:

Strange phone call this morning, just after 3 AM, asking me if I'd intercepted something. Thought he was talking about the signal from the center of Chicxulub, but when I hinted at that, he rushed to get off the line. Maybe a transmission of some sort, but what, I don't know. Anybody else get the same call?

He waited a minute, staring at his screen until Ada came out and climbed back into bed. Then he logged out and shut the system down, climbing in next to her. *Probably nothing,* he told himself.

"You promise me you'd tell me?" she said, sleepy again now.

"Yes," he said.

A few minutes later, he realized she was asleep. He lay in bed, eyes open, staring up at the darkened ceiling. It was a long time before he was able to fall asleep as well.

In the morning, logging on, he discovered all three of the others had had the same call, all well after he'd had it. Ramirez first, then Showalter, then Skud, which suggested that maybe the person making the calls was simply moving alphabetically down a list. They were all as puzzled as he was. *Ask around,* Altman wrote back. *Find out if other people had it, and what they make of it.*

By noon, they had the answer. Every scientist in Chicxulub they'd contacted had been called. Most of them had no idea what was going on, chalked it up to a crank call or the work of some paranoid. But Ramirez had finally talked to someone who seemed to know.

"He's talking about the vid broadcast," a man named Bennett said, a geologist and amateur radio enthusiast. "I figured it out right away. He called, all cryptic, fishing for something but not wanting to give away what. I said, 'You mean the vid broadcast?' He pretended not to know what I was talking about, got me to describe it, then he thanked me very politely and hung up."

Bennett had only part of the vid, a few brief seconds, something he'd come across broadcasting on not just one band but several, and so, out of curiosity, he'd recorded it. There were about three seconds of static, followed by five slightly distorted seconds of someone talking, followed by eight seconds of static. A few other people, said Bennett, had gotten other bits of it, and someone at DredgerCorp seemed to be gathering copies of all the bits. Why, he didn't know. Bennett was pretty sure it was a hoax, somebody's idea of a joke. But how they'd got it to seem like it was being broadcast from the center of Chicxulub, he didn't know. Probably a transmitter on a boat or—

"It was broadcast from where?"

"Somewhere near the center of Chicxulub crater," he said. "All part of the hoax, I'm guessing."

"Can I have a copy?"

"Why not?" he had said. "The more, the merrier." He spun it over.

It was a strange document—a man, naked, his body covered in symbols written in a substance that seemed to be blood, staring with a strange grin into the camera. "understand it—" he said, "destroy it—" And then static.

Altman watched it again. There wasn't much to it, just a few seconds. Maybe Bennett was right and it was a hoax, but there was something about the man's expression, the tightness of his features, the dead, mad emptiness of his eyes, which made Altman feel that it was not. Where was he? He watched it again. It was a small, confined space, the walls, too, smeared with symbols written with the same substance as was smeared on the man. Something at one point cast a reddish glare under the man's chin, when he bobbed forward. The lighting was industrial, harsh and unfriendly. "Understand it—destroy it," the man said. *I'm still working on understanding it*, thought Altman. *To be frank, I'm not even sure what* it *is.*

He leaned back in his chair, his elbows on the chair's arms, his fingers tented in front of his face. Maybe a hoax, he thought, but maybe not. *What if we take it all seriously? What if we try to put it all together? What will we come up with?*

A signal pulse from the center of the crater, something that hadn't been noticed before.

A gravity anomaly, also something new.

A suspicious freighter, not exactly over the center of the crater, but not far from it.

On the deck of the old freighter, a brand-new industrial submarine hoist. Also military or ex-military personnel on board.

Evidence of either seismic activity or of drilling, either in or very near the center of the undersea crater.

A vid, sent out on multiple channels, apparently broadcast from the center of the crater. On it, a man in a confined space, apparently mad, covered in odd runes, saying "understand it—destroy it."

It all seemed connected, and it all came back to the crater. Something happening at the heart of the crater that someone—probably DredgerCorp, since they were doing the asking, but maybe others besides them—was very, very interested in. Interested enough to start a drilling operation, probably illegal, to try to see what it was or to try to remove it.

That might also explain the vid fragment, Altman realized. What if the broadcast was from a submarine? He shivered slightly.

The problem was that that only raised bigger questions.

He sighed. It'd be easier, he realized, to think of it as just a hoax and stop worrying about it. Only he couldn't think of it as just a hoax. The more he thought about it, the more he pondered it, the more he thought it must be real.

He brooded, hesitating. *Your move, Michael,* he told himself. What would be the best way to flush out the secret?

In the middle of the afternoon, he hit upon an idea. It wasn't the best idea, but it had the beauty of being simple, and it was the only thing he could think of likely to have quick results.

He put a copy of the vid onto his holopod and slipped it back into his pocket. "Done for the day," he said to Field.

The man looked over, his expression like that of a dead fish. "It's only two thirty," he said.

Altman shrugged. "I have a few things to look into."

"Suit yourself," said Field, and turned back to his holoscreen.

Fifteen minutes later, Altman had a hat pulled low over his face and was sitting in the lobby of the town's youth hostel, using its single ancient terminal—a pre-holoscreen model. The deskman cast him a lazy glance and then ignored him. He wasn't paid enough to care who used the computer.

He spun the vid from his holopod to the terminal and then spent some time making sure he hadn't left a trail. Then he went onto FreeSpace and created a dummy account. It could be traced back to the monitor, he knew, but there was nothing he could do about that. It couldn't, in any case, be traced directly to him.

He prepared a message: *DredgerCorps' Illegal Doings in Chicxulub,* he typed into the subject line, and then captioned the vid, *Last Words from a Submarine Tunneled Deep into the Heart of Chicxulub Crater.* He stayed for a minute thinking and then added, *A Retrieval Mission Gone Wrong.* He then proceeded to copy the vid to every scientist he could think of in Chicxulub, himself included, and to a select few beyond.

There, he thought. *That should get their attention.*

That evening he told Ada what he had done, explained to her what they'd found out, what he thought it meant. He thought she'd tease him, tell him that he was making something out of nothing because he was bored. Instead, she just crossed her arms.

"You're such an idiot sometimes. Don't you realize it could be dangerous?" she asked.

"Dangerous?" he said. "What, you think they'd try to kill me for revealing some industrial secret? This isn't a spy movie, Ada."

"Maybe not, but you're acting like it is," she said. "Secure Web site, gangs of scientists, secret subs, signals that shouldn't exist. And then this video." She shivered. "A madman covered in symbols drawn in blood. Doesn't that make you think it might be dangerous?"

"What?"

"How do I know what 'it' is?" she asked, shaking her hands at him. "The thing at the heart of the crater might be dangerous.

Or the people who want to retrieve it might be dangerous. Or both."

"But—" he said.

"It's just—" she said, and then stopped.

She lowered her head and stared at the tabletop. He watched her hug herself, as if she were cold. "I don't want to see you hurt or dead," she said quietly.

She was motionless for long enough that he thought the conversation was over. He was about to get up and get a beer when suddenly she started speaking again.

"You have all your data," she said in a very steady voice. "You've put it together and made it mean something."

"I might be wrong," he said.

"That's not what I'm getting at," she said. "Just be quiet and listen, Michael. You scientists have only one way of looking at the world. I've got data of a sort, too, and it's just as troubling."

She started to lay it out for him, slowly weaving it together as if it were a story. The signal pulse began at a certain moment, she said, and from that moment on, everything was different. He knew it as well as she did. "Do you remember when you started having bad dreams?"

"I've always had bad dreams," he said.

"But not like these," she said. "Bloody, apocalyptic, end-of-the-world stuff every night?"

"No," he admitted. "Those are new."

"Everyone is having them, Michael. Even me. And I'm not normally prone to nightmares."

She had noticed how distracted and ill-rested everyone seemed, from the townspeople to her colleagues. She was trained to notice things like that, so she'd started asking around.

Did you sleep well last night? Did you have any dreams? Nobody was sleeping well. Nobody was dreaming anything but nightmares. And when she could get them to remember when the nightmares started, it always corresponded to when the signal pulse had begun.

"That's just the start," said Ada. "Do you know how many times over the past week you've told me that you had a headache? Dozens. Do you know how many times you've clutched your head and winced, but not said anything about it to me? Dozens more. And you're not the only one," she said. "Everybody is having them. Before the signal pulse, hardly anyone was having them. Now everybody is. Coincidence? Maybe, but you have to admit it's strange."

"All right," he said. "I admit it."

"Don't be a smart-ass, Michael," she said. "This is serious. I've spent months investigating the rituals and legends of this region, and before that I spent years reading other people's reports on them. The thing about the legends is that they've been basically the same for hundreds of years."

"So?"

She reached out and cuffed the side of his head. "I thought I told you not to be a smart-ass," she said, her dark eyes flashing. "They're no longer the same. They changed drastically once the pulse symbol started."

"Shit," he said.

"The villagers are having nightmares, Michael," she said, "just like us. But while our dreams are only thematically similar, theirs are very specifically alike. They're all dreaming of the 'tail of the devil,' which, as I mentioned the other day, is what the word *Chicxulub* means. Coincidence?"

Altman just shook his head. "I don't understand it," he said.

"I've noticed here and there, traced in the dust or freshly carved into the bark of trees, a crude symbol like two horns twisted together. When I asked what it was, people ignored me. When I kept asking, finally someone told me, almost spitting the word: *Chicxulub*."

She got up and went to the fridge, pouring herself a cup of distilled water. She drank it down and then poured another cupful, sat back down. She reached out and put her hand in his palm. He squeezed it.

"I don't know how it all fits together," she said, "nor how it meshes with your own data. Maybe it's all just weird coincidence. But all of it taken together makes me think that whatever is at the bottom of the crater is something that wishes us harm."

"You make it almost sound like a living thing," he said.

"I know it's not very scientific," she said. She took her hand back, rubbed her temple with it. "Ah, another headache," she said, and gave a wry smile.

After a moment, she went on. "The people of the town seem to have a whole mythology about this 'tail of the devil.' I don't know if the mythology has always been there or if it's something that's only recently developed. Certainly I'm only starting to notice it now.

"The only one I can get to talk about it in any detail is the town drunk, and he talks only if I ply him with booze. He claims there are stories that have been passed down from generation to generation, about a huge forked object thrust deep into the middle of the ocean. This, he told me in a mix of Spanish and Yucatec Maya, is all that remains of a great devil who surrendered his dominion upon the earth to dig down to the depths and rule over hell. His tail got caught and is still there, perhaps still alive. Some believe that this devil may still be attached to it.

"If you touch the tail, they say, you make yourself known to the devil. If the devil knows you, he will try to claim you. If you destroy more than you create, you make yourself known to the devil. 'You and your people,' the drunk told me when he was deep in his cups, 'you are known to the devil,' and then he made that strange symbol at me, a kind of curse, twining his index and middle fingers together."

She stopped and drank the rest of the water, leaving the cup on the table. "After that, he refused to say more," she said. "I tried to coax him to go on, offered to buy him more drinks, but he just shook his head. He was, he finally admitted, afraid that the devil might hear him."

They sat silently for a moment, staring at each other.

"Maybe there's a logical explanation," said Altman.

"For the stories?"

"For all of it."

"Maybe," said Ada. "But I don't know. I could, I suppose, argue that these stories are an odd mixture of Mayan and Christian belief. Maybe if I dug deep enough and thought long and hard enough, I'd have a theory about how they developed. But there's still something there, a genuine warning and sense of fear that my heart tells me we should be listening to. I love you, Michael. Promise me you will at least try to listen."

26

"We've tracked down around a dozen or so people who saw the vid broadcast," said Tanner. He'd managed to get a few hours of sleep, though his head still ached and he felt like his eyes had been rubbed with sandpaper. "Of those, about half got mostly static. The others got more. Of those, about half recorded it. But we knew that already as we used their recordings to augment our own."

"Besides you and the technicians in DredgerCorp, who else has seen the version you showed me?"

"Nobody," said Tanner. "I'm sure of it."

The Colonel furrowed his brow. "Take a look at this."

He spun the holofile to Tanner. It was a communication sent from someone with the alias "Watchdog." *DredgerCorps' Illegal Doings in Chicxulub,* the caption read. The body of the message consisted of a short bit of typed text—*Last Words from a Submarine Tunneled Deep into the Heart of Chicxulub Crater. Retrieval Mission Gone Wrong*—and a vid.

He opened the vid, saw Hennessy's blood-covered body and face, watched his strange smile and brief speech. *Oh, shit*, he thought. *The worst has finally happened.*

"Who sent it?" he asked.

"This copy was sent to Lenny Small," the Colonel said. "The list of other recipients is several pages long, mostly scientists in Chicxulub, but a few others as well."

"That vid's originally from Sigmund Bennett," said Tanner. "He recorded it."

"Do you think he's the one disseminating it?"

Tanner shook his head. "He's not the type. One of my men talked to him—it was pretty clear he thought it was a hoax. He probably didn't even think twice about it, probably just sent it to someone else because he thought it was interesting or weird. I'll have someone speak to him and find out who else he showed it to."

"Don't bother," said the Colonel.

"Don't bother? But you said—"

"Too many people have seen it already," he said. "There's no point in killing anybody now. That's more likely to hurt than help."

Tanner let out a deep breath. He was glad to know he wouldn't be asked to kill anybody. "What do we do, then?"

"We come clean," said the Colonel.

"We come clean?" Tanner felt his stomach drop out. "That's not what DredgerCorp does. Shouldn't we run this by Small?"

"Small's not running the show," said the Colonel. "I am."

"This is a disaster. I'll tell you now," Tanner said, face flushing red. "I'm not going down with the ship. I'm not willing to swallow the blame on this one. I'll fight it all the way."

"Calm down, Tanner," the Colonel said. "We don't *actually* come clean; we just pretend. If we release the story to the press, then we're the ones to spin it. We play it right and we'll be in a better position than we were in before."

"How do we do that?" said Tanner.

"Simple," said the Colonel. "Call a press conference. Claim that you've seen the video that's been making the rounds and heard the rumors and that you thought it was time to set the story straight. You give the press all the footage you have and ask them to broadcast it. You're not losing much there, since lots of people have seen bits and pieces of it—anybody gets curious enough and they'll be able to put together a good chunk of it, just like you did."

"How does that help?"

"What matters is what you say about it," said the Colonel. "You can't say that it's a hoax, because that just gives the conspiracy junkies fuel for their fire. So tell as much of the truth as you can without damaging us."

"How much is that?"

The Colonel's lips tightened. "You need me to spell it out for you? Where's your imagination, man?

"First, you say Hennessy went crazy. Not too hard a proposition to make stick once people see the vid. You say you had brought him down to Chicxulub because you were interested in testing an experimental new bathyscaphe, a borer, a vessel that can at least in theory, dig down through rock while underwater. It's something which you're certain will change the future of undersea mining, assuming that you can get all the bugs worked out. Got it so far?"

"Yes," said Tanner.

"Anyway, you chose Hennessy because of his experience with submarines and because he was a company man, someone who was reliable and who could keep a secret. Obviously, technology like this, the last thing you want is for information about it to be leaked. You came to test it in Chicxulub. . . Why?"

Tanner thought for a moment. "Because Chicxulub is out of the way," he offered. "We have a little more privacy here than we might have had in other places, and it's possible here to test how a bathyscaphe would respond boring through a variety of strata."

"Good enough for now," said the Colonel. "Polish it a little for your answer. I'll arrange for a few testing permits to be filed retroactively to cover us. So, you did a series of test runs along the coast in shallow water, with Hennessy and another experienced submarine pilot, Dantec. Everything went fine, no problems whatsoever. Then you decided, after consulting with President Small, that it was time to test the bathyscaphe in deep water.

"What happened after that, you don't know for certain. When you asked the crew to prepare the craft for a dive, they informed you that it wasn't there. When you tried to find Dantec and Hennessy, they were missing as well. You concluded that they had taken the submarine without authorization, perhaps to steal it. You looked for it, but to no avail: it was either out of sonar range or they had their engines off. You started a search, you tried to contact them repeatedly, but there was never any response."

The Colonel's lips curled back in a way that showed his teeth.

"The next evidence of them you had, you tell the press, was the transmission you intercepted. You don't know what happened, but it's clear that Hennessy came unhinged. You've managed to figure out the location of the sub: it's buried deep within the rock in the crater. So now you've contacted the military, asking them for help retrieving the bathyscaphe. If they're able to retrieve it, you say that you're committed to letting the press know what happened inside in those last fatal hours."

"The military," said Tanner. "Is that wise?"

"It's not only wise, it's brilliant. It gives us an excuse to change the scale of the operation. We don't have to work covertly anymore."

"But who do we contact?" asked Tanner. "Won't we end up losing the object to them?"

The Colonel gave another predatory smile. "You've already contacted them," he said, and pointed both thumbs at his own chest. "You're already working with them."

27

Altman had just sat down at the desk when there was a knock at the door.

"Are you expecting anyone?" he asked Field.

Field shook his head. "Not that I know of. Do you want to get that or should I?"

"I don't mind," said Altman.

He started for the door, then doubled back to log off the secure site. The knock came again. "Just a minute," he called. It came a third time just before he reached the door, louder and harder now.

Outside were two men that he didn't recognize. Locals, he would guess. They were wearing ties, and dark shoes that had been polished to a shine. One was tall and thin, with dark skin and a bristly black mustache. The other was clean shaven, his skin lighter. He held a smoldering cigarette tight between his thumb and forefinger, like it was a joint. He was sucking hard on it when Altman opened the door.

"Yes?" Altman asked.

"We're looking for someone," said the man in Spanish. "Miguel Altman."

"Michael," said Altman. "Can I ask why?"

"You are him, perhaps?" said the taller man.

"Who's asking?" asked Altman. "Who exactly are you?"

The second man sucked again on his cigarette, his cheeks shrinking in to make his face look cadaverous. "*We* are asking," he said. He reached into his pocket and removed a badge. "Police," he said.

"Has something happened to Ada?" Altman asked, his heart thudding suddenly in his throat.

"May we come in?" asked the tall one.

Altman opened the door wider and they slid past him and inside. Field watched them curiously as they came in.

"Hello, Field," said the smoker.

"Hello, Officer Ramos," said Field. "Do you have business with me?"

"With your friend," said Ramos. "Perhaps we could have privacy for a moment."

"He's not my friend," said Field. "We just share a lab." He stood and limped out the door.

The tall policeman pulled over Field's chair and sat on it. Ramos leaned against the wall next to Altman's desk.

"What's happened?" asked Altman, his panic over Ada growing stronger and stronger. "Is she all right?"

"It's nothing to do with your girlfriend. Do you know Charles Hammond?" the tall man asked. His voice was flat and uninflected. He pronounced Charles as if it had two full syllables: *Char-less*.

"The technician? I've met him."

"He says he's met him, Gallo," said Ramos. "What do we think that means?"

The tall man, Gallo, ignored Ramos. "How well did you know him?" he asked Altman.

"Not very well," said Altman. "We met once."

"He says they only met once, Gallo," said Ramos, and sucked on his cigarette again.

"What's this all about?" asked Altman.

"What indeed," said Ramos.

"Where did you meet him?" asked Gallo.

"In a bar," said Altman.

"Why?"

Altman hesitated. "He had something he wanted to tell me."

"Sounds suspicious to me, Gallo," said Ramos. "Which bar?"

"How long where you there?" asked Gallo.

"Which of you is asking the questions?" asked Altman. "You're confusing me."

"Just answer my question," said Gallo, same flat tone.

"And mine," said Ramos.

"Wait," said Altman. "I was, the bar was the one on the beach, near to here, and I—"

"The cantina, you mean," said Ramos. "There's a difference between a bar and a cantina, you know."

"Cantina, then," said Altman.

"How long were you there?" asked Gallo again.

"I was getting to that," said Altman, his voice slightly higher now. "He called me and asked me to meet him. We must have been there, I don't know, a few hours."

"How many is a few?" asked Ramos.

"I don't know," said Altman. "Two, I guess."

"The bartender says three," said Gallo.

"Well, he's probably right," said Altman. "It probably was three."

"And yet you said two," said Ramos.

"It was just a guess," said Altman. "How am I supposed to remember exactly? What's this all about anyway? Can't you get to the point?"

"No," said Ramos, "we can't."

"The point is," said Gallo, "you were the last one to see Hammond alive."

"He's dead?" said Altman.

"He's dead," said Gallo.

"What happened?" asked Altman.

"That's what we're trying to find out," said Gallo.

"You don't think I did it, do you?" said Altman. "You don't think I killed him?"

"How did you know somebody killed him?" said Ramos.

"I didn't know, but I'm beginning to suspect," said Altman.

"He could have died of accidental or natural causes," said Ramos, "but you jump to the conclusion that he's been killed."

"Where did you and he go after leaving the bar?" asked Gallo.

"The cantina," said Ramos.

"After leaving the cantina," corrected Gallo.

"We didn't go anywhere. We shook hands on the street and I went home. I don't know where he went." Altman watched the two police officers look at each other, exchanging a significant glance. "What happened?" asked Altman. "How was he killed?"

"Was Hammond your lover?"

"What? No, of course not! Are you crazy?"

"Why do you say of course not?" asked Gallo.

"I have a girlfriend," said Altman.

"What does that prove?" asked Ramos.

"Look," said Altman. "Why won't you tell me what happened?"

The two officers exchanged glances again.

"Was there anything unusual about Hammond's behavior?" asked Gallo.

"How the hell should I know if there was anything usual about his behavior?" said Altman. "I only met him once. I don't have anything to compare his behavior to."

"No need to get upset," said Ramos, "no need to get excited."

"Throat," said Gallo, and drew his finger across his own throat.

"What?" said Altman.

"You asked how he died," said Gallo. "He had his throat cut."

"He had a knife with him," said Ramos. "Do you know whose prints were on it?"

"Whose?" said Altman.

"No one's," said Gallo. "The knife had been wiped clean."

"Do you think I did it?" said Altman. "Why would I do it?"

"How would we know why?" said Ramos coolly. "We don't even know what the two of you talked about."

"What did you talk about?" asked Gallo.

"This is crazy," said Altman. "You think he might have been killed because of something we discussed?"

"How can we know until you tell us what it was?" asked Ramos.

So Altman did. He took a deep breath and then began, best as he could remember, to recount the conversation they had

had. When he said the name DredgerCorp, he watched the two officers exchange glances again. As he spoke further, he watched as first Ramos then Gallo crossed their arms.

When Altman finished, Gallo stood up from the chair and said, "Thank you, Mr. Altman. You've been very helpful." Ramos was already moving toward the door.

"Wait a minute," said Altman. "That's it?"

"What did you expect?" asked Ramos. "That we were going to arrest you?"

"We'll be back in touch if we need you," said Gallo, and then the two of them were gone.

He called Ada to talk to her about it, but she didn't pick up. He still felt unsettled. His hands, he realized, were shaking.

After a while, Field limped back in. "Everything all right?" he asked, eyebrows raised.

"Somebody I know was killed," Altman said.

"Ah," said Field. "That's terrible news."

Am I in danger myself? Altman wondered.

"Did you hear the news?" asked Field.

"What news?"

"DredgerCorp's announcement? I only just heard about it myself," said Field. "When I was outside chatting, waiting for them to get done working you over."

"What was it about?"

"You can get to it on the feed," said Field. "Tap in and take a look."

He logged in to the newsfeed. There it was, *DredgerCorp News Conference*. He opened it up.

William Tanner the man's name was. Altman didn't think he'd ever seen him before. *There's been a lot of speculation about this strange vid clip,* he said, and then showed a longer version of the clip that Bennett had shown Altman. *I wish I could say it was a hoax, but I'm afraid I can't. In any case, gentlemen, I'm here to try to provide some clarity.*

He went on to recount a story about an experimental submarine with a drilling mechanism, which had been commandeered and then sunk deep into the heart of Chicxulub. They were calling on the military to help them retrieve the submarine. His delivery alternated between confident and nervous. At the end, he claimed that *DredgerCorp is committed to finding out what went on in that submarine and why, and making sure it never happens again.* Then, ignoring the reporters trying to question him, he strode quickly off the stage.

Altman finished watching and then watched again. *Definitely blood,* he thought, upon seeing the extended vid fragment. He had to admit that what William Tanner was saying sounded plausible. It answered most of the questions he'd had. The only loose ends it left were why the pilot had commandeered the submarine and taken it. Though maybe it was enough to simply declare that to be *madness.*

In any case, it sounded good.

Indeed, it almost sounded too good to be true.

Or am I trying to make something out of nothing? he wondered.

Maybe he should just forget about it, let it go. One man was already dead, and he might end up dead, too, if he wasn't careful. Maybe Hammond had simply been killed in a mugging gone wrong and it had nothing to do with events in the Chicxulub crater.

He thought it over, then went back and watched the press conference again. On one side of the scale were the claims the press conference had made. On the other was the pulse from the center of the crater. No matter how you looked at it, the pulse had started well before the incident with the submarine. The submarine hadn't started the pulse, but maybe whatever happened on board had been what had strengthened the signal. Maybe it was all coincidence or maybe it was a big mistake on his part, but he wasn't yet ready to give up.

When he arrived home, Ada still wasn't there. He felt again the same brief thrill of panic he'd experienced when he thought earlier that something had happened to her. He tried to call her again, still got no response.

He waited nervously for her, one hour and then two. He tried to call again, then again, still no answer. *What if something's happened to her?* he couldn't help but think, even though another part of his mind knew it was nonsense, that Ada often worked late, that there was no good reason yet to assume something was wrong.

But when the door finally opened, he was close to hysteria. He started toward her, ready to berate her, when he saw she wasn't alone. She had somebody with her. A young boy.

The boy was holding her hand delicately. He started to ask her where she'd been, but she silenced him with a look. "Michael," she said, "I'd like you to meet Chava."

Altman looked down at the boy. He was young, either not yet or just barely a teenager. He was barefoot, wearing a threadbare but clean T-shirt and a pair of shorts hanging barely together. He was very thin. He had deep brown eyes and a slightly apprehensive look.

"Chava," Altman said. "What sort of name is that?"

"It's a nickname for Salvador," said Ada quickly. When Altman gave her a look, she nodded. "I know it doesn't sound like it, but it's true," she said.

"Really?" he said, and turned to the boy.

The boy nodded, but said nothing.

Altman looked to Ada for help, for some clue as to what was going on. "I thought you might like to talk to him," she said.

"Would you like to sit down?" he asked Chava.

The boy hesitated and then nodded. Altman pulled out a chair for him, and he climbed onto it.

"Would you like something to eat?" Altman asked.

The boy nodded again. Altman opened the fridge and started to look through it, then changed his mind. "Come on," he said to the boy. "Look in here. Take anything you want."

The boy approached the fridge as if it were a trap. He carefully bent his head around the door and looked in, then looked up at Altman.

"Anything?" he asked.

"Anything," said Altman.

A few minutes later he had most of the contents of the fridge piled on the table in front of him. He was tasting everything. He'd take a small bite of something, move it around in his mouth, swallow it, and then move on to the next item.

"What would you like to talk about?" asked Altman once he was done.

The boy shook his finger at him. "The lady," he said. "She is the one who said you wanted to speak with me."

"Do you think you could tell him the same story you told me?" asked Ada.

"This is not a story," Chava said with a frown. "It happened for real."

"Yes, of course, Chava," said Ada quickly. "That's what I meant."

"Okay, I will tell it," the boy said. "I was walking on the beach, very early morning. This was a day when in my head I thought, *I will walk on the beach and turn to go to town and then I will see if there is anyone who needs messages delivered.* Sometimes you, the scientists, will give me a little money to deliver messages. Sometimes, after two or three messages it is enough to buy a *polvorón* or an *oreja* at the *pastelería*.

"But this day, my feet wanted to go the other way. I could not stop them. So, instead of going in to the town, we went together out farther along the deserted beach. That is when I found something."

"What did you find?" asked Altman.

"I do not know," said the boy.

"What do you mean you don't know?"

"I mean that there is not a name for what I found. It was like a man but it was not a man. It was also like a balloon but it was not a balloon."

"How can it be like both a man and a balloon?" asked Altman.

"Yes," said the boy, and smiled. "This is exactly what I asked myself. I can see that you understand my story. The lady was good to bring me to tell it to you. It made a noise, too. Like this."

The boy leaned over the table and began to make a strange wheezing sound.

"The *bruja* told me to burn it, that it was a flea from the tail of the devil. *Chicxulub*." He crossed his middle and index fingers over each other and held his hand up for them to see. "But later . . . I found out she was dead."

"How could she tell you if she was dead?" asked Altman.

"It is like you are inside my head and seeing what I was asking myself," said the boy gleefully.

Altman waited for the boy to go on, but he didn't say anything further.

"You burned it?" he said.

"Yes," said the boy. "It burned very nice."

"What part of it was like a balloon?" asked Altman.

"Its back," said the boy without hesitation. "There were the gray sacks." He touched a cucumber on the table that he had taken a bite of. "May this come with me?" he asked.

"Yes," said Altman.

The cucumber disappeared into his clothes. He touched an onion and made a face.

"Can I ask you something?" asked Altman.

Chava nodded.

"Would you take us there, to the place where you found it?"

The boy looked at him thoughtfully. "Do you promise me that if you see me and you have a message to send that you will choose me to send it?"

"What?" asked Altman, startled. "Yes, of course."

"This is good," said the boy. "And may I take three more things from the table, but not the onion?"

Altman nodded, trying to hide his smile. Chava slipped three things into his shirt so quickly that Altman was not entirely sure what he had.

"Now I will take you there," the boy said firmly.

28

Tanner poured himself a glass of whiskey and fell back against the pillows. Finally he was going to get a good night's sleep on a good bed. Between setting up the Chicxulub office, the arrangements to get the bathyscaphe and Hennessy and Dantec to Mexico, the time spent on the freighter, the agonizing hours trying to figure out what was going on inside the bathyscaphe and all the worry afterward, it seemed like it had been months since he had had a decent night's sleep.

He sipped his whiskey. The key, he told himself, was not to think about it. The key was to relax. It was all over now. The press conference was done. The next stages of the operation had not yet begun.

His personal phone rang. He looked at it. If it was his wife, her name would come up. No name came up. Which meant it could be President Small or maybe Terry, Tim, and Tom. They were the only ones who had his number, except for Dantec. And Dantec was dead.

"Hello?" he said.

"William Tanner?" said a mellifluous voice. "I have a few questions for you about Dr. Hennessy's death."

"How did you get this number?" asked Tanner. "This is a private number."

The man ignored him. "Was there really no sign of instability before the descent? Didn't DredgerCorp's safety procedures fail you in this case? Or should I say failed Hennessy and the late Mr. Dantec?"

Tanner clicked off. After a few seconds, the phone rang again.

"Hello!" said Tanner.

"Please don't hang up, Mr. Tanner. There are important ethical issues at—"

He disconnected. He turned the telephone all the way off, left it sitting on his bedside table. If Small or the Colonel wanted to get in touch, they'd have to contact him by vid.

He took a big sip, felt the whiskey burn down his throat. He tried to relax, to empty his mind, to let himself go. He could relax now, he told himself. The phone was off; the door was locked. Finally, he could relax.

But he couldn't relax. His head was throbbing and something was gnawing at him.

He got up and swallowed three sleeping pills, washing them down with whiskey. He stared at his face for a long moment in the mirror and then climbed back into the bed.

The problem was that he agreed with the reporter. There were ethical issues at stake, things that had been done that, despite everything else he had done at DredgerCorp over the years, he was having difficulty living with.

He'd been on operations where people had died before. He'd even been on operations when they'd died as a direct result of choices he had made. Not to mention the trauma of the moon skirmishes, where everyone had done terrible things and where on more than one occasion he'd felt less than human. But these two had died and he still didn't understand why. Was it because instead of corpses that he could see and make sense of, all he had were brief, staticky images? Did he just need a little more finality? Or was it more than that?

There had been no sign of instability in Hennessy before the descent. He ran over their interactions in his head again. In his mind, if anybody had been in danger of becoming unstable, it was Dantec. Was it possible that Dantec had snapped first and that had made Hennessy snap?

The whiskey and the sleeping pills were finally starting to take effect. Things had begun to blur. Maybe there would be answers when they brought the bathyscaphe back to the surface, he thought. Maybe that would explain everything.

He was startled awake by the telephone ringing. He groped it off the nightstand and looked at the display.

The name that came up was Dantec.

His heart leapt into his throat and he was suddenly wide awake. Dantec was dead; he couldn't be the one calling. He stared at the display: it still read Dantec.

He sat up in bed, put his feet on the floor. "Hello?" he said, facing the wall. "Who is this?"

But there was only static on the other end of the line.

He waited, feeling like he might pass out. "Dantec," he said tentatively. "Are you alive?"

He stayed with the receiver pressed to his ear, listening. At some point he realized there wasn't even static. The phone wasn't even turned on.

He put the phone back on the nightstand. Immediately, even though it wasn't on, it rang again. Dantec's name came up on the display.

"Hello?" Tanner said.

There was only silence.

He put the phone back down again. When it rang this time, he just stayed there, watching it ring. *It's off,* he tried to tell himself. *It can't be ringing.* But the damned thing kept ringing.

Aren't you going to answer it? said a voice from behind him, a voice he recognized.

He felt the hairs bristle on the back of his neck. Very slowly, he turned. There was a vague shape in the bed with him that, as he looked at it, slowly became human. Crude and awkward features became more and more refined until it was, at last, Dantec. His skin was very white, almost bloodless. His lips had turned blue.

"You're not real," said Tanner.

Aren't I? said Dantec. *Then why are you seeing me?*

"But you died, in the bathyscaphe."

Are you sure it was me? asked Dantec. *Are you sure I was even in the bathyscaphe?*

Tanner hesitated. "Are you still alive?" he asked.

I'm here, aren't I?

Tanner just shook his head.

Go ahead and touch me, said Dantec. *If I'm not real, you wouldn't be able to touch me.*

Tanner closed his eyes and reached out. At first he felt only the bed, the blanket. Then he reached a little farther and felt something different, something that moved, something alive.

"It *is* you," said Tanner, smiling. "I can't believe it. How did you survive? What are you doing here?"

I've come to see you, said Dantec. *Can't a guy stop by to see an old friend?*

"Sure," said Tanner.

Also. . . .

"What is it, Dantec? You can tell me."

I hate to ask, Tanner, but I need your help. I need something from you.

"Anything," said Tanner. "What's mine is yours."

I'm having a hard time breathing, said Dantec. *I need you to share your oxygen tank with me.*

"How can I do that?"

Just make a slit in the breathing tube, said Dantec. *I'll cut mine off a few feet down and then we'll splice them together. Then we can both breathe.*

"I don't—" *I don't have a breathing tube,* he had started to say. But then he reached up and felt it; there it was.

I don't have much longer, said Dantec. Indeed his lips looked even bluer than they had looked just a few moments before.

"I need something sharp," Tanner said. "Where can I find something sharp?"

There's a pocketknife in the drawer of the nightstand, said Dantec.

"How do you know what's in my nightstand?"

I'm full of surprises, said Dantec, and smiled, his blue lips stretching and turning white.

Tanner got the pocketknife out and unfolded the biggest blade. "Where should I cut it?" he asked.

Anywhere, said Dantec, *as long as the cut's long enough. Remember, make it long.*

Tanner nodded. "Ready?" he asked.

Ready, said Dantec.

He made a long horizontal cut, almost cutting the tube right in half. "All right," Tanner said, "quickly, hand it to me."

His voice sounded strange, something wrong with his vocal cords. He coughed, spat blood. The blanket in front of him seemed covered in a pink mist. He looked down, saw that his chest was coursing with rivulets of blood.

You should have left it down there where it was safe, he heard Dantec say, his voice distant now. *You shouldn't have tried to understand it.*

"Quickly," he said, holding out his hand. "Dantec? Understand what?"

But Dantec was nowhere to be seen.

The air kept hissing out of the breathing tube and out into space. He tried to close the gap with his hand, but it was too deep—air kept leaking out. His hands were sticky, his chest, too, the hair on it all matted with blood.

He tried to call out for Dantec again, but something was wrong with his throat. He could make only a gurgling sound. He tried to get out of the bed, but everything seemed to be moving too slowly, as if he were underwater.

Very slowly, he moved one foot and slid it to the edge and over, letting it fall to the ground. There was only the other foot to worry about now. And then he would stand up and go to the mirror and take a good hard look at himself and try to figure out where he had gone wrong.

29

The boy led the way confidently, despite the darkness. He had to stop several times, waiting impatiently for Altman and Ada to catch up.

As they got closer, Chava began chattering away, saying things difficult for Altman to interpret.

"The *bruja*, he said, "she was dead but she helped us anyway. I went to find her and she came with me and spoke to me, and told me what to do. If she did not come, how was I to know what to do?"

He looked at Altman, apparently expecting a response.

"I don't know," said Altman, slightly out of breath from tramping through the sand in his shoes.

This seemed to satisfy the boy. "But she did come. And she showed us what to do. A circle," he said, and nodded at Altman.

"What do you mean, 'a circle'?" asked Altman.

The boy looked at him; then he stopped and traced something in the sand. Altman shone the flashlight on it, saw a circle.

"This is what I mean," the boy said, and then started walking again.

Altman shook his head. The boy's way of thinking was so

different that it was like communicating with someone from another world.

Suddenly the boy stopped. He made the sign of the devil's tail with his intertwined fingers and pointed.

Altman raised the flashlight. There had been a fire there, its remains half-buried in the sand. He waited for the boy to move forward, but the boy just stayed where he was. So Altman stepped around him to take a closer look.

Carefully he pushed the sand aside with his foot. There were lots of half-burnt pieces of driftwood and char and ash. Then he realized that some of what he thought had been driftwood were in fact bones. They were human, or at least human-sized, but there was something wrong with them. They were oddly twisted and deformed. There were, too, leathery bits of something—skin or seaweed, he first thought, but as he looked closer, he was less sure. The texture was wrong.

"Do you think fire could have done that to those bones?" he asked Ada.

"I don't know," she said.

He shook his head. Why was it that he kept on running up against things he didn't understand? Was it a problem with him or a problem with the world?

He dug through ash and driftwood and bone until his foot unearthed the skull. It was blackened throughout, missing the jawbone. All the teeth were missing, though it seemed less like they'd fallen out than as if they'd never been there: the bottom edge of the maxilla was smooth, socketless.

"It looked like a cross between a balloon and a man?" asked Ada.

Chava nodded.

"How was it sitting?"

Chava thought for a moment and then kneeled in the sand, hunched over, hands near his sides. "Its arms were becoming its legs," he said.

"What do you mean by that?"

"The skin was the same skin, the flesh the same flesh."

Maybe some sort of hideously deformed man, thought Altman. There was probably a logical explanation. But if it was a hideously deformed man, how had he managed to live for this long?

He suddenly thought of something.

"Where was the balloon?" he asked.

Chava, still hunched, put his hands up by his neck and waved his fingers.

"How big was it?" asked Ada.

"Very big."

"Bigger than my arm?" asked Altman. Chava nodded. "Bigger than my body?" He nodded again. "As big as a house?" Chava hesitated, then nodded.

"Sometimes it was smaller," he said, "but in the end, yes, I believe it was as big as a house."

"Can you make any sense of this?" Altman asked Ada after they had walked with the boy back to the edge of the shanty-town and left him there.

"Not any more than you can," she said.

"You think it really happened?"

"I think something happened," said Ada. "Whether it was exactly as Chava says is anybody's guess. It sounds impossible. But, then again, a lot of weird things have been happening lately. I don't know what to think anymore."

"What about the others?" asked Altman. "Have they been telling you the same story?"

"They still won't talk about it with me," said Ada. "I don't know why."

"I was really worried about you," Altman confessed.

"Once the boy started talking, I had to keep going," she said. "Any interruption might have spooked him."

Altman nodded. They walked a little farther, their footsteps soft in the dust of the road. "You know that guy I talked to? At the bar?"

"Yes," she said. "What about him?"

"He's dead."

She stopped. "Dead?" she said. "What happened?"

"His throat was slit."

She grabbed his arm, jerked it until he looked at her. "You see," she said, "I told you it was dangerous! And now somebody's dead."

"It's probably nothing," he said. "Probably just a mugging."

He saw a flicker of hope pass through her eyes, and quickly fade. "But what if it's not? You should give this up. You should stop your game of spying and do the job you were sent down here to do."

He didn't say anything, just tried to tug his arm away.

"Promise me, Michael," she said. "Promise me."

"I can't," he said.

"Why not?"

"Look," he said, taking her by the shoulders. "You were the one who brought Chava to me. I didn't ask you to do that. But every new thing I hear makes it seem stranger and stranger. I need to figure out what's going on."

At first she was very angry. She started walking, fast, staying out in front of him and wouldn't look back. He followed her, calling her name. Gradually she slowed down a little, finally let him take her hand, but still wouldn't look at him. He pulled her close and held her while she tried to push him away, very gradually giving in.

"You don't love me enough to do this for me," she tried.

"I do love you," he said. "That's not what this is about."

She pouted. Finally she put her arms around his neck. "I don't want to lose you, Michael," she said.

"You won't lose me," he said. "I promise."

They walked slowly down the street. They passed an open door, a makeshift wooden sign hanging over it reading BAR DE PRIMERA CATEGORÍA, another sign beside it, this one cardboard, reading BEBIDAS, MUY BARATAS.

They were already twenty feet past when Altman stopped and doubled back.

"Where are you going now?" asked Ada.

"I need a drink," he said. "I need to raise a glass to Hammond."

He pushed open the door. The patrons, all locals, looked up, fell immediately silent. He went up to the counter, which consisted of a stack of old crates, and ordered a beer for himself, one for Ada.

When the beers came, he looked around for a place to sit. There was nowhere. All the tables were full and people were leaning against the wall. He paid the bartender and then carried their drinks outside.

They sat on the edge of the dusty street before the makeshift bar, in the light coming through the half-open door, backs against the rickety wall, and drank their beers.

"It worries me," he said, putting his beer down.

"What?"

"This," he said. "All of it. The things going on in Chicxulub, the pulse, the submarine, the stories you're hearing, the dreams everyone has been having, the thing we just saw on the beach. I think we're in trouble."

"You and I?"

"Everybody," he said. "Maybe I'm just being paranoid."

"All the more reason to leave it alone," she mumbled.

He ignored her. He groped for his beer but suddenly couldn't find it. He turned and looked for it, but it was gone.

He turned on the flashlight and shone it into the shadows on the edge of the building, a little farther away from the door. There was a man there, his shirt and clothes filthy. He was obviously very drunk. He was holding Altman's bottle to his lips, rapidly emptying it.

"That drunk just took my beer," he said to Ada, a little astonished.

The man finished the beer, smacked his lips, and tossed the bottle off into the darkness. Then he looked at them, squinting into the beam of the flashlight.

Altman lowered it a little bit. The man held out his hand, snapped his fingers.

Altman grinned. "I think he wants your beer, too," he said.

Ada spoke to him softly in Spanish and the man nodded. She held out her beer and the man took it eagerly and upended it, quickly downed it. He tossed the bottle away then leaned back against the wall.

"Hello," said Altman.

The man carefully smoothed his filthy shirt. *"Mucho gusto,"* he said. His accent and cadence were surprisingly formal. He redirected his gaze toward Ada, inclined his head slightly. *"Encantado,"* he said.

"We've met before," said Ada. "You've told me your stories. Don't you remember?"

The man looked at her with his watery eyes but did not answer. After a long moment, he leaned his head back against the wall and closed his eyes. He stayed like that for long enough that Altman wondered if he hadn't fallen asleep.

Suddenly he asked in Spanish, "What are your names?"

"Michael Altman," said Altman. "This is my girlfriend, Ada Cortez. What is your name?"

The man ignored the question. "Thank you for the drinks," he said, his Spanish excessively polite. He turned to Ada. "Cortez, a good, vigorous Spanish name, but not one my people care for, for reasons that you must know. We have a very long memory. You must not hold it against us."

Ada nodded.

"Ada, from Hebrew, meaning 'adornment.' It is a lovely name for a woman as beautiful as you. Centuries ago, it was the name of the daughter of a notorious and handsome club-footed poet. And, a century or more later, the name, too, of a book by a famous writer."

"How do you know this?" asked Ada.

"Names were a hobby of mine," the man said. "Before drinking became my only hobby."

He turned back to Altman. "Michael, the name of the arch-angel on God's right hand. Are you a religious man, Michael?"

"No," said Altman. "I am not."

"Then we shall refer to you not as Michael but as Altman. The name Altman, it is German, is it not?"

"Yes," said Altman. "But I'm from the North American sector."

"You do not have a German face," the man said. "I hope it does not offend you that I say this. What places are there in you?"

"I'm a mongrel," said Altman evasively. "A mix of everything."

"I can see from your face that you are one of us as well," said the drunk. "The devil thinks he knows you, but he does not know all of you."

"My mother was part Indian," Altman admitted. "I don't know what tribe."

"I would say she was of our tribe," said the drunk.

"I don't know," said Altman.

"What?" said Ada. "Your mother was part Indian? You've never told me that before."

"She didn't like to talk about it," said Altman. "I don't know why. I don't think about it often."

"You are here for a reason," the man said.

"I came here with Ada," said Altman.

"That may very well be," said the man. "But that is not the reason."

"And what is the reason?"

The man smiled. "Your name," he said. "Altman. *Alt* meaning 'old,' *mann,* with two *n*'s, meaning 'man.' You are not an old man. You are a young man. Can you explain this to me?"

"It's just a name," said Altman.

"You understand the importance of a name only once you have lost yours. As I have." He leaned his head back against the wall, closed his eyes.

"There is perhaps another meaning," he said. *Alt* could mean 'ancient,' but that is not so different from 'old.' *Altman* might be an 'old man' or an 'old servant' or, if I am not taking too many liberties, a 'wise man.'" He opened his eyes again, gave Altman an intense stare, his eyes glittering in the crosslight from the flash beam. "Which one shall it be for you?"

They sat in silence. Again, Altman thought the drunk had fallen asleep.

"Ready to go?" he asked Ada.

"If you buy me another drink," said the drunk quietly. "I will tell you what I know."

"About what?" asked Altman.

"About the thing you have been asking of all over the town." He crossed his fingers. "About the tail of the devil."

Here we are, said the old man, sipping his drink, *living on the edge of the place where the devil dug down to hell, leaving only his tail behind. Perhaps you do not believe this to be true,* he said. *You, Altman, are no believer. But I have come to tell you that it is we, it is you and I and the other Yucatec Maya, who have been called to watch over the devil and to drive him back to hell whenever he appears.*

This is not the only body burned on the beach. My father told me of others. He had not seen them and his grandfather had not seen them, and his great-grandfather had not seen them, but perhaps his great-great-grandfather had. Or if not him, some ancestor before. There is a clock ticking within the devil's tail, a clock that measures the hour in its own way and judges us accordingly. When the hour is ready, the devil's tail awakens. Its curse sends our dead back onto our shores and into our heads. We destroy the messengers on the shores, and plead with those in our heads to put the tail back asleep, we are not ready to listen to it.

We do not talk of this with strangers. But you are only partly a stranger, so perhaps it is not wrong to talk to you. And I myself have become a man with no name, so it no longer matters what I do or whom I tell. For how can I be punished if I do not have a name? When I heard your name and in it heard that you were a wise man, I told myself I would speak.

I saw the creature with my own eyes. Had I a name and children, I would tell my name to them, and have them memorize it, just as my father had me do, so that they could tell their own children, and their children's children. Such is the way we learn and understand. Such is the way we remember.

I saw the creature with my own eyes. It was like a man but it was not a man. Where a man would have had separate legs and arms, its legs had joined with its arms and there was no parting them. Where a man would have a face, this creature had a hole. Where a man would have a cage of ribs to frame him, the ribs of this creature's back had opened and curled upon themselves in a scroll. Where a man has lungs that obey him and keep the same shape and form, the creature had lungs that kept swelling and swelling, rising from its back like nothing so much as an inflating balloon.

How can this be? It is not the same creature that my father told me of and made me memorize, but another. Bodies do not do what this creature did. And when it breathed air in, the air it breathed out was not the same. The air had been bled of its life and become noxious and stinking, and choking.

There are rituals associated with the appearance of the devil or his minions, ways of driving the devil out. There are forgotten languages that can be spoken and that are remembered in time of need, that the dead come whisper in our ears. This time it was a boy who led us, a boy who understood what he was doing almost not at all. There are dances and measured steps that one can take to contain the darkness. Each stage of the dance is a stage of the development of life and as we dance the development of life, the creature becomes caught in them and becomes vulnerable. When it is tight in the trap, then we destroy it.

But there is one thing that I saw about this creature that I would not put in the stories, that I would not tell to my children, did I have them, and for this reason I could not bring myself to dance with the others. One thing I saw that I cannot make fit with the stories I have heard and which I can only drive away by telling it to you. There, on what would be its arm—were it human—was a tattoo. It was a tattoo I had seen before, in a bar a few weeks before, on the arm of a sailor sitting at the bar beside me. In his cups he showed me his tattoo, the image of a woman riding on a wave, the sun cupped in her hand, the workmanship very fine. The next day he was gone, shipped out, and then his tattoo reappeared on the creature that we burned on the beach.

Now tell me this, Altman. Tell me this, wise man, if that is what you are and not an old servant instead. Was the tattoo there because the creature, through a power known only to itself, had stolen it? Or was the tattoo there because the creature had not always been a creature? Was the tattoo there because the creature had once been a man?

. . .

On the way home, his arm wrapped protectively around Ada's shoulders, both of them silent, he felt like there was too much moving around in his head, too much to consider. He tried to tell himself that he didn't believe the old man's story, that it was simply a fantasy, but he had seen the remains. He simultaneously couldn't believe and couldn't *not* believe, which made him feel like he was carrying a whole heavy indecipherable world in his head. He needed to do something. To forget about this entirely or do something.

Back at the house, after he got ready for bed and was waiting for Ada to come out of the bathroom, he switched on the newsfeed and set it for voice. Nothing interesting. Trade negotiations between the Scandinavian sector and the Russian sector. DAM announcing that it had developed and patented a new genetically modified wheat that was even better than the previous genetically modified wheat, and that it would soon be available for purchase. Problems with drug smugglers a hundred miles down the coast: a brief vid of a drifting empty boat, its deck slick with blood. The death of William Tanner, manager for DredgerCorp Chicxulub, formerly known as Ecodyne.

"Go back," he said.

The holo flipped back to the drug dealer story, opened it up.

"No," he said. "One later."

William Tanner, manager for DredgerCorp Chicxulub, formerly known as Ecodyne, was found dead this morning, an apparent suicide. According to local police, his body was discovered at nine thirty this morning with its throat slit, after Tanner failed to report to work at the DredgerCorp facility. A knife was found in his right hand. The police have not yet stated whether this knife was the instrument he used to kill himself. Though it is unusual for someone to commit suicide by slitting their own throat, it is not unheard of. Said Sergeant Ramos, "Though there is every indication that Mr. Tanner committed suicide, we cannot yet rule out the possibility of homicide." There has been a marked rise in suicide in Chicxulub and environs over the last several weeks, including—

"Off," he said.

The feed stopped. He sat heavily on the bed. One more thing to hold suspended in his head: Could be murder, could be suicide. He couldn't tell Ada about it, not so soon after their fight, not so soon after Hammond's death. It would just make her try to stop him. *It's not that I'm lying to her,* he told himself. *I'm just trying to protect her.* Ada climbed in beside him and he kissed her, feeling guilty the whole time. Then he turned off the light and braced himself for the nightmares to begin.

30

Lenny Small, president of DredgerCorp, was still sleeping when the vid-link went active. He wasn't sure how much time had passed before he became aware of it. At first he thought it was the maid, talking on her phone, and he yelled, "For God's sake, shut the hell up and get the hell out!" putting the pillow over his head.

"Wake up, Small," said a voice. It was a deep gravelly voice, a certain edge to it. Definitely not the maid.

Curious, he peeked out from under the pillow. The voice was coming from the holoscreen.

"Oh, it's you, Markoff," he said.

"Damn right it's me," said the man on the screen. Craig Markoff had white hair, slightly longer than a military man usually had, carefully combed back and gelled in place. He had an imposing, square-cut jaw and steady, ice blue eyes. He was wearing the dress uniform and insignia of government intelligence. As with all intelligence agents, his rank was not indicated even on his dress uniform.

Small stretched. He moved to the edge of the bed and got out, naked, quickly slipping into his robe. Real silk, not synthetic. Because of environmental legislation, he had had to smuggle it into the North American sector. This had cost him a small fortune, but damned if he could tell the difference.

He looked out the penthouse window and sighed. "Can't it wait until I've had my coffee?" he asked.

"We have a situation. Tanner's dead."

Instantly, Small was focused, his gaze alert, mind sparking. "How'd he die?"

"Killed himself."

"Why?"

"I don't know," said Markoff. "Guilt, perhaps."

"Not possible," said Small. "I've known the bastard for twenty years. He's handled much worse than this Chicxulub thing without batting an eye. You sure he wasn't killed?"

"I'm certain," said Markoff. "I had a camera installed in his room. He's just chatting away to himself and then he cuts his own throat. You can watch the vid of his death if you'd like."

Small winced. "No thanks," he said.

Markoff shrugged. "Suit yourself. I have a script for you," said Markoff. "Things that you can and can't say about his death. I want you to memorize it."

"Word for word? I've never been much good at memorization. It'll sound canned."

"The gist is fine," said Markoff. "Put it in your own words."

"Working with you is like making a deal with the devil," said Small. "No question as to who's in charge." He waited, but Markoff didn't say anything. "All right," Small said. "Send it over."

Markoff spun the script through the holoscreen. Small left it unopened. He'd deal with it later, after his coffee.

"Anything else?" asked Small. "Or can I have my coffee now?"

"One other thing," said Markoff. "The signal pulse has stopped."

"It's stopped? What does that mean? What do we do?"

"The gravity anomaly is still there. The object is still in place. It's just no longer signaling."

"Do you think that it's broken? Maybe those two bastards damaged it when they went down there."

"I don't think so," said Markoff. "If that were the case, it would have stopped a few days ago instead of now. No, I don't think that's it. Something else has happened. Or it's made a decision to stop on its own."

"You talk about it as if it were sentient," said Small.

"It may be," said Markoff. "I'm sure it'll surprise us in more ways than one."

"You really think you can control it?"

"I've never met anything I can't control," said Markoff. "Present company included. I don't see any reason to think this will be an exception."

"So, signal pulse or no, proceed as planned?"

"Proceed as planned," said Markoff. "I'm having the station towed into position now. It's a slow process, but it'll get there. We can start on salvage operations for the submarine and take steps to prepare the object for extraction in the meantime."

"We still split the profits down the middle?"

"Right down the middle," said Markoff. "But profits are hardly the point. Six months from now, we may well be the two most powerful men in the world." He gave Small a cold smile. "Think about that while you're drinking your coffee."

31

They ordered their beers at the counter and took them to a table in the back, all four of them: Showalter, Ramirez, Skud, and Altman. It was isolated enough that there was little danger of being overheard, and from where they were sitting, Showalter and Ramirez could keep an eye on the front door, Skud and Altman on the back door.

"So, it's gone," said Altman. "The signal pulse has stopped."

Skud made a face. "I would not say it has stopped," he said. "I would only say that *perhaps* it has stopped. *Perhaps* it has only become so attenuated as to be undetectable to our instruments."

"That's as good as stopped," said Ramirez. "It has the same effect."

"But it is not the same thing," said Skud.

"All right, Skud," said Altman. "Point taken. The first question is what does it mean that we can no longer detect the signal?"

Nobody said anything.

"The anomaly is still there," said Altman. "At least last I checked."

"Yes," said Showalter. "It's still there."

"Sure, there's currently no signal, but it could simply be part of a larger pattern yet to be determined," said Skud.

"Well said, Skud," said Altman. "So, the signal has stopped, we don't know if this is permanent or temporary. We also don't know why."

"We may never know why," said Ramirez.

Showalter and Skud began to argue with him, in muted whispers. Altman waved his hands to silence them.

"The real question is, Do we move forward now that the signal has died?"

The other three stared at him. "What do you mean by 'move forward'?" Showalter asked.

"Until now we've been investigating quietly, covering our tracks. Now DredgerCorp has made a public arrangement to dig down to the center of the crater, ostensibly to rescue their submarine. No doubt while they're there, they'll investigate whatever it is that lies at the heart of the crater."

Skud made a noncommittal grunt.

"DredgerCorp has come out into the open. Or rather, they've pretended to come out into the open. Is it time for us to do the same?"

"What?" said Ramirez. "What do you mean? You want us to knock on DredgerCorp's door and say 'Excuse me, we've been observing you and we don't think you're being entirely honest'? Sounds to me like a good way to get killed."

"I don't mean that," said Altman. "I mean we go public. The four of us together write up a rigorous and well-reasoned proposal to the North American Sector Science Foundation to investigate the crater. We cite the gravity anomaly and the pulse signal, perhaps even say something about the broadcast from the submarine. We call for a public, government-sponsored excavation of the center of the Chicxulub crater."

They sat together silent for a moment, nursing their beers, except for Skud, who had almost immediately finished his.

"What if they say no?" asked Showalter.

"Then we start approaching other granting organizations. We submit the proposal to as many places as possible, at once trying to get funding and trying to make sure that as many people as possible know about the pulse signal and the anomaly. Someone is sure to begin questioning DredgerCorp's motives. At the very least, they'll have to operate on a shorter leash."

"It could be like stirring up a nest of hornets," said Ramirez.

"Maybe," said Altman. "We won't know until we start stirring. Maybe nothing will happen. Maybe, God forbid, we will put ourselves in jeopardy. But maybe we'll find ourselves in a position to figure out what's at the bottom of that damned crater." He took a sip of his beer. "Who is with me?"

The other three looked at one another. Skud was the first to raise his hand. "I am with you," he said. Ramirez followed. Showalter hesitated for a long time and then finally nodded his head.

"Very good, gentlemen," said Altman. "Let's get to work."

PART FOUR

THE DESCENT

32

He was asleep, having nightmares again. He was running in a strange pressurized suit, through narrow, bleak halls. Part of him knew it was a nightmare for a while, but knowing that didn't seem to help him control it, and gradually he forgot it wasn't real. Something was pursuing him, something with strange tusks in the place of hands and horns sprouting at the joints of its limbs. Its body looked like it had had its skin flayed off. Or even worse, like someone had taken a human skeleton and pressed raw hamburger to it. The bottom half of its face was falling apart. Its eyes gleamed yellow, glittering and burning.

He realized he had some kind of weapon: a gun that sent out a whirling blade projected on a beam of light. He kept turning around and firing the thing, watching it cut with a grating sound through the creature's legs, spraying blood and gore all over. Its legs were gone, but it still kept coming, posting the tips of its tusks against the ground and dragging itself forward, moaning. He cut off its arms and then its head, and finally it stopped.

Thank God, he thought, and wiped the blood off his face.

He had started to turn away when he heard something behind him. The creature was still writhing, flopping this way and that, *changing*. With a wet sound, it sprouted new arms and legs. It clambered up, roaring, and was after him again.

Screaming, he turned and ran.

"Bad dreams?" asked the man beside his bed. He was a large man with a square jaw and white hair, dressed in the dark uniform of military intelligence. He was regarding Altman with a steady, aloof gaze. To either side of him were two even larger men who looked like they might be twins, dressed in street clothes. At a little distance was another man, smaller and wearing glasses. He looked vaguely familiar, but Altman couldn't quite place him.

"Where am I?" asked Altman.

"You're in your house," said the military man. "In Chicxulub."

"Where's Ada?"

"You're girlfriend? She's not here. She's safe."

"What do you mean, safe?" asked Altman, starting to get out of the bed.

The man raised a finger. Calmly but forcefully the twins to either side of him took Altman by the arms and lowered him back onto the bed, holding him down until he had stopped struggling.

Warily, Altman eyed them. "What are you doing here?" he asked the military man.

He made a gesture and the other two let go and stepped back. "I came to see you," he said.

"And who are you?"

"Markoff," he said. "Craig Markoff."

"That doesn't tell me anything," said Altman.

"No," said Markoff. "It doesn't."

"And who are they?" he asked, gesturing to the other three men.

Markoff looked left and right. "These?" he said. "These are my new associates." The man with the glasses gave a smirk. "Tim, Tom, and Terry."

"Which one is which?"

"Does it matter?" asked Markoff.

"Look," said Altman, "you can't just break in here like this. You have no right to be here. I'm going to call the police."

Markoff just smiled. When Altman reached for his phone, he said, "Tom? Tim?"

The twins moved slowly forward. One of them put his hand on Altman's wrist and squeezed until he dropped the phone. The other punched him once, softly, almost lovingly, in the side.

He fell back on the bed, gasping. Tim and Tom wandered back behind Markoff, watching Altman struggle to catch his breath.

When he had calmed down, Markoff said, "Feeling better, are we? Would you like a drink of water?"

Altman shook his head. Markoff snapped his fingers, and the man with the glasses tossed Altman a shirt and a pair of pants.

"You're in the right frame of mind now," said Markoff. "Get dressed. We're going to have a little talk."

. . .

A few minutes later, he was sitting across the kitchen table from Markoff, the other three standing next to the doors leading in and out of the room.

"It's very simple," said Markoff. "You filed a grant to investigate Chicxulub crater."

"There's nothing wrong with that," argued Altman. "That's what scientists do."

"I've already spoken to your friends," said Markoff. "Or, rather, my associates have. We've determined that the person motivating this grant application was you."

"So?"

Markoff gave him a cold look. "Don't get cocky. If I have to, I'll have Tim break your arm," he said.

"Or Tom," said one of the twins from where he stood near the doorway.

"Or Tom," said Markoff. He turned and looked at the twin. "Don't worry, Tom. He has two arms. Enough to go around." Then he turned back to Altman, looked at him with one eyebrow raised.

"I'm sorry," Altman said.

"That's better," said Markoff. "Your proposal for investigating the crater has been pulled from the grant proposal pool. It is now classified. The investigation of Chicxulub crater has become a military matter."

"So, I was right," said Altman.

"About what?" asked Markoff.

"You're not just trying to retrieve the submarine. You're trying to get at whatever is in the crater."

"You're a clever boy," said Markoff. "Maybe too clever for your own good. The reason I'm here is to find out how much you know and evaluate whether you would be a valuable member of our team. If you are, I am prepared to allow you to join us—in a limited capacity, of course. If not, I'll have to figure out something else to do with you."

"What do you mean by 'something else'?"

Markoff shrugged. "Could be ship you back to your own sector. Could be having you put in confinement for as long as it takes us to complete the project. Could be something a bit more serious." Behind him, the twins exchanged glances and smiled. "I suppose, Mr. Altman, that it's up to you." Markoff straightened in his chair, put both his hands palm down on the table. "Well, Mr. Altman, shall we begin?"

Markoff started off slow.

"How did you first realize there was something unusual going on in the crater?"

"I detected a gravity anomaly."

"It wasn't the pulse signal?"

Altman shook his head. "The pulse signal came later."

"Who told you about the pulse signal?"

Altman hesitated, tempted to lie, and then he realized it didn't matter: Hammond was dead.

And then, suddenly it clicked: he knew where he had seen the man with the glasses.

"Charles Hammond told me," he said. "I believe your associates knew him."

Markoff looked back at Terry. The latter hesitated a moment, nodded.

"But we didn't kill him," said Tim.

"No, we didn't kill him," said Tom.

"No talking shop here, boys," said Markoff. "Terry, why don't you take Tim and Tom and wait for me outside?"

The three of them quietly left the room.

"How do I know you are who you say you are?" asked Altman.

Markoff turned back, his gaze steady. "I wondered when you were going to get around to that. Either I am or I'm not," he said. "If I am, then it'll be worth your while to cooperate if it will get you on the expedition. If I'm not, then there's very little you can do about it. Whether you tell me the truth or not, you're probably in trouble either way. Tell me . . . what do you think you know?"

It's a reasonable enough gamble, thought Altman. *I know that DredgerCorp is working with the military to salvage the submarine, so chances are he is what he says he is. The trick is knowing how to tell him enough to get him to bring me aboard on the project, but not so much that he thinks he's already gotten all he can out of me, that he doesn't need me anymore.*

He took a deep breath. "I'd guess there's something in the heart of the crater," said Altman. "Not a natural phenomenon, but something else."

"Go on," said Markoff.

"Considering its location, it must have been there a very long time."

"How long?"

"It might have been there thousands of years. Or even longer."

"Why do you think so?"

"The Yucatec Maya have a kind of mythology surrounding it. They call it the tail of the devil."

He saw a gleam of something in Markoff's eye. "You've told me something I didn't know, Altman," he said. "How did you find this out?"

"I'll give you more details if you bring me in on the project."

Markoff nodded, his lips tight. "I'll let you get away with that, for a few minutes, anyway. What do *you* think it is?" he asked.

"I have no fucking idea," said Altman.

"There's no room on the team for someone who doesn't have imagination. What do you think it could be?"

Altman looked down at the tabletop, at his hands resting clasped together on it, at Markoff's hands still palm down on the other side. "I thought at first it might be a relic from some ancient civilization, but . . . I've thought a lot about it," he said, "and the only other thing I can come up with frightens me." He looked up, met Markoff's gaze. "An object, sending a pulse signal from the center of a vast crater, perhaps buried since the creation of the crater thousands or hundreds of thousands, even millions, of years ago. What if it wasn't an asteroid that made the crater but the object itself, striking the earth?"

Markoff nodded.

"Which suggests that it was something that came from outer space," said Altman. "Which in turn suggests that it was something sent here by intelligent life outside of our galaxy."

"Which raises the question of why it was transmitting," said Markoff.

"And who it was transmitting to," said Altman. "And what."

They sat in silence for a while. "If that's what it is," Altman said, "it'll change our whole understanding of life as we know it."

Markoff nodded, finally removing his hands from the table and putting them in his lap. When they returned, there was a gun in one of them.

"Ah, Altman, Altman," he said. "What am I going to do with you?"

"Are you threatening me?" asked Altman, his voice rising. He hoped he sounded tough and angry, that Markoff wasn't detecting the fear that he felt.

"You obviously have guessed too much to be let go. You've even guessed too much for me to just throw you in confinement. I have to decide whether to kill you or take you with us."

Altman slowly raised his hands. "I'd rather you took me with you," he said, a quaver to his voice now.

"Not a shocking preference, considering the circumstances. Take you or shoot you?" he mused. "I can see advantages to both. Can you tell me anything else to tip the scales? Is there something else you forgot to add?"

Altman kept his hands crossed, afraid that if he moved them, Markoff would see how much he was shaking. His mouth was very dry. His voice, when he began to speak, trembled. "There is one other thing," he said.

"Yes?" said Markoff, casually cocking the gun.

"The villagers found something. A strange creature, humanoid but not human, that they're convinced is connected to the happenings in the crater. They burned it, but there are still remains you can examine. I'll take you to them."

"Is that all?"

Altman swallowed. "That's all."

"Good-bye, Mr. Altman," Markoff said. He raised the pistol and pointed it at Altman's head, then started to squeeze the trigger. Altman closed his eyes and gritted his teeth. He heard the snap of the hammer, but no bullet came.

He opened his eyes. Markoff was watching him, intensely focused.

"All in good fun," he said. "The gun was empty. I never intended to shoot you. Welcome to the team."

He stood and extended his hand. Altman was still in shock and didn't move. Markoff pried his hands apart from each other and shook one of them.

"You will be closely watched. You won't have free run of the facility, but I want you available if and when I need you." He leaned in closer. "And if you do betray me, Mr. Altman, I will kill you," he said in a low voice. "Do you understand? Nod if you understand."

Altman understood.

"Very good," said Markoff, and started for the door. "I'll have Terry make your arrangements."

"All right," said Altman quietly.

His hand on the doorknob, Markoff stopped. He stood there a moment, his back to Altman.

"There's the question of your girlfriend, isn't there," he said.

Oh, shit, thought Altman.

Markoff turned around, looked at him with searching eyes. "What should we do about her?"

"You don't have to worry about her," said Altman. He tried to stay calm and expressionless as he said it, poker faced, but his voice, he knew, was still trembling.

"But I want to worry about her, Altman," said Markoff. "Let's just say it'd be my pleasure."

"Look," said Altman desperately. "I understand why you

feel you have to take me, but Ada's different. She has nothing to do with any of this. She even tried to stop me from taking an interest in it. Let her go."

Markoff smiled. "What you've just shown me, Altman, is that you care enough about her that I couldn't possibly think about letting her go. I believe she might come in handy."

"What are you planning to do with her?"

"Ah, Mr. Altman," said Markoff. "Questions, always questions."

He opened the door and went out.

33

Terry and the twins stood over him while he packed. They hurried him along. They impounded his phone and his holopod, as well as his terminal, the twins sealing them up in a crate and carrying them off.

"You'll have them back once Markoff has taken a look at them," said Terry. "Except for the phone."

"Can't I at least call Field and tell him I won't be in?"

"No."

"I need some time to wrap up my affairs—"

"No."

"What about my family, they'll be worried—"

"You're stalling," said Terry. "None of that other stuff is important. What's important is doing the job and doing it right. You keep stalling, and I'll give Mr. Markoff a call and we'll see how badly he wants you along."

"And then what, you'll kill me? Like you did Hammond?" Terry winced. "I resent the implication," he said. "I saw him die, sure, but I didn't have anything to do with it."

"Then it was Tim and Tom."

"Not them either," said Terry. He looked at Altman in a way that made the latter realize he was genuinely confused and strangely vulnerable.

"What happened?" he asked.

"We were just trying to question him and he flipped out," said Terry. "I've never seen anything quite like it. One moment he was running and the next he was trying to kill us." He showed Altman an angry, awkward scar on his hand. "We didn't even have any weapons. Tanner had just sent us there to talk to him." He rubbed his eyes with his knuckles. "And then suddenly he took his knife and cut his own throat. Never seen anyone cut quite that deep so quickly. Been dreaming about it ever since."

Abruptly he straightened up, his face becoming closed again. "I don't mind being blamed for what I've done, but don't blame me for what I haven't. Come on, get moving."

They walked quickly to the DredgerCorp building, Terry holding on to his arm and hurrying him along. A few people looked at them curiously in the streets, but most just ignored them or deliberately looked the other way. The building now had a security fence around it, made of welded wire mesh. The building itself had been razed to the ground and was in the process of being replaced by a structure formed of interlocking concrete and steel panels, more like a fortress than like a corporate building.

"Some changes being made," said Altman.

Terry nodded. "You don't know the half of it."

He led him around behind the construction, to a concrete

pad. On it was a helicopter, blades already spinning. They hurried to it, and Altman climbed aboard.

Ada was there, her face taut, drawn. He sat down next to her and she clung to him. *She isn't usually like that*, he thought. *She must be terrified.* Almost immediately the helicopter took off.

"I've been worried about you," he said, having to shout to be heard over the noise. "I thought they might have done something to you."

"I was worried about you, too," she said. "Are you okay?"

He offered her a feeble smile. "No permanent damage."

"Michael, do you know where we're going?"

"No," he said. "I'm afraid I don't."

"I told you," she said. "This would all end badly, I said. I told you to leave it alone. But you wouldn't listen."

"It's not over yet," he said.

He looked out the window. They had turned and were flying over the water now, were already fairly far from land. He looked around the helicopter, at the other passengers. Terry wasn't there; either he'd stayed behind or was up with the pilot. It contained eight other scientists, all people he recognized by sight, even if he didn't know them all. Field was one of them, looking like he was sick to his stomach.

Skud was there, as was Showalter. Holding on to the roof straps, he moved over closer to them.

"Where's Ramirez?" he shouted.

"They didn't have him come," said Showalter.

"What did they do with him?"

Showalter shrugged.

"Did they give you a choice?" asked Altman.

"A what?" shouted Skud. "Why are they taking us?"

"A choice?"

"No!" shouted Showalter. "We had to come."

"Do you know where we're going?" shouted Skud.

Altman shook his head. "I was going to ask you," he said.

He clambered back to his bench.

"They don't know," he said. "Nobody knows where we're going."

They flew for roughly three hours. Direction, Altman thought, judging by the sun was northwest, or west-northwest, though he wasn't exactly sure. At some point, he thought they turned south. How fast could a helicopter fly? Seventy-five miles an hour? A hundred? It seemed like they were covering a lot of distance.

Maybe they're just planning to kill us, he thought. *Just put all of us on the same helicopter and engineer a crash.* If so, he realized, there was nothing he could do. He was already as good as dead.

He sat on the bench, half-deafened by the sound of the blades, his arm around Ada. It was his fault that she was here, he knew. He was to blame. Across from him, Skud looked haggard, exhausted. Time slowed.

The hum of the blades fell an octave and the craft slowed noticeably. They all started looking out the windows. Below was a cloud of mist, almost perfectly symmetrical, clinging to the water. They started moving down toward it.

Altman began to catch glimpses of something within the cloud. A flash here and there. A strut or a bit of metal. They came down slowly, the blades of the helicopter making the mist roil. He could see the top of a large glass dome, the glass bluish, wet and iridescent in the sudden light. They came very close, hovering maybe ten meters above it, and he thought he could see a glimpse of faces inside. He could see, on the metal struts and partitions of the glass, thousands of tiny jets, each of them releasing a fine spray of mist.

Suddenly the jets stopped. The mist drifted around the structure for a moment and then slowly dissipated, revealing the dome and everything beneath it.

It was a huge floating compound, hundreds of feet in diameter, made of a series of glass or plastic domes, connected or overlapped like frogs' eggs. Much of it descended well below the surface of the water. Indeed, as much of the structure seemed to be below water as above, perhaps more.

The top of the central dome, where the metal supports met, had a flat spot. Carefully, the pilot brought the helicopter down. He touched once but with one strut off the flat spot, and they began to tilt. He went up again, came down even slower, and this time managed it.

The cabin door opened from the outside. Two guards, wearing dark military garb, gestured to them to climb out.

Altman expected the dome to sway up and down with the swells, but it was big enough that he hardly noticed anything. He climbed down onto the deck then turned to help Ada down. The others soon followed. Together they made their way to a hatch and climbed down it. By descending a short ladder, they reached a platform just under the roof of the dome. The platform had a transparent shaft in the center of it, one side of it open. As he looked at it, a lift rose up into it.

The guards gestured and herded them into it. The lift began to descend.

It was only once they were off the platform and moving down on the slowly descending lift that Altman really got a sense of how big the dome was. They were probably forty or fifty feet up, the large dome open and nearly empty, the foggy light dappling the glass walls and casting odd shadows. It was a hemisphere rather than a dome, a solid floor running along the bottom of it.

Whether there was another reversed hemisphere below, there was no way to tell from here.

Stacks of boxes and crates littered the floor along with partially assembled, or perhaps partially disassembled, machinery. Also military guards, lots of them, some of them standing at attention or employed in some small task, most of them walking or chatting idly, perhaps off duty. Here and there, a man in a white coat stood directing a group of them, getting them to lug equipment around.

At the bottom of the lift, two more guards stood waiting to meet them. Skud began to ask a question, but one of the guards interrupted him.

"No talking," he said.

They kept the group there until everyone from the helicopter had made it down, then led them across the floor of the dome. Groups of guards stopped talking as they approached, following them with their eyes. Above, Altman heard the sound of the helicopter taking off again. Immediately the nozzles began to spray and the outside world dissolved in a cloud of mist.

The ambient light in the dome dimmed, grew somber. Someone shouted a command, and banks of harsh fluorescents lined along the struts flickered on. The dome brightened with an antiseptic light, inflicting the skin of everyone around them with an unhealthy glow.

They came to the edge of the large dome and passed through a sliding door, moving into a much smaller one. Down through a pressure hatch. Into a passage running around the edge of a third dome and curving slowly downward.

Halfway around the passage, Altman noticed the water lapping up against the side of the tunnel, going higher with each step. There was a subtle change in the quality of the sound, as if everything here was lightly wrapped in cotton batting. He tapped the side of the corridor with his fingernail, heard only a dull, echoless sound. Something with a pale stretched eye veered out of the deeps and toward his hand, and then darted away again. A few steps later, the water rose all the way over their heads and closed over the top of the passage. They were completely below the surface.

They left the corridor and came into a dome cast green from the reflection of the water. Fish and other animals swam around the floating compound and here and there barnacles had begun to take hold. At a distance was a phalanx of submarines, connected by a series of cables to the floating compound, pulling it very slowly along.

"It's beautiful," said Ada.

"It's terrifying," said Altman.

The guard stuck the barrel of his gun firmly against Altman's ribs, hard enough to hurt. "No talking," he said.

They twisted to the bottom of the dome and took another lift down, to a series of adjoined chambers, squarish rooms. They passed from one to the next, the guards keeping them in a straight line and hustling them along. It felt to Altman like he was being led to his own execution. Here the water was deeper, darker. The rooms had more metal in them than glass. They were all lit by the same harsh fluorescents.

The guards hustled them into another slightly descending corridor, this one ending in a pressure hatch. Altman judged that they were back near the center of the lab, though well below the waterline now. One of the guards opened it, ushered them through.

The room inside resembled the bridge of a moon cruiser. It was a spherical chamber with a central elevated command chair. In all directions, down a few steps, were banks of controls, readouts, and holoscreens. An uninterrupted bank of windows ran along the upper half of the wall. The command chair was just enough above the rest of the lab to give an unimpeded view of the water in all directions.

The chair spun around to reveal Markoff. He looked down at them, and smiled. Here, in this environment, with his firm jaw and glittering eyes lit by the stark fluorescents, surrounded by water on all sides, he seemed like something monstrous pretending to be human.

"Ah, you've arrived," he said without any warmth. "Welcome to your new home."

It took a while, but they eventually got used to their new quarters. The lab was nicer than any he'd ever seen, and was compromised only by his having to share it, just as he had in Chicxulub, with Field. He saw this as a particular bit of sadism on Markoff's part, and even wondered if he'd brought Field along only to irritate him.

They were still three weeks away from getting to the center of Chicxulub crater. The floating compound was towed forward very slowly and sometimes, depending on weather conditions, had to be stopped. He'd initially thought the command center was the lowest point on the ship, but quickly realized that side corridors led to a tight sequence of chambers just below that. And below that, finally, was an even larger chamber, perhaps the largest chamber on the floating compound. It was carefully pressurized. It had a crane and a water opening and a very high ceiling. It was a last-minute addition to the lab, Altman learned from one of the other scientists, and had been built specifically to accommodate the object in the heart of the crater.

Everywhere Altman went, he was amazed. The floating compound, obviously built for a specific but different purpose, was being quickly retrofitted with state-of-the-art equipment. Almost hourly, boats and helicopters arrived, bringing not only brand-new equipment but also devices that were still in prototype phase. Expense was no object. Whatever was down there, they were prepared to spend whatever it took to get to it.

They ate meals in shifts at the facility's cafeteria. The researchers stayed in dormitory rooms that, generally speaking, slept six, though there were a few exceptions: Altman and Ada, the only couple on board, were grudgingly given a converted storage closet as a bedroom. It was just big enough to hold their bed and a narrow filing cabinet that they stuffed with their clothes and made into a dresser, but they were still glad for the privacy.

As Altman got to know the others, he had to admit that Markoff had assembled a first-rate team. Not knowing exactly what the thing in the crater might be, he had his bases covered.

There were a few scientists whose fields were so cutting edge that there weren't names for them yet. There were geophysicists and astrophysicists, robotics experts, geologists, marine biologists, geneticists, oceanologists, engineers of various stripes, a mining foreman, an oceanographer, a seismologist, a volcanologist, a gravitologist, a philosopher, a cognitive scientist, various doctors, a medic specializing in baro-traumatism and decompression sickness, countless mechanics and technicians, a house-keeping and kitchen staff. There was even a linguist and, with Ada, an anthropologist.

A number of them were researchers who, although once quite famous, had vanished from the public eye years before. None of them would speak about what they'd been doing in the intervening years and if pressed, spoke only of "coming out of retirement." *Retirement, my ass,* Showalter whispered to him. Altman agreed: if they were here now, it was because they had been working covertly for military intelligence in the meantime. They were given away by being the only ones who didn't seem surprised at the massive expense and effort going into the expedition: they took it all for granted.

What disturbed Altman even more were the number of military guards present and how actively they were training. It was clear—or in any case seemed clear to Altman—that Markoff had some notion that they had to be prepared for combat.

There were three possibilities for this that Altman could come up with. One, the least disturbing to him, was that Markoff was simply being a soldier himself. That he thought the military weren't needed but that as long as they were here, they deserved to be put through their paces. The second, more disturbing, was that Markoff expected someone to try to take the object away from them, that he was aware there were competing interests trying to get their hands on it, or would be. The third, and the worst of all, was: perhaps Markoff was expecting the object to fight back.

Which made Altman realize something he should have realized a long time before. Without having an altogether clear idea of what it was, Markoff thought of the object at the center of the crater as a weapon. Maybe he wasn't intending the extraction for the betterment of mankind or the advancement of science after all.

Altman talked it over with Ada, told her his suspicions.

"Does that surprise you?" she asked. "Markoff's ruthless. He thinks of everything as a potential weapon. Even people. He's a very dangerous man."

He quickly found that a lot of places were out of bounds to him. There were certain areas, certain sets of laboratories both below and above the waterline, that his keycard did not grant him access to. Sometimes he could get in following on the heels of a careless scientist or guard, but he was never allowed to remain long enough to get a good sense of what was happening. Other rooms were even more off-limits, protected by round-the-clock guards. Field was in one of these, but when Altman asked him about it, he got nowhere, less because Field was suspicious than because Field didn't see enough of the big picture to understand what was actually going on.

After just a few days, he started to notice he was being watched. It began as just a vague feeling, but grew stronger. He thought at first it was just paranoia, until Showalter noticed it as well. The guards regarded him in a different way than they did many of the other researchers, and whenever he'd spent some time alone in one of the corridors, often just to gather his thoughts, a guard suddenly showed up. Several of the technicians seemed to be paying him special attention. One man in particular, a man who always wore the same rumpled coverall, seemed always to be lingering, just behind him.

"What should I do?" he asked Ada.

"What can you do?" she said. "If they want to watch you, they can watch you. There's nothing you can do about it. You're in their power."

She was right, he knew. Who was he going to complain to? Markoff? Markoff had given him three alternatives: be part of the team, be locked up, or end up dead. Maybe Markoff had had his cake and eaten it, too: maybe he was both part of the team and locked up at the same time. The floating compound made a good prison. And it was a better alternative than being dead.

"What do you think is going on?" he asked Ada.

She rolled her eyes. "I don't want it to start all over again, Michael. It's dangerous to ask yourself these questions. So what if we can't go into certain parts of the ship? We're not the only ones in that position. Most of the researchers from Chicxulub are being treated in exactly the same way."

"Not Field," said Altman. "Field has access."

"Limited access," she said. "One room only. I've been watching. Showalter and Skud don't," she said, ticking them off on her fingers. "Lots of others don't as well."

He didn't answer, just turned away, thinking. There were ways of finding out. All he'd have to do was to replicate a card and then—

His thoughts were interrupted when she slapped him on the cheek.

"Don't," she said, pointing a finger at his face.

"What?"

"I know what you're thinking," she said. "You don't need to have full run of the place in order to do your job. If you did, you'd only get into trouble. I want you to promise me you'll leave it alone."

He looked at her for a long moment, finally shook his head. "I can't," he said.

She slapped him once more for good measure and turned away. He, not knowing what else to do, wrapped his arms around her to prevent her from going. She struggled at first, not willing to meet his eyes, but he kept hold of her until finally she began to soften a little.

"You never listen to me," she said. "I'm always right and you never listen."

"I always listen," he claimed. "I just don't always do what you say."

Finally she met his eyes. "Damn it, Michael. Promise me you'll be careful this time," she said. "Be discreet. Promise me you won't do anything to end up dead."

"All right," he said, finally letting her go. "That I can promise."

He was careful. He learned more about the floating compound, talking to some of the mechanics and engineers. It was a converted semisubmersible rig, mobile, made to float half in the water and half out. The mist, which they referred to as the blur effect, was sprayed by high-grade jets, their apertures less than one hundred microns in diameter. The water was forced through the jets and onto extremely fine needle points, causing it to atomize into droplets so small that most of them remain suspended in the air. If anyone with any sort of advanced equipment wanted to determine what was in the cloud, they would have no difficulty, but it was enough to keep at least a few of the curious ships and boats away.

On the second or third day, a sturdy man with an exceptionally frizzy red beard joined him in the cafeteria. He stretched one large hand across the table, shook Altman's hand.

"Jason Hendricks," he said. "You're new here, aren't you?"

Altman nodded. "Michael Altman," he said. "I just got here."

Hendricks gave a slow, easygoing smile that Altman immediately liked. "None of us have been here for long," he said. "I just got here a week or so ago myself."

He began to eat, and almost immediately his beard was full of crumbs and scraps of food. "What brings you here, Michael?"

Altman thought a moment about what to say, finally settled on "They're still figuring out what to do with me, I'm afraid."

"Me, I'm a pilot," said Hendricks. He rubbed his hands through his beard to work the crumbs out and then wiped his palms on his shirt. "Submarines mostly. Was trained by the navy to pilot a midsize sub. Also did some work with submersibles for a construction firm."

"You must enjoy it," said Altman.

"I like it well enough," said Hendricks. "Also spent some time in a small one-man affair working for treasure hunters in the Caribbean. Had to reconsider that line of work when I realized the treasure they had me looking for was a sunken boat full of heroin."

"Probably a good decision," said Altman.

"Probably," said Hendricks, his eyes crinkling up warmly as he smiled. "Though maybe if I'd stuck with it, I'd be rich by now. Either that or very, very high. You think I'm going to have the same ethical dilemma with this job?"

They met the next day at the same table, then the next, and soon Altman had come to think of Hendricks as a friend, as someone he could trust. After a few days, Hendricks told him more about what he was doing, that he was to be on a two-man team working with a bathyscaphe. He'd had little enough experience with bathyscaphes, but wasn't worried: there was still plenty of time before they arrived.

"I'm slated to copilot with some deep-sea explorer guy named Edgar Moresby," he told Altman. "Man's in his late sixties and has skin that looks like it's been cured. Drinks like a fish. Not much of a pilot as far as I'm concerned. Claims to be the descendent of Robert Moresby."

"Who?" asked Altman.

Hendricks shrugged. "Don't ask me," he said. "Some Brit hydrographer and naval officer. He brings it up any chance he gets."

Moresby had no interest in going out on Hendricks's practice runs, claiming he could pilot a bathyscaphe drunk and in his sleep. "And I often have," he had told Hendricks. "No better way of getting the job done, if you ask me." But as long as he had the choice, he preferred to do his drinking in the privacy of his own berth.

"That leaves me in a dilemma," said Hendricks. "I can't go out alone. What if something goes wrong?"

Altman waited for a few moments so as not to appear too

eager before answering. "I'll go with you," he said, trying to sound casual.

"Would you?" said Hendricks, and gave Altman a warm smile. "That'd be a big help."

He fully expected Markoff to find out and put a stop to it, but either news hadn't gotten back to him or he didn't care that Altman was going out in the bathyscaphe. He didn't learn much new from either the bathyscaphe or Hendricks, but he was at least keeping busy.

Plus, Altman quickly found that he had an aptitude for piloting. He knew instinctively how much to flex the controls to get the bathyscaphe to perform how he wanted it to. When asked to dive to a certain depth or rise to a certain level, he could let in just enough water or release by feel just enough pellets to do it smoothly and precisely. He found it curiously satisfying and gratifying in a way that geophysics never had been.

"You should be piloting instead of me," said Hendricks one day.

"Yeah, right," said Altman. "I don't think Markoff would ever agree to it."

But surprisingly enough, when Hendricks asked Markoff, he did agree. It'd be good to have a backup pilot, Markoff claimed, in case anything went wrong. But that was not to say that Altman was off the hook for his other tasks. He'd still be expected to follow any instructions that the lead researchers gave him and to continue to take his geophysical readings. It was just that now he might sometimes be asked to take these readings below the water, from within the bathyscaphe.

34

They were still six or seven days away from the center of the crater when Markoff decided without warning to put the bathyscaphe through deepwater tests. Hendricks and Moresby were to be carried by freighter thirty miles or so ahead of the facility. There they were to dive as deep as they could, until they reached the ocean floor, test the equipment, the air systems, the communications systems, sonar, lighting, et cetera, take a few readings, remain in place for at least an hour, then ascend. Two submarines were to go along and stand by in case assistance was required.

Hendricks showed up at Altman's door shortly before he was scheduled to leave. He looked nervous.

"I've got a problem," he claimed. "It's Moresby. He tied one on last night as soon as he heard we'd be going down."

"Is he all right to go down?"

"Right now he can't even see," said Hendricks. "I've been trying to walk him out of it, but I've got to supervise the transfer of the bathyscaphe. Do you think you . . ."

He trailed off, waited.

"Maybe you should say something to Markoff," said Altman.

"I don't want to do that," said Hendricks. "He already warned Moresby once, and I don't want to do anything to get him fired.

I know it's a lot to ask, but will you look in on him, see if there's anything that can be done?"

Altman nodded. "But I'm doing it not for Moresby but for you."

Hendricks smiled. "Thanks, man. I owe you one."

Altman clambered through the tunnels and up decks to Moresby and Hendricks's cabin. He knocked on the door. There was no answer. He hesitated, knocked again. When there was still no answer, he tried the door and, finding it unlocked, entered.

It was a narrow space with two berths, the top belonging to Hendricks, the bottom to Moresby. The room reeked of vomit. Moresby was half in and half out of the bottom bunk, as still as a corpse. Altman shook him.

At first there was no response. After a few more minutes of shaking, he groaned slightly, his eyes barely opening before closing again.

Altman shook him harder, slapped him.

Moresby blinked, coughed. "Give me a minute to steady myself," he said, and groped a bottle off the floor beneath the bed.

"You don't need any more," said Altman. "Come on, get up."

"Who are you to tell me what I need?" asked Moresby. He tried to stand up and nearly fell. "I'm a Moresby, by God, a descendant of . . ."

He was still babbling out his pedigree while Altman dragged him down the hall and thrust him, fully clothed, into the shower, turning the cold tap all the way open. A moment later, Moresby was shouting. Ten minutes later, he was dressed in dry clothes and subdued. He was pale, was sweating a sour smell, and his hands were still shaking, but he was more or less presentable.

"You're all right?" Altman asked.

"Just nerves," said Moresby. "I'll be all right once I'm down there."

Altman nodded.

"You won't tell anybody, will you?" said Moresby, refusing to meet his gaze now.

"Hendricks doesn't want me to," he said. "If it was up to me, I would."

He led Moresby to the submarine bay, where Markoff was planning to pass them in review before leaving. The submarine pilots were already there, the bathyscaphe transferred.

"You stay here," said Altman.

"Where are you going?"

"I'm going to find Hendricks."

It might have been different if he'd found Hendricks sooner, or if the other submarine pilots had kept an eye on Moresby. Or if Markoff had come right away, before Moresby had had time to have second thoughts, but it took almost half an hour for him to arrive. As it was, Hendricks and Altman made it back just a few moments before Markoff, and it wasn't until he'd started speaking that Altman realized Moresby was nowhere to be seen.

Markoff took the review very seriously. He wore a freshly pressed dress uniform and was flanked by two guards on either side. He thanked the pilots and crews and technicians for their efforts, reminded the other two submarine crews that they would stand by on the freighter in case anything went wrong and the bathyscaphe failed to rise. As for the bathyscaphe, if for any reason Hendricks and Moresby—

He stopped. "Where's Moresby?" he asked.

Hendricks looked around. "He was here just a moment ago, sir," he said.

In the end, two guards discovered him. He'd managed to find a bottle somewhere and had downed a good bit of it. Drunk, he had fallen from one of the lifts and broken his neck. *It's my fault*, Altman thought. *I should have watched him more carefully.* He looked over and caught Hendricks's eye, realized that Hendricks was thinking much the same thing, was blaming himself.

Markoff, however, didn't react at all, and rejected out of hand Hendricks's request to put the dive off for a day out of respect for the dead. "Just as well," he said when the body was brought to him. "That way we'll be sure to get the geophysical readings right. Sound all right to you, Altman?"

He had to repeat it twice before Altman realized he was being addressed. "Fine," said Altman, trying not to stare at the body, at the way the head hung at an odd, impossible angle.

. . .

They took a boat to the freighter in silence, the bathyscaphe being towed behind. Once there, the guards held the bathyscaphe steady as they loaded on.

"I'm still a little shaky," said Hendricks. "I lived with Moresby, after all. If it's all the same with you, I'll let you drive."

Though a little shaky himself, Altman was happy to have the distraction of working the instruments. He eased them slowly down. Before long they were resting steady on the ocean floor.

"How deep are we?" asked Altman.

"Not nearly as deep as we'll be in the center of the crater," said Hendricks. "Two thousand meters, I'd guess."

"Have you ever been this deep before?"

Hendricks shook his head. "Almost," he said, "but not quite."

It was peaceful there, thought Altman, soothing almost, like they had come to the end of the world. He liked listening to the quiet whir of the air recirculators, liked watching the dark, almost empty world outside.

35

A week later, they arrived, and everybody was eager to get to work. They started by taking readings from the surface, from a launch that rose and fell with the swell of the waves. Field was with him at first, taking readings of his own and double-checking Altman's, though he became greener and greener as the afternoon went on. He spent the last hour of the day hanging over the launch's side, retching.

By the next morning, a groaning, vomit-flecked Field had been shipped back to the floating compound and it was just Hendricks and Altman. They brought the bathyscaphe down a thousand meters and took their readings there, waiting for confirmation from Markoff to descend farther. When it came, they went down to two thousand meters and repeated the process.

"Seems straightforward," said Altman.

Hendricks shrugged. "More or less," he said. "Only problem is that down this deep, communication gets erratic. It's hard to know if they'll receive the data we're sending."

"We might be cut off?" asked Altman.

"It comes and goes," said Hendricks. "Really nothing to worry about as long as nothing goes wrong."

Through the front observation porthole, Altman thought he could see pinpricks of light from the excavation below, from the robotic diggers. But it was too far away to make anything out. "We could go down to three thousand meters, take readings, and then come back up," said Altman. "We've got more than enough air for it. You're the boss. Up to you."

Hendricks said, "Have you heard the stories about the other bathyscaphe?"

"I've seen the vid," Altman said.

"What do you think happened?"

"I don't know," said Altman.

"Doesn't it worry you at all?"

"I don't know," said Altman. "I want to know what happened, but I'm not worried exactly. Does it worry you?"

Hendricks nodded. "Let's take it slow. There's no point in rushing things," he said. "On the other hand, if I'm reading the data right, the pulse signal is starting again."

"Really?" said Altman, trying to keep the excitement out of his voice. "Are you certain?"

Hendricks hesitated, then nodded slowly. "It's very slight—I caught it at two thousand meters but not at one thousand—but it's there."

"What does it mean that it's back?" asked Altman. "Maybe we should keep going down after all. Who knows how long it will last? We need to record it while it's still broadcasting."

But Hendricks had one hand cupped over his earpiece. "Too late," he said. "They're ordering us back up."

They looked at each other a long moment. "You said yourself that communications are intermittent," said Altman. "How will they know we got the message?"

Hendricks shook his head. "If we don't get the okay to go down to three thousand meters, we're to go back to the surface anyway. That's protocol. If we disobey, what do you think the chances are of them letting us near a bathyscaphe again? We can't do it."

A half dozen counterarguments fired through his head and then quickly dissolved. Hendricks was right. They had no choice. The signal would have to wait.

A contingent of guards was waiting for them by the time they opened the hatch and stepped out in the submarine bay. They were hustled down to the command center, which was already occupied not just by Markoff but also by a half dozen researchers, all of them part of Markoff's inner circle. Not men from Chicxulub. They looked stern, serious.

"The pulse signal has started again?" asked Markoff. "You're sure about this?"

"Why the hell wouldn't we be?" said Altman. "The instruments don't lie." He gestured at the other researchers. "But you apparently wanted a second opinion. Why don't you ask them?"

"It's much weaker than it was before," said one of the men.

"We noticed," said Altman.

"Maybe it's not the same signal after all," said another. "Maybe it's static and feedback from the MROVs and robotic units that are handling the excavation."

"Just barely possible," said Altman. "But not at all likely. It's the same signal."

"Did you feel anything unusual? Sense anything strange?" asked Markoff.

Altman shook his head. "No," he said.

"What about you, Hendricks?"

"I don't know, sir," said Hendricks.

"You don't know?"

"When I reached two thousand meters, I started to feel a little strange. It felt like a premonition or something."

"Stevens," said Markoff, and one of the researchers came forward. He was distinguished looking, but had a relaxed, kind face. "Take Hendricks and work up a full psychological profile. If you get any sense of a problem, you're authorized to take him off duty. If he looks fine to you, we'll have both of them in the bathyscaphe first thing tomorrow."

That night Altman's dreams began again. He woke up drenched in sweat in the middle of the night and found he could not move. He was jittery, little flashes of light going off behind his eyelids, and he had a sense of dread that refused to leave him. It took a long time for him to become aware that he wasn't back at his house in Chicxulub, but when he did, the imagined shape of the room around him became amorphous and vague.

His heart began to pound heavily, and he could hear the blood in his ears. The space around him remained undetermined in the darkness. It was like he was in a place that wasn't a place at all, like he was suspended in a void. He tried again to move but still couldn't. *Am I still dreaming?* he wondered.

And then, only very slowly did he realize where he might be, in the floating compound, that sound just beside him the sound of Ada breathing in her sleep.

And suddenly he found he could move again. He got up, drank a glass of water, and got back into the bed again. Ada moaned in her sleep. He wrestled with trying to fall back asleep, when he heard a knock on his door.

It was Stevens.

"Altman, isn't it?" he whispered.

"Yes," Altman said.

"Can we go somewhere to talk?"

Altman slipped into his pants and a shirt and tiptoed out of the room, following Stevens down the hall. The man keyed an empty lab open, ushered Altman in.

"What's this about?" Altman asked.

"You haven't noticed anything unusual about Hendricks, have you?" asked Stevens.

"Is anything wrong?"

"Nothing wrong with the scans," said Stevens. "Nothing wrong with the tests either. But there's still something bothering me. I can't quite put my finger on it. He seems normal, stable, but *different* somehow."

"He seems the same to me," said Altman.

"Maybe it's just the pressure," said Stevens. "Maybe he's nervous. But it feels like he's holding something back."

Altman nodded.

"Since you're going to be alone with him in the bathyscaphe and the one to suffer if things go wrong, I thought I'd talk to you about it."

"I don't know what to say," said Altman. "He seems fine to me. I've never had any problems with him on a dive, never sensed any nervousness. I trust him. No," he said. "I'm not worried about him. In fact, I'm a lot less worried about him than I'd be being confined in the bathyscaphe with many of the other people in this facility."

Stevens nodded. "We want to be careful," he said. "You can understand that, considering what happened with the last bathyscaphe. We don't want anything going wrong. All right," he said, "I'll tell them we can move ahead."

36

"No reason to be nervous," Hendricks said. "It's just like any other day."

Altman got the feeling that he was saying it to try to convince himself. "No worries," he said. "It'll be a piece of cake."

They went down to one thousand meters, the sickly sea life at first present and then slowly dwindling. Then two thousand, the sea becoming more and more deserted, but still a few flickers of life, the photophores of a viperfish passing and spinning away into the darkness. A bony fangtooth, caught briefly in the lights, looking like a half-formed thing. A bathyscaphoid squid that resembled a disembodied head made of glass.

At 2,700 meters, they could make out the lights below, no more than pinpricks in the darkness. Slowly they grew larger. Altman was still watching them when he heard a whimper behind him.

He turned. Hendricks was pale and stiff faced. Tears were dripping slowly from his eyes. He didn't seem to notice them. *Oh God*, thought Altman, *something's wrong. Maybe I was wrong to tell Stevens to let Hendricks go ahead with the dive.*

But even then he didn't feel nervous for himself, only worried for Hendricks. Hendricks would never do anything to hurt him.

"What's wrong?" Altman asked.

"I don't want to die," he sobbed.

"You're not going to die," said Altman. "Don't worry."

"Hennessy and Dantec. What happened to them? We're not meant to be down here, Altman. I can feel it."

Altman slowed the bathyscaphe until it was descending almost unnoticeably. "If you want to go up, we can go up," said Altman in a level voice, trying to make Hendricks look him in the eye. "I'm not going to make you do anything you don't want to do. But now that we're here, we should take the readings. You don't mind doing the readings, do you?"

Hendricks took a deep breath, blinked his eyes, seemed to grab hold of himself. "Yes," he said. "I'm good at the readings. I can do that. I need something to do."

He let Hendricks busy himself with the machinery while he continued to ease the craft down. Hendricks began, running through them rapidly, Altman checking his work. The signal pulse was there, much stronger at this level. They should measure it again at two thousand feet on the way back up, Altman thought—maybe the signal was growing even stronger.

Then Hendricks tried to measure it again. This time there was nothing; the signal pulse was gone. Altman took a reading himself just to make sure. Same result. He tried yet again and it was back.

So, Altman thought, the signal was pulsing on and off, sometimes there, sometimes not. Maybe a problem with the transmitter, some irregularity or corrupted circuit. Or maybe it was deliberate. Maybe it was sending them a message.

He glanced over at Hendricks. Was he going to be able to hold it together? Should he try to get him up to the surface as quickly as possible?

"Good, Hendricks," Altman said. "These are excellent readings. Let's change our strategy for a moment. Instead of trying to record the level synchronically, let's take a diachronic profile and see if we can figure out what the pulse is doing over time."

"Would Markoff want that?" asked Hendricks.

"I think he'd welcome it," said Altman. "I think he'd congratulate us for taking the initiative."

"How long will it take?" Hendricks asked.

Altman shrugged, holding his face utterly neutral. "Not too long," he claimed.

When Hendricks nodded, he showed him how to recalibrate the device and start it recording. Altman himself kept the bathyscaphe descending, extremely slowly now. Below them, maybe fifty meters farther down, were the robotic dredgers and the MROVs. Most of the MROVs had stopped, he saw, were on standby, waiting for the next command from the surface. The signal wasn't reaching them. He made a mental note to suggest that arrangements be made to control the MROVs from the bathyscaphe rather than from the floating compound.

The machines that were still working had cleared a large circle of the ocean floor of muck and slurry, digging down to more solid rock. They had begun to break this up as well and cart it away, digging downward to form a funnel. The machines at the bottom were perhaps another two hundred meters down. It was difficult to judge; the water there was murky with mudrock particles and matter of other sort from the rock they were removing. They were deeper than Altman had thought they would be; Markoff must have started them digging well before the floating compound was moved into position.

He descended a few meters into the cone the MROVs had dug out and then stopped. If he went too much farther, he would risk being jostled by one of the robotic dredgers moving into and out of the hole. He decided to wait until he could control the dredgers and MROVs from the bathyscaphe and move them out of the way. Besides, there was Hendricks to consider.

He turned back to Hendricks. "How are you doing?" he asked.

"My head hurts," said Hendricks.

"That's normal," claimed Altman, though he wasn't entirely sure it was. His own head didn't hurt, or at least not any more than usual, and since the cabin was pressurized, their descent shouldn't have had any effect. "It's just from the pressure," he lied. "It'll go away soon."

Hendricks nodded. "Oh, right," he said, and gave a weak smile. "Normal." And then he squinted at the observation porthole. "I think my father's out there," he said, his voice filling with wonder.

Startled, Altman asked, "What did you say?"

"My father," Hendricks said again. He waved. "Hi, Dad!"

Altman started the bathyscaphe ascending, gently, never taking his eyes off Hendricks. "No," he said. "I'm sorry, Jason. It doesn't seem possible."

After a moment staring out the glass, Hendricks gave a little laugh.

"No, it's okay," he said. "He's explained it to me. He *is* dead, and so the pressure can't hurt him."

"If he's dead, he's not here," said Altman. "If he's dead, he's not anywhere."

"But I see him!" said Hendricks, starting to get a little angry. "I know what I see!"

"All right, Hendricks," said Altman, smiling and keeping his voice level. "I'm sorry."

Hendricks turned back to the observation porthole, mumbling to himself. Altman risked glancing down at the instruments. The pulse signal had increased in intensity just around the time that Hendricks had started seeing his father. He told himself that that wasn't logical, that it was just coincidence, but it was hard for him to believe that. It dipped back down again and he watched Hendricks's eyes, which had been intensely regarding the observation porthole, suddenly go out of focus. He snapped his fingers in front of his eyes.

"Hendricks," he said. "Look at me. Look here."

Hendricks began to and then stopped, his eyes drifting back to the porthole. Another glance: the signal had gone up again, was even stronger than it had been before.

"He wants to come in," said Hendricks. "He's cold out there. Don't worry, Dad, we'll help you."

"I don't think that's such a good idea," said Altman.

Hendricks got up from his chair and stumbled to the observation porthole, knocking his head against the glass. He hit it with his head again, and again.

"Hendricks," said Altman, grabbing his arm. "Don't!"

Hendricks shook Altman off and then elbowed him hard in the face, knocking him out of his chair.

"Come in, Dad!" he was shouting now. "Come in!"

Altman pulled himself up and moved to the far end of the cabin. The controls, he realized, had been knocked in the struggle; they were descending again, slowly, and he hoped he could stop it before they plowed into a dredger. Hendricks was pounding on the porthole with his fists now, stopping only to claw at its edges with his fingernails.

Altman searched frantically for a weapon. There was nothing, at least nothing he could immediately see. He searched his pockets, his person, nothing.

He crept forward, crouching. He reached past Hendricks's waist and flicked the lever even, was trying to nudge it forward to make the craft rise when Hendricks cried out and knocked him to the floor.

"Don't touch him!" he was screaming.

Dazed, Altman stared at the base of the console. *He's going to kill me,* he suddenly realized. *I was wrong. I signed my death warrant when I cleared him.*

He didn't want to die. There had to be a weapon somewhere.

Slowly, trying not to alert Hendricks, he wriggled backward and away from him. Once he was as far away as he could get, he sat up with his back to the bulkhead and removed his shoes.

The shoes were modified bluchers, with a pebbled Vibram sole but a hard heel in back, the sole flexible and with a snap to it. He stood up, took hold of each shoe by the toe box, made a chopping motion with his arms. Yes, he thought, it might be enough.

"You're not going to get him inside that way," said Altman. "You need to bring him through the hatch."

Hendricks stopped, turned around to look at him. "I thought you didn't want him to come in," he said suspiciously.

"Are you kidding?" said Altman. "I heard your father was a great guy."

"He *is* a great guy," said Hendricks, and smiled.

"Fine," said Altman. "Then what are we waiting for? Let's get him in here."

Hendricks stumbled toward the hatch, then stopped. "Wait a minute," he said slowly. "Why are you holding your shoes?"

Oh, shit, thought Altman, but tried to stay calm. "They're my favorite shoes. I thought I'd give them to your father," he said.

This answer seemed to satisfy Hendricks. He nodded once and turned toward the ladder leading up to the hatch.

As soon as his hands touched the ladder's rails, Altman was on him. He hit him as hard as he could in the back of the head with the heel of each shoe in turn, employing the shoe like a blackjack. Hendricks swayed, started to turn. Altman struck him again, then again. He crumbled and collapsed into a heap.

"Sorry about that," said Altman to his unconscious friend. "I couldn't think of any other way."

He quickly stripped off Hendricks's shirt and undershirt. He tore them into strips, twisted them into ropes. These he used to tie Hendricks's hands and arms behind his back and then hogtie his legs to his hands.

He sat down and put his shoes back on, then examined the controls. Nothing had been hurt that he could see. They were floating just above and to one side of the hole the robotic units had dug out, probably carried there by some deepwater current.

He was about to start back up again when something caught his eye. An odd fish, drifting awkwardly into his lights. It had a flayed, incomplete look. It was less like the prehistoric-looking fishes that he had seen so far on the dive than the corpse of a fish that had been dead and floating in the water a few days. And yet as he watched it, it moved under its own power.

There was something else puzzling about it. Rather than a long slender body like a viperfish or a thick bulbous one like a lanternfish, it looked like a long fish that had been folded in half and then glued together. The head was surmounted by a wavy translucent curtain of flesh that resembled nothing so much as a tail. In the place of fins, it had what looked like little spurs of bone undulating from its sides. As he watched, a snaggletooth entered the lights and the first fish darted toward it. The first fish caught the snaggletooth on its spurs and, undulating, began to tear it apart until the other fish was dead and in pieces. Intrigued, Altman pressed a button and filmed the end of the fight and the fish as it passed in front of them and into the darkness.

And then he saw something else even stranger. Here and there, floating through the water, were patches of what looked like flat, pale pink clouds. At first he thought it was a ray, but it wasn't differentiated in the way a ray was. It was just a floating, billowing sheet of something. A strange jellyfish maybe? A fungus of some kind? He nudged the bathyscaphe in for a closer look. When the craft touched it, it draped over the hull then split apart, slowly reknitting after their passage. Some of it, though, adhered to the observation porthole and remained there, caught on the rivets.

"Well I'll be damned," said Altman.

Behind him, Hendricks groaned. He was tied up, but who knew how long his bonds would hold? They had to get to the surface as quickly as possible.

He turned off the override for the pellet release valve and pressed a button. The bathyscaphe began to rise.

37

He started broadcasting a looped SOS at 2,500 meters, but got only static. Hendricks was starting to come around. By two thousand meters, he was back to his hysterical babbling. Altman tried to ignore it. Through his earpiece, Altman caught brief bits of something that he recognized as a human voice submerged in a wash of static. By 1,700 meters, it was less static than voice, but Hendricks was shouting now, straining at his bonds.

"Michael Altman, please respond," he finally heard the voice say. "Michael Altman, do you read?"

He turned the loop off and went live. "This is Altman," he said.

The other voice started to answer and was suddenly interrupted. Markoff's voice came on. "Altman?" he said. "What the fuck is going on?"

"Hendricks flipped out," Altman said. "I've got him tied up. That's him screaming in the background."

"What happened?"

"Just a minute," said Altman. Hendricks had started to work his way loose. He took off his shoes again, slowly crept up next to him. *Altman?* Markoff's voice was saying in his ear. *Are you all right, Altman?* He struck Hendricks hard in the back of the head, twice, and he stopped moving.

"What was that sound?" asked Markoff.

"That sound was the sound of me trying to stay alive," said Altman. He undid the ligature and re-hogtied Hendricks. "I'll tell you more when I get to the surface," he said. "Oh, and it might be a good idea to have a few guards on hand in the submarine bay."

Markoff had started to speak again, but Altman turned the transmitter off. He began to think. It wasn't likely that Hendricks would break free. As long as he didn't forget about him, things would be okay. He looked out the observation porthole. The tatter of the pale pink substance was still there on the rivets, undulating slightly as the submarine rose. He knew if Markoff saw it, he'd take it away for testing by members of his inner circle and he, Altman, wouldn't hear anything further about it. Same with the footage of the unusual fish.

He removed his holopod from his pocket and connected it to the console, then copied the vid footage of the fish onto it. He'd have to leave it in the system as well. Markoff and his minions would no doubt be able to tell if something had been erased, but maybe they wouldn't be able to tell it had been copied. He had to try to find some answers on his own.

The pink swath was a little harder. But a plan began to form in his mind.

He checked the pulse signal monitor. The signal had fallen off again. He checked back through the history. If the pattern continued, it should start to rise again.

What he was planning to do was dangerous. No doubt Ada would tell him to leave well enough alone, that he was only likely to get himself killed. Which was why he would never tell her about it. Maybe she was right, but his desire to know was much too great.

He slowed the bathyscaphe as he came up, trying to time it so that the signal would be strongest and Hendricks would be regaining consciousness just at the moment the craft moved into the submarine bay.

Hendricks was groaning, his eyes fluttering, by the time they were fully in. Altman knelt down and undid the ligature that hogtied Hendricks, then undid the rope around his legs but left his hands tied. He unrolled one of the ropes and tore a square of fabric off it, which he tucked into his pocket. Then he helped Hendricks get to his knees.

It was cruel, but he couldn't think of another way.

"Where's your father, Hendricks?" he asked.

The man's eyes focused briefly then moved independently of each other, wandering about the sockets.

"Hendricks," he said again. He had to hurry. The bay was almost drained down to the catwalk. Soon enough water would be pumped out and the guards would be there. "Where's your father?"

Hendricks's eyes focused again and this time stayed focused. "My father," he said. "He was just right here."

"We left him down there," suggested Altman. "We abandoned him. *You* abandoned him."

For a moment there was no response, and then, abruptly,

Hendricks let out an ungodly howl of pain and slammed his head into Altman's chest. It hurt like hell. Then he fell on top of Altman, slavering, trying to bite his face.

Altman got his hands up against his shoulders and tried desperately to hold him away, watching the man bare his teeth and shake his head like a wild animal. But he was too heavy, was bearing down too hard, his teeth getting closer and closer to Altman's face. He cried out and pushed out as hard as he could, genuinely terrified now, trying to roll him off but failing.

Just when he thought he couldn't hold him back any more, the bathyscaphe's hatch hissed open and a guard dropped in and wrapped an arm around Hendricks's neck. Altman scrambled back and away, dodging a second guard who had dropped down and scurrying up the ladder to the hatch. There was a group of guards around the hatch, pointing their weapons at him when he came out. He pushed past and, stumbling, rolled off the curve of the bathyscaphe not onto the catwalk but into the water.

He had only a few seconds. Holding his breath, he floundered briefly to the observation porthole, tugging the square of cloth from his pocket and using it to gather up the pale pink swath. Through the porthole he caught a glimpse of Hendricks struggling with the two guards, who had forced him back to the floor. He balled up the sodden cloth and thrust it deep into his pocket and returned to the surface.

He broke to shouts and cries. Hands were immediately there, pulling him onto the catwalk and out of the water. Somebody wrapped a blanket around him.

"Don't kill Hendricks!" he heard himself shouting. "He doesn't know what he's doing!" And then he was hustled out.

38

They let him stop off in his room to get a change of clothing. He managed to slip the rag out of his pocket and force it and the pink substance into an empty water bottle. He secured it in his drawer and then let the men lead him out.

He stripped his clothes off and showered. When he stepped out, he saw that his clothing was gone. When he asked the guards about it, they didn't answer.

He got dressed as the guards impassively watched. When he was done, they opened the door and gestured him out.

"Where are we going?" he asked.

"Debriefing," one said.

A few minutes later, he was on the command deck. As soon as he entered, the other people in the room started to clear out. In the end, only he and Markoff were left.

"All right," said Markoff. "Let's hear it. Tell me everything."

He told him almost everything. He mentioned the strange fish, knowing that Markoff would see the vid recording anyway. He told him about the pink swaths but didn't mention the sample he had retrieved. He told him about the problems with the MROVs, that they either weren't receiving their commands or had failed in some other way. He described the progress that had been made. Markoff just nodded.

"What happened with Hendricks?" he asked.

"How's he doing?"

Markoff shrugged. "Delirious," he said. "They're shooting him full of something to calm him down. He keeps talking about his father."

"He was doing that down there," Altman said. "He thought he saw his father outside the bathyscaphe. He wanted to let him in." He gave a wry smile. "I, quite understandably, was opposed to this."

"I thought Stevens gave him a clean bill of health," said Markoff.

"He did," said Altman. "No reason to think otherwise. I thought he was okay most of the way down. He was a friend. I'm sorry this happened to him."

"He was unstable."

"No," said Altman. "I think there's more to it than that."

He told Markoff the whole story, only glossing over the end, suggesting that it was Hendricks himself who had wriggled free of his bonds.

"We did a diachronic tracking of the pulse signal," Altman said. "The strange thing is that it seemed to correspond to Hendricks's mental decay. When the signal was stronger, he started seeing things, becoming paranoid and violent. When it was weaker, he seemed to be like he normally is. I think the signal changed him."

Markoff looked at him a long time. "That doesn't seem possible," he finally said.

"I know it doesn't," said Altman. "But it correlated perfectly. I think the pulse signal does something to the human brain."

"Why didn't it do the same thing to you?"

"Who knows?" said Altman. "Maybe I can resist it for some reason. Or maybe it's doing things that I haven't managed to notice yet."

"What do you think it is?" Markoff asked again, just as he had asked weeks before, in Altman's kitchen.

"I don't know," said Altman. "I haven't even seen it yet. But I can tell you one thing: it scares the living shit out of me."

They were both silent for a while, lost in their own thoughts. Finally Markoff looked up.

"You'll have to go down again," he said.

"Now?"

"Soon. We need to add some equipment to the console so that you can communicate with the MROVs."

"Funny," said Altman.

"What's funny?"

"I was going to suggest doing that," he said. "Adding something to the console."

Markoff gave him a quizzical look. "You did suggest it," he said. "That was one of the first things you said to us. Don't you remember? Are you all right?"

I must have been more rattled than I realized, Altman thought. He thought about how to answer Markoff, rapidly decided the best strategy was to ignore it.

"As long as it's not with Hendricks, I'm willing. I don't mind going down alone."

"Not alone," said Markoff. "I want you to take a few trips down, we'll try a different person each time."

"How do I know they're not going to react like Hendricks did? I was lucky with him. I may not be lucky next time."

"You've become more important than I expected you to be," Markoff said. "You know how to run the bathyscaphe and take the proper measurements. Which means I'm counting on you. I need you to do this."

"And in exchange?"

Markoff gave him a level stare. "No 'and in exchange.' You'll do it."

"Is that a threat?" Altman asked.

"When I'm threatening you, you'll know."

Altman closed his eyes. If it wasn't a threat, it wasn't far from one. But he knew he didn't really have a choice.

"All right," he said. "But I want a tranquilizer gun just in case. And I want whoever goes down with me to be strapped to his chair."

"Agreed," said Markoff. He stood and made a show of shaking Altman's hand. "Thank you for your cooperation. I'll be in touch."

39

Hendricks woke up in a strange place, some sort of medical facility. The last thing he could remember was being on the bathyscaphe. He and Altman were going down, and then his head had started to hurt so much, he could hardly stand it. After that, it all felt like a dream. There had been some kind of problem. He remembered Altman speaking calmly to him, remembered taking readings, but also remembered the feel of the floor. He must have fallen. Maybe they hit something.

He felt groggy. Parts of his body were numb, and parts of his brain felt like they had been torn out. There was a tube running into his forearm. Maybe they were experimenting on him.

He looked around. He was the only one there.

He moved furtively out of bed, peeling the tape off the tube in his arm and pulling it out. It burned coming out. He dropped it, left it dripping beside the bed, and stumbled to the door.

It was locked.

He stayed there, staring at the handle.

After a while he heard the sound of footsteps in the hall outside. He rushed back into his bed and half closed his eyes.

Through his eyelashes he watched the door open. A woman came in, dressed in white, carrying a holoboard. She walked straight to his bed. His mind pictured him running out the door at the far end of the room, but in the end his body did not move.

"Hello," said the woman. "How are we today?"

He didn't say anything, still pretending to be asleep.

"Oh, dear. You've torn your IV out again," she said. "We can't have that, can we?"

She bent down for the end of the tube. It was at that moment that his body decided to reach up and grab her wrist. True, he was in his body, was watching through his eyes, but it was doing things he wasn't telling it to do. He wasn't the one controlling it, which meant there must be someone else in there with him.

As soon as he thought that, it felt like everything was happening at a little distance, like he'd sunk deeper into his body, like he'd never be in control of the body again. And yet he could still feel everything. He watched the hand holding the nurse's arm pull her on top of him like she was a doll. He felt the jaw opening and the teeth closing around the nurse's neck, and then a series of wet sounds as the neck burst open and warm blood spilled down across his chin and his own neck. Her wrist, the one he was holding, he saw, was broken, crushed, and the arm attached to it was no longer sitting in the socket right. She was trying to gasp for breath, but there was a hole in her windpipe now and all that came out was a hissing and a mist of blood. Her face was there just above him, her eyes terrified for a moment but almost immediately becoming loose in their orbits as she lost consciousness.

A few seconds later, after his body had done a few more

things to her, he was certain she was dead. If he'd been asked to describe how exactly it had happened, he wouldn't have been able to say, though he was fairly certain he had something to do with it. Or not him, exactly: his body. One moment she was still alive, even if just barely, and then there was an awful blur of things happening. When they stopped, she was dead.

He padded softly to the door and tried it. It was still locked. How was that possible? She'd come through it, hadn't she?

She must have had a key. He shambled back to her corpse in search of her pockets. But he couldn't find any pockets. She was too much of a mess. Pushing his bloody hands through the sopping remains of clothing and flesh, he finally found something hard that wasn't a bone.

He had just straightened up, bloody key in hand, when he realized that he wasn't alone in the room after all. There was a shape there, in the shadows of the last bed.

"Who is it?" he said.

Don't you recognize me? a voice said.

He went a little closer, then closer still. It was as if the person was both there and not there at the same time. And then, suddenly, he felt a piercing pain in his head. He staggered. When he looked back up, he knew who it was.

"Dad," he said.

Good to see you, Jason, he said. *Come sit down. I want to have a serious talk with you.*

"What about, Dad?"

But his dad wasn't where he thought he was. He turned around and found him in another bed.

We're failing, Jason, his dad said. *You should leave that thing down where you found it. Convergence is not the only thing that matters.*

"Convergence?" asked Hendricks, then had to search frantically for his father, who somehow had moved again.

They want us all to become one, son. He gave a mournful smile, shaking his head. *Can you imagine?* he said.

"Who's they, Dad?"

We have to be very careful or there will be nothing left of us.

Then his dad smiled. It was a beautiful smile, like he used to give Jason back when he was very young, just a few years old. Jason had forgotten that smile, but now it all came flooding back.

Tell them, Jason, he said. *Tell everyone.*

"I will, Dad," he whispered. "I will."

There was some noise behind him, but he didn't want to look away from his father's face. If he did, he feared he'd never find it again. Then there was shouting. He ignored it as long as he could, but it was too powerful. He turned around and moved toward it.

There was a roar and a flash and he was suddenly on the ground, staring straight up at the ceiling. *I should get up and tell them,* he thought, but when he tried, he couldn't move. *I'll just lie here,* he thought. "Dad?" he whispered, but there was no answer.

40

"Can I have a copy of this?" asked the icthyologist, watching the vid.

Altman shrugged. "Sure," he said. "What do you think?"

"I've never seen anything quite like it," he said. "Those strange hornlike projections, I don't have a precedent for those. You may have discovered a new species. Or it may be the result of a mutation of some kind. I can ask around, see if anybody's seen anything like it, but I never have."

"So, it's unusual."

"Very unusual."

"Well?" Altman asked. He was in Skud's lab, the water bottle with him. The pinkish swath had been extracted from it and placed into a specimen tube. From this, Skud had taken a tiny sample, running a genetic test.

"It's strange," said Skud. "It's tissue."

"What sort of tissue?"

"Living tissue," said Skud. "Like flesh. It was once alive. But it has a very unusual genetic profile."

"So, it is skin that has been torn off something?"

"I don't think this is so," said Skud. "I think it was alive not so long ago. It was alive when you found it. Maybe even alive until you bottled it."

"That can't be," said Altman. "When I found it, it was just like this, but in big sheets. It couldn't have been alive."

"Yes," said Skud. "It is a very simple organism. I do not know what it is. It has no brain and no limbs and was made of almost nothing at all. But it was, technically, alive."

Altman shook his head.

"You are a doubter, I see," said Skud. "I can prove it with a simple experiment." He upturned the sample vial, leaving the pink swath lying curled on the table. He took a battery with a pair of wires connected to it, sparked them against each other, then touched them to one another. Immediately the swath jolted, moved.

"You see," said Skud proudly. "Alive."

"Don't," said Ada. "It's morbid."

"It's not morbid," said Altman. "I'm just stating the facts. This is just anecdotal, mind you, but it still must mean something."

She rolled her eyes.

"Just listen," said Altman. "Just listen and give me a hand." He held up one finger. "You were the one who started this back in the town. I'm just going to give you the same talk you gave me, more or less. Nearly everybody I've talked to on the ship has a headache. Even if I haven't heard them say it aloud, I've seen them clutching their heads. That's not normal."

"It's just anecdotal," said Ada. "It's not scientific."

"I said that already," said Altman.

"It could be a gas leak," said Ada, "or a problem with the ventilation system."

"It could be," said Altman, but most of those people have been having headaches long before that. They've been having them ever since the first signal broadcast."

He held up a second finger. "Insomnia," he said. "I've asked around about this. Showalter has it. I have it off and on. That German scientist has it. I heard the two guards outside of the command center complaining about it and then later another three in the main dome. Have you had it?"

"No," said Ada. "But I've been having weird dreams."

"That's the other thing people are talking about," said Altman, raising another finger. "Strange, vivid dreams. I've had them, too, lots of people have. And then we get to the more extreme cases." He held up two more fingers. "Attacks," he said, wiggling one, "and suicides," he said, wiggling the other. "Not scientific, I admit," he said. "But we've only been talking a few minutes and I've already run out of fingers. I've never been around a place where I've seen so many of either."

"I heard that Wenbo went crazy," said Ada. "Tried to strangle one of Markoff's men."

"I heard the same thing," said Altman. "Similar thing happened with Claerbout and Dawson. And Lumley stabbed Ewing and then painted a set of weird symbols on the walls of his own room with his own shit. And who knows what we're not hearing about, what they're covering up."

Ada shuddered. "And poor Trostle," she said. "He always seemed so stable."

"Suicides and attempted suicides. Don't forget Press."

"Frank Press? Did he attempt suicide?"

"Not only did he attempt it, he succeeded. There must be at least three or four more on that list, too. Doesn't that seem abnormal? I mean there are only two or three hundred on board. That'd put the suicide rate up over two percent. That can't be normal, can it?"

Ada shook her head.

"It's not scientific," said Altman, waving his fingers around. "But I still don't like what it's telling me. Ask around. See if I'm wrong. I hope to God I am."

A few hours later, Markoff appeared at his door. He was carrying a tranquilizer gun in his hand. It looked like an ordinary pistol but with a longer and thicker barrel, a square cartridge near the barrel's end.

"Ever worked one of these?" he asked.

Altman shook his head.

He opened the cartridge. "Darts go here," he said. "Cartridge snaps in and out. There are CO_2 cartridges in the grip, but you don't need to worry about changing those; we'll handle it. You pull this bolt back," he said, drawing back a lever on the gun's side, "and set the safety like this. It's easy to thumb off. As long as the bolt's back, it'll shoot. Aim for flesh."

"It won't go through clothing?"

"I didn't say that," said Markoff. "It'll go through clothing, but clothing means more chances of something going wrong. Aim for flesh. Or, if you're not much of a shooter, just try to push it up against the person's chest before you fire."

He handed the tranquilizer over to Altman, who held it awkwardly.

"The dart contains a strong sedative. It'll take a few seconds to take effect," Markoff said. "It'll hurt going in but probably not enough to slow a maniac down much. You sure you don't want a real gun?"

Altman shook his head.

"You leave in fifteen minutes," Markoff said.

Hurriedly he tracked down Ada and told her what was happening.

"I don't want you to go down there again," she said.

"It doesn't affect me." He kissed her again. "Besides, I have no choice."

"But after what happened to Hendricks . . ."

"I handled that all right, didn't I? We're still both in one piece, aren't we?"

She covered her mouth with one hand. "You haven't heard?" she said.

"Haven't heard what?"

"Hendricks is dead. He killed a nurse, tore her apart. They had to shoot him."

Stunned, he collapsed onto the bed. He didn't trust himself to speak. Even more so than Moresby, this had been his fault. Maybe if he'd turned back when Hendricks had first wanted, it wouldn't have happened. How many deaths would be on his conscience before it was all over?

Ada was lying beside him, stroking his forehead. "I'm sorry," she said. "I'm sorry." And then, "Michael, don't go."

He shook his head. "I have to go," he replied. "I have no choice." Turning away from her, he climbed out of the bed and made his way heavily down to the submarine bay.

PART FIVE

COLLAPSE

41

He took two trips and had to use the tranquilizer gun once. The first trip reprogrammed the MROVs, switched them over to robotic self-control, and the digging progressed at a tremendous pace, but he had to tranquilize the technician accompanying him before they reached the surface.

The man gave him a fair amount of advance warning, growing more and more irritable and then finally lashing out. He waited to tranquilize until he was absolutely sure he was violent and as a result almost waited too long. Indeed, the man was trying to choke him to death as the tranquilizer took effect and his hands slowly relaxed and he collapsed.

The other trip, strangely enough, was with Stevens, the psychologist, who applied electrodes to both his and Altman's heads, reading changes in their brain waves as they descended.

"So I guess this means Markoff agrees with me that Hendricks's mental problems might have been caused by the signal," Altman asked.

Stevens smiled. "How can I know what Markoff thinks, Mr. Altman?" he answered.

Altman stayed ready the whole time, one hand on the tranquilizer gun, but like him, Stevens didn't seem to suffer any adverse affects. He just stayed crouched over his equipment, looking up at Altman from time to time and smiling.

"Learn anything?" asked Altman.

"Yes, I did," said Stevens. "But I'd learn more if one or the other of us had an attack. I don't suppose you'd like to oblige me, would you?"

Altman shook his head.

"I didn't think so," said Stevens. "Maybe another time, then."

The next trip consisted of himself and a jovial engineer named David Kimball descending to retrieve the driller bathyscaphe, though Altman wasn't briefed until they were already on the way down.

"It'll be simple," said Kimball, patting a large chrome-plated machine that had been bolted to the console just for this trip. "Just a matter of a few minutes. All we have to do is direct an electrical pulse at the bathyscaphe."

"What'll that do?" asked Altman.

"It'll release the latches for the ballast chambers," said Kimball. "This will cause the ballast to rush out. After that, the bathyscaphe will rise on its own."

"Sounds easy enough that a robot could do it," said Altman.

"A robot could do it," said Kimball. "But Markoff thought it'd be better to have us do it."

"Why?" asked Altman.

"I don't know," said Kimball. "He didn't say."

In case anything goes wrong, Altman added in his head.

When they reached the ocean floor, they continued to move downward into the inverted cone that the robotic excavators had created. Having completed their tasks, the units now stood motionless, strange statues in the darkness. The bathyscaphe descended, the cone slowly tightening on them.

He brightened the lights and turned on the vid cameras. Altman glanced over at Kimball. He seemed like he was doing all right, though he looked a little distracted, slightly jumpy. *Nothing to worry about yet,* thought Altman, but just to be safe, he checked to see that the tranquilizer pistol was cocked and ready.

"You been down here before?" Kimball asked.

Altman nodded. "Nothing to worry about," he said.

"They showed me the vid," he said. "You seen that?"

"Yes," said Altman.

"I had no idea," said Kimball. "Do you think it'll be as bad as it looks?"

"Yeah," said Altman.

They fell silent. Down below, they could see something, a vague shape that slowly became clearer.

It was a huge structure, two tapering pillars twisting sinuously around each other and rising to a point. It seemed to be made of stone, but there was no doubt in Altman's mind that it was constructed rather than a natural phenomenon. Coming closer just confirmed it; it was covered with symbols, weird hieroglyphics unlike anything he had ever seen. They covered every inch of the object, winding downward around its body and up to the twin horns of the thing. It was massive and gave off the impression of great age. At once beautiful and vaguely menacing, it was completely alien. It had not, Altman knew immediately upon seeing it, been built by human hands. Why had it been built, and how? The stone showed no breaks or cracks or joints, as if it was a single gigantic piece. And the shape: it reminded him of something. But what was it?

And then suddenly he knew. "The tail of the devil," whispered Altman.

"Holy shit," said Kimball, awe in his voice.

The symbols were either luminescent or catching the bathyscaphe's light in a very particular way. He checked the displays. The pulse signal was negligible at the moment. *Probably a good thing,* he thought.

"Do you think it's safe to get close?" asked Kimball.

"What is it?" wondered Altman aloud. "Who made it?"

He moved the bathyscaphe slowly around just above it, filming it from all angles. It was the most impressive thing he had ever seen. Then he zoomed the camera in closer to record some of the symbols. He would have kept doing it, but Kimball's nerves were rising.

"This is freaking me out. Let's get the other sub and get out of here," Kimball said.

There it was, sunken at the base of the artifact. Altman descended farther, got as close to it as he could and shone the light into the observation porthole.

Even from that vantage, the inside of the cabin was a nightmare—blood spread over the windows and the walls, smeared in odd patterns. He moved the lights quickly away before Kimball could get a better look.

He played the lights along the side of the craft, looking for signs of damage, but the air seal seemed intact. In theory, it should rise, albeit slowly.

"Ready?" he asked Kimball.

"Ready," Kimball said.

Altman moved around until there was no danger of hitting the Marker and then fired the pulse. It struck the driller bathyscaphe full on, an eerie electric glow fizzling along its hull. Then its ballast chambers began to empty, the lead pellets pattering down and raising a cloud of silt. Slowly it began to rise. He watched it come, passing just a half dozen meters away from them, and move upward. It tilted and a disembodied arm rolled against the observation porthole.

Ready or not, he thought, and then their own bathyscaphe started up in pursuit.

42

This is getting to be a habit, Altman thought, carefully easing the chunk of rock out of the core sampler. Nobody seemed to notice. They were all too preoccupied with the interior of the bathyscaphe itself, the wash of blood and gore inside, the rotten, damaged bodies. Markoff quickly had the area quarantined, but not before Altman had gotten away with the sample.

Now he took it to his bedroom to examine it. He was certain it was from the artifact itself. It was seemingly ordinary rock, but one that he couldn't identify. The bit he held had an indentation on it, where something had been carved or inflicted on the rock, but it was too small a sample to give a clear sense of what it was.

Sneaking into an unlocked lab at night, he tested it. The substance was not unlike granite but harder, almost as hard as corundum. One face was smooth; he could see where the rest had been cut, was surprised the cutters hadn't burned out. Within the rock he found mineral veins that struck him as too regular to be natural. But if they weren't natural, what were they? In the end, puzzled, he decided to assume they were natural formations: there was no technology that he was aware of that would allow someone to manipulate solid rock in this way.

Whatever had happened to the others in the bathyscaphe, what Markoff had been able to determine about it, Altman was never told. Once quarantined, the bathyscaphe disappeared and was never seen again. No doubt Markoff and his inner circle had analyzed it to death. Altman was eager to see the rest of the vid from Hennessy, but his request to Markoff was met with silence.

Now that the bathyscaphe was up, the floating compound was frantic with preparations to raise the artifact itself. It was impossible to have a conversation that didn't turn to the monolith lying down at the bottom of the crater, and people seemed both excited and incredibly nervous. Whatever it was, whatever was down there, could change everything, and they would be the first to come into contact with it. The signal had returned but seemed to be broadcasting differently now, intermittently, on and off, in fairly regular bursts. Some researchers speculated it was a distress call, though who or what was in distress nobody dared guess. Perhaps it was a result of a failing piece of technical equipment, the artifact itself faulty or breaking down. It was, after all, very, very old. And many believed, Altman among them, that it was old enough that it couldn't possibly be of human origin, that the artifact was clear proof of alien life.

"If you'd seen it," he told Markoff in his debriefing, "you'd agree with me. There's nothing human about it."

The pulse signal was now interfering with radios and vids, creating a static communication wave and fuzzing images. Often when he descended in the bathyscaphe Altman was out of touch very quickly because of the interference, and stayed out of touch for a good part of the trip. He was piloting descents daily, with several members of Markoff's inner circle, all of whom showed no signs of cracking. He questioned whomever he was with, trying to find out anything he could. Mostly they were closed-lipped, but every once in a while they let something slip.

A scientist called him in from the hall while he was walking past a lab and, thinking he was someone else at first, began asking him questions about a winch mechanism. Was it really enough? Would it lift the thing? And what about the cable? What sort of cable would you need for something like that?

Altman played along as long as he could, finally admitted he didn't know what he was talking about.

"You're not Perkins?" the scientist asked.

Altman shook his head.

"Never mind," said the scientist, retreating quickly into his lab. "Forget I said anything."

Showalter, too, was almost as much on the outside as Altman, though he knew geophysics well enough that he was somehow consulted.

"Always just bits and pieces," Showalter confessed to Altman in a low voice over coffee. "They think if they give me just a little, I won't be able to figure it out. That'd be true if it was just them, but their colleagues sometimes consult me as well. I know more than anybody realizes."

"And?" asked Altman.

"I think we're very close to bringing it up," said Showalter. "Almost all the theoretical problems have been solved. A few more tests and they'll just be waiting for an okay."

Ada had made friends with the medical team, even helping out informally when she was needed. And she was needed more and more. In the floating compound, Ada told him, reports of scientists and soldiers beset by insomnia and hallucinations were on the rise.

"According to Dr. Merck," she claimed, "he's never seen anything like it. Violent incidents of all kinds are on the rise, nearly double what they were just a few months ago. The suicide rate has skyrocketed and the assault rate has climbed considerably."

"It's a tense time," said Altman, playing devil's advocate, the role Ada usually would play. "Maybe that's all it is."

"No, you were right. It's more than that," said Ada. "Even Merck thinks so. There are signs of widespread paranoia, people having visions of dead relatives, and more and more people speaking in a trancelike state of 'Convergence,' without being really able to explain what that meant exactly once they were themselves again. Everyone is on the verge of paranoia or panic. Goddammit, you've got me thinking like you."

Altman nodded. "Then my nonscientific inquiry was right," he said. "Everyone is on edge. Something is going on."

"What do you think it means?" Ada asked him.

"What does it mean?" said Altman. "If you ask me, it means were fucked."

43

Altman was on yet another descent, this time with a researcher by the name of Torquato, someone from Markoff's inner circle. He had with him a simple black box, homemade, with a single knob on it and a needle readout. The technology was old enough that it could have been made in the twentieth century. As they descended, Altman tried to make idle conversation to pass the time.

"You're what," he asked, "some kind of scientist?"

Torquato shrugged. "You could call it that," he said.

"Geophysics?" asked Altman. "Geology? Volcanology? Something more theoretical?"

"It's hard to explain," claimed Torquato, "and not very interesting."

But Altman was interested. He was descending into the heart of the crater with a man who was being deliberately vague. Something was up.

"So what brings you down here today?" he asked, trying to sound casual.

"A few measurements," said Torquato.

"What's the box about?" Altman asked.

"This?" responded Torquato, pushing at the box with his thumb. "Oh, it's nothing."

A few more questions and Altman gave up. They descended in silence down to the artifact and held position just above it. Robotic units had dug out under its base and were well on the way to netting it, the net itself attached to a series of cables that would eventually be hooked to larger, stronger cables on the freighter. The artifact would be reeled in, with the help of the nascent field of kinetic technology. It was to be secured and then brought through the water doors into the floating compound.

Beside him, Torquato gave the single knob on his box a counterclockwise twist. The needle immediately came to life, engaging in a rhythmic and regular movement along its graph. Torquato grunted, jotted something on his holopad.

"What is it?" asked Altman.

"Hmm?" said Torquato. "Did you say something?"

When Altman started to repeat the question, Torquato interrupted. "Take the bathyscaphe lower," he said.

"How much lower?"

"Halfway between the top of the object and its base," he said.

Carefully Altman nudged it down. The black box's needle he saw continued to bounce, but its rhythm and scope changed.

"That's good," said Torquato. "Now, can you slowly circle around, staying just at this level?"

"I can try," said Altman. He started moving the bathyscaphe slowly around the monolith, casting glances from time to time at the box.

When Torquato noticed him looking, he cast him a withering look and from then on shielded the readout with his hand.

"You're here to drive," he said. "Nothing more."

"Look, buddy," said Altman. "I'm not stealing any secrets here. I have no idea what that thing does. I'm just trying to pass the time."

Torquato didn't bother to answer. Exasperated, Altman turned away, focusing on trying to bring the bathyscaphe within a few meters of the monolith without touching it. When he looked back, Torquato was still covering the readout with his hand. *Asshole,* he thought.

Torquato's turn was different from that of the others, much more abrupt, little if any warning. One moment he was sitting there, shielding the black box's needle display with his hand, and the next he had attacked.

How he'd undone the restraint on his leg, Altman hadn't been able to figure out at the time, though later he discovered it had been cut, whether by Torquato or someone else, he never could be certain. In a flash, Torquato was free, and that was all that mattered. Altman tried to get the tranquilizer gun out and fire a dart, but Torquato had been too quick, and when he reached for it, he found the holster empty, the pistol aimed at him instead. He dived to the side, but the pistol had already fired, and there it was, the dart sticking out of his arm.

He reached down and, with effort, plucked it out. His tongue already felt thick in his mouth. Torquato was talking to him, he suddenly realized, though he was a little less clear on what he was saying. He blinked and Torquato blurred out of focus, only slowly coming back in again. The man was speaking incomprehensibly, endlessly, about the necessity for Convergence.

Altman made an effort, bit the inside of his mouth until it bled, succeeded in focusing.

"You've been here again and again, just beside it," he said to Altman, stroking his cheek. "Yet you have felt nothing. Don't you hear it calling to you? Won't you answer?"

When he regained consciousness, it was to find himself pressed up against the observation porthole, the bathyscaphe pushing up against the artifact with the motor still running until it was tilted on end. There were repeated banging noises coming from somewhere, punctuated by long moments of silence.

"It's stuck," he heard Torquato's voice mutter. And then, "I'm trying, I tell you, I'm trying."

Trying to what? Altman wondered.

The banging started again. Altman slowly pulled himself up, standing on the porthole. The cabin felt extraordinarily warm, stuffy. He scaled the side of the console and stood on it. The oxygen recirculator had been disabled, was nothing but a mass of tangled metal, sparks flying off it. He was careful not to touch it. No wonder the air felt stuffy. How long had he been out? He looked down at the console until his eyes found the chronometer. It, too, had stopped.

The ladder leading to the hatch was directly above him, horizontal along the ceiling, and he could see Torquato's feet sticking out of the passage.

The banging started up again.

Oh, shit. Altman realized, his limbs instantly going heavy: *He's trying to open the hatch. He's trying to flood the bathyscaphe.*

He clambered onto the sideways chair, nearly fell when it

swiveled. There was a brief groan, and for a moment he thought it was going to come unbolted from the deck, but it held. Carefully he put both feet on the chairback and stood.

From there, he could almost reach the fixed metal ladder. He steadied himself, reached as far as he could, but his fingers just grazed it. He'd have to leap up, hope that his fingers caught the rung and held it the first time, so that he wouldn't come down with a crash and alert Torquato.

The banging started again, Torquato screeching along with it. Altman jumped, caught the rung. He flailed his leg up, managed to get his ankle around the side rail of the ladder as well. The banging stopped.

He hung there motionless, hoping Torquato wouldn't turn around.

"It's stuck!" he shouted, apparently at nobody. "I'm trying, I tell you!"

Holding on to the ladder, Altman tilted his head back until he could see Torquato there, upside down. He was lying flat in the passage, a metal bar in one hand, a strut maybe, something stolen from the remains of the oxygen recirculator. His knuckles were bloody, and Altman could see symbols like those on the artifact, painted here and there along the passage in blood.

Torquato tugged on the wheel, then gave a little cry of frustration. He raised the bar and started striking the hatch again, at the hinge. The pressure was too great, Altman realized with relief. Unless he loosened a hinge or blew the hatch from the control panel, the seal might hold. Much more worrisome, though, was the lack of air.

Torquato stopped, breathing heavily. "A cleansing," he was muttering. "Yes, a cleansing. Start again, new and fresh."

He began pounding again. Carefully, Altman started along the ladder, back into the passage. As he got farther up, he had to bend his arms, pull himself up closer to the ladder so as not to brush Torquato's back. By the time Torquato stopped again, Altman was hanging directly over him, their bodies less than a foot away from each other. Altman could smell the man's sour sweat.

He held his breath, staring at the ladder a few inches from his face, the muscles in his arms starting to cramp. Torquato kept muttering to himself, laughing softly under his breath. Altman heard the sound of him scrabbling at the hatch, the cry of frustration, then the pounding began again.

He let go of the ladder and pushed off it hard at the same time, crashing down onto Torquato's back. It hurt like hell. He tried in the confined space to scramble around to face him, but Torquato was trying to get up, too, and for a moment his face and chest were pressed against the ladder. With a shout he pushed down as hard as he could and Torquato collapsed underneath him. He started to turn around again, knocking his shoulder against the ladder, and made it this time. Torquato was half-turned over now and groping for the metal bar, which had fallen and was under him.

Altman grabbed his head by the hair and brought it down hard. Torquato was bellowing now, struggling, trying to slip back and out of the passage. Altman wrapped his legs around him and held on, trying to keep him there, slamming his face into the floor again. Torquato had the bar now and was trying to get it up, but his arm was still pinned beneath him. He turned his head as far as he could, trying to look at Altman, and Altman saw his collapsed cheekbone and orbit, the blood that was washing over his eye. He slammed his head down again, and then a second time, until the bar slipped from Torquato's fingers and his body went slack.

Altman lay there on top of him for a while, holding him by the hair, trying to catch his breath. Knocking against the walls, he turned Torquato the rest of the way over, faceup. His face was a mess, the nose and cheekbone broken and in a pulp. He held his ear close to his mouth. His breathing was shallow, but it was still there.

Now what? thought Altman. *What do I do with him?* He could tie him up, as he had done with Hendricks, but there was always the chance he would break free. And there was the bigger problem, the lack of oxygen. With the oxygen recirculator broken, he probably didn't have enough air to make it to the surface for one person, let alone two.

Am I a killer? Altman wondered. *Am I the kind of person who is willing to kill someone so as to stay alive himself?* He ran it through his mind again, considered other alternatives, but couldn't come up with anything. It was either Torquato or him. Torquato, he told himself, would have died anyway if he'd gotten his way and managed to open the hatch, so the choice was either both of them dead or just one of them dead.

He looked at the bloody face below him. He'd done that. Maybe he'd had no choice, but in any case, he'd done it, was responsible for it. And was about to be, he realized, responsible for more.

He reached out and put his hands around Torquato's throat. It was sticky with blood. He let his hands lie there, then very gently began to squeeze.

At first he thought it would be easy, that Torquato would simply slip from unconsciousness to death without waking. But after a moment, Torquato's eyes suddenly sprang open. Altman squeezed harder. Torquato's arms began to flail and shake, striking Altman's shoulders and arms. He arched his back, knocking Altman into the wall of the passage, but Altman held on, squeezing tighter.

In the last moment before he died, a light came into Torquato's undamaged eye that Altman couldn't help but see. Human, pleading. He closed his own eyes to it and turned his head to the side. Gradually, he felt Torquato's movements slow and stop. When he finally opened his eyes again, Torquato's eyes had rolled back in their sockets. He was dead.

He dragged himself out of the passage, climbed down the wall and onto the console. There, he reversed the screws, bringing the bathyscaphe backward and away from the artifact. It slowly righted itself, Torquato's body spilling out of the hatch passage and onto the floor.

Altman climbed off the console and to the chair to start the bathyscaphe rising. The lead-pellet release was jammed, the panel all around it scarred from where Torquato had dented it. The craft started to rise, pellets slowly dribbling out, but not as fast as he'd hoped. Chances were he'd reach a certain water density and then the craft would stop moving entirely and he'd hang there suspended, slowly dying.

He recorded an SOS message and then sent it to loop and broadcast, asking them to come for the bathyscaphe, to make it rise as quickly as possible. Whether they'd get the message soon enough, he didn't know. He recorded another message for Ada, telling her he loved her and that he was sorry, just in case he didn't make it.

It was getting very warm. He wasn't getting enough air. He wondered if the best thing was to go to sleep. He'd use less air that way. He contemplated getting down on the floor of the submarine, thinking the air might be better down there.

But he just stayed slumped in his chair, staring at Torquato's remains.

And then suddenly, he saw Torquato's hand move.

Impossible, he thought. *He's dead.*

He swiveled his chair around so that he could see him better, watching carefully. No, he was dead, he wasn't moving, how could he?

And then the hand moved again.

Hello, Altman, Torquato said.

"Go back to being dead," Altman said to him.

It's not as easy as that, said Torquato. *I need you to understand something first.*

"Understand what?"

"This," said Torquato, and leapt forward.

Torquato flew up on him, choking him. He tried to pry his hands off, but they were digging too firmly into his neck. He latched his own hands on to Torquato's neck, squeezing with all he had; then he blacked out.

He came conscious to find his hands around the neck of a corpse. It was rigid and cold, had been dead a very long time. *What is going on?* he wondered.

He tried to stand up to get away from the corpse, but couldn't. He moved his fingers away and rolled off, lying just beside it. He hoped he was close to the surface, but there was no way to tell from here.

Suddenly he saw something strange. A woman. She looked a lot like Ada, though it wasn't her. It was obvious when he looked close. But maybe it was her mother, back when he had first met her, before she had cancer.

But that's impossible, he thought. *Ada's mother is dead.*

I'm hallucinating again, he thought. *Just like with Torquato.*

Hello, Michael, she said.

"Aren't you dead?" he asked.

How can I be dead if I'm here with you?

For a moment he wanted simply to accept what she was saying, but then found resistance welling up within him. "Who are you, really?" he asked. "Why am I hallucinating you?"

Ada's mother didn't answer either question. *I've come to give you a message,* she said. *About the Marker.*

"What's the Marker?"

You know what it is, she said. *You've come near it again and again, but somehow you've resisted it.* She crossed her index and middle fingers, held her hand toward him.

"Tail of the devil," he said. "The artifact, you mean."

She nodded. *You need to forget about it. The Marker is dangerous. Above all, you need to leave it where you found it.*

"I don't know what the hell you're talking about," said Altman. "What do I have to do with the Marker?"

Not just you, she said, and spread her arms wide. *You. Whatever choices are made will affect all of you.*

She cocked her head in a manner very similar to the way

Ada often did. A tremendous pressure built rapidly in his head; then it was gone.

"What's the message?" asked Altman.

Convergence is death, she said. *You must not give in to the Marker. You must not allow it to begin Convergence.*

"What does that mean, Convergence?

It means you shall finally begin, from the new beginning.

"The beginning of what? And just me?"

She again spread her arms wide. *You, all of you,* she said. Then, for a moment, she seemed almost exactly like Ada in a way that he found very disturbing. *I love you, Michael,* Ada's mother said. *I'm counting on you. Please help me stop it. Please don't fail.*

And then, as quickly as she had appeared, she was gone. He tried to get up again, fell back. The world around him was growing dark, as if seen through a black veil. Slowly it grew darker still, and then, suddenly, it was gone.

44

He woke up with an oxygen mask strapped to his face, surrounded by a series of seemingly identical men dressed in white, their faces covered by surgeon's masks.

"He made it," one of them said. "He's alive."

"Any evidence of brain damage?" asked another.

Altman tried to speak, but couldn't get his tongue around the words. One of the doctors put a hand on his shoulder. It was Stevens, he realized; he could recognize him by his eyes. "Just relax," he said. "You're lucky to be alive."

He closed his eyes, swallowed. And then a terrible thought hit him: What if this was just another hallucination?

He tried to move his arms, but couldn't. He opened his eyes, looking desperately around.

"He's confused," he heard one of them say. "Disoriented. He doesn't know where he is."

What was it she had said? *You must not give in to the Marker. You must not allow it to begin Convergence.* He had to tell them. "The Marker," he whispered. Markoff leaned close. "The Marker," he repeated.

"The Marker?" said Markoff. "What Marker? He's talking nonsense. Give him another shot."

Altman shook his head. Or tried. Whether his head moved or not, he couldn't say. Either it didn't move or they ignored him. He watched one of them fill a syringe and prime the needle, without being able to do anything about it.

He tried to speak, made instead a gurgling, inarticulate cry.

"It'll be okay," said Stevens, patting his arm. "Don't worry, Altman, we're here for you."

And then he felt the prick as the needle punctured his flesh. His arm burned a moment, and then went numb. The men in white were there for a moment longer; then they slowly blurred and ran together and finally disappeared entirely.

When he came conscious again, the room was empty, except for three men: Stevens, Markoff, and another man from Markoff's inner circle whose name he didn't know. He was as large as Markoff but thicker, with a brutal, flat face. They stood to one side of the bed, speaking in whispers impossible for Altman to make out.

Stevens was the first to notice he was awake. He gestured at him and whispered something. The other two stopped talking. In unison, all three moved closer and stared down at him.

"Altman," said Markoff. "Still alive. You seem to lead a charmed life."

Altman started to respond, but Markoff held a finger up to stop him. He reached down, removed Altman's oxygen mask.

"Are you feeling up to speaking?" asked Markoff.

"I think so," Altman said. His voice sounded like it no

longer belonged to him, or belonged to someone that was him but much older.

"You remember Stevens," said Markoff. "This is Officer Krax." Altman nodded.

"It's very simple," said Markoff. "I want you to tell me everything."

He did, starting with the moment when Torquato had suddenly attacked and moving through to his hallucinations.

"Tell us more about these hallucinations," said Krax.

"Does it matter?" asked Altman. "They were just hallucinations."

"It does matter," said Stevens. "Indeed, it matters a great deal."

So, Altman, too tired to argue or make up a lie, told them. When he was done, the three men withdrew to the far side of the room, started whispering again. Altman closed his eyes.

He was on the verge of falling back asleep when they returned.

For a moment they just stared at him. Stevens started to say something, but Markoff touched his arm and stopped him.

"I want you to tell Stevens everything from here on out," he said. "Any dreams, hallucinations, anything at all out of the ordinary, you contact Stevens right away."

"This is crazy," said Altman.

"No," said Markoff, "it isn't."

And then they were gone, leaving Altman behind to brood. He felt more confused and apprehensive than ever.

But a few minutes later the door opened, and a distraught Ada rushed in, and he had other things on his mind.

45

After nearly dying in the bathyscaphe, it was as if he was living a different life, as if the world he had known had become overlapped by another, ghostly one. He began to see more people whom he knew to be dead: his father, sister, a teacher he'd been close to who had committed suicide, an old friend killed by a car in high school. They would appear, looking nearly as real as anybody, and offer vague and sometimes puzzling messages. Some spoke against "Convergence," urging him to hurry and "focus your attention correctly" (as one of them put it) before it was too late. Others spoke of unity, suggesting to him that it was somehow too late, that he had misused the resources given him and showed no signs of learning from his mistakes. All urged him to leave the Marker alone. He told Ada about seeing her mother. At first it made her angry, and then it made her cry. But then, a few hours later she asked him to tell her about the experience in detail.

"But why you?" she asked. "Why not me?"

A day later he woke up in the middle of the night to find Ada staring at him. "I saw her," she said, her face radiant. "Like a vision. She was as real as you or me. She was standing right over there, near the door."

"What did she tell you?"

"That she loved me. And that we needed to leave the Marker alone, to forget we ever found it. It must be dangerous. Or powerful, anyway. What do you think the Marker is?"

He explained to her what he knew, described the way the Marker had looked underwater.

"It's all connected," she said. "The stories in town, these visions we're having, the artifact in the center of the crater. I'm sure of it."

At first she was ecstatic about seeing her mother. It had been, Altman realized, an almost religious experience for her in a way that it hadn't been for him. For the rest of the night she was manic, elated. But by the next morning her mood had begun to turn. She was moody, depressed.

"Why can't she be here all the time?" she asked. "Why can't she stay with me?"

"But it's not her," said Altman. "It seems like her, but it isn't. It's a hallucination."

"It *was* her," said Ada, with a sense of conviction that worried him. "And I need her. I need her back."

And just when Ada was at her most depressed and listless, her mother came back. Altman was in the room at the time, beside her, and saw it as well. Only what he saw was not her dead mother but his own dead sister. They both agreed that something had happened, but had experienced it differently. They were each shown whomever they wanted to see. The words spoken were different as well, phrased to fit the way the person herself spoke when she was alive. But it all, with a little interpretation, fit into the idea of one crowning event, Convergence, though the dead were less clear about what exactly that was, or what could be done to stop it.

Altman was suspicious. "It's not real," he tried to tell Ada. "We're being manipulated, used."

"I know what I saw," said Ada. "It was as real as anything I've ever seen." She wanted her mother back from the dead so much that she wouldn't listen. It was strange, Altman thought, that the hallucination—or vision, as she called it, was constant for her, always her mother, when his kept changing from one loved one to another. But perhaps it was simply because he was too skeptical to accept the hallucinations as anything but delusion and so it had to keep trying different strategies.

As he'd been ordered, Altman told Stevens about his hallucinations, mentioning Ada's as well. Stevens just recorded what he said and nodded. He seemed tired, overworked.

"What do you think it all means?" Altman asked.

Stevens shrugged. "You and your girlfriend are not the only ones having them," he said. "Others are experiencing the same thing, and more and more frequently. Only dead people, loved ones—the sort of people that you'd want to take seriously. Some people, like you, believe they're hallucinations. Others, like Ada, believe they're something more."

"Whatever it is, it wants us to do something," Altman said. "But it doesn't know how to communicate it properly."

"Not only that," said Stevens, in one of his rare moments of openness. "Our hospital ward is full of people suffering from psychosis and the suicide rate is sky-high. Either it wants a lot of us mad and dead or what it's saying is literally destroying us."

There was, he noticed, a shift in the way people interacted with one another aboard the floating compound. There was a growing feeling that something was happening, something that they couldn't begin to understand. Some people began clumping together in groups, sharing their experiences with the dead, speculating that the boundaries between heaven and earth had been broken. Others dismissed them as a function of the signal emitted by the Marker, similar to a drug trip. Others seemed to be having a bad trip: they became withdrawn, confused, even violent.

He was in the laboratory, charting the moments when the signal pulse was strongest and trying to see if his hallucinations were occurring at those same times, when he noticed through the open door people rushing down the hall.

He stepped out to get a better look, saw at the far end, against the door, surrounded by a crowd now, a scientist named Meyer, someone he didn't know very well. He had a laser scalpel in one hand, very close to his own throat.

"Now, Meyer," another scientist was trying to say. "Put the scalpel down."

"Stay away!" Meyer shouted. His eyes were wild, darting about in his head. "Just keep your distance! You're with them, I know it!"

"Who's 'them,' Meyer?" the man asked. "Put the scalpel down and I'm sure we can sort this all out."

"Go get the guards," someone said.

But Meyer overheard. "No guards!" he shouted, and lunged

forward, cutting off two of his friend's fingers with the laser scalpel.

The man screamed and fell backward, and Meyer turned in a circle, brandishing the scalpel until everyone stood at a little distance from him. He brought the scalpel back to his throat.

"It's too late," he hissed. "We're all dead or good as dead. We cannot escape. Get out now before you become one of them."

And suddenly, with a swift, vicious movement, he whipped the scalpel through his neck.

The wound was bloodless at first, slightly cauterized by the scalpel, but then the blood began to pulse, a thick jet of it spurting from his severed carotids. He gave a ghastly, gurgling scream, the air hissing strangely from his mouth and from his slit windpipe, and then took a step forward and collapsed.

A few moments later, guards were there, covering up the body and hustling everyone away.

"What happened?" Altman asked one of the scientists passing back by his door.

"Meyer went crazy," the man said. "He started screaming in the lab about the end of the world and then he stabbed Westerman through the arm with a broken pipette. Then he grabbed that laser scalpel and ran here."

"But why?"

The man shrugged. "Who knows," he said. "It's just like when that guard shot a technician last week for no reason then shot himself. These things just happen."

He sometimes found himself on the edge of a group, listening to them expounding. The focus was usually on the Marker, the name that Altman had learned to call it from his hallucination having caught on with others as well. Altman didn't know who had first suggested that the Marker was the product of alien technology, but the idea had caught on quickly, and now many of the researchers in the facility were convinced of it. There was a good deal of speculation about the originators of the Marker, why it had been left there, what it meant, and whether they should tamper with it or leave it alone.

One day, on his way from his room down to the submarine bay, he found the hallway blocked. Six or seven people were gathered in the hallway, a group consisting of both scientists and guards. One of the six, an older scientist, addressed the others. When he saw Altman coming, he fell silent.

"Excuse me," said Altman, and slowly pushed through, the people shuffling out of the way and allowing him to squeeze past. It was strange. He was, he was sure, interrupting something, but wasn't sure what. Mutiny maybe?

The answer came when, just as he reached the edge of the group, the scientist began to speak again.

"You must free your flesh, and unify with the divine nature of its construction. . ."

A religious meeting of some kind. Some crazed sect, no doubt, or perhaps members of different faiths getting together. He hadn't seen anything resembling a chapel in the floating compound, though Altman, not a religious man himself, hadn't realized this until now. He slowed, kept listening, trying to get a sense of who these people were.

"We must lose ourselves to find ourselves," said the scientist. "Convergence is the only salvation. For I hear this in its whispers, unless you can understand what it means to become one with the Marker, you shall not have eternal life."

The word *Marker,* coming at a moment when he expected to hear a deity referenced, made Altman shiver. He continued hurriedly on. Only once he'd left the corridor did he realize that what he had witnessed was the beginning of some kind of new religion, this one based on the Marker. It scared the shit out of him.

In the days that followed, he overheard such talk more and more frequently, even from Ada. Their opposing philosophies of the Marker had come between them to an even greater degree than his unwillingness to stop doing things that might be dangerous. In a matter of a few short days, their notions of the world had become radically different. He realized at a certain point that they'd begun to avoid each other when they could. He still loved her, but he felt like he was losing her and didn't know how to get her back. Despite that, he was still surprised the first time he saw her on the fringes of one of the religious groups.

"Can we talk about this?" he asked her, drawing her away from the crowd.

"I've been trying to talk to you about it," she said, "but you just won't see the light."

"That's not talking," he said. "That's preaching."

They fought and fought, and Ada threatened to leave him. Even though he knew it was hopeless, that their relationship was in the process of dying, he agreed at least to hear her out.

It was in listening to Ada that he began to get a clear sense of the believers' philosophy. They believed the Marker to be divine, that it had been sent to them by God, for humanity's benefit. *We must believe in it and bend ourselves to its will and then it will heal us. It will unify us and make us free and perfect.* A strange mishmash of Christianity and paganism, it gave people something to hold on to in the face of the uncertainty and anxiety about the Marker. Soon, Altman realized, a new problem would emerge, as everyone on board, just like he and Ada, would be split between believers and unbelievers.

At first Markoff's guards ignored this, but as the groups became larger and more dynamic, they started to break them up, presumably on Markoff's orders. But this only seemed to make people want to meet more frequently. It seemed an indication to many that there was something the military didn't want them to know.

Meanwhile, plans to raise the Marker continued. There was still a great deal of excitement, but it had metamorphosed into fervor on the one side and apprehension on the other. Altman went down in the bathyscaphe twice more, both times alone, both times to supervise the robots attaching cables to the net that now contained the Marker. Twice more, hovering near the ocean floor, he hallucinated Ada's mother. She repeated what she had said before, but it was no clearer this time.

"Where exactly shall we leave the Marker?" he asked her.

The Marker, as long as it lives within this sphere of gravitation, is where it must be.

What the hell does that mean? he wondered.

"What is going to happen to us?" he asked.

You must not study it. If you do, you will succumb to Convergence, she declared. *Perhaps it is already too late.*

"If we converge, what will happen?"

You shall finally begin, from the new beginning.

"What does that mean?"

You shall be made one and you shall lose yourself.

He came back up to the surface feeling even more confused than before. He thought maybe the believers were right. That the Marker was something divine. He thought, *What if it's a homing beacon for an alien race, something to call them down to us, the forerunner of our own destruction?*

No, he was not the sort of person who was easily given to belief. He didn't know if he believed in God, and he certainly didn't believe in organized religion.

Late one night, while he was getting ready for bed, Ada nowhere to be seen, probably hiding from him, a knock came at the door.

He went to the door. "Who is it?" he asked.

"Field," said a voice through the door. "Let me in."

Field? Why would Field want to see him? They hadn't gotten along well since they'd first come to the floating facility.

When he opened the door, it was to find Field flanked by a dozen others.

"What is it?" asked Altman upon seeing them.

"We need to talk to you," said Field. "Please let us come in."

Not knowing what else to do, Altman did. They filed solemnly in, one by one, standing in place or sitting on the bed, filling the room.

"We've come to ask you to lead us," said Field.

"Lead you? Lead you in doing what?"

"You've seen it," said someone from the crowd, Altman didn't see who.

"Seen what?"

"The Marker," said Field. "You've spent more time around it than anyone else. We know what happened on the bathyscaphe. When it killed others, it left you alive. We know that it converses with you. You have been chosen."

"How do you know what happened on the bathyscaphe?" Altman asked.

"We have brethren not only among the general population," said Field. "We have many close to Markoff. You understand, more than anyone else. You must guide us. You are our prophet. It is the Marker's will."

"Let me get this straight," said Altman. "You want me to lead you as the prophet of your religion?"

A rumble of assent shivered through them. For Altman, time seemed to have slowed to an excruciatingly slow pace. He moved back until he was touching a wall.

"Did Ada put you up to this?" he asked.

"Please," said Field. "Tell us what to do."

"No way," said Altman.

A collective groan arose from the crowd. "Are we not worthy?" asked Field. "What must we do to be worthy?"

"I liked you better when all you did was sit at your desk for eight hours a day," said Altman. "And I didn't like you much then."

"You shall lead us," said Field. "You cannot abandon us."

"I don't believe in the shit you do," said Altman.

They stared at him, astonished. When he looked back at Field, he saw a crafty expression had fallen over his face.

"This is a test," he said. "He is testing us."

"I am not testing you," he said evenly.

Field smiled. "We understand," he said. "Now is not the time. We shall watch and wait. When the moment comes, we will be ready to come to your side."

"I'll say it again," said Altman. "I am not a believer."

"But you will be," said Field. "I know. You may be a reluctant prophet, but you are a prophet nonetheless. I have seen it in a vision."

"Now is not the time," said Altman. Get the hell out."

They filed slowly out, each stopping to lay a hand on his arm or shake his hand, touching him as if he were some sort of good luck charm. His skin was crawling.

46

He watched from the bathyscaphe as the robotic units finished threading the Marker in cables. There it lay before him, bound and trussed, but somehow still imposing despite its metal net. *This is the cause of my problems*, he thought. *And now my problems are only going to get worse.*

He watched from five meters above it as the larger cable, the one running curved up into the darkness and to the ship above, grew taut. The MROVs had dug around the base, but there was no telling if it would come up. In a way, he hoped it wouldn't. He held his breath. The Marker sagged lower in the net, and for a moment he thought the net would not hold. It creaked and swayed slowly in the darkness, and they came up with a large grating sound, oddly distorted by the water, and began to rise.

He followed it up, relaying messages and corrections to a series of submarines, which, in turn, relayed them upward and to the surface. At first the Marker twisted as it rose, the water naturally channeling around the two spirals of the Marker and making it turn, creating an invisible whirlpool in its wake.

It could, Altman realized, soon become a problem, tangling the cables, so he slowed the towing down to a snail's pace and it stopped. After a while, it was moving regularly, ascending slowly but straight upward.

This is it, thought Altman.

Slowly it rose through the darkness. Only once they were halfway to the surface did he realize he hadn't experienced any hallucinations. His head, for the first time in months, didn't ache. He checked the readings, found that the signal had stopped broadcasting around the time it began to rise.

Maybe we've disconnected it, he thought. *Perhaps we're doing something right, perhaps this was what we were supposed to do. Maybe it was transmitting so that we would find it and bring it to the surface. Maybe that was its purpose.*

For a moment he felt reassured, and then unanswered questions began to assail him. If that were really the case, then why would there have been any hallucinations at all? And why would they affect people most strongly when they were close to the Marker itself? *It's almost as if it wants to keep us at a distance. And what do the dead's warnings of Convergence have to do with any of it?*

Maybe we've done something right, he thought, *or maybe we've done something very wrong.*

Soon they would get close to the surface, and the Marker would be drawn onto the freighter itself. Already the water had changed, the darkness receding, and he could see the Marker more clearly than he'd ever seen it before. In the light, it was even more impressive, covered with symbols and laterally striated by dark lines cut into the rock. He still could see no evidence of joints or cracks. It still seemed like it was formed out of a single large rock.

When the station was five hundred meters above them, Markoff ordered the ascent stopped.

"What's wrong?" asked Altman over the audio channel. "This wasn't how it was planned."

"Thank you for your help to this point, Mr. Altman," said Markoff. "A deepwater craft is no longer required. Return to the submarine bay."

"What? I think I'll stay here, Markoff, if you don't mind," said Altman.

There was silence for a long moment and then the vidscreen crackled into life. He saw Markoff's face.

"You've been an asset to me to this point. Now you risk becoming expendable."

"What's going on?" Altman asked.

"That is none of your concern," said Markoff.

He opened his mouth and then closed it again. Markoff, he knew, was capable of having the bathyscaphe torpedoed. Perhaps it was time to flee, dive deep and head for somewhere safe.

As if he could read Altman's mind, Markoff added, "Do you need something tangible to convince you to behave? Your girlfriend?"

For a moment, he hesitated. In a way, he had already lost Ada to the Marker, to her desire to be one of them. It was just a matter of time before he lost her completely.

All the same, he still loved her and couldn't live with her being dead because of him. With a sigh, he cut the signal and began to head for the surface, leaving behind the Marker, hanging in its gigantic metal net. On the way up, he passed a trio of submarines dragging a new cable. It led back, he could see, to the gigantic below-water chamber of the floating compound, the chamber that had been off-limits to everybody except for Markoff's inner circle ever since they'd arrived. What Markoff had planned, Altman had no idea.

47

As soon as he had left the bathyscaphe, he made for the chamber that he knew would house the Marker. Centrally located and the biggest of the below-water chambers, it had four ways in. But three of those ways, he discovered, had been welded closed, permanently sealed. The fourth, the main entrance, already had two guards stationed in front of it. He tried to bluff his way in.

"I'm supposed to be in there," he said. "To bring the Marker up."

"Do you have a pass?" asked one guard.

"Nobody gets in without a pass," said the other.

"I left my pass back in my room," he said. "I don't want to be late. I'll bring it back and show it to you later?"

"No pass, no entrance," said the guard.

Another man, a scientist, sidled past him, flashing his pass, and was nodded through. Altman watched as the doors slid open, but saw only an airlock on the other side. The man stood there waiting, and the door slid shut.

"Please," said Altman. "I need to—"

"We already told you," said the first guard. "No pass, no

entrance. Now move along or I'll have you thrown in the brig."

He went back down the corridor. He couldn't get in, but maybe he could at least get some idea of what was happening. He went from lab to lab, trying doors until he found one that also had a window facing toward the chamber.

Looking out, he saw the Marker hovering just below the chamber, being slowly drawn up and in. But he couldn't see into the chamber itself. Something had been done to render the glass semiopaque. He could see vague shapes and the sense of movement and then, as they began to reel it in, the shadowy rising shape of the Marker, but little more.

"You see," said Field, "we knew you would come around to the truth."

Altman hadn't come around. He still thought that Field and his believers were insane, but saw no point in telling Field that. The Marker had been in the station less than twenty-four hours, but ever since the Marker had been raised and secured, the whole feel of the station had changed. Even before he'd entered the submarine bay, a series of researchers had been declared inessential and had been shipped back to the DredgerCorp land compound, which rumor had it was serving now less as a research facility and more as a holding tank for scientists for whom Markoff had no use but whom he didn't want to release into the larger world. Ada had been among them, which meant he hadn't gotten a chance to see her and make sure she was okay. Altman suspected he, too, might have been among them if the bathyscaphe had arrived slightly earlier. As it was, he'd been told to pack his things, that he'd be among a batch of researchers to be shipped out early the next morning.

"I need a favor," he claimed, his hand on the chunk of Marker that he carried in his pocket. "There's something the Marker wants from me. I have to see it."

Field's face fell. "It's being guarded," he said. "It's very hard to see it."

"You said the other evening that some of the believers were in Markoff's inner circle."

"Yes," said Field, "that's true. But—"

"It's important," said Altman. "I wouldn't ask if it wasn't." He took the chunk out of his pocket and showed it to Field. "This is a piece of it," he said. "It needs to be returned."

Field reached out and very gently touched it. "Can I hold it?" he asked, his voice filled with awe. Altman handed it to him. He took it delicately in both hands, like he was holding a newborn child, his face lit up with a joy it frightened Altman to see. He crooned to it, a soft chant, something that Altman couldn't make out, and then reluctantly handed it back. He knelt before Altman.

"Stand up," said Altman. "And not a word to anybody about what I plan to do."

But Field refused to stand. "Thank you for choosing me," he said, his head bowed. "I will do all I can to help you make the Marker whole again."

Around three in the morning, a knock came at his door. It was Field, and another man with him wearing the black garb of one of Markoff's inner circle. He was carrying a package under his arm. Altman vaguely recognized him. "This is Henry Harmon," Field said. "Mr. Harmon, Michael Altman."

"I know who he is," said Harmon dryly. "You're sure this is absolutely necessary?"

Altman nodded. Harmon tossed him the package. He tore it open, saw an outfit identical to Harmon's own. "Put that on," he said.

Altman stared at it. "How's this going to help?" he asked. "Won't they recognize me, in any case?"

"Maybe," said Harmon, "but they won't try to stop us. They won't question the pass as long as you have the uniform. If we have trouble, it'll be afterward, which is a risk I'll have to take."

He put it on and they set off.

Field followed them, but Harmon turned briefly, shook his head, and Field, a look of disappointment on his face, disappeared.

He checked his chronometer. "There are four guards total, two at the door outside the chamber and two inside, all armed. We're lucky: the two guards inside are with us, though that's far from being generally known. The two outside, though, aren't. Shift changes in about fifteen minutes and all bets are off. If we stay longer than ten, chances are good that one of the guards will get curious and place a call to check on our authorization. Understood?"

"Yes," said Altman.

"Here's your pass," he said. "It's not the best, but the guards outside should only glance at it. The men inside will go with whatever I say."

Harmon was right. The guards outside the room seemed hardly surprised that someone was coming to see the Marker in the middle of the night. They looked at Harmon then glanced at both passes and waved them in. The guards inside didn't even bother with that, withdrawing discreetly to the other side of the room as soon as they entered.

There it was. A series of catwalks had been built up along the walls to make it easy to get a close look at any part of it. Massive and towering, it dominated the whole chamber. Seeing it out of the water, he got a fuller sense of its bulk and strangeness. It was like nothing he had ever seen, a kind of impossible object that was nevertheless there. A power seemed to emanate from it. It was dangerous.

At the same time, he felt his scientific impulses kicking in. It was amazing, and he genuinely wanted to study it. A piece of extremely advanced technology, something predating humanity.

He took out his holopod and began to vid it.

"What are you doing?" whispered Harmon. "Nobody is allowed to vid it."

"That's what I came for," he said.

"But it's not allowed."

Altman shrugged once, then ignored him. Either Harmon would stop him or he wouldn't. He filmed the whole structure at first, then ran the lens in close-up over the sides closest to him. As he did so, he tried to spot the place where the piece of rock he had in his pocket was from, but couldn't find it.

He felt like he'd only just begun when Harmon grabbed his arm. "We've got to go," he whispered.

Altman nodded. He slipped the holopod back into his pocket and headed for the door, Harmon pulling him along. Harmon nodded once to the guards on the inside and they resumed their stations. The guards on the outside he saluted.

"Why do you need a vid of it?" asked Harmon as they walked away. "I have half a mind to turn you in."

"It's important," said Altman. "Trust me. You'll see."

Five minutes later, he was back in his room, hastily packing. The hunk of rock he kept on his person. He backed up his holopod onto a memory stick, which he hid in the lining of his jacket, just in case. And then he lay down on the bed and waited.

But sleep wouldn't come. Every time he closed his eyes, he would see the Marker there, towering above him. It was powerful, it was dangerous, it wanted something from them. Why did Ada worship it? To worship it would be just to put yourself even more fully at its mercy. And it was not the sort of thing, Altman felt, to grant mercy.

Soon, in an hour or two, a knock would come at the door and he'd be escorted to the launch and sent back to the land compound. He stared up into the darkness, thinking. Once there, he could forget all about this, pretend like the Marker was no longer his problem and let Markoff do with it what he would while he went back to his life. Or he could figure out a way to smuggle out the vid that he'd taken of the Marker, make it available to the general public, and try to make the Marker a matter of international scientific inquiry rather than a toy for the military.

The first possibility would mean safety, a chance to lead a more or less normal life. Probably he could patch up his relationship with Ada. Maybe with time, miles away from the Marker, separated from the hallucinations of her mother, she would begin to come to her senses. She would stop thinking about it, would regain her sanity. Everything could turn out okay. That is, assuming nothing went wrong with the Marker.

The second might mean danger, even death. Markoff and his goons wouldn't hesitate to kill both him and Ada if they became, as Markoff liked to say, expendable.

He already knew which one he would take. He'd never been the sort to take the safe route. Now all he had to do was figure out how to get the news out.

48

Markoff went from holofile to holofile, looking for some good news. So far nothing. So far the Marker had remained unresponsive and mute.

They had tried everything they could think of. They had begun to experiment on it. A team of cryptologists was attempting to decipher the symbols on the Marker, but without any idea of what the symbols referred to, they weren't making any progress. They had subjected it to an electric current, without result. They had tried irradiating it, subjecting it to radio waves, microwaves, electromagnetic waves. Nothing, always nothing.

Or almost nothing. The Marker, the researchers had told him, had begun to broadcast again. Very slight now, but definitely present. Some of the scientists working on the Marker seemed to notice it; others did not. According to Stevens, those who noticed had begun to be visited by dead relatives, just as Altman had been in the bathyscaphe, all with some variation of the same message: leave the Marker alone, do not try to make use of it. The scientists themselves didn't understand it any better than he did, and after conveying the message to Stevens, they had started speculating about it among themselves. It was a warning, some felt, and should be taken at face value: nobody should touch the Marker, nobody should try to harness its technology; if they did, they would unleash something they couldn't imagine. But maybe it was simply that they weren't ready, others felt, that once they proved themselves worthy, the secrets of the Marker would be revealed to them.

There were many more in the latter camp. A mystical belief in the Marker had started to grow. Whenever they could, the believers gathered together and worked themselves up, convinced as they were that the Marker was the path to eternal life and oneness with the divine. Some argued that this was what it meant by "Convergence." So far, the movement had been held in check by the guards, but even some of them, Markoff realized, had started to become believers. He was in danger of losing control of his project.

They needed to find a simple way to harness the power of the Marker and do it quickly. He was sure the technology, once harnessed, would be the pathway to tremendous power, even domination of the world, not to mention the moon. Even the solar system.

But now a group of believing scientists was trying to put down strict rules about how the Marker could be examined. Only *respectful interaction* with the Marker should be tolerated, nothing that might threaten or damage it or cause it to think less of humanity. *We needed to show the Marker that we were worthy of it so that it would begin to teach us.* It was a ridiculous list of demands, and Markoff dismissed them out of hand, but he couldn't stop people from talking. There was a palpable shift in how people approached the Marker, even if Markoff had refused the believers' demands. Indeed, he was surprised at how many people in the facility seemed to feel an almost religious awe for the Marker. Something was changing, shifting, in a way that didn't respond to his usual tactics. He had to figure out a new way to approach the situation.

He put a vidlink through to Krax. From how quickly he answered, it was clear he'd been waiting beside the monitor for the call.

"You've had a chance to look over the data?" Krax asked.

"Yes," said Markoff. "What is your recommendation, Officer Krax?"

"An unequivocal refusal to meet any of their demands. Once we begin to do so, we'll never stop. They're crazies. They shouldn't be tolerated."

"It won't end there," said Markoff.

"Maybe not," said Krax, "but we have the firepower and they don't."

"All right," said Markoff, "see to it."

Two days later, Krax had a call from one of the guards in the Marker chamber.

"It's the scientists, sir," he said. Krax could hear a steady rumble of noise in the background. "They're protesting. They won't leave the chamber."

"Make them leave," said Krax.

"It's not as easy as that," said the guard. "There are a lot of them. We've had to call for reinforcements. What should we do?"

"Don't do anything until I get there," said Krax, and disconnected.

By the time Krax and his team reached the chamber, things had become more serious. The scientists, led by a pudgy man named Field, had encircled the Marker. They had locked arms and were attempting to keep the guards at a distance. The guards had their weapons out. Many of them were visibly upset.

"What is it?" Krax asked one of them. "What happened?"

"You'll have to ask that one," he said, and gestured at Field.

"All right," said Krax. He removed his plasma pistol from its holster and walked forward to the line, to where the man was.

"What's the meaning of this?" he asked.

"We sent you our demands," said Field.

"We read them and rejected them," said Krax.

"We're here to protect the Marker until you agree to them."

"Starting an insurrection, are you? This will surely end poorly for you."

A few of the men in the line rustled and looked at one another, though fewer than Krax hoped. Field looked a little nervous, but his voice was still steady when he spoke.

"We're trying to do what's right," he said.

"What's right," said Krax, "is for you and your friends to go back to your quarters."

"You'll respect our demands, then?" said Field.

Krax levelly met his eye. "You shouldn't be interfering in something you don't understand," he said. "I'll ask you again to break your line and go."

Field gulped and then shook his head. *Honestly,* thought Krax, *to look at the guy, you wouldn't think he had it in him. But belief makes people unpredictable.*

"I'll ask once more," said Krax. "After that, I'm done asking."

Field had started to sweat. His eyes seemed strangely glazed, but still determined. He tightened his lips into a white line and shook his head.

Krax smiled. Raising the pistol slightly, he shot Field in the foot.

He went down in a heap, screaming, and the room broke into chaos. A plasma beam fired by one of the believers cut close across his cheek, singeing his hair, and struck a guard just behind him full in the face. He went down, bleeding, blinded. Krax crouched, shot another scientist in the leg. Shots flew back and forth on both sides.

And then Krax had an idea. He fired directly at the Marker, watched the blue fire splat on the surface and flicker about before going out.

He darted forward to Field and knelt beside him where he lay grimacing in pain. He forced Field's head around to look at the Marker and then fired at it again.

"No!" said Field, clearly terrified. "You'll hurt it! Don't!"

"Tell them to stop!" shouted Krax. "Tell them to put down their weapons and surrender or I'll have every guard in here shooting the thing." And to show he meant business, he fired at the Marker a third time.

Suddenly he was overwhelmed with pain, his head feeling as though it were ready to explode. He gasped for breath. People all around him were doing the same. Field screamed and then began to yell for the believers to listen to him, to stop the violence, to put their weapons down. At first the believers were too distracted by pain, but gradually they gathered themselves and stood as if stunned. Krax bellowed and raised his open palm to stop his guards from resuming firing. God, his head hurt.

"For the good of the Marker, we must concede the battle," said Field, wincing from the pain in his leg. "Lay down your weapons, brothers. Do not resist."

Krax was amazed when he found that, to a man, they did. *Just more proof,* he thought, *that religion is a dead end.*

The next twenty minutes were spent imprisoning the believers and attending to the wounded. There were four dead: two guards and two scientists. He ordered them dragged off to the morgue.

Krax smiled. He hadn't had so much fun since the moon skirmishes. It had been a very satisfying day. If only his head didn't hurt so much, it would have been downright perfect.

49

"It's started again," said Altman. "The pulse. I'm sure of it."

He was clutching his head when he said it, clearly in pain. Ada, too, was rubbing her forehead, though absently, not suffering as much.

"You're sure?"

"I'm sure," he said.

"Then I'll see her again? My mother will come back?"

Altman turned away, frustrated. They were in the land compound, which had become, as they immediately found out, more like a detainment center than a research facility. Their labs were empty, containing only the most basic equipment. There was only one way out of the center, and that was guarded day and night by a rotation of the three men who had originally corralled him for Markoff, before he had come to the floating compound. All had names that started with *T*. Terry was thin with glasses, but he carried a large-caliber gun. The other two, Tim and Tom, were brothers, large men who looked enough alike to be twins.

On the first day, Altman had tried to go outside and was stopped. "But I just want to—" he started to say.

"Nobody in or out," said the bespectacled Terry. "That's the rule until the boss says otherwise."

When he tried later, with either Tim or Tom on duty, he met a less verbal refusal, was simply pushed back and then, when he persisted, punched in the stomach.

"Go away," Tim or Tom said.

There were maybe twenty of them in the compound, including nearly all the scientists from Chicxulub except for Field and, for some reason, Showalter. They tried to continue the research they had been doing on the floating compound, but without proper equipment, it was impossible. Instead, they compared notes, shared information and research.

Like Ada, many of them had become believers. Many of them had been part of Field's flock and looked up to Altman, recognizing him as a reluctant prophet.

"The Marker has chosen me," an icthyologist named Agassiz confided in him. "I don't know why, but I know it to be the case."

"Why are you telling me this?"

"I know you speak to it," said Agassiz. "Ask it about me."

Others were like that as well, approaching him, hoping for a sign or a blessing. At first he tried to tell them that it wasn't possible, that he wasn't a prophet, but it was difficult enough to convince them that he found a few cryptic words or a muttered blessing was quicker and would get them to leave him alone.

Speaking with Agassiz, he realized that it would be a simple matter to manipulate them. He could tell Agassiz that he had a role and that his role was to obey Altman. There were enough believers that he could use their belief to get them to help him break out. But he hesitated. If they were to try to leave now, they might manage to overpower whichever of the three guards was on duty, but probably not before a few of them were hurt or killed. The last thing he wanted was more deaths on his conscience.

Despite the lack of equipment, Skud somehow managed to create a limited set of research equipment, partly by stripping out the wires of the security system, including something to provide a crude measurement of the pulse. He was able to confirm that yes, in fact, the pulse was up and functioning strongly.

"I cannot say exactly how strongly," he said. "There is a limitation of equipment."

"Yes," said Altman, "but within that limitation, you can confirm that it seems strong."

"There is a limitation of equipment," Skud insisted.

But as it turned out, Altman didn't need Skud to tell him. He could tell by the way the people around him changed, becoming either withdrawn or violent. And by the fact that he kept turning the corner and running into ghosts.

Help us, they pleaded. *Make us whole.*

He brooded, wondered what he could do. He had to go public, but how? He couldn't escape.

And then suddenly, late one night, walking down the hall, he realized that the guard on duty at the front door, Tim or Tom, was talking to himself. He watched him gesture to empty air and then hold out his rifle and let go of it. It clattered to the ground and he just left it there, and then went rapidly down the hall, passing Altman without a second glance. Nobody was guarding the door.

He didn't hesitate. He grabbed his wallet, his holopod, and Ada's hand and immediately rushed to escape. Sure enough, there was still no one there, the key left in the lock. With shaking fingers, he turned it and opened the door.

What if it's a trap? he couldn't help but think. *Maybe it is a trap, but it might also be my only chance.* He crossed the threshold and ran, dragging Ada reluctantly behind him. He was already formulating his next steps: a car or bus out of town, then a flight back to the North American sector. He'd have to move quickly, but if he did, he might get word out. It was time to go public.

50

Tim was on duty, standing watch at the outer door, when his father appeared. This didn't surprise Tim, apart from the fact that his father had been dead for twenty years and, when alive, had lived several thousand miles away.

Hello, Tim, he said. He was smoking his pipe and wearing the sweater that he had always worn. Well, not always, but a lot.

"Dad," he said, "what are you doing here?"

I came to see you.

"You didn't need to do that, Dad. You didn't need to go to the trouble."

I've been worried about you, Tim, he said. *About you and your brother.*

"Why, Dad? Tom's okay. I'm doing okay, too. We're both working. And we're making good money."

It's not that, said his father, drawing deep on his pipe. *It's just that, well, I don't know how to put this, son, but are you sure that you're ready?*

"Ready for what, Dad?"

If you have to ask that, you're not ready, son. And what about your brother?

"I haven't talked to him about it," said Tim. "I'm not even sure what you're talking about."

Things are going to change around here, son, said his father. *Which team will you be on? Will you be on the winning team? Do you have good hustle?*

"I want to be on the winning team, Dad," said Tim eagerly. "I'd like to think I have good hustle."

Your brother, I think he may have dropped out of the game, said his father. *Are you ready to sub for him?*

"Tom?" he said, his voice rising. "What happened to Tom?"

I can't rightly say, said his father. *One minute we were talking and the next moment he wouldn't speak to me. He was listening to the opposing coach at the same time as me. I think he got confused. He was like that when you were kids, too. Tom always did tend to misunderstand what I said. You won't do that, will you?*

"Where's Tom, Dad? Tell me what happened to Tom."

But his father was already gone, vanished into thin air. Or maybe he was still there but right behind him, always just behind him, just out of sight. "Dad?" he said. "Dad?"

He paced back and forth anxiously for a moment but he couldn't stop thinking about Tom. Tom was his older brother, born nine minutes earlier, and he had always looked up to him. And they had always looked out for each other. It was almost like they weren't a full person unless the other one was there, that together they were two people but that one of them taken separately wasn't even one. Which was what made guarding the compound door alone so hard sometimes.

What was it his dad had said? That Tom had stopped talking. Maybe he was just mad at Dad. Tim didn't understand how you could get mad at Dad, Dad was a great guy, but Tom often had been, and sometimes stopped talking to him. Maybe that was part of being the older brother.

By maybe it was more than that. Maybe there was something else wrong. He owed it to Tom to check on him. After all, wouldn't Tom have done the same thing for him? And if he didn't do it and then something turned out to be wrong with Tom, how would he ever manage to forgive himself?

There was only the problem of the door. He was guarding the door. He needed someone to watch the door while he was gone.

"Dad," he asked, "could you do it?"

Why, sure, son, said his father. He was just lighting his pipe. *What do you want me to do?*

"Take this," said Tim, and gave him the gun. His father couldn't hold on to the gun, dropped it on the floor. That was okay, Tim thought, he could pick it up later, after he'd finished with his pipe. "If anyone comes," he said. "Pump them full of lead."

His father grinned. *Will do, son,* he said, and gave Tim a little wave.

Yes, sir, thought Tim as he headed down the hall in search of Tom. His father was a good egg, that was for certain. He was certainly understanding. Not everybody was lucky enough to have a father like that.

He smelled his brother before he saw him, though he didn't know it was his brother at first. All he knew was that he smelled blood. And that it was coming from their room.

He went into a crouch and moved in, balanced on the balls

of his feet, ready for someone to attack. But the attack never came.

His brother was in his bed, turned on his side.

"Tom," he said to him. "Dad said you weren't talking to him. Is anything wrong?"

Tom didn't say anything.

"Tom?" he said.

Not only did he not say anything, but he didn't even move. Tim moved forward and touched his shoulder.

He was cold to the touch. Tim suddenly couldn't breathe. Tim pulled him toward him and he came all at once, and Tim saw that his throat was cut, and that there was a knife in his hand.

51

"Have you seen this?" asked Stevens. Krax was with him, standing just behind.

"Seen what?" asked Markoff.

Stevens reached out and opened the vid. "It was just broadcast," he said. "Still fresh." They stood there together, watching it.

It showed Altman before a podium at a press conference. The tickers on the bottom ran the line SCIENTIST ACCUSES MILITARY OF COVER-UP and then ALIEN LIFE CONFIRMED? Altman was describing the Marker and the expedition.

"Where is this?" asked Markoff.

"Washington, D.C.," he said.

"How the hell did he get to Washington, D.C.?" He turned to Stevens, who in turn looked at Krax.

Krax shrugged. "Security failure," he said. "Not my men," he claimed. "Leftovers from Tanner."

. . . every evidence that what we are talking about is the first evidence of alien life, said Altman. *But this is not something that the military should be investigating. This is something that should be investigated by scientists from all the sectors, a coalition of experts from all over the world. . . .*

Altman's image disappeared, was replaced by images of the Marker itself, taken from within the underwater chamber.

"Where the fuck did he get those?" asked Markoff.

"I don't know," said Krax.

"Find out who does!"

. . . *the military wants to cover it up*, Altman was claiming. *They want to control the investigation so as to use the alien technology to manufacture weapons. We cannot let this happen. There needs to be a public inquiry about the Marker's use and its function.*

Below him, on the ticker, were the words MICHAEL ALTMAN: WHISTLEBLOWER OR PARANOID?

Krax had already started for the door, when Markoff stopped him. Stevens was speaking to Markoff, whispering quietly, both of them just far enough away that Krax couldn't hear anything. He watched Markoff nod, then nod again.

"Belay that," said Markoff to Krax. "You can worry about it when you get back. Find out what hotel Altman is staying in and make whatever arrangements you can to book us into the neighboring room. Handpick three additional men. I want all of us on a plane fifteen minutes ago. We need to stamp out this problem right now."

PART SIX

HELL UNLEASHED

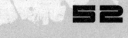

52

It had been a long day. First the press conference, then other questions, individual interviews. The first one he tried with Ada at his side, but her obsession with the ghost of her mother made her come off as a nut. For the others, he tried to stick to the basics. Yes, there was an alien artifact that they had dubbed "the Marker." Yes, it had been found at the heart of the Chicxulub crater under layers of rock, which suggested that it might well be older than human life. No, this was not a hoax. Yes, he was convinced that the military was trying to cover up the existence of the Marker. What the rest of the government did or did not know, he couldn't say.

He did not bring up the hallucinations. He wanted to avoid the notion that the Marker was sentient, and in any case, he wasn't sure the hallucinations really came from the Marker—maybe they were simply triggered by it. He didn't talk about the strange creature on the beach or show them the sign of the tail of the devil, or tell them that the Yucatec Maya believed the devil's tail was deep beneath the waves, just where the Marker had been found. Most media outlets, he quickly realized, saw him as an interesting curiosity, an extremist whom they could parade before their viewers and listeners. They were more interested in poking holes in his story. Couldn't the vid be faked? How did they know that it was actually the size he said it was? Size could be simulated on a vid, and there were no human figures in the vid to compare it to. Hadn't he gone to Chicxulub to work on a university research grant? Then how was it he had ended up working for the military, living on this alleged floating island? Didn't that sound a little too much like something out of a sci-fi novel?

But there were a few people who asked more serious questions. And once he had answered, they looked at him in a different, more thoughtful way.

They arrived at the historic Watergate Hotel late, past midnight. There was another round of interviews the next day, requests still coming in over the phone. Also a meeting with a lawyer about possibly filing an injunction against the government. Public opinion seemed to be building; maybe it would be enough to apply the right amount of pressure on the places that needed it.

"It's going to work," Ada said as he opened the door. "Markoff won't be able to keep the Marker for himself. Everybody will know about it now, everyone will have a chance to share in its message."

Not knowing what to say, he didn't answer. They opened the door. He flipped on the light and then stopped dead.

One of the walls had a large hole in it, plaster scattered all about the floor. Just behind it, sitting in a chair beside the bed, was Markoff.

"Hello, Altman," he said.

Altman started to turn toward the door, but found a gun with a silencer on its end pointed at his eye, another pointed at Ada's chest. Krax was holding one, a guard he didn't recognize the other. There were two more guards deeper in the room. They came forward now.

"I don't need to tell you that I'll shoot your girlfriend first. No screaming," said Krax. "Nothing but polite silence unless you are spoken to. Do you understand?"

Altman nodded.

"Move into the room," he said. "Get on the bed."

They moved in, were pushed onto the bed. Krax stepped back and sat in a chair that he'd set up across the threshold of the bathroom, keeping his gun trained at Altman.

"I take it you've seen the press conference," said Altman.

"Shut up, Altman," said Markoff. "Nobody likes a smart-ass."

"It's too late, Markoff," hissed Ada. "Word is out."

Markoff ignored her. "Let's have a little talk, Altman," he said. "Talking can't hurt, can it?"

Altman didn't say anything.

"I don't suppose we could encourage you to drop everything," Markoff said. "Hold another press conference, let them know that you were only joking, that there is no Marker, that there is no conspiracy, that you've been the victim of an incredible hoax."

"No," said Altman.

"If you do," said Markoff, "we could come to some sort of arrangement. You'd be allowed to come back to research the Marker." When Altman didn't say anything, he added, "With total access."

Total access? It was tempting. But no doubt Markoff was lying. And in any case, he was far enough along that there was no going back. The Marker had to be investigated openly.

"He doesn't answer to you," said Ada. "He answers only to the Marker."

Markoff reached out, cuffed her hard. "Shut up," he said.

"Don't touch her," said Altman.

"What's your answer, Altman?" asked Markoff.

"I'm sorry," said Altman. "No."

"I'm sorry, too," said Markoff. "That's it, then. You're going to have to come with us."

"I don't think so," said Altman.

"We're not asking you if you want to come or not. We're giving you the choice between coming or dying."

"Then kill me," said Altman without hesitation.

Markoff looked at him coolly. "Call me superstitious, but I think that Marker has something in store for you. I don't want to kill you yet." Markoff nodded toward Ada, and Krax's gun slowly swiveled until it was pointed at Ada's head. "But I don't have the same reservations about your girlfriend."

Altman looked over at Ada. She didn't look afraid, but it was that very fact that made *him* afraid. She was eager to die a martyr. "So the choice is either both of us go with you or just I go," he said.

Markoff smiled. "Got it in one," he said. "Krax here has a sedative for both of you." He gestured to the others. "These fine boys will repair the hole we made, make everything as good as new. As far as anybody knows, you simply got cold feet and disappeared."

"You're a real bastard," said Altman.

"Takes one to know one," said Markoff. "Now be a good boy and take your medicine."

53

And so Altman was back where he'd started, though also a little surprised that they hadn't simply killed him. He suspected a trap, something awful they were saving him for, but didn't know what it would be. He wondered if his press conference or his disappearance following it had had any effect, but doubted he'd be able to find out while inside the floating compound.

As for Ada, when he awoke from the drug, she was gone. When he demanded to see her, they just laughed.

"She'll be safe," Krax had said. "As long as you cooperate."

A few hours after waking up, still a little groggy, he had found himself in Stevens's office. The latter sat with his elbows resting on the arms of his chair and his fingers tented in front of his face.

"Why am I here?" Altman asked. "Why am I still alive?"

"Markoff is curious about you," Stevens admitted.

"Curious?"

"You have some resistance to the effect of the Marker, a resistance that most of your colleagues don't have. Markoff realizes you might be of use for his project."

"And what project is that?"

Stevens smiled. "You can understand why he might wonder about you," he said. "You've survived trips in the bathyscaphe that have driven other people mad. Even when you've had headaches and hallucinations, they haven't caused you to degenerate into violence or madness the way so many of the other hallucinators seem to do. Many of the believers on board have an almost religious awe of you. And I have to say that I find myself half sharing their belief. I suspect that a few of my colleagues feel similarly."

"That's insane," said Altman.

"They think you're a reluctant prophet," said Stevens.

Altman shook his head. "The Marker is dangerous," he said. "I'm sure of it."

"And yet you're fascinated by it," said Stevens. He leaned forward. "We still suspect you know things that you're not telling." He opened his desk drawer and removed from it the chunk of rock from the Marker. "This was found in your jacket pocket while you were unconscious," he said. "Care to explain?"

"No," said Altman.

Stevens nodded. "Up to you," he said. "If you don't want to explain to me, perhaps you can speak with Krax."

But Krax didn't seem to want to talk exactly. "You know why you're here?" he asked.

Altman nodded. "You want to know about the chunk of the Marker."

"That's part of it," he said. He led Altman to a chair with leather straps affixed to the arms and legs. "Sit here," he said.

"Why?" said Altman. "Where's Ada?"

"Don't worry about Ada. Just sit," said Krax, pushing his chest lightly so he tipped back into the chair. "Now I'm going to strap you in," he said.

"There's no need to strap me in," said Altman, panic starting to rise in him. "I'll stay as I am."

Krax shook his head and began affixing the straps. "You won't," he said. "I'm afraid, Mr. Altman, that this is going to be a bit of a bumpy ride."

"What do you mean, a bumpy ride?"

"How do they feel?" Krax asked as he tested each strap in turn. Not uncomfortable? Not too tight?"

"I'm fine," said Altman, "but what—"

Krax pulled the left wrist strap painfully tight, then the right. Altman could feel the strap cutting deep into his flesh. "How about now?" he asked.

And then he left the room. For a moment Altman was alone, straining against the straps, and then he stopped. Maybe he could tip the chair over, break it somehow. But when he tried to rock it back and forth, he found that it had been bolted to the floor.

A moment later, Krax was back, bringing a wheeled cart with him. On top of the cart was a tray covered in a white cloth. Krax brought it close, pulled the cloth off it with a flourish. Beneath was a row of scalpels and knives, a pair of pincers as well. Krax ran his hands slowly over them.

"You didn't think you could just waltz off and report on us and suffer no consequences, did you, Mr. Altman?"

Altman tried to speak, but his mouth had gone suddenly dry.

Krax selected the smallest knife. "Let's start small and work our way up, shall we?" he said.

"I'd rather you didn't," said Altman.

"Just a few small cuts at first, Mr. Altman. Just something to make it interesting and to make you respect my artistry."

He grabbed hold of Altman's index finger and very carefully crosshatched the tip of it, the knife just cutting through. At first it didn't hurt, just felt warm. And then the finger began to throb, a drop of blood forming on the tip. He went on to the next finger and then the next, just three or four small cuts per finger, hardly deeper than papercuts. Altman watched a drop of blood collect at the end of each finger, the hand feeling like it was on fire.

"We're going to be here for days and days, Mr. Altman. We'll get to know each other very intimately."

He left the room again. Altman tried not to look at the hand, tried to ignore its throbbing, but he couldn't help it. Before it was all over, it would, he knew, become much, much worse. He'd wish he were dead.

And then Krax was back, a bowl full of salt in one hand.

"Have you heard the expression 'rubbing salt into a wound,' Mr. Altman?"

Altman felt his hand clench involuntarily. He closed his eyes. Krax slapped him. "You'll want to watch this," he said. But Altman kept his eyes closed.

Suddenly his hand was burning, his fingers being ground into the salt. He couldn't help but gasp. He clenched his eyes tighter. "Fine-grain salt works best," Krax explained in a calm voice. "Sea salt in particular. Iodized, of course."

Krax released the hand. "That's it," he said. "You can open your eyes."

He did. The light in the room seemed abnormally bright through the pain. "What do you want to know?" asked Altman through gritted teeth.

"All in good time," said Krax. "No need to rush things." He returned to the cart, placing the bowl of salt on it. He replaced the small knife, ran his hands over the knives that remained. "I love my job," said Krax, smiling, and then plucked a slightly larger knife from the tray and came toward him. "Open wide," he said.

Markoff was alone on the command deck, standing in his usual spot. To someone coming in, it might look like he was staring out through the observation window and into the dark water. What he was really doing was monitoring a series of holovids, set up to be seen only from that one position. They showed various parts of the ship, cycling rapidly between them.

Something was up, he could tell. A disturbance in the Marker chamber. "Stay with that," he said, and one of the holovids dedicated itself exclusively to that chamber. Lots of guards and scientists shaking fists. Where was Krax? He was supposed to keep shit like this from happening. And then he remembered Krax was with Altman and smiled.

The door slid open and Stevens stepped in. He stood there a few tiers down, waiting, until Markoff gestured him forward.

"We've got problems," admitted Stevens.

"Tell me something I don't already know," said Markoff.

"The believers are getting restless. Somehow they know Altman is back on board. They're demanding to see him."

"Absolutely not," said Markoff. "I've given him to Krax to play with."

"If we don't let him make an appearance, we're likely to have another riot on our hands. Besides, Krax has already found out enough. He knows where he got the chunk of the Marker and how—it didn't take long for Altman to give that up. I've watched the vids, had Altman's microexpressions analyzed. I don't think Krax is likely to get much more out of him." Stevens came a little closer, put his hand on Markoff's shoulder. "I know you hate him," he said. "We all hate him. But we can use him."

Markoff just shrugged the hand off.

"He'll be a distraction to the believers," Stevens said. "He's more useful to us that way than he is dead."

Markoff focused his hard stare fully on Stevens. Stevens met it placidly.

"How do I know you're not one of them?"

"One of whom? The believers? Do I seem like a believer to you?"

"All right," Markoff said. "He can be useful. Get him from Krax. But if anything goes wrong, I'm blaming you."

In the middle of the sixth knife, two guards showed up. He was released suddenly and without warning, hands and feet sore and bleeding, cuts on his back and thighs, but basically in one piece. "We'll see each other again soon," Krax promised.

The guards bandaged him and hustled him down to Stevens, left the two of them alone.

"It would have been easier to tell me," said Stevens. "Keep that in mind next time you have a choice."

"Screw you," said Altman.

Stevens smiled. "I can send you back to Krax anytime," he said. "Keep that in mind as well."

Altman didn't reply.

"The only reason you're here now," said Stevens, "is because I have a use for you. There was a skirmish between believers and unbelievers the other day that left people dead. People are taking sides. If it goes on like this, more people will die. I'd like to keep that from happening. I think you can help."

"How?"

"The believers trust you," he said. "They may listen to you."

"The pulse signal is broadcasting again," said Altman. "The conflict between the believers and the unbelievers is hardly your biggest problem."

"No," admitted Stevens, "but the two feed one another. You're here instead of with Krax and his knives because Markoff thinks you may have a chance of keeping things stable."

"And if I say no?"

Stevens shrugged. "Then you go back to Krax. And if you misbehave or try to stir the believers up, I'll shoot you myself. But keep things stable and you'll prevent a lot of people ending up dead. And it goes without saying that we'll be watching you at all times."

"I want to talk to Ada first," said Altman.

Stevens hesitated for a moment. "No," he finally said.

"Why not?"

"You'll have to trust me that she's safe," said Stevens. "If everything goes well, I'll let you talk to her."

. . .

Field was there, many other scientists he recognized as well, all of them happy to see him again. It was Field who told him about the firefight with the military, the deaths. He showed him, too, where he had been shot in the foot, but didn't remove the dressings.

"That must hurt," said Altman.

Field smiled happily. "Without the morphine, I wouldn't be able to walk," he said. "But that's not important," he said. "I'm not important."

"Of course you are," said Altman, patting him on the shoulder as if he was crazy.

Field shook his head. "What's important is that things have begun to change. A lot of us are dead now and a lot of us are crazy. Those of us who are left have a different perspective." He clutched Altman by the shirt, pulled him closer, the weird morphine smile still plastered clownlike across his face. "Those of us who are left," he said in a stage whisper, "*believe*."

"If you say so," said Altman, trying to free himself.

"It's the Marker," said Field. "It talks to us." He gave Altman a searching look. "It spoke to you, too. That makes you a believer. It's separating the sheep from the goats. Either you believe or you die."

"That's crazy," said Altman.

"Is it?" said Field. "Look how many people are dead now. Look how many are mad. Is that normal? Can you explain it any other way?"

"There are other explanations," said Altman. "There have to be."

"Like what?" asked Field. When Altman didn't answer, he

said, "Be one with the Marker, Altman. Accept its message of oneness and unity. Join with us."

Finally he let go. Altman took a step back, trying not to reveal to Field how disturbed he actually was. Mad or dead or religious—what the hell kind of choice was that?

"More and more people believe in our unitology," Field said with his same mad smile. He reached clumsily into the neck of his shirt, grasped a leather thong. He tugged it out. At the end was a crude sigil: two slivers of metal twisted together to form a representation of the Marker.

"When we are weak," said Field, "we call on this." He wrapped it in his fist and squeezed it, then closed his eyes, whispering something over and over again, a ritual chant or a prayer, soft enough that Altman couldn't quite make it out. He didn't want to make it out. He looked away from Field and saw that most of the others around them were doing the same thing, each holding something and whispering toward their clenched fists, their eyes closed. Slowly and quietly he shuffled his way free of the group and got the hell out of there.

His interactions with the researchers were radically different than they had been before. Before, there had been a separation between Markoff's inner circle and the rest of the scientists; now everybody seemed inclined to work together. There was a new sense of urgency, a sense—largely from the hallucinations (or "visions" as the believers called them)—that time was of the essence.

For the first day or two, he just listened. Researcher after researcher approached him, telling him what they'd been able to discover. Most of them had faces lit with zeal, either religious zeal or the zeal of discovery. Either way, it scared him.

As he listened, started seeing data from the tests, and began to interact directly with the Marker itself, he became convinced that he'd been right to begin with, that the Marker had a purpose that had nothing to do with the good of humanity, though what that purpose was he was still unable to say. Lying in bed at night alone, wondering where Ada was and whether she was still wrapped up in the madness of the Marker, he turned it over in his head, becoming more and more worried. All the talk of Convergence and everlasting life that had started with the hallucinations was not so much a lie as it was something related to the Marker trying to express itself in human means, manipulating the imprinted memories of loved ones and conforming to their words. But what was that something? The Marker itself? The beings that had created it? Some sort of protective mechanism? Something else entirely? And whatever it was, something was being lost in the translation: nobody was sure what the Marker wanted from them. Becoming more and more nervous, he opened a vidlink to Stevens.

Despite the late hour, Stevens did not look like he'd been woken up. His voice when he spoke was as mellifluous as always.

"Altman," he said, not a hint of surprise in his voice. "What can I do for you?"

"You're awake?"

"Don't sleep much these days," said Stevens. "Too busy talking to the dead."

"I have something I need to talk over," he said. "It's about the Marker, about the messages it seems to be sending through hallucinations. I don't know who else to ask."

"Go ahead," said Stevens. "I've been thinking about it myself."

"I wonder about its purpose. I don't know that we should trust it."

"Go on."

"I think we read what the Marker says positively because we are prone to believe in a life beyond this one and because it speaks to us through voices of people we are close to."

"Fair enough," said Stevens. "Clearly it wants us to think of it in a positive light."

"But if you listen closely to what the hallucinations are saying and try to think of them as being the words of an alien presence channeled through human memories, and try to forget that you're being told them by someone you know and love, there's another interpretation for Convergence, for becoming one."

"Yes," said Stevens.

"What if Convergence means not eternal life or transcendence, but radical subordination? What if it means unity more literally, the destruction of the individual to a larger communal self?"

"Like the way some insect colonies function," said Stevens. "The individuals all subject to the will of the colony, a kind of hive mind in control of all the individuals."

"Yes," said Altman. "Or maybe even more extreme. What if it's being literal? What if it means somehow to transform us from many creatures into one?"

"That doesn't sound feasible," said Stevens.

"This is new territory," said Altman. "We hardly know what's feasible and what's not. In any case, it's dangerous. We may not be heading for utopia but instead toward destruction."

"Which raises an important question," said Stevens quietly.

"What's that?"

"Whatever we're looking for from the Marker, whether we see it as something to be mined for power or something to be worshipped or an object of scientific inquiry, are we using the Marker or is the Marker using us?" For the first time, Stevens's smooth exterior broke, and Altman saw something like a glimmer of anxiety burst through. He covered his eyes with his hand. When, after a moment, he moved his hand away, the smooth exterior had returned.

"One other thing," said Stevens. "The dead talk to some about unity, others about a ticking clock. What does this refer to? How does it relate to Convergence? Is the Marker awakening now to punish us for not making the most of our time here?"

"I don't know," said Altman. "It may be something less threatening, but I think it might be more. The dead act as though we have been facing a deadline. A deadline that we have evidently crossed. Convergence is talked about as starting over, but I don't know that it's likely to be a fresh start for us. Maybe it'll just be a fresh start for the Marker, or whatever controls it. Maybe Convergence means wiping us out to start some new cycle, some new phase of whatever strange process we seem to be a part of."

"If you're right," said Stevens, "the human race is on the brink of extinction. Either way, this Convergence represents the end of life as we know it."

"Yes," said Altman.

"So what do we do?"

"It should be stopped," Altman said. "But I don't know how. Now that it's active, I don't think it would help to simply sink the Marker again. We have to satisfy it enough to make it fall silent and leave us alone for a while, but not enough to move completely forward into Convergence. I don't know what else to do but try to keep understanding what it's saying to us before it's too late. Maybe once we understand what it's saying, we can figure out how to talk to it."

"But you may be wrong," said Stevens. "The Marker may actually be promising us eternal life."

Altman nodded. "I may be wrong," he said. "But I don't think I am. You told me yourself: suicides are up, violent crimes are up. Some people's headaches are so bad that they try to stop them by banging their heads against the wall until it cracks open. All the infirmary beds are filled and there are still people screaming and with nowhere to go. Once respectable scientists are painting their walls with their own shit. Does that sound like eternal life to you?"

Stevens sighed. "It could be just an intermediate stage. Do you know Pascal's wager?" he asked.

"Who's what?" asked Altman.

"Blaise Pascal," said Stevens. "Seventeenth-century philosopher. Mostly forgotten now, though one of the first ships destroyed in the moon skirmishes was named after him. His wager argues that since the existence of God cannot be determined through reason, an individual should live as if He did exist since he has very little to lose if God does not exist and everything to gain if He does."

"What does that have to do with—"

"I'm getting to that," said Stevens. "I can either believe what you're telling me or I can believe that the Marker has our best interest at heart. If I believe what you're telling me, then that means that most likely humanity is a lost cause anyway and I'll spend my final days beating my head out over a problem that can't be solved. If I believe the Marker has our best interest at heart, then I move forward full of hope, toward my own salvation."

"Oh my God, you've become a true believer," said Altman.

"Why else do you think I convinced Markoff t3o have you released? I have to wish you the best of luck," said Stevens. "If you're right and I'm wrong, I hope you can figure it out and save all of us. If you're wrong and I'm right, then I have everything to gain by believing."

"That's not how belief works," said Altman. "You can't just decide to believe."

"Apparently, *you* can't," said Stevens. "But I can. I hope you're wrong." Altman watched him reach out and cut the link.

Stevens's attitude, Altman realized, was likely be shared by many, though very few would be as rational-sounding or as coherent in the way they managed to deliberately shut their eyes to the danger. By raising it with his colleagues, he risked their resentment and, even, their attacks. Even if they believed him, it might well mean that panic and fear and depression might compromise their ability to work.

No, he was going to have to make a little gambit of his own: Altman's wager. He'd wager that he could pretend to proceed as if he agreed, pretend to move forward with fulfilling the Marker's will, and then at the last minute, once he'd learned enough to defeat it, turn things around. If he won, then life would probably continue on roughly as it was. If he lost, then he'd probably be dead, and maybe everyone else would be as well.

Not good odds, but they were the only odds he had.

It was Showalter who made the initial breakthrough by suggesting a possible function for the Marker. The symbols, he theorized, were mathematical codes that symbolized DNA. The Marker itself was a representation of a DNA sequence.

The scientists set about decoding the sequence. Another scientist, a radio astronomist named Grote Guthe, made the next breakthrough, suggesting that the Marker's signal could be read as a transmission of a sequence of genetic code. Field made sure that Altman heard about both.

Showalter's team sequenced the Marker itself, and came up with a genetic profile that was, so he told Altman, remarkably similar to that of humans.

"So something like humans?" said Altman.

"Maybe," said Showalter. "Maybe even something exactly like humans. I think that the Marker has the DNA code for our ancestors."

"So it records our genetic code," said Altman. "So what?"

"Not just records," said Showalter. "We think the pulse transmits it as well, deliberately changing genetic structure slightly in existing human organisms. It may, in fact, have been the beginning of human life."

Altman didn't know what to say. It was staggering to think that human life had neither evolved naturally nor been a gift from God but was, instead, based on the Marker.

"But why would it be rebroadcasting our genetic code?" asked Altman. "We've already evolved. What would be the point of that?"

"Have you talked to Grote Guthe?" asked Showalter. "He's hit a snag. For God's sake, go talk to Grote."

And so he did. The German scientist was not what he expected he would be; he was small and very thin, and had a skin condition that had left him hairless. He looked harmless, almost helpless. He seemed to be expecting Altman.

"Yes," he said, "Herr Doktor Field has told me about you. You are one of us, yes?" Altman neither nodded nor shook his head, but Guthe went on. "You want to know about the pulse," he said. "Whether my team has decoded the pulse. Perhaps Herr Doktor Shovalter has said something, yes?"

"Yes," said Altman.

"We have decoded the pulse, perhaps. But we have struck a complication."

"What's the complication?"

"My team has decoded the signal and we think it is decoded correctly. We understand it to be a code and we understand what that code is. Herr Doktor Shovalter thinks he has decoded the signal and he, too, thinks it is decoded correctly. The complication is that we have different answers. For him it is a code that is a step upon the sequence to human life. For me it is something else entirely, not correlatable to a known species. I am making a synthetic version of mine now, to get a closer look at it."

"Perhaps one of you is wrong," said Altman.

"Perhaps," said Guthe. "Or perhaps the pulse signal is transmitting a different code than is recorded on the Marker." He leaned forward and gave Altman a steady look. "I must say something to you," he said. "I am a believer, you must not doubt my belief. But I am also a scientist. I have looked carefully at Herr Doktor Shovalter's calculations and I have looked carefully at my own. Our calculations are correct. If the Marker was the beginning of human life, then it has no need to be broadcasting this now. And yet it is communicating a pulse, one with an unfamiliar genetic code. Perhaps it is communicating a pulse, but perhaps it is a flawed pulse with a flawed genetic code. Perhaps this Marker has begun a process of deterioration."

"The Convergence," said Altman.

"But maybe it has simply become confused," said Guthe. "We must try to understand it. We must work with it."

"But what if this is what it's meant to do?" said Altman.

Guthe groped his necklace out of his shirt, clutched the icon of the Marker in his fist. "No, it cannot intend this," he insisted. "The Marker is here for us. It has simply become confused." And then he looked at Altman for guidance.

Altman just nodded, and left without another word. *I'm surrounded by madmen,* he couldn't help but think. *Fanatics.*

But later that night, he began to have doubts. What if Guthe was right? What if the Marker *was* just broken? Maybe they could fix the Marker by returning the core sample to its rightful position.

That's ridiculous, he thought. *It was transmitting its signal before the core sample was taken.*

He lay in bed staring at the ceiling until another idea came to him. *But maybe it was transmitting a different signal then, the correct signal.*

He couldn't sleep until he at least tried.

He woke up Showalter, explained what he wanted to do.

"Already been tried," said Showalter. "Doesn't make a difference."

"But maybe—"

"The missing piece isn't crucial," Showalter explained. "In fact, no single piece is crucial. The Marker is a complex but internally replicated structure in the same way, for instance, that the pattern of a nautilus replicates even as it tightens. Even if parts of it are broken or damaged, it still works. Probably the only way to stop it from working would be to pulverize it."

Depressed, Altman went back to bed. Chalk one up for the Marker. Not damaged, or at least not damaged in a way they could understand. Which meant it must be acting the way it was for other reasons. Either it was working for their own good or for their destruction.

55

Herr Doktor Guthe had been up for hours. With the help of his team, he'd sequenced the synthetic strand and then had it biotically assembled by a nanosystem. Then he'd meticulously gone over the results to make sure it was right. It was rough, hardly the kind of job that he would be proud of, but it was accurate. If he could get it to replicate, he'd be able to make some extrapolations about the original strand, about the purpose of the mutation, and this might in turn tell him if the Marker was broken or if it was working intentionally.

His team had stuck with him around the clock until the moment when they'd injected the sequence within a proxy nucleus into four dozen embryonic sheep cells, followed by chemical encouragement to get them to divide. After that, there was nothing to do but wait. Either it would work or it would not. For the first time in several hours, he looked around at his team, saw that they were haggard and frazzled by turns, some of them barely standing. So he sent them to bed.

Herr Doktor Guthe had intended to go to bed himself. Only he wasn't tired. In fact, he couldn't remember the last time he'd been tired. He hadn't slept for days.

And so he had stayed on, alone, in the laboratory. He waited, motionless, sitting on his stool. He felt as though he had entered a completely different state of mind, one that did not need sleep. He expected never to have to sleep again. This, he was sure, was due to the Marker.

Upon thinking the word, he pulled the necklace out of his shirt and clutched the icon in his fist. Would she come? If he thought hard enough, would she come?

And then she stepped out of the wall and toward him. At first she was no more than a blur, but as he squeezed the charm and concentrated, she began to change. The shadowy air around her was cut away and she became herself—tall, thin, a perfect face save for one small scar just above her left cheekbone.

I missed you, she said.

"I missed you, too," he said.

She smiled, and a little blood dripped out of her mouth, but not too much. He tried to ignore it. Except for the blood, he loved the way she smiled.

What are you doing? she asked.

"An experiment," he said. "I'm trying to understand the thing that brought you back to life."

How flattering, she said. *But I wish you wouldn't.*

"I wish I would have spoken to you then," he said. "Back when you were alive. I watched you, you know. I followed you everywhere."

I know, she said.

"And then you died and I thought I had missed my chance. But now you are here again."

I'm just a projection of your mind, she said. *You know that. You told me that yourself. You know that I'm a construct made from your memories.*

"I know," he said. "But you seem so real."

She smiled again, wider this time, and blood began to slip down her cheek and to her chin. He had found her like that, twenty years before. He hadn't even known her name. Then, as now, he was unsure of what had happened to her. Then, she was as good as dead when he found her. Now she kept dying but kept being brought back to life again.

You musn't . . ., she started, and then she slowly faded and was gone. He sighed. He never got much further with the message the Marker sent, never heard as much of it as his colleagues had. He figured it was because his desire to see the girl was too strong, too intense.

He took a look in the cooker, was surprised to see that all forty cells in all forty receptacles had multiplied. That was unprecedented. Also unprecedented was the speed with which they multiplied—he had never seen anything like it. It had been only a few hours, and already the sample was visible to the naked eye.

He stayed for the next hour watching them until each of the receptacles was teeming with a pale pink substance like nothing so much as biological tissue. Should he take a closer look? Why not: there were plenty of samples. What would it hurt to look at just one?

He opened a receptacle, ran a mild electric charge through it. The pinkish substance withdrew, as if it felt it. Maybe it did.

He upturned the receptacle, poured it onto the table. The substance lay there, undulating slightly. Carefully, he cut it in half with a scalpel. He watched an empty furrow appear between the two halves, then watched the substance run back together again into a single sheet, leaving no visible line or scar. *Marvelous,* he thought.

He was still experimenting with it when his grandmother's face appeared, hovering just over the counter. Startled, he jumped.

Sure, he loved his grandmother, but not nearly as much as he loved the girl. Or maybe it was just different: he had known the girl for only a moment, and so his love for her was pure and unadulterated. His feelings toward his grandmother were much more complex. After his parents died, she had taken him in. She had treated him all right, but she was old and grumpy, and sometimes she did things that he had a hard time understanding. And then one day, when he was a little older, she had simply disappeared. Even then he basically understood that something must have happened to her, something that she couldn't help, that perhaps she had even been killed. But part of him had a hard time not resenting her for not coming back.

"What do you want?" he asked in German.

Is that any way to treat your grandmother? she said. She was speaking in a heavily accented English, even though he knew that if she had been real, she would be screeching in German.

"I'm sorry," he said. "You've come, I imagine, because there was something the girl was unable to express. You know I love you."

That's more like it, she said, and held out to him a cellophone-wrapped sweet. She had always been doing that when she was alive. He tried to take it, but his hand met empty air.

It's time, she said. *You've learned too much. It's time.*

Time for what? He hadn't felt whole since he lost his grandmother. And now she was here again, but not here at the same time. He could see her and hear her but not touch her or smell her. His whole life had been like that, a life of loss, first his parents gone and then his grandmother. In the end, all that was left was just his laboratory, the only thing he could count on. His laboratory had never let him down.

Are you listening to me? she asked, snapping her fingers. *Do you understand what I'm saying? You must stop this research at once!*

Stop his research? He felt a rage rising in him. She had never understood what he was trying to do, so why should it surprise him that she didn't understand him now? "But I'm doing important work," he said. "I'm making discoveries beyond human imagination."

What you are doing is dangerous, she said. *Trust me, child. I say this for your own good. The Marker will destroy you. You must stop before it is too late.*

His eyes were stinging with tears. Stop his work? What else did he have? *It's not really her,* he told himself. The Marker has just borrowed her image and voice. Why couldn't it have stayed with being the girl? He had loved her but never really had her, so he couldn't miss her in the same way that he missed his grandmother. And now it was trying to manipulate him, trying to use his grandmother to get him to stop.

"Please, go away," he said, trying not to look at her. "It's too much."

Too much? she was saying. Her voice was a little shrill now, grating on his nerves. *I need you to listen to me, Grote. This is very important.*

He groaned. He couldn't listen; he couldn't bear it. He covered his ears, but somehow he could still hear her anyway. He shook his head back and forth and started to sing as loudly as he could. He could still hear her, could still tell she was saying words, but couldn't hear what they were exactly. But she just stood there, still talking, refusing to go away.

He closed his eyes, her voice still humming on. What could he do? He was so tired, he just needed a rest. How could he drive her away?

Confusedly, he told himself she was a mental construct: his mental construct. If he simply stopped thinking, he could drive her away. All he'd have to do was knock himself out and he'd be all right.

There was a syringe in the drawer, a fresh needle. He had to uncover his ears to reach for it, and suddenly her words were spilling louder through his head. *No, Grote!* she yelled at him. *Stop this foolishness right now! You haven't understood at all. You're going to do yourself harm.*

He shuddered. He needed a sedative. There it was, already on the table.

Grote! she said. *Can't you see? This is what the Marker wants! You are not thinking straight. Stop and listen!*

"Leave me alone," he mumbled.

He affixed the needle and sucked the fluid up and in. It was thicker than he thought, hard to get into the needle. Still listening to his grandmother's yammering, he tied his arm off and flicked the vein, then held the needle to it.

Grote, why are you doing this? she asked.

"I just need to sleep," he said, and plunged the needle in. "Just a few hours' sleep."

It burned going in, and then his arm began to tingle. His grandmother gave him her awful, heartbroken stare.

You think that is a sedative? she said. She shook her head and drew back, a look of horror on her face. *That is not what it is. You have hastened the Convergence. You must hurry to the Marker,* she said. *Surrounding the Marker is a dead space that will stop this thing in you from progressing. Go there and show the others what has happened to you and warn them. You must convince them to leave the Marker alone. You must try to stop the Convergence before it is too late. It is urgent that you convince them, Grote. Very, very urgent.* And then slowly she faded away into nothingness.

He sat there for a moment, relieved, before realizing that she wasn't saying it just to needle him; she was telling the truth. *Oh, God,* he thought, staring down at the empty receptacle, the empty syringe, realizing what he'd just injected. He looked at his arm, the strange swelling in the vein, the painful undulating movement that was not his own now deep within his arm.

He reached out and triggered the alarm, but then found he couldn't sit still. Something was wrong. Something was already starting to change. His arm was tingling, had gone numb, and the undulating movement was larger now, had spread. He had to get out, had to see the Marker, had to talk to it. The Marker would save him, his grandmother had said.

He rushed out and down the passage, took the spiral down. The alarm was howling, people starting to appear, confused. He stumbled through two laboratories he had a passcard for, then through a transparent corridor with the move and shift of the water playing on its walls.

There, at the end, was the door to the Marker chamber, two guards standing in front of it.

"Let me in," he said.

"Sorry, Professor Guthe," said one of them. "There's an alert. Can't you hear it?"

The other said, in a strange voice, "What's wrong with your arm?"

"I sounded the alert. That's why I have to get in. The arm," he babbled. "I need to talk to it about the arm."

"Need to talk to what?" said the first guard suspiciously. Both guards had their weapons raised.

"The Marker, you idiot!" he said. "I need it to tell me what is going to happen to me!"

The two guards exchanged looks. One of them began talking into the com unit very quickly; the other now actively pointed the gun at him.

"Now, Professor," he said. "Calm down. There's nothing to worry about."

"No," he said, "you don't understand."

There were other people in the hall now, people behind him, watching, puzzled.

"All I want is to see it," he pleaded to them.

"What's wrong with his arm?" someone behind him asked.

The arm was twisted now, his hand facing backward as if it had been cut off and flipped over, then reconnected. It was not just in his arm now, but in his shoulder and chest, too, everything changing.

He tried to speak, and it came out as a deep retching sound. The alarms were still going off. He took a step forward, and now the guard was shouting. He held his arm out in front of him and they shrank back, moving slowly out of the way. *I'll shoot! I'll shoot!* one was yelling, but he didn't shoot. Guthe was at the door now, swiping his card. A bullet thudded into his leg, but it didn't matter, he hardly felt it. And then the door opened and he fell in.

The chamber was empty except for him and the Marker. He moved toward it, his injured leg s3uddenly giving out underneath him. He pulled himself along on his knees until he could touch it.

Whatever was happening in his arm seemed to have stopped. It wasn't getting better, but it wasn't getting worse. The Marker was helping. The Marker was stopping it. He breathed a sigh of relief, then winced from the stabbing pain in his leg.

He would stay here, protected by the Marker. Once he figured out what had happened, he could put his team to work helping him to get better. If worse came to worst, he would have the arm amputated.

The alarm stopped and he found he could think better. He would have someone move his laboratory down here and would continue his work. He moved his leg, winced from the pain. Out of the corner of his eye, he saw the door to one side opening. He turned, recognized one of the leaders, the man who ran the guards, the one with the brutal face. What was his name again? Ah, yes, Krax. He was just the one to help move his lab. And he had brought others with him, lots of men, healthy strapping lads. They could all help.

He was just opening his mouth to speak when Krax lifted a pistol and shot him through the forehead.

. . .

"That wasn't necessary," said Markoff from behind him.

"Funny," said Krax. "You never really struck me as the squeamish type."

"I'm not," Markoff said. "But his condition was worth investigating while he was still alive."

Krax shrugged.

Markoff gave him a cool look. "Give them the body to examine. And watch your step," he said. "Don't start assuming you're not expendable. You're more expendable now than you were ten minutes ago." He turned on his heel and left.

Krax watched him go, feeling at once a little contemptuous and a little scared, and then started out the door himself.

"Take the body," he said to the guards. "Carry it to one of the labs and leave it there." He looked at the crowd of researchers. "Which of you have dissection experience?" he asked. Nearly all of them raised their hands. He singled out three of them at random. "Take a closer look at it and tell me what was happening to him." And then he pushed through the already dispersing crowd and left.

Guthe's body started changing shortly after the guards bundled it onto a stretcher and carried it away, but as it was hidden beneath a sheet, they didn't notice. There were strange sounds coming from it, popping and crackling sounds, which they just took for the sounds of strain in the stretcher or the scuffling of their boots in the passageway.

They took it to one of the labs and slid it onto the table, the sheet still on top of it. The three dissectors had followed them at a distance, whispering, holding on to their icons. They filed into the room as the guards left.

"We should contact Field," the first of them said. "He'll want to know."

One of the others nodded. "I'll contact him," he said, and activated the room's comlink.

A strange, wet sound came from under the sheet, followed by a snap, like a bone breaking. The sheet fluttered.

"What's that?" asked one.

"Just the body settling," claimed another.

"It didn't sound that way to me," said the first.

"Hello, Field?" said the third into the comlink. Field's tired face appeared on the holovid.

"Hideki," he said. "Why are you calling me so late? What's wrong?"

Another crack came from the sheet, even louder this time. The shape underneath it had changed noticeably.

"What was that?" asked Field.

"Just a minute," said Hideki.

"That's more than a body settling," said one of the others.

"You're right," said the third.

Slowly, they moved forward. One of them reached out, tugged the sheet off, let it fall to the floor.

What lay beneath hardly looked human anymore. The head was still there, but was now embedded in a curtain of flesh, some deformation of what had once been the shoulders. It was animate, moving slightly, what was left of its chest heaving up and down with rapid movements. The legs had atrophied and the arms had lengthened. The body had flatted and ribs and skin seemed to have spread out to create a winglike structure between the wrist and what was left of the ankle, like the body of a manta ray. It was an unhealthy, morbid color. The eyes were sunken in and had a strange gleam to them.

"Professor Field, are you seeing this?" asked Hideki.

"What is it?" said Field.

"Oh my God," said one of the other two.

There was another cracking noise, and the body changed further, what was left of the face receding, becoming lost except for the eyes and the mouth, which was now little more than a hole. It split open at the end, dissolving there into a mass of tentacles or antennae now, almost insectoid. The hands and feet shriveled, and hooks of bone sprouted in their place. It made a shrieking sound and began to struggle.

Field shouted at them to run. The alarm started to sound again. Professor Hideki Ishimura fled, his only thought being to get as far away as quickly as possible.

The other two researchers were paralyzed with fear. "Run!" Field kept yelling at them. "Run!" But they didn't move. The creature flipped itself over. It sat there, draped over the edge of the table, wheezing slightly, body bobbing up and down.

One of the scientists gave a little cry and rushed for the door. The creature leapt, wrapping itself around his shoulders and face, pressing itself wetly against his face. He was screaming, and then the scream was suddenly stifled. Through the vid feed, Field watched as a strange proboscis suddenly sprouted from it with a tearing sound and stabbed through the researcher's eye and deep into his skull. It pulsed, pumping something in.

The other slid into the corner and, moaning, clenched his eyes shut. "Run!" Field screamed again, but he didn't pay any attention.

The first researcher had collapsed in a heap, the creature retracting its proboscis and slowly moving off him. A minute later, maybe even just seconds later, he started to change, his body beginning to shake. As Field watched, his skin changed to a deep lavender, almost purple. There was a wet tearing sound, and blades of bone sprouted from his shoulders, his upper arms suddenly fading into his chest, his forearms and flexing fingers now seeming to sprout from his stomach wall. His hair fell away, his eyes growing hollow, his ears oozing down his face to join with his neck.

Slowly it stood and stumbled toward the lab door.

The last scientist was still crouched in the corner, whimpering slightly. The creature that had been Guthe, clumsy on the floor now, dragged itself awkwardly toward him, and then leapt. Field cut the feed so as not to have to listen to the screams.

57

He was dreaming. He was walking down an empty beach, holding Ada's hand.

Michael? she asked.

"Yes?" he said.

Do you love me?

He didn't know how to answer, so didn't. He loved Ada; he was sure of that. But he didn't understand how she had changed. How they had moved apart.

I need you to do something for me, she said.

"What?" he said.

I want to have a baby, she said.

"Are you serious?" he asked.

She nodded. *That's what I need,* she said. *It'll bring us closer together.*

And then in the dream there began a faraway insistent sound. At first he hardly noticed it, but it grew louder and louder. Ada was still speaking, almost as if she didn't hear it, but he could no longer hear what she was saying. And then both she and the beach around them began to be eaten away by darkness, slowly coming unraveled, and he woke up.

The sound was still going. Someone had triggered the alarm again. He got out of bed, got quickly dressed, and went out into the hall. It was deserted. In the room behind him, he heard the comlink go live.

"Altman?" it said. "Altman, this is Field. Are you there?"

He went back, switched the visual on. "I'm here," he said.

"Something's gone wrong," Field said. His face was bone white. "I saw it, but can't hardly believe what I saw. It's horrible, absolutely horrible. Get to safety, Altman, as quick as you can."

"Calm down, Field," said Altman. "Tell me what you're talking about."

"It sprouted swords," said Field. "Just had them sprout out of its back like—"

Somewhere in the background came a scream. Field whirled around, and Altman saw he was holding a gun. The vid clicked off.

Down the hall he heard screams. He poked his head out, saw a researcher running toward him.

"What's wrong?" Altman asked. "Wait a minute. Stop!"

But the man kept running. "They're everywhere!" he called back over his shoulder. "You shoot them and they still keep coming at you." And then he was around the corner and gone.

I'm still asleep, Altman thought. He closed his eyes and shook his head, and then opened his eyes again. No, it was still as it had been, more screams and now even the sound of gunfire.

He rushed back into the room and looked around for a weapon. Nothing there. He went out again and down the hall in the direction the man had run, walking very quickly. Rounding a corner, he saw the corridor barricaded by a laboratory table turned on its side. He headed for it, and shots rang out, thunking into the wall beside his face.

"Don't shoot!" he cried, raising his hands above his head. "It's me, Altman."

A chorus of shouts, and the firing stopped. Someone from behind the table waved to him, and he moved to the table and pulled himself over it, down among them.

"Altman," said Showalter. "I'm glad they didn't get you."

"Get me?" said Altman. "What's going on?"

"I don't exactly know," said Showalter, his eyes darting nervously from side to side. "I've only seen one of them, but I wish I hadn't. It was monstrous. It had bone scythes instead of arms and legs and it scuttled like a spider. Its head just hung there, swinging, staring down at the floor, but it seemed to see us anyway. I don't know who it used to be, but you could tell from the remnants of clothing that it used to be someone, that it used to be human. It sure as hell isn't human now. Something's gone horribly wrong."

"I gathered that," said Altman. He looked around. One of the other men was someone he vaguely recognized. White, he thought his name was. The third he didn't know.

"Here," said Showalter, and handed him a gun. "Got this off a guard who had his head torn off. Don't know that it'll help much. When you shoot them, they don't seem to die. They just keep coming."

Altman took the weapon. "How many people left alive?" he asked.

Showalter shrugged. "How do I know? The four of us counting you," he said. "Probably a few guards. There's a few others running around."

"Field vided me not long ago, so he's still alive," said Altman. "It must have started down here. Maybe it hasn't made it to the top part of the facility yet, to the part above water."

"Maybe not," said Showalter.

"Vid Field," said Altman. "Tell him to get up there and seal the lock, wait for us on the other side. We'll fight our way up and once we're there, he can let us through."

Showalter passed the order along to one of the other two men with him, someone called Peter Fert, who took out his holopod and got to work.

From the far end of the hall came an eerie bellow and then something shuffled around the corner. It stood roughly as tall as a man, but the arms it had looked like the arms of a child. They protruded from its stomach. From its shoulders had sprouted two jointed scythes of bone, like the wings of a featherless bird. Its skin was mottled and seeping, disgusting to look at, and it smelled faintly of rotting meat. It was humanoid, but Altman wouldn't have guessed it had once been human if the tattered uniform of a guard weren't still clinging to its torso.

"Holy shit," whispered Altman.

"Keep trying to contact Field, Fert," said Showalter, keeping his voice low. "We'll hold it off. Oh, and if you can help it, men, try not to send too many bullets into the walls of the passage. Last thing we want is to be flooded out."

White, Altman saw, was holding his gun so tight that his knuckles were white.

The thing shuffled slowly in their direction and then stopped dead. It made a grunting sound and then, with a cry, rushed at them.

"Fire!" screamed Showalter.

All three of them fired at once. The shots slowed it a little, but didn't seem to permanently harm it. It just kept coming. Altman aimed carefully for the head and fired three times quickly. At least two of the shots connected—he saw the bursts of flesh and blood as they went in—but the creature continued forward unfazed.

And then it was on them, looming over the barrier. They crouched down and kept firing, trying to keep it at a distance, but with remarkable ease it leaned in through the hail of bullets and plucked up White.

The man screamed and tried to run. The creature's scythes were gouging into White's back, which had already grown bloody. It pulled him close like a lover and leaned in to bite his neck.

It was terrible to watch, White flopping like a fish out of water, screaming in a way Altman had heard only once before, when a rabbit had been shot in the head but lived long enough to realize it was desperately hurt. The creature was making a grotesque mumbling sound, drooling as well as biting, and shaking its head so bits of flesh and gore spattered about.

Altman's first impulse was to run. The only reason he didn't was because of a fleeting selfish thought. *If I don't kill it*, he thought, *I'll be next*.

He moved as close as he could and put the gun's barrel up against the creature's neck and rattled off four shots. It was enough, at point-blank range, to tear the thing's head mostly off, to get its teeth away from White's neck. But even without the head, the body kept moving.

"Don't these things ever die?" shouted Altman.

Showalter just grunted. He was imitating what Altman had

done, holding the pistol at the joint of the scythe. He pulled the trigger and fired and the blast tore it off.

"That's it!" said Altman. "Maim it!" He brought his gun low and shot three times, until the thing's leg collapsed and it tilted to one side and went down, taking White with it. Altman vaulted the barrier and was on top of it. He fired and stomped on its remaining limbs, kept stomping until it was in enough pieces that he didn't think it could do any damage. Even then, he wasn't sure it was dead. He was only sure that it was incapacitated enough that it couldn't hurt him.

He stepped back, stunned. His shoes and legs were slick with blood, blood spattered on his chest and arms, too. White, he saw was still alive, but in shock, his back a bloody mass. Altman knelt down beside him and slapped his face, tried to get him to pay attention. The man's eyes flicked slightly and then clouded over. He was dead.

"Is he all right?" asked Showalter.

Altman opened his mouth and gave him artificial respiration for a moment, trying to breathe him back to life, tasting the dead man's blood on his lips.

Showalter touched his shoulder.

"Leave him," he said.

He looked up and shook his head. He was just turning back toward the mouth when he heard a crack, saw White's torso convulse.

He pushed away from it and scrambled back. The body seemed to be going through a fit, shaking and contorting. And then it began to change.

Altman watched, horrified, trying to keep his panic under control. "What the hell is going on?" he said.

"He's changing," said Showalter. "He's one of them now."

"Let's get the fuck out of here," said Altman.

"I'm afraid there's one more thing we have to do," said Showalter.

"What's that?" asked Altman.

"We need to take steps to make sure he doesn't come after us."

Altman nodded, his lips grim. "You mean . . ." he said.

"We're going to have to dismember him."

The two of them were standing together, breathing heavily, staring down at blood and gore on the floor, the pieces of the creature, and of the partially transformed White. *I'll never be the same,* thought Altman, and he could tell by the way Showalter dodged his gaze that he felt similarly. He'd been having nightmares before, but he had material for an entirely new set of them now.

"I got through to Field," said Peter Fert. "He says as far as he can determine, the creatures are still all in the lower levels. He'll try to get to the airlock and shut it, and then wait for us to contact him."

"If we're going to make it, we'll need something other than guns," said Altman. "Bullets don't do enough. They barely even slow the things down."

"What do you have in mind?" asked Showalter.

"We raid the labs and janitorial closets as we go," said Altman. "See what we can find. Anything that'll cut off a limb or get partway there."

They found, in the first lab they came to, a handheld plasma cutter, which, by unscrewing the guard, could be made into a close-combat weapon. Showalter recalibrated a laser pistol taken off a dead guard using the tools of the next lab to give it a wider beam, something with a little slicing power. Peter Fert dug up a laser scalpel, modified it to cut through an object as thick as a wrist.

"Probably won't stop them," said Altman.

"First thing I'm worried about is cutting through their scythes," said Fert. "If I can get that far, I'll be lucky."

"All right," said Altman. "What do we have to lose? Let's go."

58

"You've got two seconds to explain what in the living hell is going on, Krax," said Markoff. He was gesturing to a series of open holovids strung over the console that showed the floating compound in chaos. Here, a table was overturned, researchers and guards alike crouched behind it. There, a man was being skewered by a strange creature that looked like a cross between a spider and the whirling blades of death. Another showed a scene of carnage, bits and pieces of bodies strewn all up and down the hallway. In another, a group of humanoid creatures lurched back and forth, at a loss.

Krax looked panicked. He was sweating, his eyes darting left and right. "We're being attacked. Monsters of some sort. I don't know who or what."

"What the fuck are they, and how did they get on board?"

"I don't have any idea," said Krax. "I've never seen anything like them."

"They look familiar," said Stevens. "Haven't you noticed?"

"Familiar?" said Markoff, and squinted at one of the vids. "Yes," he said, nodding. "I see what you mean."

"That one there," said Stevens, "that used to be Molina. You can tell by what's left of the face. They're all wearing bits of clothing, too, scraps of it."

"They used to be human?" asked Krax.

Stevens nodded. "But they certainly aren't now."

"What's behind it?" asked Markoff.

"Right now I'm debriefing Hideki Ishimura, one of our astrophysicists," said Krax. "He was the first one to witness one of them—the first one still alive, anyway. But he's scared half to death—I'm not getting much out of him. He keeps saying Guthe's name, though, over and over again. I thought he was babbling, but if they come from humans maybe Guthe was the first."

"Hurried along, no doubt, by you shooting him in the head," said Markoff. "Where's this Ishimura? I want to talk to him."

"He's right here, ready to be evacuated. We have to get out of here, sir."

"I don't like to run from a fight," said Markoff.

"You're not dealing with anything human," said Krax. "You shoot one of these things two or three times in the head and they keep coming. You tear its head clean off and it keeps coming."

"That's impossible," said Markoff.

Krax shook his head. "How can you fight that?"

"So a tactical retreat," said Markoff. "We'll get out and then regroup. I suppose there are often setbacks like this on the way to major discoveries."

"This is not a setback, sir," said Krax. "This is a disaster."

Markoff gave him a hard stare. "How many men all told? One hundred? Two? Even with all or almost all transformed into those hideous creatures, it's not much in the grand scheme of things. Just a setback. We'll be back in operation before you know it."

"Are you kidding?"

"Let's take advantage of all these cameras set up all through the facility," said Markoff. "Set them up to transmit to the escape boat. No reason we can't watch and learn. It should be very instructive."

"You can't possibly be thinking—"

"The Marker exists," said Markoff. "Either we make something of it or someone else does. The losses we've had and will have are acceptable losses."

"I suggest we leave, sir," said Krax, voice strained.

"You've already made yourself clear, Mr. Krax," Markoff said. "Stevens and I will prepare to evacuate. I'm still considering what to do with you."

"You're not thinking of leaving me, are you?"

"Indeed I am. As I told you before, you're far from expendable, Mr. Krax."

"Craig," said Stevens in his soft, pleasant voice. "There's no point in leaving Krax here. He'll be much more of a help to us alive than dead. You'll not only be punishing him but punishing us as well."

Markoff hesitated a moment. "Always the sensible one," he said. "Have you at least got a clear escape route prepared for us, Krax?"

"I do," said Krax. "We're ahead of the tide. If we leave now, we can avoid it."

"All right," Markoff assented. "Lead the way."

59

"What about Markoff?" asked Altman.

"What about him?" asked Showalter.

"What's he think about all this?"

"I don't know," said Showalter. "Been trying to contact him off and on for quite a while. Nothing doing. Dead maybe?"

"I'd be surprised," said Altman.

They were traveling through a sequence of laboratories, moving first into the control station and then, through the safety door, into the lab itself. They had seen a few more of the creatures but had succeeded in dodging all but two of them, which they'd managed to carve up without losses. The first lab had been normal, nothing to worry about, but as soon as he opened the door to this one, Altman knew something was different. Something was *off*.

And then he saw it. Growing out of one of the air ducts and spilling onto the floor was a strange mass of tissue. It had spread along the floor itself, had seemingly become a part of it.

He gestured at it with his cutter.

"It's starting to get around," he said. "Spreading through the vents."

A few seconds later, the lights flickered and went out, leaving only the emergency lighting on, the room now cast in thick shadow.

"They're getting to the power grid now," said Showalter. "We'd better hurry."

They were almost to the door to the next lab when they heard a scuttling in the vents above them. The grille just above them was kicked out, and something fell down onto the deck, just missing them.

It was formless and pulsing, a kind of mound that at times stretched flat and looked like little more than a puddle. It slid slowly across the deck. As it crossed the floor, it left a sizzling stain inflicted on the deck itself. Anything it touched was either sucked in and disappeared or was stripped to bare metal. In the slow roll of it, Altman glimpsed from time to time a human skull, stripped to bone, and even once what looked like a laughing human face.

"How do you cut the limbs off something that doesn't have any limbs?" asked Fert.

It moved slowly toward them, attracted perhaps by the vibration of their voices or propelled by some other means. It wasn't aggressive; it seemed to have another purpose. As it eased them back, making them feel trapped, Altman began to wonder what it was. It stripped the deck bare, got rid of all features. Transfixed, he couldn't help but watch, thinking they were finally out of time. It destroyed everything in its wake, living or dead. And he wouldn't be surprised if, when it did, it *grew*. How big would it get? Were there any limits? Would it consume the entire world?

"We should go back," Showalter said.

Altman nodded, and they started back toward the door they had come from. Fert was just about to open it, but Altman stopped him.

"Not yet," he whispered. *"Heard something."*

He pressed his ear to the door's panel. Yes, definitely something out there, just on the other side of the door, and from the scraping and moaning sounds, he was pretty certain it wasn't human.

What now? Altman wondered, his eyes casting around the room for something to get them out. Maybe they could leap the creature and run around it. Maybe they should simply leave the room and start firing at whatever was outside, trying to incapacitate it before the creeper caught up with them and engulfed them.

And then he realized Fert was pointing and gesturing. There, just shy of the edge of the creeper, was a hydrogen tank, a torch screwed into its nozzle. Altman reached out and grabbed it, dragging it back with him.

He spun the nozzle as open as it would go, sparked the torch alight, and adjusted it to give him the longest spurt of flame possible. He dipped it down, near the floor, and sprayed the creeper.

Where the flame touched it, it caught fire, burning and bubbling black. Elsewhere the creeper withdrew from the flames, trying to get away. He moved forward, spraying it, coughing in the acrid smoke it raised. Even where it was black and burning, it didn't stop moving exactly, the burnt portions folding under into the core and disappearing. But at least it was moving in the other direction now.

"I can hold it at bay," he called back to Showalter and Fert.

"But I can't get rid of it."

Fert had just started to respond when the door crashed in. Still waving the torch, Altman glanced back over his shoulder to see Fert lopping off a scythe with his laser scalpel. Showalter was backing away, firing the laser pistol steadily, a half dozen of the shambling things coming at him with their bladelike arms. Fert was in the middle of them, surrounded on all sides, doing his best to cut his way free, but there were too many. Altman watched as one of them plunged his face into Fert's neck. Fert, screaming, tried to pry it off and finally did, knocking it back and cutting into its mouth with the laser scalpel, but another was instantly in its place. Fert was screaming. A moment later his head had been torn free, his decapitated body collapsing onto the deck.

Two were down. Another was crippled, one arm and one leg inoperative, but it still dragged itself forward, hissing. Showalter stomped on it.

That left three. Altman gave the creeper a last blast and turned, dragging the cutter out. One was just bringing its bone scythe down whistling toward Showalter's back, but the cutter caught it in time, shaving the appendage off close to the body. Another scythe tore a gash in his arm, and he almost dropped the cutter. Cursing, he managed to hold on to it and sliced the creature's legs out from under it. A laser blast flashed by his head and left the arm of the last one half disarticulated, but with a cry it sprang forward, brushing past Altman and charging at Showalter.

The latter stumbled back, his laser pistol going off and singeing the wall. Together Showalter and the creature fell, toppling backward and into the creeper.

Altman immediately fired up the torch and rushed forward, but it was too late. Showalter was engulfed and simply gone, part of the pulsating, shifting mass. Weirdly enough, it did the same thing to the creature, engulfing it just as quickly and dramatically, swallowing one of its own.

He stomped on one of the creatures that was still moving and then lay down a blast of flame along the creeper's side. It withdrew, moving back enough to allow him to sidle past and out the door.

Just me now, he thought. *Down to one.*

It was hard not to feel that there was no point going forward. It was inevitable—one of them would catch him, tear him apart.

But he kept going. He was limping now, though he wasn't exactly sure why, not sure what had happened to his leg. He'd bandaged his arm with a first aid kit from the lab, stopping every once in a while to drive the creeper back with the torch.

He'd been lucky. Creeping through the half dark of the emergency lights, he'd met five of the bladed creatures since Fert and Showalter had died, never in sets of more than two, never in a place where one could get around behind him while the other tore him up from the front. The single one had been easy, but the pairs had been harder, and he couldn't help thinking when it was all over that if the cutter had just once gone a little high or a little low one of the creatures would have sunk its maw into his neck and that would have been the end of him.

And then he saw Ada. She contacted him by holovid, a static-thick message.

"Michael," she said. "Are you there?"

"Ada," he said. "Is that you?"

"I'm here," she said. "I'm safe for now, but I don't know what they're going to do with me. If you get this, please hurry, Michael."

"Ada, where are you?" Altman said.

But she didn't seem to be listening. She reached out beneath the camera, and the image flickered and shorted out, then began again.

"Michael, are you there?" she said.

A recording, then, being rebroadcast over and over. Still, it was enough, just enough, to get him going again.

As he moved higher in the facility, he saw fewer of the creatures. Those he did see, he either hid from or killed as silently as he possibly could, trying to avoid attracting the attention of the others.

Nevertheless, he was surprised when he realized that he was one hallway shy of the airlock. Suddenly he began to believe he might make it out alive after all.

There was only one problem. He almost walked straight into a creature assembled from not just one corpse but several. It looked like a spider, but with the scythelike appendages of the other creatures serving as legs, seven of them in all. The body proper consisted of overlapped and buckled torsos awkwardly melding with one another. Two heads dangled weakly at one end, as if ready to drop off.

He hid partly behind the doorframe, furtively examining it. On its underside was a pulsing yellow and black lump, maybe a tumor of some kind.

Rush forward, start cutting, he thought. Not much of a plan, but it was all he could think of.

He stayed for a long moment hesitating and then, taking a deep breath, rushed out and at it.

It immediately turned to face him and hissed. It scuttled toward him, the tips of its bonelike appendages thunking against the tunnel's floor.

But before he'd gotten close enough to hit it with the cutter, something unsettling happened. One of the heads that had been dangling loose scrambled to the top of the body and launched itself at him. It struck him in the chest, wrapping a set of sinewy tendrils around his neck. It started to squeeze.

Holy hell, he thought. He stumbled back, trying desperately to pry it off. The spiderthing was still coming, still scuttling forward, its other head alert and on top of its body now as well. He struck the one already on him hard with the side of the cutter, again and again. It loosened just a little, enough that he could breathe, and he forced his hand in between it and his neck and tore it off.

It tried to crawl up his arm and back to his neck, but he held it tight by its writhing tendrils and didn't let go. The other head launched itself at him and he batted it down to the ground with the first head, stamping it to a pulp. The head in his hands he slammed into the wall, then cut in half with the plasma cutter.

The rest of the spiderthing was on him now. He sliced off the tip of one appendage, and it reared back on its three hind legs and struck at him with the remaining four. He managed to parry two of them successfully and dodge the third. The fourth, having just lost its tip to the plasma cutter, struck him hard but bluntly in the chest. He fell to the floor, the wind knocked out of him.

Then he was beneath it as it danced about, trying to skewer him. He cut off one leg, then another, but it didn't seem to hurt its balance. He kicked it hard and knocked it back and scrambled back himself and then, knowing it would do little good, just to buy time, he whipped out the plasma pistol and started firing.

The shots flashed off its legs or entered the flesh of the body with a hiss, but hardly seemed to slow it. It was nearly over him again, and he kicked it back with both feet this time, succeeding in turning it off balance and flipping it over.

As it struggled to right itself, he saw again the pulsing yellow and black lump. He fired at it.

The lump exploded, the blast knocking him back through the doorway, deafening him. Bits of the creature struggled about, including one whole enough to come at him. He stood, stumbled toward it, sectioned it with the plasma cutter.

The blast had stressed the corridor, covering the walls with hairline cracks. Stumbling up, he inspected it for leaks. For now it seemed to be holding.

Limping, still deafened, he moved to the end of the corridor and pounded on the airlock hatch. No answer. "It's Altman!" he called. "Let me through!"

When there was still no answer, he realized there was an easier way and established a comlink to Field through his holopod. Immediately the airlock slid open and he stumbled through.

· · ·

"Altman," said Field. He was clutching his Marker icon tight in one hand, closing the airlock behind him with the other. "Thank the Marker. I had just about given up hope."

"Where's Ada?" was the first question Altman asked.

"What do you mean?" asked Field. "Still confined to the mainland, I presume. I haven't seen her in days."

"But I saw her," said Altman. "I saw her vid. She was right here."

"I'm sorry," said Field. "I haven't seen her."

Maybe it was the Marker, he thought. But how could that be? The Marker only showed dead people. But Ada wasn't dead. And then his blood froze as he realized what he'd known ever since he'd dreamt of her earlier: Ada was dead.

Field grabbed his arm. "We have to go," said Field. "I don't know how long we'll be able to keep them contained."

"Where's Markoff?" Altman asked.

"I don't know," said Field. "I think he must have packed up and left. Either that or he's dead. Doesn't matter much to me either way."

Altman nodded.

"We'll have to come back, you know," said Field.

"What?" said Altman.

"We need to go get help and come back. We have to make sure this is contained. We have to protect the Marker."

Altman followed him away from the airlock and upward, through a series of open chambers and then around a curving corridor to the main dome. They got on the lift and prepared to take it to the top, but it didn't move.

"What's wrong?" asked Altman.

Field shook his head. "Apparently the lift won't run on the auxiliary power," he said. "We'll have to climb. After you."

Altman slung the cutter over his back and started up the access ladder, Field right behind him. It was a narrow climb, not much room between the ladder and the wall, and it quickly became an arduous one as well. Already exhausted by what he had just been through, Altman found he had to focus on putting one foot in front of the other. Behind him, Field wasn't doing much better; he was wheezing like he was about to pass out.

"Everything okay, Field?" Altman called down.

"I'll live," said Field. He started to say something further, then made a choking sound and was suddenly cut off.

Altman glanced down and saw that Field was being choked by something that looked like a whitish gray snake or a length of intestine. One end was curled tight around the ladder, the other tight around his throat. Field was scrabbling at his throat with one hand, trying to hold on to the ladder with the other. Altman started down toward him, shouting, while Field let go of the ladder, both hands on the strangler now.

Altman was still clambering down, just heaving the cutter off his back, almost ready to cut the thing in two. But Field wasn't holding the ladder. If he cut through the creature, Field would fall.

"Field!" he cried. "Grab hold of the ladder!"

But Field didn't seem to hear him. His face was purple now, and Altman saw that blood was leaking slowly from his ears. Altman stretched down and stamped on the end of the strangler holding to the ladder. It squirmed beneath his foot but didn't let go. At the other end it gave a little wrenching jerk, and Field's head popped off like a grape, thunking down to the floor below. The body, knocking against the walls and the ladder, swiftly followed it.

He watched the strangler slither down, moving swiftly and sinuously. When it reached the bottom, it moved in twisting undulating motions until it reached Field's headless corpse. He watched it prod his stomach and then one end of it narrowed to a point and it stabbed through the skin. Slowly, throbbing, it forced itself into Field's belly. The belly swelled and slowly distended, until with a last wriggle the creature had disappeared entirely.

Altman felt sick. He clung to the ladder a moment, staring down. He might have hung there for longer, but then a thought occurred to him. *There might be more of them.* Glancing nervously about him, he forced himself to continue up the ladder.

When he reached the hatch, he opened it and clambered out onto the deck, making sure it was securely closed behind him. He hoped the creatures wouldn't be capable of opening it, but he didn't know for sure.

He started clambering down the side of the dome, following the narrow steps cut in the glass. Below was the boat platform, slopping up and down with the swells. Most of the boats were gone, but one was left. He undid the mooring and climbed in.

The motor started immediately. Only then did it start to seem real, like he might actually get away, like he might actually survive.

And then he remembered Field, dead because he had waited for Altman. *We'll have to come back,* Field had said. *Make sure it's contained.*

No, thought Altman. *I'm free of it. I'm not going back.*

And then suddenly he felt a presence in the boat beside him, just behind him, just out of sight. He was afraid that if he turned, he would see Field, his head loose, in place but not connected to his neck, threatening to fall off at any moment.

Hello, Altman, someone said.

"Leave me alone, Field," Altman said.

Are you coming back for me? Only, when he thought of it, it didn't seem exactly like Field's voice.

"You're dead, Field. I can't come back for you."

But what about me? it said.

Definitely not Field's voice. It was the voice of a woman now. He turned his head, saw Ada.

"Where are you, Ada? Who killed you?"

I'm right here. I need you, Michael, she said. *I need you to finish what you started.*

He shook his head. "You're not Ada," he said. "You're a hallucination."

It's not finished, Michael. Everyone is in grave danger. You have to stop the Convergence.

"What is Convergence?" he asked.

You've seen the Convergence, Ada said. *You need to stop it.*

And then she disappeared. He put the boat in gear and pushed the throttle down hard. Damned if he could figure out what exactly she wanted from him. What *it* wanted from him. *I'm not going back,* he told himself, *I'm not going back.*

But he already was afraid he would.

60

When he landed at the docks in Chicxulub, someone was waiting for him. Chava, the boy who had told Ada and him about the body on the beach. He was standing there in the dim light, shivering. Beside him was the town drunk who had lost his name.

"I knew you were coming," said Chava as Altman tied the boat off. "The *bruja* told me. She is dead and yet she told me. She has asked me to tell you that you must go back."

"I don't want to go back," he said.

"You must," said Chava, his eyes innocent and sincere. "She needs you."

"And why are you here?" said Altman to the drunk.

He wasn't drunk now, or at least didn't appear to be so. He crossed his fingers and made the sign of the devil's tail.

"The only way to beat the devil," the man told him, "is to take the devil inside you. You must open yourself to the devil. You must learn to think like the devil."

"I don't have time for this," said Altman. "I need to find help."

"Yes," said Chava. "We will come with you."

He left the docks and set off, the old man and the boy following him. When it became clear that he was heading toward the DredgerCorp compound, Chava hurried to catch up, tried to hold him back.

"You will find no help there," he said.

He shook the boy off and kept going, heading for the gate. When he looked back, he saw the boy and the old man had stopped, were standing motionless in the dusty road.

"We will wait for you here," the boy called after him.

He tried his card on the gate and it opened. He crossed the stretch of empty ground to the compound and tried the card on the door, without result.

He knocked, pressed the buzzer, then waited. For a long moment there was nothing and then the vid panel next to his face flashed on, to show a wavery black and white image of Terry.

He stared at Altman, pushing his glasses back on his nose.

"I'd like to come in," said Altman.

"I'm sorry," said Terry. "No admittance for anybody at the moment."

"It's important," said Altman. "Something's gone wrong with the facility," he said. "We need to do something about it."

He heard the sound of someone speaking, a voice too low to make out, just outside the frame. Terry turned his head and looked offscreen. "It's one of them," he said to someone on his left. "I don't know which one, I don't remember his name. Alter, I think." He was silent, the other voice rumbling again. "Yeah, that's it," he said. "Altman." He listened intently and then turned back to Altman.

"You can come in," he said.

"Who were you talking to?" asked Altman.

"Nobody," he said. "Don't worry about that."

"I need to know I'll be safe," he said.

"You'll be safe," said Terry after a moment's hesitation, but by the way he looked sideways as he said it, Altman knew he was lying.

He had almost reached the outer gate by the time Terry opened the door. He kept going, not even turning around. "Wait a minute," asked Terry, "where are you going?"

"Sorry," said Altman. "Can't stay."

"I've got a gun," said Terry. "Don't make me shoot you."

Altman stopped.

"Now be a good boy and turn around and come back," said Terry.

He did. He turned slowly and went back. Terry held his gun casually, almost desultorily. The safety, Altman noted, was off.

"What's that you're holding?" he asked, glancing down at the plasma cutter.

"What's this about?" said Altman. "First I can't come in and then you're insisting I come in?"

"Orders," said Terry. "You're to come inside and stay put." He gestured at the plasma cutter. "I think you'd better drop it," he said.

"Whose orders?"

Terry just shrugged.

"I don't want to come in," Altman said, moving slightly forward. "There's something I need to finish first."

"And I don't want to shoot you," said Terry. "But I will. Drop that thing and put your hands up."

Suddenly the gate started to rattle, someone banging on it. Terry's eyes flicked toward it just for a moment, just long enough for Altman to lunge and knock the gun to one side. It fired, the bullet sparking off the fence, but Terry didn't drop it, indeed was already starting to bring it back to bear on him. Altman flicked the plasma cutter on and flashed it toward him in the same movement. The energy blade sliced through his forearm, the gun and the hand holding it tumbling to the ground.

For a moment Terry was too shocked to realize what had happened. He just stood there, unable to figure out what had happened to his arm. And then, it hit him. Eyes wide, he stepped back and took in a deep breath to scream.

Altman, not knowing what else to do, ran, trying not to hear the screams of the man behind him. He darted out the gate and was joined by Chava, who ran along beside him.

"I came and knocked for you," he said, "and now you come."

"A good thing you did, too," said Altman. "Where's the old man?"

"*El Borracho?*" asked Chava. "He had to go. He was thirsty."

He started back down the street, the boy following him. *What now?* He turned and crouched beside the boy.

"I have to destroy some devils," he said. "Like the thing you saw on the beach."

"I will help you," said Chava. "Together we will kill them."

"No," said Altman. "It is not a game. You cannot come. I must find weapons and go alone."

The boy thought a moment and then smiled. "You will come with me," he said. "Follow."

The boy led him down through the streets and to the shantytown and then to the edge of the jungle. He went to a particular tree and put his hand on it and then carefully pointed himself in a particular direction and, stiff-legged, started to walk, pounding his footsteps hard against the ground. When the sounds of his footsteps changed, he stopped.

"Here," he said, and pointed at the ground. He crouched and began to brush the dirt away until he had uncovered a steel ring and a wooden trapdoor about two feet wide and six feet long. He gestured to Altman to open it.

He put the plasma cutter on the ground and reached down and pulled on the ring. The door creaked up on its hinge, revealing underneath it a coffinlike space lined with rocks. One half was full of guns and rifles, maybe a dozen in all. The other held axes and mauls, tree-spikes, a machete, a can of fuel, an old-style chain saw.

"You may use these," said the boy solemnly. "But you must bring them back. They belong to my father."

"What exactly does your father do?" he asked.

"He is for the people. He is . . ." For a moment he couldn't think of the words, and then it suddenly came to him. "Ecological guerrilla."

"Thank God for tree huggers," said Altman.

He took the chain saw, left the rest where it was, though this confused the boy.

"These monsters," he asked, wide-eyed. "They are trees?"

At first Altman thought to answer him properly, but when he started speaking, he suddenly realized how complicated the response would be. He just nodded and said, "Yes, trees."

But this created new complications. "How can trees be monsters?" the boy wanted to know.

"It's hard to explain," said Altman.

"And what kind of tree?" he asked. He began to rattle off Spanish tree names, following Altman.

Altman ignored him. He was almost back to the boat, the boy still following him, when his holopod sounded. When he answered, Krax's face appeared on the holoscreen.

"Altman," he said. "Hello."

He switched off. Krax called again immediately. He thought of not answering, but knew Krax would just keep calling until he did. So he answered. But this time he kept walking.

"This thing you did to Terry," said Krax. "Hardly subtle. I could have you arrested."

"Somehow I don't think you're going to do that," said Altman.

"Probably not," he admitted. "But I have to say, I think you overreacted. We just wanted to talk to you."

"You didn't just want to talk to me," he said. "You wanted to keep me there."

"It's for your own good. Don't do anything foolish, Altman. Come back."

"No," said Altman.

"What about your girlfriend, Altman?" he said. "What about Ada? Would you come back for her?"

Altman stopped. "Put her on," he said.

For the first time, Krax's composure cracked slightly. "She's not available right now," he said.

"You can't because she's dead," said Altman.

"Don't be ridiculous, Altman. Why would she be dead?"

"I started hallucinating her," said Altman. "Either you killed her or she killed herself. Which was it, Krax?"

"Hallucinations don't mean anything," Krax insisted. "She's alive."

Altman started moving again. "Show her to me, then," said Altman. "If I see her, I'll come back."

"As I said," said Krax, "that's not possible. You'll just have to trust me. Your girlfriend's life is in your hands."

He was at the dock now. "Good-bye, Krax," Altman said, and disconnected, powering the holopod all the way off.

He loaded the gear into the boat and climbed in himself. Chava tried to clamber in, but Altman stopped him.

"Stay here," he said. "I already have enough deaths on my conscience."

61

As he navigated the boat through the swells and felt the spray on his face, there was a lot of time to think. *I'm crazy,* he thought at first. *I shouldn't be going back. I was lucky to escape alive the first time.* And indeed, he might have stayed on land if Ada hadn't been dead. But no, as it was, there was no reason to go back to land. He felt he had to end it.

And then he began to think of what the old drunk had said when he met him on the dock: *The only way to beat the devil is to take the devil inside you. You must open yourself to the devil. You must learn to think like the devil.*

And how would the devil think? Or how, in this case, would the Marker think?

If anyone would know, Altman thought, it would be him. He had seen the Marker many times, had survived close proximity to it even when it was broadcasting fully. It had spoken to him by way of hallucinations again and again.

What had it said most recently, through his memories of Ada? *I need you, Michael. I need you to finish what you started.* That was vague—like most of what the ghosts told him, it was hard to pin down. Earlier, in the dream, it had been much more specific. But was it really the Marker speaking to him through the dream or was it only a dream, or even something else? A dream was a far cry from a hallucination.

But maybe the dream was his subconscious mind trying to tell him something. What exactly had Ada said? *I need you to do something for me,* she had said. *I want to have a baby. That's what I need. It'll bring us closer together.*

But was a dream the same thing as a hallucination? Maybe it was a different force altogether—maybe not his subconscious at all but something else. What did she mean by having a baby? Were these creatures, the crewmen that had been transformed after death into monsters, the Marker's offspring? Well, yes, he supposed so, in a manner of speaking, if he was right in thinking they'd been created by the Marker's transmitted code. But unless he was mistaken, his dream about Ada had not raised the issue with him until after the creatures, whatever they were, had been spawned. Indeed, he must have had the dream *just after* the creatures had appeared, even though Altman hadn't known about them until a few minutes later, when the alarm woke him up.

Maybe he should take the dream literally. Maybe that was exactly what the Marker was demanding of them: that they reproduce it. Maybe if he could convince the Marker that he understood, that he could reproduce it, things would return to normal.

It was simple, he thought.

And then doubts assailed him. He was basing it all on a dream, and it didn't jibe perfectly with what his hallucinations had been telling him. It could mean nothing, or even be something else, another force, trying to manipulate him. It was almost too simple. And even if he was right, who was to say that if he did what the Marker wanted things would go back to normal? Maybe they would just get worse. What if the Marker had no stake whatsoever in the survival of the human species but saw humans only as a means to an end? *If that end is fulfilled*, he thought, *will it still need us, or will it crush us, almost without thinking, as if we were flies?*

What if we're trapped between a rock and a hard place? he wondered. *What if humanity is going to die either way?*

He shook his head. It was the best he could come up with. He'd have to take a chance. But what choice he would make, what he'd choose to risk, he didn't know. *Altman's wager*, he thought. In any case, the Marker was the key. There was no choice but to return to the Marker, no matter what stood in the way.

It was nearly dark now. There, up ahead, were the lights of the floating compound, dim, running on the emergency backup, but still there. Soon he would be there as well. Soon he'd either have his answer or he'd be dead.

PART SEVEN

THE END OF THE WORLD

62

Even before he had opened the hatch, he could hear a skittering sound from inside, could see through the glass dim shapes moving below as well.

Here goes nothing, he thought. He threw open the hatch and went in.

He was only a few steps down the ladder when something dropped onto him. It struck his shoulder, and he had a glimpse of it before it wrapped itself around his face. It consisted of a human head, stretched and rubbery, on a network of tendrils. It immediately started to smother him.

He couldn't see. He tried to bat it off with the plasma cutter, but it simply wrapped its tendrils tighter. He banged it against the rungs of the ladder, but it still wouldn't let go. *Shit,* he thought, *I'm going to die.*

Blindly, his hand found the trigger of the cutter and started it up. He raised it slowly, trying not to cut through his own face and succeeded in nearly cutting all the way through the side rail of the ladder. He was beginning to black out. He tried again, closer to the face this time and felt the blade go through the creature's flesh. It loosened its grip and he shook it off, watching it bounce off the rung just in front of him and tumble down.

The worst part about it was that as it fell, he recognized the face. It was stretched and red, severely deformed, but he was sure it had belonged to Field. As he watched it strike the rungs below him and then spiral down, it was like he had killed Field himself.

He caught his breath and then continued descending.

The emergency lighting cast shadows everywhere. He kept seeing things moving in them. He heard a noise, at a little distance, then closer. Something was slithering up the side of the ladder. He looked down and tried to see it, but saw nothing. He stayed still, listening, but heard nothing. *Maybe I'm just imagining it,* he thought.

But when he took another step, he heard it again, and looking down he caught a brief glimpse of the same sort of sinewy pulsing thing that had popped Field's head off. And then it disappeared, was on the other side of the ladder. He tried to get around to see it and caught a brief glimpse and then lost it again. The sound, though, was closer now.

He wrapped one arm around the ladder and hung there, waiting. *Where was it?*

And then suddenly he saw it, just a few feet below him now, its gray body blending in with the ladder. As he watched, one end of it left the ladder and started wavering like a charmed snake, looking for flesh to grab on to. And then suddenly it whipped up and wrapped around his foot.

It wrapped itself tight and hard, almost dislodging him,

leaving him hanging by one arm, legs dangling in the air. He tried to swing the plasma cutter down to saw it off, but it was too low—he'd have to let go to get down to it, which would mean falling. It had started pulsing, tightening, and then began working itself up his ankle and onto his leg. Struggling for a foothold with the other leg, he finally managed to find it. He lifted himself on his toes as far as he could go, the ankle feeling like it might tear off, and swung his arm loose, grabbing hold again a few rungs down. That was enough; he could reach now. He sawed it in half with the plasma cutter. Ichor jetted from it, and then it fell.

Feeling dizzy, he clung on tight. He might have stayed like that forever except his head, pressed against the ladder's siderail, heard a dull pounding. Something else was coming. Still dizzy, he looked down. Two others were already starting up the ladder, these more humanoid, the kind with scythes sprouting out of their shoulders. They held on to the ladder with the tiny hands sprouting from their bellies, their scythes waving madly back and forth as they climbed.

He climbed frantically up, back the way he had come, trying to get to the level ground of the platform, knowing all the time that they were gaining on him. He could almost feel their scythes slicing up and taking off his legs.

Then suddenly he was at the top, on his knees and panting. He slung the cutter's strap over his back and let it hang, pulling the chain saw around. Precariously balanced, he tugged on the rip cord. The first time it didn't catch, nor the second time. The first one was already there, the tips of its scythes visible over the edge of the platform, its head just coming into view. He tore the rip cord back hard, and this time it caught. He revved it and then leaned down and pushed it into the creature. The chain blade whipped the blood in all directions, spattering him from head to toe.

He stepped off the ladder, the chain saw sputtering in his hands. Were there others? It was a big room, poorly lit.

He moved cautiously toward the passage to the labs that would lead him down to the airlock. There were spills of flesh here and there around the walls, near the vents. Living, it seemed. He prodded one with his boot, but it didn't seem to respond, just sat there. He stamped on it, but it didn't seem injured by that either.

He was almost to the door of the lab when it came, rushing at him with an almost unholy cry. In the darkness and shadows, he had a hard time seeing it at first; it was just a blur. He revved the chain saw, trying to keep the blade between him and it, and struck it full in the head.

It was the most terrible of the beasts he had seen so far. It backed quickly away, hissing. Its jaw was distended, its teeth having grown long and predatory, the flesh having torn all the way back to the hinge. Its arms had become forelegs, its body thickening in the front and narrowing in the back. It had a single, overly muscled leg in the back, the other leg stretched and emaciated and lashing like a tail, the thinned toes fanned out and flexing at the tail's top.

It took a few steps sideways, then gathered itself and leaped. He tried to take its head off with the chain saw but was only partly through when the chain caught on something chitinous and the weapon was torn from his hands, almost dislocating his shoulder. The neck pulsed and spat fluids over his chest, the head leaning to one side and still snarling. The forelegs scratched and tore at him. He groped for the chain saw but couldn't get to it, wasn't certain that he'd be able to get it started again anyway. He kicked the creature back and it circled slowly, its head hanging like a loose sack, before springing again. Blinded, it struck just a little to the left of him, smashing into the wall. He was already scrambling up, trying to get the plasma cutter into his hands and turned on. It knocked him down and into the sickly smelling tissue that covered the deck and then reared back, looming over him. He rolled to one side but couldn't avoid its claws tearing through his shirt and the shoulder beneath, pinning one arm down.

And then suddenly he had the cutter on. He struck once hard, tearing off the foreleg pinning him. It balanced awkwardly over him on its remaining two limbs. He chopped into the other foreleg and it crashed down.

He pushed it back and stumbled away, the shoulder really starting to ache now. He circled it slowly, waiting for a moment to dart in and cut the last leg when it did a curious thing: it got its remaining leg planted but rather than using it to leap at him as Altman expected, it flipped the whole body over, landing it on its legtail. It stayed there motionless, perfectly balanced, the last leg contracted back, like the leg of a dead arachnid. *It must be dead*, Altman thought.

He came cautiously forward, but it didn't move. Carefully, he reached out and touched it with the edge of the cutter, and the leg sprang out hard, catching him in the chest and hurling him back against the wall.

He lay there for a moment, stunned. His chest felt like it'd been caved in. Slowly he sat up. The creature was still there, still balanced on its tail, its one remaining leg contracted again.

Fuck it, he thought. Gathering his weapons, he circled around it, giving it a wide berth, and made for the door.

The laboratory beyond the door was a shambles, everything turned over and collapsed, pure carnage. Bodies and pieces of bodies were everywhere. He moved through it cautiously, careful not to touch anything, and out the next door.

The next room was almost completely intact, which, somehow, made him almost more nervous. He moved past the central table and to the observation booth. From there he connected to the vid system, still running on emergency power.

He flicked quickly through the cameras he had access to, saw more of the creatures in almost every place he looked. The airlock door between the upper and lower decks, he saw, was open and shooting sparks. In the space just before it, just one room beyond where Altman was now, between him and the airlock, moved a creeper, maybe even the same creeper that he had seen before—though if it was, it was bigger now, and growing. It moved slowly forward, consuming everything, converging everything.

Shit, thought Altman. *No going that way.*

He asked the system for alternative paths, but there weren't any. The facility had been very deliberately constructed with one connecting point between its upper and lower halves. As long as the creeper was there, there was no way forward.

Unless . . .

Unless I go through the water, he realized. He flicked the vid display to the submarine bay. If he could get there, he could get in. It was what, twenty meters down? A long swim by any standard, and pressure would be strong as well. And once he was there, he'd have to enter the chamber and close the doors and wait for the water to be pumped out. If that wasn't enough to kill him in and of itself, the cold of the water very well might.

Then the display he was looking at was interrupted, cut into by another feed. A face appeared, a grainy black and white feed. "Who's there?" the man said. "Who's in the system?"

The man was vaguely familiar. It was, he realized, the man who had taken him to see the Marker in its chamber for the first time. What was his name? *Harm* something. Yes, that was it, Henry Harmon.

He switched on his vid feed so the man could see him.

"Harmon," he said. "It's Altman. You're alive?"

"I thought I was the last one," said Harmon. "It's great to see you."

"Where are you?"

Harmon looked around distractedly, as if for a moment he couldn't remember where he was. "I'm in the Marker chamber," he said. "I thought I was trapped, but for whatever reason, those things won't come near the Marker. I'm glad I'm not the only one left alive."

"I'll come get you," said Altman.

"That's not possible," said Harmon. "Before you even go a few steps, they'll tear you to bits."

"Can you do me a favor?" asked Altman. "Is there a way you can open the submarine bay doors from there? Do you have authorization?"

"Sure," said Harmon. "Why?"

"Open them and leave them open," Altman said. "That's how I'll get to you. Oh, and one other thing."

"Name it," said Harmon.

"Gather everything you can from the system about the Marker. Signal, composition, dimensions, makeup, anything at all."

"All right," said Harmon. "It'll give me something to do."

"I may have figured out what the Marker wants," said Altman. "I'll know when I get there. If I get there."

Harmon started to say something, but Altman had already switched off. He made his way out of the lab and back in the direction from which he'd come. He searched through lockers and cabinets, looking for either oxygen or a wet suit, but found nothing. He'd just have to risk it. He looked at the chain saw. It was hardly the ideal weapon; when the chain had caught, it almost got him killed. In any case, he couldn't take it. The water would ruin it. The plasma cutter, though, was another matter. It would probably work even after having been through the water.

He found two fifteen-meter coils of rope and hooked them over his shoulder. Then he started climbing the ladder again, back to the hatch.

63

He climbed down the dome to the boat platform, bucking now with the swells. The submarine bay was below and a little to the left. He went to the far edge of the platform and looked down for it.

There, there it was. He could just make out the glow coming out through the open bottom of the hangar.

He tied the two coils of rope together, tugging on either side of the knot until he was satisfied, and then carefully measured its length. He tied the plasma cutter's strap onto one end of the rope, double-knotting it just to be safe. The other end, he hitched fast around a mooring.

Carefully, he lowered the plasma cutter and the rope into the water until they were gone, little more to see than the first few meters of rope. He stripped to the waist and carefully limbered up, thinking.

He'd have one chance, he knew. Once he'd gone a certain way down, he'd be committed. Either he'd make it into the submarine bay or he'd drown.

He breathed rapidly in and out and then dived, letting the air out through his nose as he went. He swam as quickly as he could straight down, following the rope. The pressure built quickly, his head feeling like it was being squeezed. It felt incredibly slow, like he was making no progress, like he was still just a few meters below the platform.

He kept swimming, trying to keep his strokes even and steady and his heart rate constant, trying not to panic. He could hear the blood beating in his ears now, a steady thudding growing slower and slower. Were his limbs slowing down, or did they just feel like they were?

He saw lights. He was close to the submarine bay. *No*, he thought, *don't look, stay focused, just keep swimming down.*

He felt his lungs struggle, wanting to breathe in air that wasn't there. He made a gurgling sound, had to force himself not to breathe in water. Things all around him seemed slower, much slower.

And then he saw it, floating near the end of the rope, the plasma cutter, like a shadow in the darkness. His heart leapt with exhilaration and things started going dark around the edges and he thought for a moment he was going to pass out.

But when he reached it and grabbed hold of it, he realized he'd never be able to struggle it into the bay with him. He didn't have enough air left, didn't have the strength. He'd have to leave it behind.

He let go. He looked to the side and there it was, just a few meters away: the open submarine bay. He left the rope and swam for it. He would never make it, he realized. He might make it into the submarine bay, but he didn't have enough strength left to close the floor and then wait for the time it took to pump the water out. It was pointless.

But something in him kept him swimming anyway. He

crossed through the opening and into the bay. He was just heading for the door lock when he caught a flash above him and suddenly had an idea. He shot up as quickly as he could, striking his head hard against the roof, almost knocking himself unconscious. But there, in the corner, was a thin layer of trapped air. He put his face up against the roof and took a gasping breath, water lapping against the sides of his mouth.

He hung there, floating, breathing in more, until he stopped wheezing, until his heart stopped pounding. It was okay. He was going to be okay.

When he felt calm, he dived back into the water and swam down. But instead of swimming to the floor controls, he swam through them and outside. For a moment he was lost, disoriented in the open ocean, and thought he'd gone in the wrong direction. And then he caught sight of the shadow of the rope, realized he was looking too high. He looked down a little and there it was.

He swam to the plasma cutter and grabbed it, immediately striking back for the submarine bay, dragging the rope along with him. With the rope, it was too heavy, the progress very slow. For a moment he considered abandoning the cutter, and then an idea struck him. He turned and switched the cutter on and cut through the rope with it.

The cutter was heavy, making it so he could use only one arm to swim. It threatened to drag him down. He made it to just beneath the bay floor and then swam desperately up, kicking hard with his legs, a little panicked. By the time he got his fingers around the edge and pulled himself in, he was nearly as exhausted as he'd been from the initial swim down. He thrust it into a corner and then swam quickly for the controls for the floor.

He pressed the button and held it down. The emergency lights in the room began to flash. Slowly, he saw, the floor was sliding out of its channel and coming across, coming closed. He swam up for the pocket of air and for a moment couldn't find it. Where was it? He swam back along the ceiling and found a pocket about the size of his fist, just enough to get his face into. He sucked it in, then breathed quickly out, the pocket growing larger. Below him, he heard the water-dulled clang of the submarine bay floor closing and then the gentle throb of the pumps.

The water level began to drop and he got his head completely out, took a deep gasping breath, and immediately blacked out.

Michael, the voice said. *Michael. Wake up.*

He opened his eyes. It was his father. *I asked you to get up,* his father said. *How many times do I have to ask?*

In a minute, Dad, he said. His voice sounded strange, hollow, as if coming from a distance.

I said now, said his father. *Get up or I'll drag you out of bed myself.*

He didn't move. His dad shook him. He moaned, shook his head. *Dad—*

Get up! His father was screaming now, so close to his face that he could smell the liquor on his breath. *Get up!*

He came conscious facedown, half-on and half-off the catwalk running the edge of the chamber. He had been lucky. He was alive and coughing up water rather than floating facedown in the center of the room, dead.

He struggled and leaned back against the wall, gathering himself. Then he inched to the edge of the catwalk and jumped off and into the water.

He couldn't find the plasma cutter. Maybe something had gone wrong. Maybe it had shaken loose when the doors were closing and had slid out into the water. Maybe it was gone.

He resurfaced, holding on to the edge of the catwalk, and then went down again, searching more carefully this time. He found it wedged behind a float, all but impossible to see until he was almost touching it.

He worked it free and surfaced again, pulling himself out and onto the catwalk. Then he lay there on the grille a moment, breathing, trying to recover.

When he got up, he was still shaky, his nerves jittery. He wiped the droplets off the wall com unit with his palm and connected to the Marker chamber.

"Hello?" said Harmon, his voice a little panicked now. "Hello?"

"It's me, Altman," he said.

Harmon squinted at the screen. "Altman," he said. "I wondered if you were still alive. You still are, aren't you? This isn't a vision, is it? You look different."

"I'm still alive," said Altman. "Just a little wet."

"Where are you?" he asked.

"Submarine bay," said Altman. "Not far."

Harmon nodded. He pulled a holofile up and spun it so that Altman could see it.

"Here you are," Harmon said, and a red blotch appeared on the map. "It's simple," he said. "Down this hallway, the one with the slight slope. Then into a new hall, past these two labs. A final hall and there you are."

"What's between you and me?" asked Altman.

"Close to the Marker, nothing," said Harmon. "They won't get close to the Marker. If you can get into the final hallway, you should be all right. Before that, it might be a little trickier."

He flashed Altman a view of the hall just outside the submarine bay lock. The camera made a slow sweep, showing a pile of corpses, a pallid batlike creature fluttering above them, and then dissolved into a wall of static. "This was just before the camera was destroyed," he said. "Who knows what's there now."

The view changed, two separate cameras, two labs. In one, a spiderlike creature like the one he'd killed before, only this one had a third head and a ridge of spines along its back. In the other, two of the creatures with the scythelike blades. They lay on the ground motionless, perhaps dead. "These are current," Harmon said. "I'd suggest being quiet going past the labs. The hall itself, and the hall after it, seem to be empty."

Altman took a deep breath. "All right," he said. "Here goes nothing."

He stopped the airlock mechanism when it was only slightly open and looked through. The hall outside was dim, some of the emergency lights fluttering, others burnt out completely. But he could see from the dim shapes and tell from the sounds being made that they were there.

And then an arm reached through the opening and grabbed him, wrapped itself around his own arm and pulled hard, dragging him against the airlock.

Or at least at first he thought it was an arm. As he tried desperately to pry it off, he realized it wasn't an arm at all, but something more like a bundle of sinew stretched long and hardened somehow. He tried to get the plasma cutter up, but his arm was flush against the hole, no space to cut. It tugged again and almost tore his arm off. He pulled back hard but couldn't get any purchase. Not knowing what else to do, he kicked the lever to continue opening the door.

As soon as the opening was large enough, the sinew pulled him through. The hall had been remade, was covered in an organic layer, smeared with an approximation of flesh. It was like he was being tugged down an intestine. He cut at the sinew with the plasma cutter, but the blade didn't go all the way through. The sinew jerked, just dragged him farther down the hall. He cried out in pain, cut again, and this time cut through.

There was a roaring sound. The rest of it slid rapidly down the hall and disappeared into an air duct. The piece that he had cut off was still digging tightly into his arm, cutting off the circulation. To get it off, he had to carefully section it.

It was like walking through a nightmare. Blood and flesh everywhere, no idea where they were going to strike at you next. He was becoming jumpy, he knew. He needed to relax, needed to calm his nerves, or they'd get him. But how could you relax in a hell like this?

Aching all over, he stumbled down the hall, wading through a kind of putrid slurry, trying not to touch the flesh-coated walls or ceiling. There was a corpse blocking the way. He tried to kick it out of the way, but as soon as he touched it, it hissed and lashed out at him. He stumbled back and slipped and then it was on him, trying to slash his head off with its scythes, scythes that had been hidden beneath the water. He raised his knees and turned to see it up and over him, its drooling mouth just centimeters from his throat. He somehow got his hands between it and him, held it away. It hissed and shrieked in frustration, leaning hard on its scythes and trying to get closer, its breath enough to make him want to retch.

With a groan, he gave a mighty push and threw it to one side, then spun over and pulled the cutter out from under him. It was already looming over him again, but he had the cutter now and lopped off one of its scythes. It kept coming at him with the other scythe and the stump. He brought the casing of the plasma cutter down hard, pulping its head. It kept coming. He scrambled back and away from it, stopped only to swipe at it. He took the rest of the stump off, then most of the other scythe. It thrashed for a while, half buried in the muck, and then stopped.

It was only then, in the brief quiet, that he realized there was something coming up behind him. He leapt to his feet and turned, and a scythe cut through his forearm, making him drop the plasma cutter. He screamed and struck the thing open-palmed in the chest, hard, feeling the sickening smack of its dead flesh. It staggered back a little and he managed to get the cutter up again, wincing with pain. It rushed again and he dropped to avoid its scythes, which whistled over his head, and kicked its legs out from under it.

It fell on top of him and for a moment, trapped in the muck and beneath its stinking, rotting flesh, he had the impression that he was already dead, that he was wandering the afterlife, living out a peculiar hell for all he had done wrong in this life. The cutter was trapped between his body and the creature above him. The creature was gnawing at his shoulder, working its way over to his neck, and was trying to prop itself on one bone scythe so as to swing the other through him.

He pressed the trigger for the cutter, hoping it wasn't too low and pointing down rather than up. The blade sprang between his knees and he angled it up hard and through the creature's pelvis, forcing it up bit by bit, sawing it slowly in half. It fell to either side of him, but he still had to get up and stomp each of the halves before it stopped moving.

He stumbled up. Blood was still spilling out of the cut in his arm. He tore off the bottom of his shirt and awkwardly bandaged himself. It wouldn't stop the bleeding, but it would slow it, and that would have to be enough for now.

Two more hallways, he thought. *That's all.*

He went to the end of the hall. He had to cut away the growth around the door to find the controls, but once he'd done that and scanned his card, it opened fine.

He looked in. Harmon was right—the hall looked fine, nothing there. There, to the side, were the two lab doors. He would just move forward as quietly as possible, past them, and then he would be safe.

He eased into the new hall, moving slowly, squishing sounds coming from his shoes from the muck in the other room. He could hear movement behind the first door. He held his breath. And then he was past it, almost to the second door. He could hear a sound from behind that as well, a crackling sound and then a low, long whine. He hurried his step a little, was soon past that as well.

He'd already reached the door at the end when one of the doors opened. He didn't look back to see which one it was, just pressed his card against the scanner and prayed the door would open soon enough.

The low whine came again, louder this time, closer. The door began to slide open and he rushed through it and into the final hall, casting a glance back to see the three-headed spiderlike creature, just standing there near the end of the hall, watching him. It was different from the other one. Its back, he saw, was covered with spikes, which as he watched began to stiffen and stand up. One spat off its back and shot toward him, embedding itself in the wall next to his face. All three of the creature's upside-down heads hissed in unison, but it didn't move forward. And then the door between him and it slid shut.

He reached the door at the end of the hall and engaged the comlink.

"Who is it?" came Harmon's voice.

"Who the hell do you think it is?" said Altman.

"Altman?" he said. "How can I be sure it's you?"

"Come on, Harmon. Open up."

"No," he said. "You have to tell me something that nobody but you, nobody but the real you, would know about me."

What, was he crazy? "I don't know you that well, Harmon. I don't have anything to tell."

"I'm sorry," he said, "I can't open it," and cut the feed.

Altman reengaged the link. When Harmon picked it up, he said, "Don't disconnect. Turn on the vid feed and you'll see it's me."

Harmon did. Altman saw his worried face squinting, peering at him. One hand was clutching something at the end of a necklace.

"I don't know," he said slowly. "A vid can be faked."

"You're paranoid," said Altman, and then realized that yes, that was exactly what he was. The Marker was making him that way. But, he remembered, Harmon was also a believer.

"Look," Altman said quickly, "you were the one who told me that the creatures can't come close to the Marker, right? If that's true, I must not be one of them. If I was one of them, I wouldn't be able to get this close. The Marker will protect you if you believe in it. In the name of the Marker, open the door."

Harmon gave him a long, solemn look that Altman couldn't interpret; then he reached out and pressed a button ending the vid transmission. A moment later the door opened. Altman walked in slowly, his hands up.

"Ah, it is you," Harmon said. "Marker be praised."

64

"I knew you were coming," said Harmon. "I just knew." He was, Altman noted, sweating profusely. His responses were disconnected, his voice zigzagging back and forth between being affectless and flat and a panic-stricken roar. He was clearly not in his right mind.

"Actually, I called you and told you I was coming," said Altman.

"No!" Harmon said, his voice rising. "You didn't tell me! I knew!"

"Calm down," said Altman. "How do you know I'm the one?"

"You're the only one who has come," said Harmon, speaking with a calm simplicity. "It has to be you because you're the only one. Everyone else is dead."

Altman slowly nodded. He might be able to play Harmon's belief in the Marker to his advantage, he realized. He wanted Harmon to believe whatever he had to believe to allow Altman to do what he needed to do.

"I came here," said Harmon. "This is the first place that I came and then, when I saw that they couldn't come near me, I understood why. The Marker wanted me here. I used to mistrust the Marker, but I was wrong. The Marker is protecting me. The Marker loves me."

"And me," said Altman.

"And you," Harmon agreed. He reached out and took Altman's arm. His hand was feverish, burning hot. "Do you believe?" he asked.

Altman shrugged. "Sure," he said. "Why not."

"And have you understood my message?" he asked. He looked at Altman expectantly, clearly waiting.

"Message received," Altman finally said.

Harmon smiled.

"I asked you to gather some information," said Altman. "Do you have it?"

Harmon gestured to a holoscreen.

There was a series of holofiles, some of which Altman had seen and some that he had not. There were vid images of the interior of the first bathyscaphe, taken after the bathyscaphe had been brought up. He had seen bits of it before, first in the intercepted vid from Hennesey and then later, from the outside, through the window. As the camera taking the images scanned slowly, he recognized the scrawlings in blood as symbols from the Marker. But, he also realized, they were not in the same order or sequence as they appeared on the Marker. What he'd seen before as a symptom of madness now actually struck him as rudimentary calculations and seemed to contain a glimmer of sense.

In addition, there were analyses of the Marker's structure and density, hundreds of dissections of its transmissions, speculations, unproven theories. There was information about the different genetic codes that Showalter and Guthe had read into the signal and the Marker. There were, in the end, more files than he could read—even more files than he could skim. Thousands and thousands of pages and images and hours and hours of vids. What was important and what wasn't? What was he going to do? How was he to start?

Harmon was crouched on the deck beside his chair, staring at the Marker. "Have you ever seen anything like it?" asked Harmon.

"No," said Altman.

"It's good," said Harmon. "It loves us, I can tell. I touched it and when I touched it, I felt its love."

"You felt something?" said Altman.

"I felt its love!" insisted Harmon, shouting now, apoplectic. "It loves us! Touch it and you'll see!"

Altman shook his head. *"Touch it! Touch it!"* Harmon was still screaming. And so Altman, not knowing how else to calm him, stood up, walked across the chamber, and did.

It was not love he felt, but something different, something that was not a feeling at all. At first it was as if he was experiencing all the hallucinations he had had at once, as if he was experiencing all the experiences any of the others had had, all laid over one another. Most of it interfered with itself, created a kind of blinding static that blotted itself out, but beyond that, and in spite of it, he could see something he hadn't seen before. He could see that the hallucinations were not a function of the Marker but of something else that stood in opposition to it, of something that was ingrained in his own brain. The hallucinations had been trying to protect them, but they had failed: the process had begun. Now all he could do was try to satisfy the Marker enough that the process would stop but not do enough to lead to full-fledged Convergence.

And then, suddenly, something cleared and he could see past the hallucinations to glimpse the Marker itself. It was as if it were changing the structure of his brain, reworking connections, rewiring circuits, to make him understand. Suddenly he felt he could see the structure of the Marker from the inside, and in a way that gave him a complex appreciation of it. It filled his head and set it aflame, and then it poured out through the cracks in his skull and took him with it.

When he came conscious, Harmon was over him, stroking his head, a beatific smile on his face.

"You see?" he said when he noticed that Altman's eyes were open. "You see?"

Altman pushed him away and stood, stalking quickly over to the monitor. He began to type frantically, sketching a structure out as well. His hands were moving faster than his brain, working on different bits and pieces of it all at once, flipping from holofile to holofile and back again. He was, he realized with a shock, recording the basic rudiments for a blueprint of a new Marker. It was sloppy and skew. There were a lot of unanswered questions, a lot of mysteries to be sorted out, but that was definitely what he was doing.

"What is it?" Harmon was asking from behind him. "What's going on?"

"I've figured it out," Altman answered. "I thought I'd figured it out before, but I was still struggling to understand what it meant. Now I know."

He worked awhile longer; how long he couldn't say. His

head was spinning, his fingers aching. When he had finished, he turned to Harmon.

"I need your help," he said.

"What is it?"

"I need you to help me translate what I have here, best as you can, and feed the signal back to the Marker."

At first Harmon just stared and then he slowly sat down, took a closer look. He went through it, slowly. Suddenly he glanced up at Altman, the first coherent look he'd given since Altman had entered.

"This is the Marker," he said, awe in his voice. "You understood it, just as she asked you to do."

Altman nodded.

"You want me to transmit to the Marker the image of itself?" he asked.

"Yes," said Altman.

"Marker be praised," said Harmon. And then he added, "Altman be praised."

It made his skin crawl to hear Harmon say his name like that, but he bit his tongue, said nothing. What he had done was far from complete, would require years and years more work, but hopefully it would be enough right now to stop the process of Convergence.

It took a few hours more, and a few attempts to transmit in different ways, before something connected. The Marker sent out a short, intense burst of energy, and then, as suddenly as it had begun broadcasting, it fell silent.

"What's wrong with it?" asked Harmon.

"It's resting," said Altman. "We've done what it wanted us to do. We've saved the world."

65

After it was over, he sat there for a long time, thinking. Why did the Marker want to be reproduced? What effect would it have? What did it mean? And if the hallucinations, the visions, weren't from the Marker but were opposed to it, where were they from? Which of the two was on their side?

He still didn't trust it. No, what he had felt when he touched the Marker was not love but nothing—total absolute indifference to the human race. They were a means to an end. What that end was, he wasn't certain, but felt, more than ever, that for the Marker they were expendable, a necessary step on the way to something else. When the new Marker was constructed—and he had no doubt that that was what the Marker intended—what would happen then? He had stopped the Convergence, but perhaps by doing so he had jump-started a discovery that would lead humanity to an even worse fate.

Then again, another part of him responded, *what if you're wrong? What if you're being paranoid?* Or what if the love Harmon had felt was his own feelings, his own emotions mirrored back to him: his own religious love for the Marker being reflected as the Marker's love for him? What if the indifference Altman sensed was not something inherent to the Marker, but something integral to himself, reflected back?

He sat there thinking, thinking, but getting nowhere. What was he going to do now? Now that he'd given the Marker what it wanted, had he inadvertently made things worse for humanity?

"We'll have to go," he said to Harmon. "The Marker wants us to leave."

"How do you know?"

"It told me," said Altman.

Harmon nodded. He went to the Marker and touched his lips to it. He was no longer paranoid, no longer jumpy, no doubt because the Marker had stopped broadcasting. But he was still a believer.

"Where are we going?" Harmon asked.

"To the control room," said Altman. "I have something to take care of, and then we can leave."

He didn't know what he expected—maybe that when the Marker stopped broadcasting the creatures would lose power, would collapse, even fall apart. But it wasn't like that. When they left the Marker chamber and went down the hall and opened the door at the far end, it was to find the strange spiderlike creature still there, still waiting for him. It was a little slower maybe, a little more listless, but it was still there, still eager to kill them both.

Seeing that only strengthened his commitment to do what he planned.

They opened the door and saw it, and the creature's back began to bristle. Altman grabbed Harmon, pulled them both behind the doorframe. The strange conical projections it cast from its back whipped down the hall and past them, whunking into the walls.

He stuck his head back out and waited for what it would do next. All three heads, he saw, were loose now, scurrying toward them.

He thumbed on the plasma cutter.

"You might want to stay back," he said to Harmon, and then stepped into the doorway.

He caught the first with the blade as it leaped at him, separating the head from its tendrils. The head, still grimacing, bounced and richoted off the wall and he crushed it with his foot. The second he caught with an upward thrust as it scurried along the ceiling just above the doorframe. Then he had to step back and press against the wall again as the creature slung more barbs at him.

The last, he had to pry off Harmon's neck. It had gotten past him somehow, he didn't know how. He didn't even know it had attached itself to Harmon, and wouldn't have known if Harmon hadn't grabbed him from behind and shook him. He'd turned, saw Harmon going purple, thought *Not this again*, and sliced the thing in half, somehow managing not to take Harmon's face off along with it.

Harmon coughed, rubbed his throat. "Altman be praised," he suggested in a hoarse whisper.

"Stop saying that," said Altman. "Altman doesn't want to be praised."

He glanced again around the door frame. The creature was moving forward now, its spearlike legs rattling down the hall and coming toward them. He put his finger to his lips, warning Harmon to be quiet, then flattened himself against the wall.

He heard it coming, the tapping of each leg a kind of complex, echoing rhythm that suddenly made it difficult for him to tell exactly how close it really was. He heard it pause at the doorframe. He kept expecting it to sidle through, but for some reason it didn't. Instead, it turned around and started back the other way.

Shit, thought Altman, *so much for ambushes.* And rushed around the door frame and after it.

It spun around, surprisingly quick despite its many legs. He sheared off the one nearest to him, then threw himself to the floor as its back bristled and it spat its barbs. He sliced off another leg on the same side, almost lost his foot as it stabbed one of its remaining legs down. Another swipe and it crashed to one side, disabled. He dismembered it, careful this time not to cut into the yellow and black tumor.

He went back for Harmon and they continued down the hall. They passed the laboratory doors and saw that they were open. Inside the second one, two of the creatures with scythes turned about in circles, performing a strange dance, as if the Marker, before falling silent, had sent them a message that they could not interpret and now they were caught in some kind of glitch, forced to perform the same motion again and again. Not knowing what else to do, Altman moved quietly past. If they noticed him, they didn't show it.

Instead of going through the next hall and into the submarine bay, they took the side passage and cut up and back, toward the command center. There were two more of the scythers, these directly in the hall, same lost movements, blocking the way. But as soon as he touched one with the plasma cutter, both of them attacked. Harmon turned and, wailing, fled back down the hall. Altman cut the legs out from under one, but couldn't get the weapon around before the other on was him, its scythes wrapped around him and drawing him in, its mouth pressed to his neck and tearing at it, making a moaning sound, the neck burning as well from whatever fluid the dead mouth was secreting. He cut into its chest and through its torso and its legs fell off but the top half of it continued to cling. The other one, legless and all, had dragged itself forward by its scythes and was trying to climb up his legs. He tried to pull the head of the first away, tried to drag it off his neck, but couldn't. The cutter was still trapped.

He held down the button and brought it up, carving slowly through the creature's torso then over to the side to cut off one of the scythes. From here he could shake it off, then stomp both it and its companion out of existence.

He stumbled back down the hall until he found Harmon. "Come on," he said tiredly. "Let's go."

He didn't have authorization to open the command center door, but Harmon did. The command center was clear, empty inside, perhaps because the Marker was there just above it. He went over to the console, found what he was looking for.

He entered the sequence in, found himself locked out. He entered it in again.

OVERRIDE? Y/N the holoscreen asked him.

Y.

ENTER AUTHORIZATION CODE.

"Harmon," he asked. "Do you have an authorization code?"

"Why?" said Harmon. "What do you want it for?"

"I don't want it," said Altman. "The Marker does."

After a brief pause, Harmon gave the code to him. He entered it.

Immediately an alarm started to sound.

FLOODING SEQUENCE WILL BEGIN IN 10:00. CANCEL SEQUENCE Y/N?

"What did you do?" shouted Harmon.

N.

The countdown began. SEQUENCE CAN BE CANCELED AT ANY TIME BY PRESSING N.

Harmon was screaming behind him. "What are you doing?" he was shouting over and over again.

Altman grabbed him and shook him. "I'm sinking it," he said.

Harmon had a hurt look on his face, seemed ready to melt into tears. "Why?" he asked.

"To protect the Marker," lied Altman. "It was down there for a reason, to keep it safe. And to kill these creatures. I promise you, Harmon, this is what needs to happen."

"You have to stop the countdown," said Harmon.

"No," said Altman.

"Then I'll stop it," said Harmon.

"No," said Altman, holding the plasma cutter up near his face. "You're coming with me. Either that or I'll kill you."

The pressure inside the station had already started to shift. There was a trickle of water in the corridor as he entered, the process starting slowly, nothing that couldn't be reversed.

The system, he knew, would not commit fully until the full ten minutes had passed.

At first Harmon was in a rage, and then overcome with tears, which slowly reduced to sniffles and then petered out entirely. Altman thought for a moment he'd have to kill him, but finally he allowed himself to be coaxed, prodded along.

Altman looked at his chronometer. "We don't have much time," he said. "I don't know what creatures are still alive on the decks above or how long it'd take me to kill them. We'll have to go out the submarine bay."

"I didn't know there was still a submarine there," said Harmon.

"There isn't," said Altman.

"Then how—"

"We're going to swim," said Altman. "I'll flood the bay and open the doors. As soon as they open, swim out as quickly as you can and make for the surface. There's a rope. If you see it, follow it up. It'll lead you to the boat platform. I've left a boat moored there. I'll be right behind you."

Eyes wide, Harmon nodded.

They moved out. Altman took the lead, stayed on watch. Nothing. There must be more of the creatures in the facility, but he wasn't seeing them. He kept expecting them to crash their way out through a vent or to hear a door slide open behind him and find one suddenly looming over him, but no, nothing. That was almost worse than if there was something. It kept him tense, expectant, a coiled spring of energy that never could release itself.

By the time they reached the door of the submarine bay, there were two minutes left. The water was up to their knees in the corridor and when he tried to open the bay doors, they wouldn't respond. He threw the override and forced the doors open enough that they could slip through, the water from the hall pouring in along with them.

He tried to shut the door, but couldn't get it shut. As long as it wasn't shut, he wouldn't be able to flood the chamber. He called for Harmon to help him, but the man just stood there, motionless, staring down over the edge of the catwalk. Altman finally had to yell at him, threaten him. Together, with Altman working the manual controls and Harmon pushing the door along, they forced it shut.

"Swim higher in the chamber as the water rises," Altman said. "Keep your head above it until you get to the ceiling, then, once it starts to cover you, dive down and swim out the bottom. Got it?"

Harmon didn't respond.

Altman slapped him. "Got it?" he yelled.

Harmon nodded.

They began to flood the chamber. At first Harmon just stood there, watching the cold water rise, swirling up around his legs, and for a moment Altman just expected him to stand there, watching, not moving, and drown. But when the water reached his chest, he suddenly took a deep gasping breath and began to paddle.

"Remember," called Altman, floating now himself. "Up to the ceiling and then down and out the bottom and then all the way up to the surface. But not too fast."

He tried to keep his breathing slow, measured. The water all around him was swirling and foamy, and it was some effort to keep above it. He watched Harmon, but he seemed to be doing all right now. Twice he disappeared beneath the surface, but he reappeared again almost immediately.

And then Altman's head grazed the ceiling. He looked up at it and grabbed on to the grating there, holding still, breathing slowly in and out until the water covered his face.

He dived, stroking back to the controls, and opened the bay floor. Harmon was already down there, he saw, knocking against the metal of the floor, trying to get out. As soon as the floor split, he was through it and gone. Altman quickly followed.

The water was much darker than it had been earlier. He struck through it blindly, trying to go straight out, and then turned and started to rise too soon, striking the underside of the bay. He swam out farther and then made for the surface.

It wasn't as hard as going down, but it was difficult. The temptation was to go too quickly, which would have left him cramped and shivering and probably killed him. So, he went up slowly, all the while aware of the way his air was running out, his heart beating slower and slower. By the time he finally broke the surface, his lungs felt like they were on fire. There was a sliver of moon, just enough to see by. He looked around, saw the ghost of the boat platform, but no sign of Harmon. He spun his head around but didn't see him.

"Harmon!" he called as loud as he could.

He kicked up, trying to pull himself as far out of the water as he could. Even then, he wouldn't have seen it, if it hadn't been for the way a dip caught the platform and showed him the head floating on the other side.

He swam to the platform, climbed the ladder up onto it, and stumbled along the swaying platform to its far side. The facility now had started to settle strangely, listing in the water.

There was the roar of water rushing into it, or maybe the roar was from something else, the whole structure creaking, too, as the change in buoyancy shifted its weight, putting pressure on girders and links.

"Harmon!" he called again.

But the man didn't hear him, perhaps couldn't hear him over the noise. Altman dived in, swam to him, touched him.

"Harmon," he said, "come on!"

He was confused and seemed dizzy, in a state of shock. Altman slapped him, pulled him toward the platform. He got him swimming again, though somewhat lethargically, and had to practically drag him up onto the platform once they arrived.

The platform was already listing, half submerged in water, being dragged down by the sinking dome. He pulled Harmon over to the boat and dumped him in, and fell in himself. Then the dome behind them creaked noticeably lower and the platform was underwater, the mooring rope between it and the boat stretched taut, the boat listing hard to one side, threatening to turn over. His fingers shaking, he picked at the knot, but the pressure had tightened it too much for him to loosen it. His eyes cast desperately around for a knife but he didn't see one. There was an anchor, though, and he grabbed it up and began striking the mooring with it as hard as he could, trying to break it free.

The boat tipped farther, very close to taking on water. "Get to the far side of the boat!" he cried at Harmon, but couldn't look around to see if he did. He kept hitting the mooring with hard, smashing blows.

Suddenly the boat bobbed back and threw him to the boards. It was only after scrambling up again with the anchor that he realized the mooring and rope were gone, that he had succeeded.

The boat began to swirl. There was a sucking sound as the facility began to go down now in earnest. He leapt into the driver's seat and started the craft, throwing the throttle down hard. The boat leapt forward, but it was heading wrong, directly toward the dome: he corrected it, but there was still something wrong. They were caught in a vortex, some sort of whirlpool that the facility was creating as it went down.

Instead of forcing the rudder against it, he turned and followed it, trying to edge carefully free. The last dome slipped all the way under and was gone. He felt the drag on the rudder but kept it steady, trying not to look to the side, trying not to panic. For an instant he felt the boat resisting him, threatening either to turn and plunge downward or to flip over, but then suddenly they were free.

He sped away, looking back over his shoulder. The inside of the compound, the little he could see of it through the waves, was flashing and sparking, the electrical systems and generator still in the process of shorting out. He had just a glimpse of it and then it was gone. He took the boat in a long curve then headed back toward Chicxulub.

He was just thinking he should check on Harmon when he realized that he was standing there behind him. He turned and was struck in the side of the head by the anchor, knocked out of his seat.

"You were lying, Altman," Harmon said. "The Marker didn't want to be sunk. You don't love the Marker, you hate it."

No, he tried to say, *no.* But nothing came out.

He saw Harmon bend over him. He roughly took hold of Altman's hands, put them together, began to tie them.

"I thought you were my friend," said Harmon. "I thought you were a believer. But if you were really a believer, why don't you have one of these?" He touched the Marker pendant hanging from his neck. "I shouldn't have trusted you."

I saved you, Altman tried to say. *I could have left you to die, but I saved your life.*

"Now I'm going to get some real help," said Harmon, and he stood and took the controls.

Altman lay there, eyes glazed. A warm fluid was puddling up against his cheek and his mouth. It was only when he tried to swallow that he realized it was blood. It took him another minute to realize it was his own.

Okay, he thought. *I've been in worse situations.* He tried to move his hands, but couldn't feel them. It was as if his body had become disconnected from his head. *I'll just rest a moment,* he told himself. *I'll just lie here and then, in a moment, I'll wriggle free of these ropes.*

His vision started to go dim, and then slowly faded away. He listened to the sound of the engine, then that slowly left him, too. He lay there, feeling the movement of the boat through the waves. After a while, it seemed to come only from a distance. A while longer and even that was lost. He lay in the boat, seeing nothing, hearing nothing, feeling nothing. The whole world had dissolved around him. He tried as long as he could to focus on the taste of blood in his mouth. But soon he couldn't hold on to even that.

Epilogue

And then it began again. It started first with a pinprick of light in the darkness at a great distance. He watched it, trying to determine if it was getting closer or farther away, but was unable to say. He watched it a long time, or what felt like a long time, until it disappeared again.

Darkness. Plain and simple. But a sense, too, of a body. Of *his* body, the limits of it.

I'm dead, he thought. *This is hell.*

There was a long moment in which nothing happened. The pinprick of light came back again. He did not notice it reappear exactly, just knew that it was there, and knew it had been there for a while. He watched it. This time it grew slowly larger. It was moving slowing toward him. Suddenly, it became excruciatingly bright.

Things began to take shape around it. A thin silvery casing from which the light itself came. Something pinkish nestled around it, which he began, slowly, to realize was a human hand.

"A little response," said a voice, flat, uninflected. "Up the dosage."

He felt something, a stinging somewhere on his body. Suddenly he could move the muscles on his face.

Where am I? he tried to ask, but what came out was a dim, inarticulate sound.

"There we are," said another voice. The light pulled back and he saw a face, half-hidden behind a surgical mask. Behind it were other faces, maybe a half dozen in all.

"Where am I?" he asked, and this time the words came out.

"You're alive," said the muffled voice through the surgeon's mask. "That's all you need to know."

He tried to move his arm, found it strapped down. The other arm was strapped, too, his legs as well. He struggled against them, arched his back.

"There, there," said the voice. "You won't be able to break them. Just relax." The surgeon's mask turned to address someone behind him. "Go get Markoff," it said. "Tell him that Altman is awake."

He must have drifted off again. When he opened his eyes, there were three people over the bed, looking down at him: Krax, Markoff, and Stevens.

"Congratulations, Altman," said Krax. "You still seem to be alive."

When he opened his mouth and spoke, his voice was hoarse, his throat sore. "You killed Ada," he said.

"No," said Krax. "Ada killed herself. She started hallucinating and then cut her own throat. She wasn't strong enough. She wasn't worthy."

"Worthy?" Altman asked.

"We need to have a little talk," said Markoff.

Altman narrowed his eyes. He watched him, warily.

"We've talked with your friend Harmon," said Krax. "He told us everything that happened."

"You sank the Marker," said Stevens. "Why would you do that?"

"It was dangerous," said Altman, his voice barely above a whisper.

"It's not dangerous," claimed Krax. "It's divine."

"You're crazy," said Altman.

"No, he's right," said Stevens. "I'm afraid that's the conclusion that all three of us have reached."

Altman turned his head slightly in Markoff's direction. It hurt to move it. "You don't believe this, do you? How can you believe it's divine now that you've seen what it's capable of?"

Markoff offered him a hard, glittering smile. "It created life," he said. "I saw that for myself, saw it take dead flesh and bring it back to life."

Maybe he doesn't actually believe, thought Altman. *Or maybe he's pretending as a way of bending the others to his will. Just as I did with Harmon.*

"But what kind of life?" asked Altman. "It was monstrous."

"There must have been a glitch," said Stevens. "The Marker must have gotten damaged somehow. But as a principle, it's sound. All we have to do is fix it."

"Or if not fix it, make a new one," said Markoff.

"After all," said Stevens, "every indication is that when it was originally working, millennia ago, it established life on earth. Once we have one that's working properly, it will allow us to evolve beyond our mortal form. It will lead us into eternal life."

"No, it's not that. It's not that at all. You're wrong," whispered Altman. "It wasn't damaged; it was doing what it was meant to do. It meant to destroy us."

"Then why did it stop?" Stevens asked. "And why did it stop when you began to broadcast its own code back to it, showing that you'd figured out how to replicate it?"

"How do you know about that?"

"You don't think we left the facility without making sure that we could record everything that went on in it, do you?" said Krax. "We watched the whole thing. We have footage of everything."

But Altman just shook his head. "You're wrong," he said. "It'll destroy us."

"The Marker wants to help us," Stevens claimed. "Harmon has told us what you figured out: the Marker wants to be replicated. It was broken and must have known it was broken. It wants us to make it again so that it can help us. But we'll improve the technology, Altman. We'll make one that works and then make it even better." He leaned in closer. Altman could feel the man's breath on his face, could see in the man's eyes traces of fanaticism that belied his calm exterior. "There are sure to be other Markers, somewhere, on other worlds," said Stevens. "They will lead us forward. In the meantime, we'll do our best to try to understand this one and duplicate it."

"You've done a lot to help with that," Markoff said.

"But this one is sunk," said Altman desperately.

"It was sunk before," said Markoff, "and we got it up. You know that as well as anyone. All you did was slow the inevitable down slightly, by a few weeks, a few months."

"You don't have the research," said Altman. "Everything

must have been destroyed by the water and the pressure. You'll have to start over."

Krax shook his head. "Altman," he said. "You're so naïve."

"Remember Harmon?" said Markoff. "What do you think Harmon was doing while he was in the Marker chamber? He was recording everything, making sure that none of the data would be lost. And then he carried it all away in his pocket. If you'd thought to check his pockets or simply left him to die, you might have set us back. But you didn't. You're far too trusting, Altman. We have everything."

"We also have all of Guthe's research," said Stevens. "We can learn from it what went wrong with the Marker and learn how to repair it. We ran our first experiments, synthesizing and reproducing the creature's DNA, while you were still unconscious. Hermetically sealed labs, a variety of fail-safes. We're being a great deal more careful about it than Guthe was, though most likely hallucinations were to blame for his rashness."

"And to be frank," said Krax, "watching you struggle past them taught us a great deal about how to control them. We wouldn't be nearly as far along without you."

"You're making a terrible mistake," whispered Altman. He was very tired. He was helpless, couldn't do anything. But maybe soon. All he had to do was regain his strength. Once he regained his strength, he'd do everything he could to stop them. "If you go ahead with this, it'll mean the end of humanity. Maybe not right away, but soon."

"That's what we're hoping for," said Stevens. "If we go ahead with this, we'll reach the next evolutionary stage. We won't be human; we'll be better than human."

"Good-bye, Altman," said Markoff. "You've been a worthy adversary. But this time you've lost."

Once the three of them had left, a doctor who had accompanied them to the door returned and whispered in the surgeon's ear. The surgeon nodded his head, and then filled and primed a hypodermic. He pushed it into Altman's arm. The world grew gray, slowly faded away.

2

When he woke up, he was still strapped down to a bed. He was alone in a small room, something very like a cell. He struggled against the straps, but they were firm.

He slept, he woke, he slept again. Occasionally a nurse would come in and change the bag of fluids hanging beside him. His head throbbed. Once when the nurse came, she took out a small pocket mirror and held it so he could see himself.

His head was wrapped in bandages. He hardly recognized his own face.

"There, see," said the nurse, and gestured to the top of his head. "That's where you had your accident."

"Accident?" he said.

"Yes," she said. "Where you slipped and fell."

"It wasn't an accident," he said.

She smiled. "After head trauma, sometimes things can get confused," she said.

"No," he said. "I know exactly what happened."

Her smile looked painted on, fake. "I'm not supposed to talk to you," she said. "Those are the rules." She backed slowly out the door.

A few minutes later, the door opened and a man with a hypodermic entered.

When he woke up again, he was in a different place, a place that didn't just look like a cell, but was one. The bandages were no longer on his head, though a lump and a healing wound were still there. They had unstrapped him, had left him lying on the floor. He got unsteadily to his feet, his muscles weak from disuse.

The room was white, without mark or other design. There was one door, small, in the middle of one wall. High above him and out of reach was a vid recorder. A small toilet in the corner, a food dispenser just beside it.

He went to the door and pounded on it. "Hello!" he called. "Hello!" Then he pressed his ear to the door. He heard nothing.

He waited, tried again. Nothing happened. And then again. Still nothing.

Hours went by, then days. The only noise that did not come from himself was the clunk when food came down the slot. There was no way for him to control when it came, no button to push. Suddenly there was a clunk and the food was there. He saved the containers and they slowly filled one side of the room.

He felt like he was the last man on earth. He felt like he was going mad.

He withdrew deeper and deeper into himself, paid less and less attention to the outside world.

Then the dead started to return, one by one, to keep him company. All the people whose deaths he felt responsible for, sitting around him, judging him. There was Ada and Field, Hendricks and Hammond, and others he couldn't recognize. It was just him, and his guilt, and the dead.

And then he awoke to find that he was no longer in that room, that instead he was sitting in a chair at a large table. His hands were cuffed to the arms of the chair. Across from him, on the other side of the table, were Markoff and Stevens.

"Hello, Altman," said Markoff.

He didn't answer at first. It was strange to be in a room with living people, almost unbearable. He couldn't believe it was really happening.

"Altman," said Stevens. He snapped his fingers. "Here, Altman. Focus."

"You're not here," said Altman. "I'm hallucinating you."

"No," said Stevens. "We're here. Even if we're not, what will it hurt you to talk to us?"

He's right, said Altman. *What will it hurt?* And then he remembered Hennessy, dead from listening to a hallucination; Hendricks, dead from listening to a hallucination; Ada, dead from listening to a hallucination. On and on and on. His eyes filled with tears.

"What's wrong with him?" Markoff asked.

"We broke him," said Stevens. "I told you it was too long. We're real, Altman. What do we have to do to prove that we're real?"

"You can't prove it," said Altman.

"Do something, Stevens," said Markoff. "He's not any fun like this."

Stevens darted forward, slapped him hard, then again. Altman reached up and touched his cheek.

"Did you feel that?" asked Stevens, his voice gently mocking.

Had he felt it or had he only imagined feeling it? He didn't know. But he had to make a choice: either speak to them or ignore them.

He hesitated for so long that Stevens, or the Stevens hallucination, slapped him again. "Well?" he said.

"Yes," said Altman. "Maybe you're real."

And as he said it, it was almost as if they became more real. But if he had insisted they were hallucinations, would the reverse have happened? Would they have merely faded away?

"That's better," said Markoff, his eyes starting to gleam.

"Where's Krax?" he asked.

Markoff waved the question away. "Krax made the mistake of becoming expendable. What we're here to talk about, Altman, is you."

"What about me?"

"We had to figure out what to do with you," said Stevens. "You've caused a lot of trouble."

"That stunt you pulled in Washington," said Markoff. "That was in very bad taste. I wanted to kill you for that."

"Why didn't you?"

Markoff glanced briefly at Stevens. "Cooler heads prevailed," he said. "As it turned out, they were wrong."

"I'm the first to admit it," said Stevens.

"You were no better once you came back," said Markoff. "You meddled with experiments, caused a tremendous amount of property damage, did everything you could to get in the way. Once the setback occurred on the floating compound, I thought, *Well, they'll tear him apart and transform him into one of them, and I'll be at home with my popcorn and candy, watching it on the screen.* But that didn't work either. Instead you sank a billion-dollar research facility."

"We almost had you killed when we picked you and Harmon up from the boat, but Markoff wanted your death to be the perfect thing," said Stevens.

"Yes," said Markoff, "the perfect thing."

"You're both crazy," said Altman.

"You've used that one before," said Markoff. "You need to come up with a better insult."

"Would you like to hear our plans?"

"No," said Altman. "Send me back to my cell."

Stevens ignored him. "Once we have the secret of the Marker worked out, once we have the new Marker replicated, we'll share it with the public. Until then, we'll give them little tastes, something to prepare them for what's coming."

"That's where you come in," said Markoff.

Stevens nodded. "Seen in that light, you have played right into our hands. It's not enough for just us to believe. Since it's a matter of the salvation of the human species, we need to spread the belief. What better way to do that than to start a formal religion? That way, when the right time comes, they'll be ready."

"Not everybody has to know the full extent of what's really going on," said Markoff. "Indeed, it's better if only a few of us really know the details, only a select inner circle. It's always better to maintain a little mystery, initiate people slowly, gradually. Keep the power in the right hands."

Altman found his hands were shaking. "But I got the word out," he said. "I went public. People will know."

"Yes, you did," said Stevens. "Thank you for doing that. The word you got out was that the government is hiding something that the people should know about. Think about it. We've looked back over all the footage, all the interviews you did. You were conflicted enough about whether the Marker was something to be feared or something to be studied, and so you remained vague. We can spin your comments any way we want. By the time we're through with you, not only will your little stunt not hurt us: you'll be considered a saint. You got the word out first, Altman—you're the one who started it all. Everyone will believe that you were the one who founded the religion."

"I'll never go along with it," said Altman, dread rising in him.

Markoff laughed. "We never said we needed you to go along with it," he said.

"Like any prophet, you're more useful to us dead than alive," said Stevens. "Once you're dead, we can let the truth—our truth—build up around you and you can't do anything about it. You'll be larger than life. We'll write histories of you, holy books. We'll erase what we don't like about you and make you fit what we want. Your name will be forever associated with the Church of Unitology. You'll come to be known as our founder."

"Which will allow the rest of us to stay in the background and get things done," said Markoff. "I must admit I find it very satisfying to think of your name leading the movement that you tried so hard to destroy. It almost makes all the trouble you caused feel worthwhile."

"You'll never get away with this," said Altman.

Markoff smiled, showing the tips of his teeth.

"You can't honestly believe that," Stevens said. "Of course we'll get away with it."

"You have officially become expendable," said Markoff. "We've decided to donate your body to science. We have a particularly vicious death planned for you."

"You'll find this interesting," said Stevens. "Using a variant of the genetic material that Guthe produced, we've developed a specimen that we'd be interested in having you meet. It was made by combining the tissue of three human corpses with the DNA. We've named it after one of the corpses. We're calling it the Krax. The results, as I'm sure you'll be likely to agree, are rather surprising."

Altman tried to lunge across the desk but succeeded only in turning over his chair. He lay there with his face pressed against the floor.

After a moment, Markoff and Stevens got up from their chairs and heaved him back upright.

"Krax, by the way, was lying to you when he said he didn't kill your girlfriend," said Markoff. "What was her name again? Doesn't matter, I suppose. He did kill her. A generally inconsistent character. Which is why he became expendable."

Altman didn't answer.

"So there's your motivation," said Stevens. "Revenge. Kill the Krax, and Ada's death will be avenged. Should make for a good show." He smiled. "It seems fitting, doesn't it? An appropriate way for you to meet your end? Who could ask for anything more?"

"You may think we're going to throw you in there defenseless," said Markoff. "If you think that, you're wrong. We have a weapon for you." He reached into his pocket and pulled out a spoon, forced it into Altman's closed fist. "Here you go," he said. "Good luck."

And then, without another word, the pair stood and left the room.

3

The chamber they dumped him into was circular, about six meters in diameter. They pushed him through a pressure door and had left him there, gripping his absurd weapon, for too long. He had tried to make it a little less absurd, scraping it against the walls and sharpening its edges, giving it a point, making it a makeshift knife.

The observation chamber was directly overhead, the same size and shape as the chamber below. The glass ceiling of the lower chamber served as the glass floor of the upper one. He could see Stevens and Markoff above, looming over him. They were drinking glasses of champagne, smiling.

It's one thing to be killed, thought Altman, *but dying knowing what infamy will be done in your name after your death is another thing entirely. Better to be like the old drunk in the town and have no name.*

The second door of the chamber slid open to reveal a dark corridor. He stayed where he was, near the door he had been pushed through, waiting for something to come through. Nothing did.

The world is a hell, thought Altman. *You can do everything right and cheat death, and then be ruined by one false step.* Those, apparently, were the conditions of life. Of his life, at least.

The smell suddenly reached him. It was a rank, rotting odor, putrid to an extreme. He gagged.

And then he heard a heavy scraping sound, and the creature pulled itself in through the door.

It scraped against the sides of the passage as it came. He could see, here and there, reminders that it had once been human, a foot that had been stretched and split and now projected from the joint of the creature's chitinous gigantic arm. Finger-like tentacles throbbed over its face. And there, in the middle of its pulsating abdomen, was a large callus that looked like Krax's screaming face.

It pushed the rest of the way into the room and howled.

Oh, God, he thought. *Let this be a hallucination. Let this be a dream. Let me wake up.*

He closed his eyes and then he opened them again. The creature was still there. It roared, and then it charged.

ACKNOWLEDGMENTS

This book would not have been possible if Frank and Nick Murray hadn't provided me the perfect place to write at just the right time. Thanks are due to them and to *Le Trèfle Rouge*, and to the fine folks at Visceral Games/EA for trusting me with the best bit of first-person SF/horror dismemberment out there. And applause is due especially to my editor, Eric Raab, for his excellent, tireless, and thankless work.

For more fantastic fiction, author events,
exclusive excerpts, competitions, limited editions and more

VISIT OUR WEBSITE
titanbooks.com

LIKE US ON FACEBOOK
facebook.com/titanbooks

FOLLOW US ON TWITTER AND INSTAGRAM
@TitanBooks

EMAIL US
readerfeedback@titanemail.com